BURNING UP

ST. MARTIN'S GRIFFIN ≈ NEW YORK

NINA BANGS

CHERYL HOLT

KIMBERLY RAYE

and PATRICIA RYAN

BURNING Up

FOUR NOVELLAS *of* EROTIC ROMANCE

Library of Congress Cataloging-in-Publication Data

ISBN 0-7394-3571-X

CONTENTS

THE FLAME

by

NINA BANGS

CHAPTER ONE

Serenity So-Fine hoped the sex object was here, because she was *not* walking back down that mountain in the dark without it. During her five years as curator for the Galactic Museum of Erotic Art, she'd never come home empty handed, and she didn't intend to start now.

She pounded on the massive door with her wooden stake. No way would she get anyone's attention with just her fist. What kind of barbarian would live in this crumbling stone monstrosity? *A doddering, old, eccentric sculptor.* With no doorbell or knocker? *A doddering, old, eccentric misanthrope.* She sighed. Okay, so maybe this wouldn't be as easy as she'd thought.

Serenity had raised the stake to pound again when the door slowly creaked open. No surprise. This was not a door anyone would ever fling open. Everything about this place said old, a fitting setting for the old man—no, old *genius*—who lived here.

Serenity pasted an I'm-thrilled-to-be-visiting-this-backwater-time smile on her face and drew in a deep breath, then lifted her gaze to the man in the doorway.

"Hi, I'm . . ." Uh-oh. Major miscalculation. Museum records had put the sculptor at seventy-eight years old in 2005. Of course, in 2700, seventy-eight wasn't old. But in this time it warranted some wrinkles and withering. She did a quick body scan. Nope, no withering. The records were a few years off.

Early thirties, tops. Attractive in a primitive sort of way. Sensual lips tight with anger. Gray eyes narrowed in warning. Fine, he was more than just attractive. Maybe she should hold her breath so his pheromone attack wouldn't flatten her.

"How'd you get here?" He glowered.

By the World Time Travel Agency's evening express. "By taxi." A half-truth. She'd gotten from the small town at the foot of the mountain to his gate by taxi. But even a half-truth made her uncomfortable. Everyone told the truth in 2700, and lying was only permissible when traveling through time because lies were acceptable in primitive cultures. The ancient philosophy of "When in Rome."

"Bet he took you to the gate, then hightailed it back down the mountain." The tilt of his lips would almost qualify as a smile. It didn't reach his eyes.

She frowned. "He did seem overly anxious to leave."

The only light came from the hallway behind him, casting the surrounding forest into deeper shadows. The wind picked up, lifting his tangled mass of dark hair from his shoulders and separating it into shining strands.

"How'd you get through the gate?" He clenched his fists, his brief stab at good humor obviously over.

Fascinating. This was the first time Serenity had ever seen a physical expression of anger. She wished she could take the visual back to her associates to share.

"The electronic components wouldn't keep a child out." Of course, she meant a child from 2700.

"What about the dogs?" He took a step forward.

Serenity took a step back. Intimidation. Another new experience. Humans in 2700 never used this primitive technique to get what they wanted. It was effective, she had to admit. She gripped her wooden stake tighter. "I used a mind soothant."

"What's that?" He moved closer.

Dumb, dumb, dumb. She should've remembered that mind soothants were invented in 2100. He'd rattled her. No one had ever disturbed her calm, logical thinking processes. No one had ever tried. She must get to the point, then return to her time.

"It's not important. Are you Justin Hill?" A servant? Did they still have servants in 2005, or had robots replaced them? She couldn't remember.

His nod was almost imperceptible. His anger was not.

"Lady, you'd better be here to warn me the world will end in five minutes, because anything less will really steam me." He moved into her personal space, with no permission and no apology. A manners breach of major proportions in her time.

Then he leaned down.

He was so *big*. Serenity felt the first ripple of unease. Another new sensation. There was nothing in her period that could possibly make her feel uneasy. It was a time of undisturbed peace.

"And when I get steamed . . ." His voice was a husky murmur. "I get violent."

Violent? *Violent.* The most dreaded of human traits. Extinct for almost three hundred years. Serenity didn't know how to counter this kind of savagery. She wished they made sooth-ants for humans.

She drew in a deep, calming breath, and regretted it immediately. His gaze dropped to the lift of her breasts, and her nipples hardened to sensitive pressure points in response. Very strange. She didn't experience physical reactions to men. Never had. In 2700, humans had moved beyond the physical to the mental. The only things Serenity So-Fine lusted after were more sex objects.

You are one big, hairy liar. What about all the times in the museum when—? Serenity slammed the door shut on that particular thought, but she couldn't stop it from rattling the knob.

This whole experience was starting to . . . disturb her. *Nothing* disturbed her. If she stayed here much longer, she'd regress to prehistoric grunts.

She drew herself up to her full height, which only reached to about his shoulder, and tried for a confident, professional expression. "I'm Serenity So-Fine, and—"

His soft laughter mocked her. "Serenity So-Fine? You're kidding, right?"

She stared at him, shocked. He was ridiculing her name. She'd never heard ridicule used before. It made her feel . . . She wasn't sure, didn't want to explore the feeling. "Serenity is a positive emotion, and positive emotions make excellent names." Her last name was problematic. "The So-Fine name has a long, respected history. It traces back five hundred years. Legend has it that when my ancestor first saw the woman he'd marry he said, 'You are *so* fine, lemon drop.' It was a quaint and archaic compliment, but in that time it was traditional to take as a last name the first compliment a man gave to his chosen mate." Perhaps her ancestor should've given more thought to his first words.

He raked his fingers through his hair, and she followed the motion, noting the flex of powerful shoulder and arm muscles. She'd never seen a man with this much physicality.

"Five hundred years ago, people didn't run around telling women they were so fine." His gaze dropped to the stake she still clutched. "So, are you a reporter, a sales person, or a Buffy wannabe?"

She kept forgetting she was in 2005. Okay, so she was officially panicked. And he was bombarding her with so many new emotions, she couldn't keep up with them. She needed to tell him why she was here before he made her forget.

"I'm here for your sex object. And—"

He didn't give her a chance to finish.

"Sure. I'll just rip my clothes off, and you can go at it. I don't believe you, lady." His eyes had darkened to the angry gray of the approaching storm. A rumble of thunder punctuated his fury.

She blinked. His anger said he *did* believe her, even if he'd misunderstood her. His anger made her nervous.

Her gaze touched his face. Hard, uncompromisingly male. She couldn't hold his stare, so she allowed her glance to hop and skip over the rest of his body. Total impression? Tall, muscular, scary. *An alpha male.* Extinct in 2700, but like the Tyrannosaurus rex, a subject of fascinated conjecture.

Well, no primeval, testosterone-breathing dragon would stop her now. "I'm the curator of the Galactic Museum of Erotic Art." Her baby. During her five years as curator, she'd sent her assistants throughout the planetary systems and back to Earth's primitive past to acquire erotic treasures.

"What?"

"Don't interrupt."

His expression said *no one* talked to him that way.

"I've sent a total of three trusted assistants to purchase your sex object and none of them returned. Their messages? They were having too much fun. *Fun?* What kind of an excuse is that?" They'd been weak. Probably lost track of their purpose while they wallowed in the sensual hot tub that predominated this period. Exasperated, she'd finally come herself.

"Galactic Museum? Never heard of it." He moved closer, if closer was possible. Justin Hill was way beyond just invading her space. He overwhelmed her with his in-your-face maleness and the heated realness of his sexuality. It wasn't anything he'd said; it was who he was. And, even across the span of 695 years, the female in her recognized him.

She sighed. Of course she couldn't tell him anything that would confuse him. He wouldn't sell her squat if he thought she was crazy. First, she had to make it clear what she'd come for.

Stepping back, she raked him with what she hoped was a contemptuous gaze. Unfortunately, it grew less contemptuous as it drifted lower. When it reached his groin, it stalled altogether. Men in her time wore loose, flowing garments that hid any proof of their gender. Of course, men in her time didn't *have* much proof. But that was okay, because sexuality wasn't really important. The mind defined the man.

It was very clear what defined *this* man. "I've come here to purchase the greatest of all sex objects." She speared him with her glare. "And *you* are not it." A flash of lightning followed by booming thunder made her announcement a little more dramatic than she'd planned. A few drops of rain started to fall.

She didn't intend to stand here getting wet while he decided whether to invite her in or leave her outside to be washed down the mountainside. Serenity picked up her travel pack. "I'll just step inside so we can discuss your monetary reward for handing over *The Flame*." She stepped around him and into his home.

Serenity half expected him to close his fingers around her neck, yank her out of his hallway, and heave her into the stormy night. It would do him no good. She'd just pick herself up and offer him more money.

When she heard no sound behind her, she turned. He stood as if frozen while the storm broke around him.

The wind whipped his long dark hair into a tangled glory and plastered his sleeveless T-shirt against his broad, muscular chest. Suddenly, the heavens opened, and sheets of rain soaked him. Water ran down his bare arms, making his skin gleam like a statue of some pagan warrior.

Serenity would've enjoyed studying the musculature of his thighs and legs as well, purely from an aesthetic perspective, but his hard stare held her prisoner.

She pushed a shiver of fear away and tried to deny her inner voice of truth. Its whisper reached her anyway. This was not one of her time's gentle and supremely civilized men. Justin Hill looked at her from the eyes of one of Earth's ancient predators. Did one enter the house of a predator? You did if he had something you wanted. And that was the bottom line for Serenity So-Fine.

"Umm. Maybe you should come inside, too." After this, she could have changed her last name to So-Stupid.

He held her gaze as he strode into the house, then pushed the door shut behind him. Despite his obvious strength, the door didn't slam, but merely eased shut with an ominous click.

"Come in and sit down." His voice made plain this wasn't a friendly invitation. He walked past her and disappeared through one of the many doorways lining the long, dim hallway. He didn't look back to see if she followed him.

Serenity hesitated. All she had to do was reach for the time travel disk secured around her neck, press "return," and she'd be safe once again in her sane time. *Without* *The Flame*.

She wouldn't do it. Slowly, she followed him.

The room was an eclectic mix of comfortable seating and other furniture, with a large blazing fireplace to take away the chill of the cool, wet night. But that's not what riveted Serenity's attention. Scattered around the room, on tables, on the fireplace's mantel, and even on the floor, were metal sculptures. Justin's artistic DNA was stamped all over them. Emotional, energetic, and brilliant. But none of them were erotic. Where did he keep *The Flame*?

Serenity eased into the overstuffed armchair closest to the door, then set her pack and stake beside her. Not that she'd have anywhere to run if she decided on a quick getaway.

He stood with his arm propped against the mantel, staring into the fire. "Now, tell me what you know about *The Flame*." He didn't look at her.

Uneasiness slid up her spine. His demand didn't make sense. The whole world knew about it. All the records they had indicated *The Flame* had caused a sensation in 2004 because of the innovative technique used to create it and the incredible emotion conveyed by the sculptor.

"Everybody's talking about it. *The Flame* is probably the greatest erotic sculpture the world will ever see." From her perspective in 2700, she could state that with some authority.

"And what year did I finish . . . *The Flame?*" He still didn't look at her, but his fingers once again curled into fists.

Something wasn't right here. What if he'd already sold it to someone else? According to the records, he still owned it in 2005, but old records could be wrong. His tenseness was a living, breathing extension of the man. She squirmed in her chair.

"You finished it last year." Serenity was on safe ground now. "And I'm here to offer you whatever you want for it." She'd done her homework well. People in this time worshipped money, and she could afford to outbid anyone else who wanted the sculpture.

"When exactly was 'last year,' Serenity So-Fine?" He finally looked at her, and something frightening blazed in the depths of those gray eyes, something that reflected the fury of the storm now muted by the house's thick walls. There was nothing muted about Justin Hill's emotions.

Suddenly, what had seemed so simple as she sat in her comfortable museum office now took on sinister dimensions. Was he crazy? Maybe *he'd* sent the messages from her assistants. Maybe he'd murdered them and buried their bodies in the cellar. She shook off her mind's overreaction. Museum records would've noted if he were a serial killer. He'd asked an easy question; she'd give an easy answer.

"Two thousand four." Serenity willed herself to relax, but she wished the house wasn't so silent. Didn't anyone else live here?

He pushed away from the mantel and took a step toward her. Even that slight motion pushed her back in her chair, made her dig her nails into the arms as an anchor.

"The year is two thousand three, and the only place *The Flame* will probably ever live is in my mind." His smile was no smile at all, merely a baring of his teeth. "How did you know what was in my mind, Ms. So-Fine?"

"Two thousand *three*?" Serenity widened her eyes until she felt her face must be one huge eyeball. How had the time travel agency made that kind of mistake? She closed her eyes, pictured herself scribbling the information on a note and giving it to her assistant, Tranquillity. She must've made her five look too much like a three. Why hadn't she made the arrangements herself, the way she arranged everything else in her life? Too late now for should-haves.

"You may as well open your eyes, because you have some questions to answer." His voice sounded close.

Too close. So close that his warm breath moved across her tightly closed lids. For the first time in her twenty-eight years, Serenity So-Fine wished she could curse. A curse wicked enough to shrivel his no-doubt oversized sexual organs. Unfortunately, no one cursed in 2700, because to use an effective curse, one had to have a worthy recipient.

She opened her eyes and met his silver stare framed in dark seduction. Where had that thought come from? Seduction wasn't part of her normal word bank. But no other description seemed a fitting tribute to his gray eyes with those thick dark lashes. It was a good thing he didn't live in 2700, because he'd disturb the calm, even tenor of every woman's life.

"What're you thinking?" His voice was soft and controlled, but his eyes said something else entirely.

She swallowed past the boulder in her throat. "I was thinking that a vile curse might be appropriate for the moment, but I don't know any vile curses."

His lips slanted up in the first real smile she'd seen from him, and she drew in a deep, fortifying breath. She'd never quite understood the true meaning of "lethal." She understood now.

"I'll give you a few you can use." He bent closer, even as he planted his hands firmly on the arms of her chair.

Trapped. He was so close that, if she chose, she could lean forward and slide her tongue across his full lower lip. She frowned. Even during her two government-mandated sexual encounters, she'd never thought in terms of her mouth on any part of a man's body.

The truth behind her mind's closed door had given up on doorknob rattling and was now whispering through the keyhole. *What about all those nights alone in the museum with only the paintings, the sculptures, and your imagination? You wondered about all the ways—*Serenity stuffed the keyhole with her resolve *not* to think about those nights.

"Who the hell are you, and how do you know about *The Flame?*" His lips moved slowly, carefully enunciating each word.

Wonderful lips. If she lived in this time, she might even be tempted to taste those lips. Of course she didn't, and she wouldn't. "I'm *still* Serenity So-Fine, and I know about *The Flame* because its existence is recorded in the museum's data base of erotic treasures."

With a muffled oath she didn't quite catch, he pushed away from her chair, then raked his fingers through his tangled hair. "I know the names of all the major museums, and there is no damned Galactic Museum of Erotic Art."

"I don't care what the hell you know, but in my time there damned well is a Galactic Museum of Erotic Art." She hoped she'd used the curses correctly.

"And what *is* your time?" He shook his head, and his wet hair shifted across his shoulders. "I can't believe I asked that."

A total disaster. Nothing else would describe this whole thing. Not only was she in the wrong time, but Justin Hill, aka The Savage, sounded like he might never create *The Flame*. Civilization couldn't lose such a great work of art. Even though she wouldn't be able to stay long enough to see him finish it, she had to make sure he started. Then she could send an assistant back to claim it in 2005. She'd choose a very old assistant this time, one who wouldn't be tempted by the carnal nature of this time, *of this man*.

"I asked a question, and I don't like to wait for answers." His tone suggested that people usually didn't keep him waiting for anything.

"Too bad." Once again, she noted his startled expression. For the first time, she wondered what happened to someone who talked back to him. Maybe she didn't want to know.

She'd have to tell him the truth. This wouldn't be so tough. The travel agency always prepared time travelers for this eventuality by sending along a list of major events that had happened within five years of the targeted time period. The list was supposed to convince skeptics who didn't believe in time travel. It sounded great in theory. Then why was her heart pounding at about a thousand beats a minute?

Serenity took a deep breath. "I'm from the year 2700. Now, before you tell me you don't believe it, let me get you some proof." Refusing to look at him, she bent down to her pack and rooted around in it. The list had to be here somewhere. If her hands weren't shaking she could do a better job of searching.

Why wasn't he shouting and threatening her with a mental health facility? She wasn't going to look up and find out. At last, her fingers touched the list. As she glanced at it, a sense of inevitability settled around her like a toxic cloud. The list spanned the years 2005 to 2010. Fat lot of good that would do.

Suddenly, he crouched down in front of her and put his hand on her knee. A large hand with strong, blunt fingers. Not the hand of an artist. Not the hand of a man from her time. "Calm down. I believe you."

"You do?" Why would he believe her? Everyone needed proof.

"I believe you because I've never talked about *The Flame* to anyone." His eyes glittered with suppressed excitement, not the disbelief and panic she'd expected.

"Oh." Her vocabulary seemed to shrink with every moment she spent near this man.

"Tell me about *The Flame*." His fingers still lay on her knee, a warm reminder of her vulnerability in his house.

"The museum only has two views of *The Flame*, the back and one side. It shows a nude man and woman wrapped in a sexual embrace. They're standing, and the man has the woman's hands clasped above her head." She'd always wanted to see their faces. Did their expressions mirror the passion of their embrace?

He nodded, and she had the feeling his thoughts were turned inward.

"And they're surrounded by the symbolic flames of their desire." His murmur was an affirmation of his inner vision.

She nodded. Maybe this trip had been worthwhile after all. Perhaps she hadn't wasted all those hours spent studying the speech patterns and culture of this time. If she could give him the nudge he needed to create *The Flame*, then she would have done a service to mankind. The thought energized her. "So why don't you do it?"

He stood and, for the first time, seemed to realize his shirt was soaked. In one swift motion, he stripped it off and dropped it to the carpet. "I don't create on demand. *The Flame* is in my head. It doesn't become real until it's here." He tapped his chest.

Serenity did the eye-widening thing again. Nudity didn't cause embarrassment in her time because so much of the fixation on the sexual nature of the body didn't apply anymore. A great mind was sexy, not a great body.

Of course, there were bodies and there were bodies. She'd never seen a man's body that was so . . . *there*. How could she concentrate on his mind when her senses had attached themselves to his tanned, muscular chest like tiny, immovable suction cups? He oozed elemental maleness on a scale she'd never experienced.

For the first time in her life, Serenity considered the possibility that her time might not have it all.

"What?" The wicked slant of his lips said he knew exactly what she was thinking.

Drawing in a deep breath of resolve, she dragged her senses kicking and screaming from the candy jar of their choice. "I'm here for you, Justin. I have three days to move *The Flame* from head to heart. Now, what do I have to do?"

"Three days, huh?" He studied her, giving away nothing. "What do you know about me, Serenity?"

"Well . . . nothing. Museum records are pretty incomplete about your personal life. They even had your age wrong. I thought you were seventy-eight."

He frowned. "Your records probably mixed me up with my grandfather. He's done some impressive sculptures of the human body."

Serenity searched her memory. "Evidently, he didn't do anything important enough for us to have records on."

"I bet that would shock the hell out of him." His lips were set in a grim line.

For a moment, she wondered about his relationship with his grandfather, then pushed the thought aside. She was here for *The Flame*, not to get involved in the artist's family life. "I'm dealing with a time limitation here. In 2700, every citizen on Earth is allotted a three-day trip through time. We're only allowed one trip to keep time travelers from cluttering up the past. So I've got to make these three days count, because I won't get a second shot."

He nodded, his gaze thoughtful. "You sound like anyone I'd meet on the street. Why?"

If it made him more comfortable with who she was, she'd answer his questions. "I studied the speech patterns and vernacular of this time."

His expression didn't change, but Serenity swore she saw a gleam of amusement in his eyes. "Is that why you called *The Flame* a sex object?"

She looked away. "I wanted to use terms that would convince you I was from this time, so I tried to use your slang. Not all slang terms are explained in our language program." She sighed. "I thought the phrase 'sex object' sounded self-explanatory. I was wrong."

"And the stake?" His amusement was open now.

Serenity didn't know if she'd ever get used to being laughed at. It almost made her . . . mad. She frowned. Anger had never touched her. How would she handle it? "I stopped at a small store in Carlton to get directions, and the lady there sold me the stake. She said that no one knew who lived here now, but that legend said this was once the home of a vampire." She shrugged, a little embarrassed. "I don't believe in vampires, but in my society everyone must be polite to others, so I took the stake."

"And now you're going to help me create *The Flame*."

His gaze assessed her, stripped her of all her pretensions, and exposed the doubt. The doubt that hadn't existed before Justin Hill had opened his door to her.

"Yes." She'd do whatever it took to bring *The Flame* into existence.

"You can try, Serenity So-Fine." Challenge gleamed in his eyes. "You can certainly try."

A lightning flash was followed immediately by booming thunder that seemed to shake even this house's thick walls. Suddenly, the lights went out, leaving them in darkness.

Serenity sucked in a breath of panic. Fear of the dark was a primitive trait. She was *not* afraid of the dark. So, of course, her shriek of terror when someone touched her arm came as a complete surprise.

"It's okay, Serenity. I'm here."

That's what she was afraid of. Candlelight flickered into life beside her, and, in its glow, she saw Justin. His incredible eyes, his face framed by his fall of demon-dark hair, all seemed disembodied within the circle of wavering light. The darkness shifted and moved, a living thing whispering night secrets. At this moment, vampires seemed a very real possibility.

"Come with me." His voice was a soft murmur of sensuality.

"Where are we going?" Her question was meaningless because she'd follow him anywhere he led. She didn't intend to be left alone in this dark room populated with the Vampires-of-Christmas-Past, the vampires she absolutely did *not* believe in. She picked up her pack and stake, then stood.

"I'll take you to your room, then go to start up the generator. The lights go out a lot up here on the mountain. You'll find a flashlight in the drawer beside your bed if you need it." He held the candle so she could see the flight of stairs as it wound up into the darkness. "So, how do all the . . . sex objects you collect make you feel?"

She shrugged, then remembered he probably couldn't see the gesture. "If you mean do they affect me sexually, the answer is no. I admire them only on an aesthetic level." In her mind, beady eyes peered at her from beneath the closed door. Accusing eyes. *Lying is wrong, wrong, wrong.* Serenity chose to ignore the eyes. "Our culture has progressed beyond the need for sexual responses."

"Let's hear it for progress."

She chose to ignore his muttered sarcasm and concentrated on not tripping as he led her down a long, dark hallway.

"Are you a virgin, Serenity?" He stopped at the end of the hall.

Virgin? An archaic word, but one whose meaning she knew from her study of erotic art. "Is that the usual question you ask guests?"

"No." He didn't hide his amusement. "But then, you're not anyone's usual guest. So, are you a virgin?"

"Of course not. The government suggests that we have two sexual encounters so we can make an informed decision about whether married life and parenthood should be included in our life plans." She didn't want to acknowledge the unease she felt discussing sex with him, even though erotic art was her life.

"Did you enjoy the sex?" A door clicked open, and, when he swung it wide, she stepped into the room.

Where was he going with these questions? "No one lies in my time, and sometimes that creates . . . problems. After my first encounter, I explained to my partner that his foreplay technique needed restructuring, and he compared me to an arctic ice flow. My second encounter didn't even reach con-

summation. He left right after I suggested that a penis extension would make his sexual experiences more rewarding."
Uncertain, she glanced at Justin. "Should I have been less
truthful?"

He laughed out loud. "God almighty, woman. In two thousand three, you'd be known as the Great Emasculator."

Serenity was *not* amused. She was used to the admiration
of others. People praised her for her cool and analytical ap-
praisal of the erotic art in the museum. Her directness and
adherence to truth were legendary. Now this barbarian was
making fun of her.

She plopped down on the massive bed he'd led her to. She
couldn't see much of the room, but that was probably for the
best. What she could see of the antiquated four-poster bed
was enough.

He loomed over her. "You challenge me. And I haven't
felt challenged in a long time."

Was that good? Did it mean he'd start on *The Flame*?

Justin reached out and drew a line of sizzling surprise along
the length of her jaw. "You have a lot to learn—about life,
about me."

She could only swallow hard. As an afterthought, she realized she'd probably swallowed her voice along with her
courage.

"Sleep well, Serenity So-Fine." His wicked grin was made
more dangerous by the candlelight's pale glow. "And believe
in things you never believed in before . . ." He strode to the
door, then glanced over his shoulder. "Even vampires." Then
he was gone, and not even a soft click marked the door's
closing.

She was *not* afraid. Serenity stripped off her clothes and climbed beneath the covers.

She was *not* intimidated. She closed her eyes and willed sleep to come.

She did *not* believe in vampires.

She opened her eyes, leaned over the side of the bed, retrieved her stake, and shoved it under her pillow.

CHAPTER TWO

Justin sat cross legged on the floor of Serenity's bedroom and sketched her as she slept. The cool light of dawn cast its first pink rays across her bed.

He smiled. She'd like him to believe she was like the dawn, cool and calm, a woman untouched by passion even though surrounded by the Earth's most sensual art. He didn't believe her.

Justin paused to consider what else he didn't believe. She said she was from a far distant future. His reason refused to accept that. But his reason had no explanation for how she knew about *The Flame*. Believing she was some sort of mind reader was as much of a stretch as believing she'd come from the future. Since he thought of himself as a pragmatist, he'd accept her at her word until he found out differently. His doubts wouldn't stop him from enjoying Ms. So-Fine.

Justin smiled every time he thought of her last name. She'd hate knowing how much it fit her. And he was in a prime position to make that call.

Her long blond hair fanned across her pillow, and she'd kicked off the covers during the night. Who would've guessed Serenity So-Fine had so much woman hidden beneath her long, flowing dress of yesterday, and that she'd make it so easy for him to see all that woman this morning? He'd have to explore the so-much and so-easy possibilities later. She was either very naïve or very calculating to sleep nude in his house.

He amended that last thought. Nude except for the small medallion attached to a silver chain that circled her smooth throat. His alter ego would find her throat an irresistible temptation.

Justin concentrated on sketching the curve of her breast, a breast that would fill his palm without overflowing it. Firm, with smooth, warm skin and a nipple puckered by the cool morning air. If he went to her now and touched her nipple with his mouth, would she wake to . . .

He tried to shake the thought away, but his body was like a bulldog with a bone. It growled and hung on. He knew better than to argue with his body when it was in this mood, so he simply unzipped his cutoffs to let his body expand on its vision.

"What are you doing?" Her voice was still warm and soft from sleep.

"Not what I'd like to be doing." Reluctantly, he slid his gaze to her face.

She frowned, and he could almost see her sluggish thoughts wrapping themselves around his words and trying to make sense of them. If she'd told the truth about the future thing, she might not understand sexual innuendoes.

Pushing herself to a sitting position, she scraped a few strands of hair from her face. "No, I meant why are you in my room? It's wrong to invade my personal space." She made no attempt to cover herself.

"I'm not anywhere near your personal space, but I'm about to be." Justin rose in one motion, strode to her bed, and sat down beside her. He made no attempt to zip up his cutoffs.

Curiosity tugged at him. What would it take to get a sexual response from Ms. So-Fine? She certainly hadn't worked hard to get one from him. But he was starting to realize that where Serenity was concerned, his cock was easy, shallow, and definitely not interested in the So-Fine mind.

Reaching out, he touched the medallion with the tip of his finger. Did she flinch, or was that just wishful thinking? "Considering that you shucked everything else before climbing into bed, I'm surprised you kept this on. Valuable?"

She nodded, and her hair trailed tangled paths across her bare shoulders. "It's my ticket home. When my three days are up, it'll send me back to 2700."

He narrowed his gaze on the small blue stone in the medallion's center. "And if you're not wearing it?"

She shrugged. "It goes home without me."

Leaning forward, she glanced at his sketch and her scent touched him—an elusive blend of warm female, hot promises, and cool Appalachian breezes. "Why are you drawing me?" Her hair followed the bend of her head and tumbled around her face. Impatiently, she pushed it behind her ears.

That gesture blew Justin's calculating woman theory. She had to know how that incredible tumble of blond glory affected a man and wouldn't carelessly tuck it away. Then again, if her story was true, she had no idea what affected a man's sexual response.

"You want me to start on *The Flame*, so I'm putting myself in the mood to transfer the image from head to heart." Not exactly the truth. He was sketching her because she was the first woman to catch his imagination in a long time. An intriguing mix of naïveté and determination wrapped in a lithe, seductive package. And if her story was a fake? Hey, he lived a make believe life on a daily basis.

"Oh." Her expression said she didn't get it.

"Do you always sleep in the nude?" Just saying the words compelled him to touch her. "Do you understand what happens to a man's body when he sees a woman bared to his gaze, her legs spread, open to whatever he wants to do?" He slid his hand along her outer thigh and felt her muscles tense beneath his fingers.

If he'd expected her to curl into a frigid little ball, he'd made a mistake.

"I'm sorry. I forgot I wasn't in my time. Bodies no longer trigger sexual responses in twenty-seven hundred, so we're comfortable with nudity. But if it bothers you, I'll cover up." She offered him a tight smile as she pulled the covers up to her chin.

Well, hell. If that wasn't a kick in the crotch. "You bet it bothers me." He knew he was snarling but he couldn't help it. She'd relegated him to oversexed Neanderthal. Exhaling sharply, he let it go. Maybe oversexed Neanderthal wasn't a bad place to be.

Her blue eyes widened in alarm. "I'm definitely not criticizing you. All that sexual drive allowed primitive people to create wonderfully moving, sensual works of art."

"Primitive people, huh?" Irritated, he stood and zipped up his cutoffs. Her gaze never left his face. "How do your people create 'wonderfully moving sensual works of art' when your sex drive has taken a hike?"

Her glance skittered over his bare chest, but he figured

bare male chests weren't a turn-on to Ms. Arctic Ice Flow. Too bad his chest didn't know that. His stomach muscles tightened in the hope her gaze would drop lower.

"You're right. That is a problem. Great art has to have great passion behind it." She bit her lip.

"I feel your pain. Great passion is out of stock in your time. Bet it isn't even back-ordered." He fixated on the glistening fullness of her lip, and in his imagination sucked on its pouty fullness before slipping his tongue into the heat of her mouth. "I guess that's why you travel through time pillaging the past of its treasures. How does it feel to be a sex-object pirate?"

Serenity's narrowed eyes said she was *not* amused. "We aren't pirates. We pay for what we get. You'll be a rich man after I pay you for *The Flame*."

Her gaze finally drifted down to his groin, and he could swear his cock was trying to unzip his cutoffs from the inside in its frenzy to fulfill its destiny. "I'm already a rich man, and I don't remember saying I'd sell *The Flame* to you."

Justin strode toward the door, satisfied that *The Flame* was no longer in his head. His problem? It had bypassed his heart and raced directly to his Go spot. It hadn't collected its two hundred dollars and was pretty steamed about that. He had to find a way to route it back to his heart.

"You'll sell. My research indicates that money could buy anything in this time." Her voice oozed annoying self-confidence. "And I'm not surprised you're rich. Those sculptures I saw last night were amazing."

He smiled at the thought of getting in the last word on Ms. Serenity So-Sure-Of-Herself. "I've never sold *any* of my sculptures. No one knows about them except Clara . . . and you." His smile widened. "I don't think you want to know how I make my money." He pulled open the door and stepped into the hallway. "There's coffee down in the kitchen and stuff to eat if you root around. I have work to do." He closed the door quietly behind him.

Who was Clara? Serenity stared at the closed door as she let the covers slip from her shaking fingers. It had taken all her self-control to maintain her calm veneer and not yank the covers up to her nose when she'd found him sketching her. But she had a reputation for remaining composed in any situation, and no six feet plus of primitive intimidation would shake her from her normal reactions. Her trembling hands, however, hinted calmness might be a state of mind lost to her forever if she spent much more time around Justin Hill.

And what if he refused to sell *The Flame?* She'd never considered that possibility. He *had* to sell it. She'd already made an honored spot for it in her museum.

Once out of bed, she stood at the window, staring at the forested mountain that was Justin Hill's lair. How could he be rich when he'd never sold any of his work? And if he was rich, why was he living in the local vampire's crumbling former residence? Serenity couldn't imagine him outside this setting, though. She wished his life records had been more complete.

Sighing, she headed for the bathroom. Only when she stood beneath the shower's warm spray did she allow herself to consider the most disturbing part of Justin's visit.

She'd reacted physically to him. When she'd woken to find him sitting on her floor, she'd had no time to think, to raise any protective barriers. In her mind, she'd climbed from her bed and stretched, watching his gaze sear a heated path over her breasts and stomach, then touch between her parted thighs. She'd felt the fullness, the wet need for what this man could give her, and wondered why need had never touched her before. *Because you've never met such a completely sexual animal before.*

Sexual animal. Serenity closed her eyes, and the slide of warm water over her body became his fingers, a glide of pleasure that heated every bare inch of her flesh.

What would *he* look like? Not like the men of her time. Without clothing, he'd be all tanned skin and hard muscle, a body gloriously equipped to give pleasure. He would be the taste of rich cream, a slide of sensual excess that would never be good for her, but was, even in her time, irresistible.

She touched her nipples, sensitive to the very thought of him, then glided her fingers the length of her body. Sexual curiosity. An unknown quantity in her life's equation. What if she satisfied it here, in this time, with this man?

Her fingers had no allegiance to her brain as they slipped between her thighs to tease a spot that had little experience with teasing. Her body welcomed the new sensations with enthusiasm, its slick readiness announcing its joy over her sexual fantasy.

Sexual fantasy? Serenity opened her eyes and blinked away the stream of water along with the sensual fog that wrapped her in layers of silken possibilities, then drifted away, leaving only the echo of its laughter. She'd never fantasized about anything beyond the acquiring of new and wonderful erotic objects.

She'd *never* fantasized about a man. But this man? The sexual scenarios were tumbling over themselves in their eagerness for . . . For what?

Abandoning the warm water, she stepped onto the plush rug, and dried herself with his fluffy towel. Plush and fluffy. That's how she'd think of herself for these three days.

Her main focus was still *The Flame*, but he'd said himself he'd need to move the concept from head to heart. And all her research confirmed her belief that, during this time period, men's hearts and sexual organs were interchangeable.

So, if she could arouse sexual need in him, wouldn't that translate into a need to create *The Flame*? Sounded logical to her. And, if she worked things right, his need could segue into her wish fulfillment.

Feeling suitably righteous, she dressed. Sort of. What would be considered sensually exciting attire in 2003? Was she being too . . . ? What was the common term? Was she being too slutty? She firmed her lips and stiffened her spine. Bring on the sluttiness.

As she reached the door, honesty tapped her on the shoulder. It asserted with prim outrage that she had no right to try to seduce Justin Hill so that she could live out a few sexual fantasies. Besides, she'd probably fail. She hadn't been a rousing success with her first two sexual encounters.

Serenity narrowed her eyes and reached for the doorknob while honesty continued to natter in her ear. Fine, so this time she wouldn't be so forthcoming with her opinions. Justin could never live up to a fantasy, but, if they got as far as a sexual encounter, she'd swallow any negative comments and make chirpy sounds of ecstasy. She tried to push aside the memories of her own sexual inadequacies and thoughts of what Justin might say about her probably amateurish night performance.

Honesty sputtered into silence, rendered speechless by Serenity's intention to lie.

Justification rode to her rescue. This was really all about getting *The Flame*. She had a duty to the museum to use any methods necessary to secure this national treasure. And if she had to sacrifice herself on the altar of duty, then she'd do what needed doing, no matter how . . . distasteful.

As Serenity left her bedroom, she tried to ignore honesty's snort of disbelief.

She'd eaten a banana because that was the only food she recognized, and now Serenity prowled the huge old house. Sexual fantasy fulfillment would be kind of tough if she couldn't find her fantasy man. Obviously, she hadn't left Justin slavering with lust for *her*. But that was okay because she had enough lust for both of them.

There, she'd admitted it. She'd leaped from the comfort zone of her own time, with its societal expectations into this time, where sensuality thickened the air and made each breath a panting desire. Did that make sense? Probably not. Serenity only knew she'd landed in this time running. She'd experience all that needed experiencing in 2003 and return to her time a sated woman. An added plus. All this hands-on practice would make her a better curator, more in tune with the museum's creations.

She wandered long hallways that were dimly lit by flickering electric lights intended to imitate candles burning in wall sconces. Old faded wallpaper, worn hardwood floors, and time-darkened paintings of ancient battles added up to an atmosphere that could only be described as . . . foreboding.

Serenity smiled. This whole house sent shivery chills down her spine. Fear. An extreme emotion. Until she'd landed on Justin's doorstep, she'd never realized how bland her life's sensations had been. No fearful shivers, no fist-clenching anger, no pulse-pounding excitement. Now, she'd experience it all. Maybe when she went home, she could pass the emotions on to a few talented artists to help in their creative processes.

She reached the end of the third-floor hallway and glanced out the window overlooking the back of the house. A helicopter sat on a concrete pad. Its gleaming newness clashed with the old house. At least she now knew how Justin got off the mountain.

Distracted by thoughts of where he could've made enough money to pay for the helicopter, she turned the knob of the door nearest the window. She'd tried other doors, but they'd been locked. This one wasn't.

Serenity stepped into the room, then froze. She'd found a portal to hell.

It had no windows. Walls and ceiling were painted blood red, and the thick, crimson pile of the carpet swallowed her footsteps as she edged further into the room. Artificial lighting meant to mimic leaping flames flickered and danced across the walls and ceiling. In the center of the room, a black marble throne rested on a raised dais.

But none of this was enough to make her heart beat madly, her breath catch and freeze. None of this was enough to draw her into the room.

Masks. Dozens of shining silver masks lined the flame-licked walls. She almost ran across the room while her brain shouted helpful advice like: Are you *crazy*, sister? Get your behind *out* of here. She ignored her brain. Her brain had no artistic curiosity. It was completely focused on survival.

She touched the first mask with reverence. A light metal, meant to be worn, not just admired. A creature from some grotesque nightmare. Evil watched from behind the slanted eyeholes, the twisted mouth murmured terrifying promises, and fangs dripped silver drops of blood. Beautiful. Wicked. *Genius*.

Vampires. Serenity drew in a deep calming breath as she moved from mask to mask. All depicted fanged creatures of the night; all were magnificent, if you could think of evil as magnificent. Her shudder was instinctive, a reflexive action.

"What do you fear, Serenity So-Fine?"

His soft, husky whisper fanned the back of her neck and hinted she'd waited too long to run. She turned.

He stood behind her.

Even though he still had on the cutoffs he'd worn as he sat on her floor, he looked different somehow. He towered over her, his sweat-sheened torso taking on the heat and menace of the flickering flames, the rise and fall of his chest becoming the rhythm of sex and sin recorded in ancient tales of demons who stalked the night.

She lifted her gaze. A stranger looked out of his eyes. Eyes that reflected the fire, heated to molten silver from within. She wasn't sure it was safe to know what burned in him.

"I asked what you fear." He reached out and slid his fingers through her hair. The gesture and the question were charged with erotic intent.

I fear what I want to do with you. Since she wouldn't tell him the truth, she resorted to a lie. She'd never realized that lies were so easy to tell.

"This room is sort of scary, but your masks are incredible. I'd like to buy some of them to take back to the museum." *What about you? How much would you cost?*

"The masks aren't for sale." Leaning down, he touched the base of her neck with his lips where her pulse beat strong. "I use them."

"Use them?" Uh-oh. She'd swear she could feel the hot rush of her blood beneath the warm pressure of his lips. Could he feel it, too?

His soft laughter heated her throat. It made her want to pull him close, so she could see what else he could heat with he drhis laughter. It made her want to push him away, until he explained exactly *how* he used his masks.

"You never asked how I make my money, Serenity." He nibbled a path across the top of her shoulder.

Okay, nibbling was good. She could get into nibbling as long as fangs weren't involved. "You said I didn't want to know. I took you at your word."

Lifting his head, he captured her gaze and held it with ruthless ease. "So let me get this straight. You don't know a thing about me except that I created *The Flame*. You're alone with me, and . . ." his lips tilted up in the beginning of a smile ". . . you're standing here in just your bra and panties." His gaze warned that you should never tease a wolf . . . or a vampire. "Don't you feel the danger?" His smile widened. "If you leave right now, you can still run screaming into the night."

She blinked. "It's daylight."

His smile held secrets. "Wrong. I bring the darkness, Serenity So-Fine."

Her literal roots struggled to interpret his smoke-and-mirrors imagery. "I've never experienced danger . . ." *Before.* The first tingle of unease worked its way down her spine. "I've never been afraid . . ." *Before.* "Should I be afraid of you?"

His smile turned wicked, and she knew the memory of that smile would keep her warm and toasty on cold winter nights. Well, maybe not warm and toasty. How about hot and sweaty?

"Always, sweetheart. Always." With one finger, he drew a sizzling line along the top of her bra. "Why'd you decide to go with just the bra and panties?"

Another lie? She didn't think for a minute he'd believe she forgot to put on her dress. Besides, she'd spent a lifetime telling the truth. It was time to get back to basics and hope he was enough of a sexual creature that he would at least be intrigued.

She stepped back, but stepping back didn't succeed in freeing her thoughts from his sensual pull. He was erotic quicksand.

"I noticed that the more of your body you exposed, the more . . . interest I felt." She shifted her gaze to a point beyond him. Okay, call her a coward, but she couldn't say what she was saying and meet his gaze. "I thought I'd dispense with some clothes and see if you felt a reciprocal interest . . ." She sneaked a quick peek down. Yep, he did.

"And your point is?" He stepped forward so he filled her total field of vision.

He couldn't force her to meet his gaze. She stared at his navel, visible where his pants hung low on his lean hips. "I decided I could achieve two goals. If my lack of clothing could arouse . . ." *Poor word choice.* "If it could excite . . ." *Oh, what the hell.* "If it could stir your interest, you might be motivated to begin work on *The Flame*." Now, her explanation got harder.

"Hmm."

Since she wouldn't lift her gaze, she had no idea what expression went with his "Hmm."

"And I will admit to a certain amount of sexual curiosity about . . . you. I have a few fantasies that . . ." What did a person do when all meaningful thought evaporated in the middle of a sentence?

She didn't resist when he put his finger under her chin, forcing her to meet his gaze. "Do you have a fantasy about this room, Serenity?"

Amusement glittered in his eyes, but behind the laughter was something else entirely. Something hot and very interested.

A fantasy? Did she? Serenity glanced around the room. She did. "I'd like to have a sexual encounter with a masked stranger in this room."

He frowned. "A sexual encounter?"

What was wrong with that? Sexual encounter was the term used in her time unless two people decided to marry, then the description changed to making love. She certainly didn't want to marry Justin Hill. Instinct told her that an emotional attachment to him would come with infinite layers of complications. The only emotional attachment she wanted was to her beloved museum.

"A masked stranger?" He abandoned her and touched one of the masks. He didn't look at her as he smoothed his fingers over the cool silver features. "I don't need the mask, Serenity. I *am* a stranger to you." Finally, he lifted his gaze to meet hers, and the danger he'd hinted at burned in his eyes. "More of a stranger than you could ever imagine."

"I *want* the danger." Surprised, she realized she'd answered the promise in his eyes. "I've studied erotic art, Justin. I know that other emotions enhance sensual enjoyment. I want it all." Her vehemence amazed her.

Without commenting, he strode to the door and pushed it shut, triggering soft music. Dark and rich with night whispers, the melody promised it would haunt her future dreams. She believed the promise.

Suddenly nervous, she rushed into speech. "You wanted to tell me how you made your wealth. And what about this throne? Let me guess, you rule a kingdom of one." That wasn't even close to being funny. She swallowed hard. With the door closed, his size expanded exponentially to fill every shadowed corner. What exactly had her flapping lips wrought?

Instead of returning to her, he wandered over to the marble throne. He didn't glance at her as he casually rid himself of his shoes, then unbuttoned his pants and slipped them off. "You're wrong, Serenity. I rule a kingdom of many."

Her unblinking gaze fixed on his fingers as he hooked his thumbs over the top of his briefs, then paused for thought. "Of course, it's a kingdom of darkness, but I suppose you already knew that." The touch of amusement in his voice eased a little of her tension.

Serenity's desire for him to rid himself of the briefs must've zapped him with a silent compulsion, because he slid them down his lean hips and muscular legs. He left them lying on the scarlet carpet, a stark white contrast to the room's overwhelming redness.

She controlled her childish urge to scoop them up so she could put them under her pillow when she returned home in the hopes the orgasm fairy would put an erotic dream under her pillow. She didn't need them now.

With the controlled motion of a man at ease with his body, he sat on the marble throne. His lazy sprawl looked right for a naked dark lord.

She slid her glance the length of his body. She *wanted* this. And, since her gaze was riveted between his open thighs, she didn't have to question what *this* was.

Serenity lived and breathed erotic art. She'd seen the good, the bad, and the ridiculous. Artists in her time tended to exaggerate the size of the male sexual organs. She wasn't sure why. Maybe as a silent revolt against the dwindling interest in sexual organs taken by society as a whole. Penises big enough to double as a national monument were *not* sensual. Of course, she'd seen the real thing on beaches and during her two sexual encounters. Smaller, less imposing, boring.

Nothing boring here. He was—

"Serenity, look at me."

"I am." He was—

"At my face." He didn't attempt to hide the laughter in his voice.

"Why?" Reluctantly, she lifted her gaze to his face. She'd been enjoying her analysis of his sexual organs. From a purely aesthetic perspective, of course.

"I want to tell you how I make my money." His gaze grew shuttered.

"It's not important now." Her gaze slid down to what *was* important.

"Now is when it *is* important. I don't want any emotional outbursts or accusations later, when it's too late."

Offended, she met his gaze. "I've *never* had an emotional outburst."

"Too bad." He sounded sincere.

"What human characteristic is most dreaded in your time?" He leaned forward, his interest fully engaged in her answer, even though his body seemed intent on its own agenda.

She didn't have to think. "Violence. Can we get back to our sexual fantasy now?" That sounded overeager, even to her ears.

He exhaled deeply, then sat back. "That's what I was afraid of."

Puzzled, she watched him lean forward again. His eyes shone silver, the leaping flames reflected in their depths. "Come to me, Serenity So-Fine." His soft command allowed for nothing other than obedience.

Warily, she approached him. She stepped onto the raised dais where the throne rested, then stopped.

She felt it, the smooth slide of his power, like the low throb of the music. It wound around her with a sensual promise that touching the warmth of his flesh would bring her more pleasure than all the treasures in her museum.

She doubted it.

"Not close enough, Serenity." His husky mockery dared her.

She met his gaze and accepted his dare. Stepping between his open thighs, she made the mistake of dropping her gaze to the smooth expanse of his chest, then to his hard muscled thighs spread to accept her and the hard jutting proof that he could indeed bring her much pleasure.

Her knees trembled. More pleasure than her museum's treasures? She doubted it less every minute.

"Do you know what I am, Serenity?" He didn't wait for her response. "I'm the dark shadow in your dreams, all the violence you've imagined but never seen."

As he leaned further forward, his hair shifted. For the first time she noticed a small tattoo on his right shoulder. She focused her gaze on it. Anything rather than look into those silver eyes and see what expression went with the soft menace in his voice.

A bat? He had a small bat tattooed on his shoulder. What—

His lips moved against her ear. "I'm a purveyor of orchestrated violence, Serenity So-Fine."

She shivered as his warm breath touched her neck. "I don't—"

His laughter held no amusement. "I'm a professional wrestler, sweetheart."

"Wrestler?" Flinging people around rings? Sweaty, grunting displays of primitive . . . *A wrestler?*

"You're alone with the Night Creature, lemon drop."

CHAPTER THREE

He watched her eyes widen, but she didn't turn from him.

"A wrestler." She said the words again, probably trying to get used to the sound of violence. "Why would you want to do something like that? You could hurt your hands." She shrugged. "Besides, wrestling merely panders to the primitive mind's need to view savagery."

Why the hell didn't she get upset? He could probably tell her he was Clethor, Destroyer of the Universe, and it wouldn't knock her out of calm and reasonable mode. Amusement warred with anger. "I wear gauntlets. And don't be so quick to put down the primitive mind, lady. You're looking at a charter member of Barbarians, Incorporated. I'm physical. I'm emotional. I enjoy throwing people around a ring, then coming home to a day of creating sculptures with all that emotion you love."

Amusement won the war. "You'd be surprised how violent my creative process is." He dropped his gaze to where her hips fitted perfectly between his bare thighs. "My sculptures are fire and heat." He lifted his gaze to see the fire and heat image ignite in her eyes. "Free your emotions, Serenity So-Fine, and burn with me." His harsh demand hung between them.

She licked her bottom lip with the tip of her tongue, and his need to capture that lip and confirm every one of her preconceived beliefs about savages, emotions, and self-control almost overwhelmed him. He drew in a deep breath of temporary patience and leaned back in his throne.

She nodded, and he wondered what she was agreeing to. Justin smiled. He doubted even she knew.

He slid his finger over the thin material of her panties and enjoyed her shiver of anticipation. "Take the panties and bra off, Serenity."

She shook her head. "In my fantasy, *you* take them off."

Justin dropped his gaze to her bellybutton. Cute. "Fantasies are reciprocal in this time." He watched her stomach muscles clench beneath his stare. "I'd suggest shucking your bra and panties fast before I rip them off with my teeth." Did he sound calm and reasonable? Sure he did.

"With your teeth? Really?" Those wonderful lips tipped up at the corners.

"Take the damned things off." That sounded pretty much like a growl. He was dropping fast on the evolutionary scale.

Serenity must've thought so too, because she stepped away from him. His body acknowledged the cool sense of loss between his thighs.

"Men in my time wouldn't demand their own way." She didn't sound upset. She was just stating a fact.

He knew his smile was predatory. "Welcome to two thousand three, where men have lots of demands . . ." His glance shifted to the masks. "And women have even more."

His gaze returned to her silky black panties, to the woman inside them. Was she wet where his finger had pressed? Could he wait more than thirty seconds to find out? "Lose the panties and bra, then choose a mask." So much for slow, sensual sex talk. He couldn't remember ever being this hot for a woman.

She stood there forever. Plenty of opportunity for him to think about perceived time passage in relation to real-world time.

When he'd just about decided to up his estimate of how long she would stand there to infinity, she lowered her gaze and reached for her bra.

She fumbled with the front clasp. Perceived time, one month. Actual time, thirty seconds.

"I'll get you a pair of scissors." Where had he put the damned scissors? After the bra, she'd probably take another month to slide off her panties. "You can cut the panties off, too."

She raised startled blue eyes to his face. Whatever she saw there stilled her fumbling, her wide-eyed nervousness. "I didn't know a man could *want* that much." Her voice was whispered surprise.

Justin drew in a deep breath, then exhaled some of his need to dismember whatever idiot had designed bra clasps. He closed his eyes for a regrouping moment. When he opened them, she had finally mastered the clasp. He watched as she slipped off the bra and dropped it to the carpet.

He couldn't control the flare of his nostrils, the baring of his teeth that he hoped to God she interpreted as a sensual smile. "I want more than you can ever imagine, Serenity So-Innocent."

Her breasts were perfect: for his hands, for his mouth. The soft flicker of the artificial flames cast constantly changing images of warm flesh and shadowed mystery, each incredibly tempting.

"I never realized that each movement a woman made could be erotically stimulating to a man." Her voice had a low huskiness to it as she slid the panties down her slim hips and long legs. She left them lying beside her bra.

"I'm surprised." Justin skimmed his open palm over his chest, his stomach. He lifted his gaze from the shadowed promise between her thighs to assure himself that she was following the path of his hand. "You're an expert on erotic art. You should know that great art is never static. And sensual movement is always . . . stimulating." He slid his index finger the length of his erection, touched the drop of anticipatory moisture crowning its head, then allowed his hand to rest against his inner thigh. "Doesn't the art in your museum touch you, Serenity?"

"Not erotically." She swallowed hard, her attention fixed on his hand, on his body. "That's why I'm such a great curator. I can judge the artistic value of the artwork without any hormonal input. It's a strength." She lifted her gaze, challenging him to disagree.

"It's a weakness." He was always up for a challenge from a beautiful woman. "Erotic art was created with hormones in mind."

Her narrowed gaze was her only response. What would it take to make her really mad? Spitting, hissing, throwing-things mad? He'd explore that some other time. Right now, he wanted another emotion from her.

"Choose the mask you want me to wear." He didn't tell her the mask would only be making a token appearance, because the things he wanted to do to her body required mouth-to-body contact.

"I've already chosen." Her smile teased, hinting that she was getting a handle on *her* motion and *his* erotic response.

Turning, she paused for effect, then walked to the wall. The sway of her bare bottom was magic. He wanted to fling himself from the throne, fall to his knees, then cup each sweet cheek in his hands. He didn't know what would happen next, but he was damned sure his mouth and cock would be involved at some level.

"How the hell can someone be so at ease with their bare body and not be tuned into their sexual self?" The question burst from the heart of his frustration with her.

Calmly, she lifted a mask from the wall, then turned back to him. "When you don't think of your body as sexual, the naked part isn't a problem." She moved back to him, the mask held in front of her like some ancient idol.

She stopped just short of him and held out the mask. He took it, his fingers skimming hers. And, in that moment of touching, he felt it—the pounding excitement, the anticipation of explosive release.

"The naked part *is* a problem when I'm with *you*." Her quiet admission drew his gaze to her face. Something shimmered in her eyes that he hadn't seen there before.

Carefully, he put on the mask. His alter ego took its first deep breath and smiled. Only his senses would guide him now. And his emotions. "Come here, woman." He knew his voice echoed hollowly behind the mask and became the voice of the stranger she longed for. He refused to use her name, further distancing himself. *But only for a few minutes, lemon drop*.

He sensed her unease with him, with her own fantasy. Good.

She moved closer, her doubts bright in her eyes.

He reached out and, with the tip of his finger, trailed a leisurely path—starting between her breasts, moving down the soft swell of her belly to the spot between her legs where his finger had rested earlier. Wet, but not as wet as she would be.

She shivered, but she didn't attempt to cover herself. Brave lady.

"Make me want you." His demand was a harsh whisper. "Make me need to plunge deep inside your body more than I need to feed. No one has ever kept me from the night when it called. Can you do that?" He slid his finger between the already swollen lips that protected all the responsive woman in her. Her gasp shuddered through him. "Are you more than all the others?"

He saw the moment unease shaded into excitement. "Who are you?" She touched his mask, sliding her fingers over the cool metal as if memorizing its features.

"You chose me, called me to you. In the dark corners of your soul, where secrets hide, you know me." He flexed his hips, easing the growing pressure, watching her gaze slide across his arousal like the roughened tip of a cat's tongue.

"I want *you* to tell me." The beginning of urgency gave her voice a breathy quality. "I can make you."

Make me, Serenity So-Sexy. Make me. He remained silent,

knowing silence was his greatest ally. When he sensed her tension stretched tight, he laughed softly.

His laughter challenged and mocked her. She responded as he'd hoped.

"I can make you forget the night, your hunger." She stepped between his legs, tipped her head back, and closed her eyes. "I can make you forget all those other women." She began to move.

And he believed her.

Cupping her breasts in her palms, she stroked her nipples with the pads of her thumb. "Taste me, touch my flesh with your mouth."

"Temptations. Love them." He didn't know if she'd heard his murmured comment as he removed the mask, hung it on the corner of the throne, and then leaned forward.

Pushing her hands from her breasts, he touched one puckered nipple with his tongue and drew pleasure from her soft moan. He was barely aware when she buried her fingers in his hair and pulled him closer. Justin closed his lips over her nipple, just as he'd done in his imagination so many times since finding her naked that morning. Nipping gently, he slid his tongue across the hard nub. When he moved to her other nipple, he gently rolled the one he'd abandoned, still damp from his mouth, between his thumb and index finger.

The smooth softness of her breast, the wet heat of her nipple, and the scent of warm woman and need scattered any future planning he might have attempted. It was action and reaction, a driving desire to lay her naked body on the blood red carpet and drive into her until she screamed his name.

But what name would she scream, the one she knew or the one that drove him now?

Justin sucked in a deep breath as she moved her hips in a slow slide of temptation, back and forth across the head of his cock. Opening his thighs wider to maximize the contact, he shook as the trail of sensation shuddered through his body, shut down everything not centered between his legs, and tore the breath he'd just drawn from his body.

Her eyes remained shut, and he wondered what images moved behind her closed lids. Did she see him, or the fantasy he'd created? And why did it even matter? Then the thought was gone.

"Tell me who you are and why I need . . ." She opened her eyes, heavy lidded and glittering with all the things she'd never done with a man.

"Shh." He hushed her by drawing his finger across her parted lips.

She closed her lips around his finger, her teeth holding him captive to the heat of her mouth. Now, he was the one to close his eyes as the heat flowed downward and pooled in his groin, then drove his hips upward in an instinctive search for an end to the building pressure.

Suddenly, she released his finger. He opened his eyes as she made an inarticulate sound, then straddled his tensed thigh. Spreading her legs wide, she rode him. Leaning forward so that the exact spot she wanted touched his flesh, she slid back and forth, searing a path of hot desperation that shook him with its intensity.

Enough! Without warning, he scooped her up in his arms, stood, then laid her on the thick carpet. The dark music he'd always hated flowed around him as he dropped to his knees between her spread legs. For this moment and this woman, it seemed right.

"You're heat and fire, woman. How can you live in a time that doesn't recognize your passion? Why would you want to?" His voice was thick with his need. He leaned toward her, sliding his erection between her breasts, over her stomach, feeling the scrape of his balls across her flesh.

Her answer was a pleading whimper as she arched her hips, pressing into his groin, wringing a groan from him.

He leaned back on his heels, his breath coming in harsh gasps.

She opened her eyes wide at his withdrawal, her gaze suggesting his life would end quickly and unpleasantly if he dared leave her. "Come back here right now."

He slid his gaze the length of her open, welcoming body. "Bossy." He didn't try to disguise his predator's smile. "I like that in a woman." His gaze returned to hers, holding her, promising her things he wasn't sure he should be promising.

Reaching behind him, he slid the foil packet from the pocket of his cutoffs. She watched him prepare with avid interest.

"I know. Primitive." He clenched his jaw as he fumbled with a task that before he'd always performed with quick efficiency.

Her smile was a slow slide of anticipation, her eyes the heated blue of a flame's center. He worked with fire on a daily basis, knew the power of blue flame. A few more seconds and he'd be hot ash.

"Now." To illustrate exactly what she wanted *now*, she

reached between his thighs, ran her nails lightly the length of his cock, and circled it before making the return trip. "Or else you'll see primitive on a scale you can't even imagine."

She didn't give him a chance to respond, which was a good thing, because his power of speech had just exited out the same door as his self-control.

Hesitantly, as if discovering her power for the first time, she wrapped her fingers around his cock, squeezed gently, then began the up and down rhythm that made him jerk hard. He gritted his teeth. She was dealing in overkill now. "Where did you learn that?"

"From museum exhibits. Do you have an appropriate term for what I want you to do, or should I just scream?" Her breath caught on the words.

He growled some kind of unintelligible reply as he slid his hands beneath her bottom and lifted her to meet his thrust. This wasn't how he'd planned it. He'd wanted slower, with lots of touching, but his mask persona ruled in this room. He was out of control.

"Fine. I'll scream."

Her comment ended on a moan as he drove into her. Hard. The explosive pleasure dragged a grunt from him. He was barely aware of her cries as he withdrew, then plunged again and again.

Friction, heat, the tight clench of muscles around his cock, squeezing until he shouted out what he wanted. *Needed.*

Every one of his senses merged into his body's free fall toward that one ultimate moment of screaming, mindless pleasure. A kaleidoscope of impressions whirled past him. Her breasts, a sheen of sweat making them gleam in the flickering light. The arch of her body as she met each of his thrusts. The room's redness melting, absorbing him into it. And the masks, always the masks. They watched. They approved. He was one of them.

Then even the impressions were gone. The spasm rocked him, lifting him high, then slamming him down with enough force to stun him. He held his breath, reaching for infinity as pleasure washed in slowly receding waves over him, pinning him to her body beneath him. And, as the final wave receded, he realized infinity had eluded him. Maybe next time. Because even with his diminished faculties, he knew there *would* be a next time. He would bet money on it.

As reason returned, he lifted himself off Serenity, then lay on his side beside her.

She turned her head to stare at him from eyes wide with questions. "What happened?"

He shrugged because he hadn't had time to make sense of his emotions. "It's what happens when you have a sexual encounter in two thousand three."

"Is it always like this with your sexual encounters?" Her gaze was straightforward. She expected him to tell the truth.

He shrugged again. A shrug wasn't truth-specific. Sex had never been like this for him. The ramifications of his admission could have ripple effects he didn't want to deal with.

"I assume your first two encounters weren't like this?" Okay, so he was fishing. He reached over to push a strand of her hair away from her face.

"No." Her voice was soft, wondering. "No, they weren't."

Her gaze slid from him to the masks lining the crimson

walls, then to her mask of choice, still hanging from the throne. "Who are you?"

Disappointment stabbed him. She was talking to the mask, and the mask wasn't who he was. Not really. But then she wasn't here for him. Only his art interested her. He couldn't fault her for that.

In order to cover his conflicted feelings, he stood and retrieved the mask from the throne. Then he sat cross legged beside her. "This is Upir. He's supposed to have two hearts." His most horrific mask. The crowd loved it.

She sat up, and he watched the shift of her breasts as she reached for her bra and panties.

"Interesting. He could love . . . and not love at the same time. Convenient." She slipped her bra on with a lot more dexterity than she'd removed it. Practice made perfect.

"I don't think our boy here had loving on his mind." With a sense of inevitability, he watched her stand and pull her panties on. Did she seem a little overanxious, a little more aware of her nudity than before? He hoped not. He sort of liked her unembarrassed take on the human body.

She sat down again facing him. Not so close as before. "He's like you." She seemed pleased with her discovery.

He frowned at the mask. "I don't think so."

"Sure he is." Her gaze touched his face, slid down his body, and came to rest between his spread thighs.

Encouraged, his sex system huffed and puffed to recharge its batteries. He frowned. He wanted to concentrate on her conversation, but with all the activity down below he might start to lose it. "I don't think Upir had a cock." He was making that up. Justin didn't give a damn what Upir had or didn't have.

Her glance popped back to his face, and he could swear a flush tinted her cheekbones. Probably his imagination.

"No, I meant the two hearts thing." She talked to his mouth instead of meeting his gaze. "You're a wrestler and a sculptor. You love two opposites."

"Not as opposite as you'd think." He looked down at the mask. "I feed on emotion, Serenity So-Fine. So maybe I'm more like this guy than I think. When I'm in the ring, the crowd gets me going. My sculptures? I have to create the emotion."

Her gaze followed his down to the mask he held. "What emotion did you use to create him?"

"Upir?" Justin traced the mask's features. He'd see Serenity So-Fine's delicious body reflected in the shining metal face long after she returned to her time. "I don't remember, but I was probably pissed off at someone. There's nothing like a shot of healthy anger to get the creative juices flowing." He frowned. "Don't get attached to him. He only lives in my imagination."

She shook her head. "I don't think so, Justin. He's a part of who you are."

"Right. A part of me." Whoever *me* is.

Her conversational ball of twine seemed to have unraveled for the moment, so they just sat, absorbing the echo of sex in the red room.

"Did you build this room to feed your emotions?" She eyed the black throne.

Justin's head-of-sexual-readiness paused to consider what

it would be like to do it on that throne, then got back to the energizing process with renewed vigor. "Nope. I'm not that creative. My grandfather takes the credit for this."

"Why?"

Since her gaze had once again dropped to observe the creative process in action, he wasn't sure which "why" to address first. "Grandpa only wants to do one thing before he goes to the Great-Art-Critic-in-the-Sky. He wants to sculpt the greatest erotic piece man has ever seen." He offered her a shrug. "After what you've said, I guess he can forget it. But I wouldn't want to be the one to tell him."

He glanced around the room, seeing it through her eyes. "Once these walls were lined with erotic images. This house is full of rooms like this, rooms that were supposed to drive him into a sensual, ergo emotional, frenzy. The frenzy was supposed to feed his creative forces so he could pop out his dream. Didn't work, so he left."

Okay, now he'd answer her other "why." "And I'm hard again because you drive me crazy, lemon drop."

She stared at him with wide startled eyes. She hadn't expected him to answer her question so directly. He was sure in her time men were circumspect. Bunch of anal retentive jerks.

"Yes, well . . ." Her gaze skittered away from him.

He was making her nervous. Progress. Justin wanted to drag every one of her petrified emotions into the light of his time and watch them bloom.

"I don't want to keep you from what you were doing." She scrambled to her feet and edged toward the door.

Translation: I can't believe I screamed, begged, and had

hot, sweaty sex with a stranger. Justin shrugged. "I was working out, practicing some falls, when I heard you moving around down here."

She paused with her hand on the doorknob. "Umm, all that emotion we just stirred up . . . Did it make you want to start on *The Flame*?"

Justin beat down his urge to grin. "I thought about it. But it'll take a lot more stirring up before I move from thought to action." His urge to grin died a quick death. Had she made incredible love with him just so he'd start on her damned sculpture? No, her response had been too enthusiastic. Nothing fake there. He relaxed.

She bit her lip and looked worried. "A lot more stirring up, huh?"

"Maybe months. But you could hurry along the process." He allowed her a moment to consider that. "The keys to the other rooms are in the kitchen drawer next to the sink. I'll meet you in the kitchen as soon as I shower and change."

Justin thought about sharing his shower with her, then dismissed the thought. He really wanted to show her the rest of his house, and a side trip through his shower might put his plans on hold. "We'll take a look at the rooms and see if any of them . . . stir us."

The sound of pounding on the front door stopped whatever response she would have made. He cursed silently as he rose and pulled on his pants. "That's Clara. Comes once a week to clean."

She nodded, pulled open the door, then paused again. "I'll meet you in the kitchen."

He suspected his smile was prime Night Creature. "Dress casual." His gaze skimmed her. "And light. Very light."

CHAPTER FOUR

"*Damn. What* the hell happened back in that room?" Serenity addressed her question to the parade of stern-faced Hill ancestors whose portraits lined the walls at carefully measured intervals. They hadn't a clue.

Damn. Hell. As she entered her room, she applauded the full, rounded sound of the primitive expletives. Justin had shouted a few new ones during their mutual plummet into orgasmic ecstasy. She'd have to try them at an appropriate moment.

She did know one thing. Her sexuality, never a moving force in her life outside of her museum, had jumped up and smacked her in the face. And other places. Serenity loved Justin Hill's body. She *wanted* that body. Over and over again.

For the first time, her body was asserting its sexual independence. Serenity's nipples still felt sensitive from his mouth, his fingers, and *her* complete buy-in to all that was Justin.

And below her waist? Unimaginable upheaval. Every inch of flesh clenched around the wonder of having his body between her thighs. Closing her eyes, she had no difficulty remembering the fullness, the intense sensation, of him moving inside her. Never again would she be able to ignore the sexuality of her body. Never again would she be able to stand naked in front of him and even pretend that she lacked awareness of that sexuality.

Okay, so she understood her body's awakening. But what had happened above her neck? Her mind was still analyzing data. Her mind wasn't as much of a pushover as her body.

A quick shower left her refreshed but unenlightened. She changed into another flowing dress. Red. It was a red kind of day. She added a red scarf to punctuate the dress's statement.

On her way down the winding staircase, she tried to make sense of her feelings. She'd expected to enjoy her encounter, but enjoy was a weak sister to what she'd felt. She'd prepared for a cozy virtual fireside experience and instead been flattened by a firestorm.

The really scary part? Beyond the incredible sexual connection she'd felt with Justin was her need to know everything about him. Who he was shouldn't be a priority. Only *The Flame* should be important, but she'd forgotten all about it until the end.

Serenity paused at the bottom of the stairs. Music coming from the kitchen reminded her that the keys were there. She followed the sound and found Clara busy cleaning the sink.

"Hi, I . . ." Serenity's greeting died as Clara turned to face her. She narrowed her gaze on the older woman's cheery smile. "You . . ."

"Sold you a stake to protect you from the big, bad vampire." The woman's grin widened. She pushed a strand of impossibly red hair away from her face. "It probably came in handy for pounding on Justin's door."

"Do you always take advantage of tourists?" Serenity couldn't work up a real mad in the face of the woman's cheerfulness.

"Sure. The vampire house on top of the mountain is big business. Could sell you a cross, holy water, and some garlic, if you'd like my Vampire Special." She wiped her hands on a towel, then turned down her CD player. Her smile grew sly. "Course, the garlic might discourage Justin a wee bit. Wouldn't want to do that. My philosophy? A bite a day keeps boredom away. Some dangers are worth the risk."

Serenity wasn't going there. She retrieved the keys from the drawer, then headed for the door. She'd wait for Justin in the hallway.

"Going to take a peek at his granddaddy's fancy rooms, are you? Won't find the real Justin there. You'll find Justin's heart in the attic and in the metal building beside the house." Clara's advice followed Serenity out the door.

Serenity smiled. So he had two hearts after all. As she left the kitchen, Serenity wondered why Clara thought she'd want to find Justin's heart.

She had barely closed the door when she felt him. It wasn't a physical touching, but a warm slide of awareness that sent conflicting messages. *I'll keep you safe* warred with *Consider me dangerous and take appropriate action*. She didn't know which to believe. Did she even have a choice?

"Ready for the grand tour, Serenity So-Fine?" Justin's soft question heated the back of her neck and promised that the tour wouldn't be the grand part at all.

He guided her up the wide staircase to the second floor, his palm a sizzling pressure point on the curve of her hip, then stopped at the first door. Taking the keys from her, he unlocked the door and swung it wide.

She stepped into a jungle scene, complete with trees and

shadowed pool. Behind her, Justin flipped a switch, activating jungle sounds and the tumble of water over a small waterfall.

"So does this stir you, Serenity So-Fine?" He moved up beside her but didn't touch her.

She waited for the rush of emotion, the intense reaction she'd felt in the room of fire and demon masks. Nothing. "It's beautiful, but . . ."

"Yeah." He nodded as though she'd completed her thought. "Clara said she used to make Grandpa mad when she told him that fancy rooms wouldn't inspire him. He needed a real, live, flesh-and-blood woman to do that." He shook his head and chuckled. "Grandpa fired her once when she told him his sculptures didn't have heart."

Serenity thought about why a woman would trek up the mountain to this house for so many years. "Clara was in love with your grandfather?" *Did he look like you, Justin? Could he heat a woman from the inside out without touching her like you do?*

Justin stepped further into the room. "She still is." He turned toward Serenity. "Maybe Grandpa should've spent more time in the kitchen with Clara, instead of up here searching for his muse." He grinned. "Grandpa can sculpt perfect bodies that're doing sexy things, but that's all. You never get the feeling the bodies are seriously into the moment."

She backed from the room, and Justin followed her. He cast her an amused glance. "No stirring?"

Serenity shook her head as he unlocked another door. This time, the door swung open on a bordello scene done primarily in red velvet, mirrors, and erotic paintings of women who needed some serious body sculpting. She winced at the heart-shaped bed draped in red velvet that dominated the room. Again, she shook her head.

"You're a hard woman to stir, Ms. So-Fine." To test her hardness, he pushed her hair aside and kissed the sensitive skin behind her ear.

She drew in a deep breath. No hardness in sight. In fact, if he touched her again, she'd probably melt onto that hideous bed. She didn't want anything to do with that bed because . . .

"Let's try another room." He sounded relieved when he closed the door on the red bed and overendowed women.

Serenity bit her lip as they continued down the hall. Something wasn't right. Both of those rooms screamed "sensual premise." Why hadn't they triggered any panting sexual need?

In fact, all they did was make her more curious about Justin's relationship with his grandfather. "How does your grandfather feel about your two careers?"

He stopped. When he turned toward her, his face was all shadowed planes and hard edges. "He hates the wrestling. He got all bent out of shape when he found out. Said it was no fit career for a grandson of his. Said he didn't want to see me again until I got the foolishness out of my system." His laughter rang hollow. "Clara and he are the only ones besides you who know who the Night Creature is. He'll never tell anyone because it would tarnish his almighty reputation as a 'serious' artist."

Justin's bitterness told Serenity all she needed to know about his love for his grandfather. Inexplicably, his hurt moved her. "What about your sculptures? Isn't he proud that you've followed in his footsteps?"

She wanted to draw her finger across the tight line of his

lips, watch them relax into the sensual smile that touched her in all the right places.

"He doesn't know about the sculptures. No one does except Clara and you. He can damn well come here and see them if he cares about what I'm doing." His lips relaxed a little. "Guess I'm as hard headed as the old man."

He opened the next room, but Serenity only gave the fake harem scene a cursory glance. "What does Clara say about your sculptures?"

He closed the door of the harem without bothering to go inside. Evidently, nothing about these rooms stirred him either. "Clara says I need to find a focus for all my emotions before I can reach my potential."

Serenity thought about what it would cost a woman to be the focus of Justin's emotions. Worth it? Definitely.

She almost let him walk past the next door. "What about this?"

He shrugged. "That's my room. Nothing of interest there."

Nothing of interest? He was kidding, right? "I'd like to see it."

For a moment, he hesitated, then threw open the door.

She stepped inside and instantly felt the connection, the rightness. The plain brass bed with the rumpled white sheets spoke to her. It whispered of naked bodies slick with heat and sex, of cool mountain breezes moving the sheer curtains and sliding across the lovers who lay tangled in the sheets, of the scent of passion and white cotton. "*This* room stirs me, Justin."

"Why?" His expression was puzzled as he watched her walk

to his old, battered bureau and run her fingers over the horse sculpture he'd set there.

She didn't answer him directly. "I wondered why those other rooms didn't affect me like the one with all your masks. Now I know." Anticipation made her impatient with her need to explain. She turned to face him. "Don't you see? It's *you*. You're part of this room and the mask room. I can *feel* you in this room."

His gaze darkened with a promise that she'd soon feel him in a much more direct way. As he advanced into the room, he stripped off his T-shirt and flung it to the floor. Without speaking, he quickly slipped her dress over her head. It joined his T-shirt on the floor.

She purposely pushed all thoughts of her job, and what this might mean to her future, into a corner of her mind where they wouldn't interfere with the power of the present.

As soon as he'd freed her from her bra, panties, and red scarf, she moved to the window. While she absorbed the sound of him removing his jeans and shoes, Serenity raised the window, then turned to face him.

If she remained curator of the Galactic Museum of Erotic Art for the next hundred years, she'd find nothing in the universe to equal him.

The breeze from the open window lifted his demon-dark hair from his shoulders. He towered over her, a hard-muscled, flesh-and-blood testament to the fact that art could *never* touch the reality of Justin Hill.

He offered her a slashing smile. "Aren't you afraid all the magic will escape out the window?"

"I think we need to leave it open." She walked to where

he stood beside the bed. His hot gaze touched her breasts, her belly, and between her thighs. For the first time in her life, Serenity So-Fine felt beautiful in a totally sexual way. "You generate the heat of a thousand suns, Justin Hill, and spontaneous combustion is a real danger. We'll need some cool air to lower the temperature."

"The heat of a thousand suns?" He raised one brow as he drew her down to the rumpled white sheets.

"I suppose that could be considered an exaggeration." She smoothed his dark hair away from his face as he rose above her. "Okay, so it's only the heat of ten suns."

She lost track of time, space, and superheated heavenly bodies, as Justin did his best to reduce her to glowing ash with his mouth and tongue. And, as she arched to meet his first thrust, the sheer curtains moved gently in the cool mountain breeze.

Serenity stood at the foot of the attic stairs and considered the wisdom of searching out Justin in one of his "heart" places. She'd already left a part of herself in his room with its brass bed, white cotton sheets, and billowing curtains. Could she afford to lose more?

She started to climb the stairs.

He liked hot chocolate, fast horses, and snow. As she'd snuggled next to him on his bed, she'd remembered her childhood, when she'd loved the same things. That was before her society taught her that life wasn't about fun and sensory pleasure.

She continued climbing.

When she'd finally returned to her own room, she'd tried

desperately to refocus on museum business. She'd sort of succeeded.

Serenity's only reason for being here now was to remind Justin of her urgent need for him to start on *The Flame*. *Right. And you'd better get some professional help for your compulsive lying problem when this is all over.*

Serenity paused at the top of the stairs. Muffled sounds came from behind the closed door. Okay, she needed a plan. She'd knock. Then, when he opened the door, she'd ask how work on *The Flame* was going. No, too pushy. When he opened the door, she'd ask when they were going to have mind-altering sex again. No, too direct.

Perhaps she was overthinking the whole thing. She'd just knock and go with spontaneity. She knocked. Nothing. The muffled sounds continued unabated. Time for Plan B. She turned the doorknob and pushed the door open.

Good thing she hadn't bothered planning any logical and lengthy explanations for her presence, because it would've been wasted effort. She would've swallowed her words along with her heart.

The periphery of the large room looked like a workout area. Machines meant to drive the human body to sweaty exhaustion lined the mirrored walls.

But this wasn't what left her gaping. A square raised ring, probably like the one Justin performed in, took up the center of the room.

And a man stood in the ring staring at her.

Not Justin. This was the Night Creature. He held a stake in his hand, and his muscular body was bare except for brief black trunks with the outline of a bat across the front. The bat's voracious eyes and tiny fangs were set at an appropriate spot. The Night Creature wore gauntlets and another one of the masks from the red room. No two-hearted Upir here. This vampire was evil in ways she couldn't even begin to imagine. Her shudder had nothing to do with fear and everything to do with excitement.

"Why are you here?" The husky voice behind the mask suggested that interrupting the Night Creature was not a good thing.

Serenity considered a lie. She was lost? No, too ordinary. She'd heard the noise and thought mutant squirrels had gotten into the attic? No, too bizarre.

In the end, it would be easier to tell the truth. "I was looking for you." He could probably figure that out for himself. Maybe she needed to be a little more specific. "Clara mentioned this workout room, and I wanted to see how you prepare for a match." *I wanted to see, to touch your naked body again*.

He lifted the mask from his face, and a part of her mourned. But one glance at his expression revealed that the layer of himself he'd just stripped away had been the kinder and gentler one. "Come here, Serenity."

His harsh command wakened something in her. Something she would never have acknowledged in her time. In 2700, she would have run from the implied threat in his voice and the blatant power of his bared body, because that was what her society expected. This was a different time with different expectations. And the savage, gleeful creature whispering wicked suggestions in her ear was . . . Serenity allowed herself a totally evil smile. Was a perfect match for the Night Creature.

"I'm coming." She strode toward the ring, and, with each step, she shed the rules and beliefs of twenty-eight years.

When she reached the ring, he leaned down and helped her up. She noted the slight flare of his eyes. He recognized the new Serenity So-Fine. *Too late to escape now, Night Creature.*

She stood in the middle of the ring, feet spread, hands on hips, and head thrown back. "Show me some moves, Night Creature."

He hesitated, and she knew he wanted to ask why.

Don't. Don't ruin this moment with questions. Don't make me think about what I'm doing, feeling.

The moment passed, and he merely nodded. "I practice here. In tomorrow's match, the other guy will threaten me with a stake. I'll take it away, then beat him with it until the referee makes me stop." He dropped the stake.

"Beat him with it?" She frowned. "Isn't that against the rules?"

"I make my own rules. You should try it sometime." His gaze was silver challenge.

"Oh, I will. I definitely will." Her smile was a potent promise.

"Anyway, I need to smooth out my moves. That's why I have the mirrors. It has to look realistic. This is contained violence."

There was nothing contained about what Serenity was feeling. "Show me."

An anticipatory smile touched his lips. She'd make sure

those lips had the workout of their life. They'd be too worn out to whisper.

"That dress won't last." His smile widened. "It didn't earlier."

"It won't have to." Her smile challenged him. Deliberately, she pulled the dress over her, head and flung it away from her. Her black bra and panties were perfect matches for his color of choice. Except she didn't have a bat. She wanted a bat.

"I'm going to bounce off the ropes and take you down, then we'll do a somersault and you'll land on top of me. Got it?" His smile had widened to a grin.

She blinked at him. "I don't do somersaults."

"You do now. Don't worry, I'll control the action." He moved toward the ropes.

Not if I can help it. She paused from thoughts of conquest to watch him walking away. The smooth expanse of his back, the muscular strength of his legs, the compact perfection of his . . . ass. She congratulated herself for remembering that word from a magazine she'd found in her room. Justin Hill had a perfect ass. She felt hot and wet just thinking of it bared to whatever she chose to do.

She had a moment of sanity. *When you lose it, So-Fine, you lose it big time.* Okay, moment of sanity over. "Bring it to me, Night Creature." She was pulling out all the stops on her idiomatic usage of the common dialect for this time period.

When he turned back to her, he was still smiling. "Bring it to me?"

He wouldn't be smiling long. "Get your . . . ass over here, big man."

He was laughing openly as he bounced off the ropes, then flung himself toward her.

Serenity didn't even have time to squeak out her alarm before he brought her down, somersaulted over her, then launched her over top of him. She didn't know how it had happened, just that she was on top. *In control*. Serentity So-Fine was about to morph into Evil Woman.

Straddling his hips, she sat back on her heels and stared down at him. His powerful sweat-sheened chest rose and fell with his effort; his smile slowly faded as he stared into her eyes. Good. He was starting to get the picture.

The urge to slide forward, until the head of his erection slid into her with all its stretching and filling sensations, almost overwhelmed her. She felt an anticipatory spasm just thinking about it. Small problem. There'd be no "into her" until she got rid of her panties. Kick her if she ever wore panties under her dress again.

Besides, she couldn't lose herself in his body until she explained a few things to him. She wasn't sure why an explanation was important; she just knew it was.

"Let me tell you about my life, Night Creature." She touched each of his nipples with the tips of her index fingers, felt his nipples harden, and gloried in the sharp hiss of his indrawn breath between his clenched teeth. Sex was strange. Everything hardened on the outside, and melted inside.

"I hope you had an uneventful life, because if you go on for more than three minutes, we're in trouble." He shifted his hips, drawing her gaze to the bulge of his sex that stretched the bat to menacing proportions.

Firmly, she pressed her palm over the bat's beady eyes. "He's staring."

Justin jerked against her hand, his curse somewhere between laughter and a groan. "Get rid of him if he bothers you."

What a . . . delicious thought. Hooking her fingers beneath Justin's waistband, she waited for him to lift his hips, then slid the offending material down his strong thighs and long legs.

She studied the hard length of his cock, the taut fullness of his balls . . . Cock and balls, not expressions she'd choose, because what she felt went beyond those descriptions. But emotions didn't always translate well into language.

"What are you thinking about, Serenity?" His voice was a husky murmur.

"Cock and balls." She frowned at the harsh sounds of the consonants. Words to describe his maleness should glide over the senses with soft *s*'s that slid across the tongue. Full, rounded vowels should fill in the empty spaces.

"What happened to the story of your life? Not that I mind the change in direction." He reached up and pulled her bra straps off her shoulders.

Her life? Right now, she was convinced it began the moment he opened his door yesterday evening. Closing her eyes, she forced her memory past that moment to her life in 2700.

He took advantage of her closed eyes to deftly unsnap her bra. She allowed him to slip it off. That was the last thing she would allow until he understood.

Serenity opened her eyes to find his hot gaze fixed on her breasts. She'd never thought of her breasts as a source of pride. She did now. Arching her back, she felt their thrust and lift, watched his gaze turn molten, a searing, liquid silver that touched her nipples, her heart. She backed up. Not her heart. Her nipples might be near her heart, but his gaze touched something much lower, much less complicated.

He lifted his gaze to her eyes. "Your life?"

Serenity nodded. "My life." She removed his gauntlets, then grasped his strong wrists in her hands. Leaning forward, she forced his arms above his head. He let her. Probably because he realized as she leaned forward that her breasts would be poised within easy reach of his lips.

He closed his warm lips over one nipple, and she sucked in her breath at the jolt of pleasure that was almost pain.

"Stop." She grated the command through lips that in another moment wouldn't be able to form an intelligible word.

He released her nipple. And waited.

She drew in a deep, calming breath and willed her heart to slow, her brain to function. Still leaning over him, she met his gaze. "I want you to know about me."

"I know some things about you already, Serenity So-Beautiful." He didn't try to free his hands to touch her. "I know what your hair feels like trailing across my skin."

For the first time, she realized her hair spilled over his chest, skimming his body with each breath he took. Did he find the slide of her hair erotic?

"I know the scent of your flesh. A man would never feel alone if he could wake in the night and bury himself in all that warm woman scent." His eyes promised he'd do much more than bury himself in her scent.

Alone? Did he ever feel alone? Her need to know about him was a scary thing.

She did some mental head shaking to clear away her urge to lean back and wallow in the luxury of his words. Men in her time would never mention her hair or scent. They wouldn't think to include her and a bed in the same sentence. No man of her time would think of her while he lay alone at night. Instead, he'd compliment her brilliance in obtaining another erotic treasure and her dedication to the museum, then go to bed and think about how much that treasure was worth.

Okay, enough deep thoughts about the men of her time. She needed to get this conversation back on track. "Don't say another word."

He raised an expressive eyebrow but remained silent.

"I've spent twenty-eight years being what everyone expected me to be: cool, calm, dedicated. . . ."

"I guess that's admirable." He didn't sound convinced.

"I don't have fantasies about the men I know. I don't want to see them naked, and I don't want to have sex with them. I'm totally dedicated to my job. In my time, nothing comes before career." Her breath came hard and fast with the exertion of saying all this before her courage evaporated.

He narrowed his gaze on her. "So if dear old granny needed you to help her move some furniture at the same time you had a business meeting scheduled . . ."

"I don't have a granny. I only have a few distant relatives, and they're scattered across the galaxy." She paused for thought. "My friends know better than to call at work." She shrugged. "Besides, we have robots to handle heavy labor, and the furniture floats on air pads, so my mythical granny wouldn't need me."

"Your life doesn't sound like a hell of a lot of fun." Even frowning, his lips were a source of wonder to her.

She removed her hands from his wrists. "Don't move."

Once again, he raised his brow, but he left his arms stretched above his head.

"I was a successful professional woman of my time." *Was*. Strange how one little past-tense form of the verb *to be* could signal monumental life-altering possibilities. "I . . ." She ran the fingers of both hands through his thick dark hair, feeling the texture of each strand, its strength, its silky temptation. "Was . . ." Greedily, she dug her fingers into the muscles of his shoulders, felt their power, and gloried in it. "A repressed . . ." With open palms, she slid her hands over his chest, a smooth expanse of warm skin she intended to make her personal playground. " . . .woman." She punctuated her sentence by gliding her hands low on his stomach. She paused.

He swallowed hard before speaking, and Serenity smiled at this physical proof of how her touch affected him. Her smile faded as she remembered that exerting power over others was a primitive trait. But no one had ever told her it felt so good.

"How can you be repressed when there's never been anything to repress? Don't ask me for more logical thoughts because I'm just about—"

"I'm not finished." She made little patterns with her fingers around the base of his cock.

Serenity was sure she caught the words "hell" and "long-winded" in his muttering.

Leaning down, she touched his full bottom lip with the tip of her tongue. "During the day, I was a repressed . . ." she searched for a term in his vernacular strong enough to describe the cold emotionless facade she wore during her workday ". . . bitch."

His lips turned up, and she followed their curve with a feeling of wonder. His hands still remained above his head, a silent permission to do what she wanted with him. For the first time, she realized that having control over this man's powerful body would give her more joy than returning to her own time with *The Flame* clutched in her hands. She didn't explore where that joy would take her.

"But, at night, I became something else entirely." She explored the warm, sensitive spot beneath his ear with her tongue, then whispered into his ear. "At night, I stalked the dimly lit galleries of the museum, studying the artwork. All the accumulated knowledge of how men and women gave each other sexual pleasure filled room after room." She slid her tongue along the side of his neck until she reached the spot where his blood pounded hot and strong. "I memorized everything I saw." She played with his nipples, felt them harden beneath her fingers, felt the thrum of excitement in her blood. "And I imagined."

"You're killing me here, woman." His voice was a strangled gasp.

"Oh, I haven't even begun." She sat back on her heels in an attempt to slow her raging impatience. "I didn't really fantasize, because I had no man's face or body to put to the fantasy. But I imagined what it would be like, and I memorized all the things those men and women did to each other."

She stood. Time to get rid of the final barrier between them. As she slipped off her panties and the red scarf, she allowed thoughts of the *true* final barrier to slip into her mind. One more day to decide what she would do with the rest of her life. She pushed thoughts of time and destiny aside. Right now? She was into the moment.

"*I* wanted to do that." His tone was gruffly accusing.

"With your teeth?" She smiled down at him.

"With my teeth." He pierced her with a gaze hot with need.

This wasn't a man who hid his emotions. He put what he felt out there, and that was one of the things she . . . liked about him.

"Next time." And there *would* be a next time.

"Get back down here. Now." His glare would have done credit to the masks in his red room, but he didn't move his arms from above his head.

He was allowing her power over his naked body. She'd been taught from birth that to want power over someone was shameful. No one had mentioned the total sensual impact the feeling of power could give. Okay, so only *this* man would give her that thrill.

"Turn over and spread your legs . . . slave." Would he allow her this fantasy, only the second she'd ever had? She'd never even *wanted* to put a face to her desire before.

He turned over and spread his legs wide.

She clenched around the sight of his powerful back, tight sexy buttocks, and muscular thighs. All hers, bare and waiting.

"What I've been getting at . . ." she slipped to her knees

between his thighs ". . . is that I have all the sexual knowledge of the ages in my head." She leaned over him, enjoying the slide of her sensitized nipples across the smooth skin of his back. "And all the want of twenty-eight years between my legs." And all the *love* in her heart, too? She didn't know, wasn't sure. Right now she couldn't separate her body's needs from what her heart felt. Later.

"I don't know if I can live through this fantasy." His voice was strained.

"You will. For me." And somehow she knew he would. How could she have complete belief in the strength of this man she'd known for all of two days? But she did. Go figure. "You'll give me your body tonight. Completely. Without reservation. And I'll use it in whatever way I choose." Her need drove her. "You see, you're not the only night creature here tonight. I have a taste for your flesh, your sex." Unable to resist, she nipped his shoulder and reveled as he flexed his muscles in response. "By the time I'm finished, you'll be drained . . ." she pushed his hair aside and glided her tongue across the back of his neck ". . . and I'll be a sated woman."

"Give it your best shot, Serenity So-Crucl." His voice was a soft rumble of challenge. "Go for it, but then it'll be *my* turn."

CHAPTER FIVE

"*What do* you think a mistress would do with a disobedient slave, hmm?" Serenity picked up the discarded stake and slid the sharpened point lightly down the length of his back. She paused at the base of his spine.

He clenched his buttocks against the implied threat.

She leaned over, deliberately allowing her hair to glide across his flesh, and whispered in his ear. "Speak to me, slave."

"Anything she wanted." His answer sounded like it was forced between gritted teeth.

"Anything she wanted?" Serenity leaned back on her heels, then barely touched his skin as she drew abstract patterns with the stake's point on each firmly muscled cheek of his tempting bottom. She sensed his silent flinch. "Do you know what I learned from all those nights in the museum?"

"How to torture a man." He sounded certain of that fact.

Her laughter was low in her throat because she couldn't seem to force it higher. "The museum's treasures taught me that true erotic pleasure rarely has one face. It isn't just a man and woman coupling. Almost always it has nuances of other, darker elements."

"You know an awful lot for a repressed woman." He turned his face to the side so he could see her and shifted his hips to ease the pressure on his groin.

She smiled, hoping it was a smile full of wicked intent.

"I'm analytical. I wanted to know what caused so much excitement in primitive societies. It had to be more than just the urge to procreate."

"Hmmph." His comment could be interpreted in different ways.

Serenity chose to interpret it as a desire to get on with her fantasy. "There are many methods to punish a slave, but the best is one that brings sensual pleasure to the slave's mistress."

A sheen of sweat delineated each gleaming muscle in his tensed back, but he kept his arms above his head as if ropes truly bound him. The mental picture merged with the reality, and she became one with her fantasy.

"Open to me, slave." Her order was harsh need.

There was momentary hesitation, then he spread his thighs wider, exposing himself, making himself vulnerable in a way that almost took her out of her fantasy. *Almost.*

His sacs lay heavy between his muscular thighs. Large, stretched tight around all that made him male. His cock was thick with his need, a searing, smooth velvet pleasure for any woman who liked to play with fire. *Bring on the flames, Night Creature.* Serenity bit back a moan at the mental picture of him sliding deep into her.

"What punishment could I administer that would make me hot and wet?" Serenity offered a shrug meant to demonstrate her complete disinterest in any opinion he might offer. She was really getting into this fantasy thing.

"One of the museum's paintings depicted an interesting take on sexual pleasure." She slid the blunt edge of the stake between his cheeks, spreading them, then paused at a particularly vulnerable spot. She applied light pressure and felt his desire to clench his buttocks against her intrusion. She waited, but he remained open to her. "The woman in the painting had strapped a double-ended phallus to her so that she could bring herself pleasure at the same time she used the man beneath her."

"Is that part of your fantasy?" His voice betrayed nothing.

"No." Serenity cast the stake aside. "But, of course, there're always whips." She reached for her discarded scarf. "Whips and passion are a repeated theme in many of the museum's treasures. I don't know why." Slowly, she drew the scarf across his shoulders, his waist, then between his cheeks. When she slid it over his balls and the head of his cock, he clenched his fists and groaned. "Then again, perhaps I do know why."

She leaned over him, letting her breasts and hair slide over the flesh of his sweat-sheened back. "Your reaction excites me, Night Creature." Serenity had to make a conscious effort to keep her voice from quavering.

All those nights as she'd stood studying the exhibits, she'd wondered what past generations had found erotic in the acts, but now she knew. It wasn't the act itself. It was the person you shared it with.

Serenity was frantic for his body. She could never get close enough. She wanted to crawl deep inside him and never leave. Since that wasn't possible, she settled for clamping her teeth into the hard muscle of his shoulder. He bucked beneath her, and she spread her thighs wide so she could feel his buttocks pressed into her, touching the spot that was more than hot, wet, and willing.

"I'm losing it here, lady." He sucked in a deep breath before explaining further. "If you spend much more time trying to prove you're the connoisseur of carnal cruelty, I'm going to blow your fantasy to hell." He started to turn over.

"No." Her hissed command was born of desperation. "I haven't tasted you yet." Of course, he could technically interpret her teeth in his shoulder as tasting, but she didn't think it qualified.

He stilled, waiting.

Serenity closed her eyes, willed herself back into her fantasy. With eyes still closed, she glided her hands down the muscled length of him, then kissed the path her fingers had taken. When she reached his buttocks, she squeezed gently. He groaned in response as she traced a tight circle with her tongue over each cheek. Who would ever have guessed that sliding her tongue over warm male skin could cause this . . . ?

She couldn't put a name to her hunger. It had gone way beyond a simple need to touch his flesh with her mouth and fingers. Beyond a need to hold him inside her.

"Turn over." She opened her eyes to the sinking feeling that she'd really miscalculated her pacing. She'd worked herself into such a frenzy over his back that she wouldn't be able to do justice to his front.

He flung himself onto his back, his breath coming in short pants. "You can stop trying to think up punishments, because you've got the torture market cornered. I thought I had stamina, but any minute now I'm going to explode. So you might want to fast-forward whatever you have planned."

She knew he was mumbling something about punishment

and hurrying, but damned if she could concentrate. He'd spread himself before her—open, wanting. She glanced down. Yep, definitely wanting. He still had his hands stretched above his head, was still giving her a chance to complete her fantasy. Which was? Oh, yeah, the mistress-punishing-slave fantasy.

She stood on trembling legs and looked down at him. If she didn't put some distance between them, she'd pounce on him like a favorite lollipop, and it would be all over. How many years, how many lifetimes, would it take to get enough of his body, his *heart*.

Serenity needed to shut out the heart part. This wasn't about her heart. She didn't *want* it to be about her heart. Purposely, she picked up the discarded mask. She handed it to him.

"Wear this." She knew she owed him an explanation. "I can't stay in the fantasy if I can see your face. I need to make love to your body. Your face is a . . . distraction." *Make love?* It had been a slip of the tongue. *How about a slip of the heart?*

His gaze touched her with a wisdom she refused to acknowledge. "I feel it, too. And covering my face isn't going to stop it. You know that, don't you?"

"No." Probably the biggest, fattest lie she'd ever told in her brief lying career. Onward and upward.

His lips curved in a smile that didn't reach his eyes. He shrugged. "Hey, who am I to deny you your self-deceit?" He took the mask from her, then paused. "Kiss me before I put it on."

If she were really into her fantasy, she'd ignore his order.

She couldn't. Holding his hot gaze, she covered his body with her own.

Everything almost ended right there. The breast to thigh contact with his hot, hard body was more than one woman could endure. Her nipples were sensitive nubs of pleasure-pain against the smooth wall of his chest, her soft belly was a perfect balance for the ridged strength of his abdomen, and his erection prodded between her legs, energizing a part of her that was already a whirling dervish of frenzied need.

He stepped out of the fantasy to tangle his fingers in her hair and pull her down to his mouth. He was way beyond gentle seduction. His mouth was heat and hunger, barely controlled savagery, as his tongue plundered whatever breath she still had left. When he finally broke the kiss, her lips felt swollen from the intensity of his need.

The damp temptation of his full lower lip almost drew her back to his mouth, but he slid the mask over his face before she could act on the thought.

"You have three minutes, tops. Use it wisely, Serenity So-Fine." His voice echoed from behind the mask like the Ghost of Christmas Past in the ancient tale, *A Christmas Carol*. "And you're only kidding yourself if you think the mask will keep things impersonal between us. It's too late for that."

Use it wisely. Would she return to her museum and sit at her desk thinking about him, wondering if she'd used her time wisely, asking herself why she'd left?

Serenity silenced her questions by making love to his body. She'd wanted this to be a slow, sensual exploration, but her own compulsion drove her. It would be closer to his three-minute limit than she'd like.

She touched his nipples, chest, and stomach with her tongue. Memorized the male taste of him, the smooth texture of his skin, the warm tanned beauty of it. She kissed the small bat perched on his shoulder, the white line of a scar that ran across one hip.

And beyond the explosion of sensual impressions was the vibrant life of Justin Hill. She felt it, would always feel it. Knew that existence in her time would seem drab without his life force giving it color and meaning.

Sliding further down between his legs, she kissed a path the length of his hard inner thigh, savored the heat and scent of sex as she neared his groin.

"The clock is ticking." His reminder was a tortured groan.

Time. Her enemy. She was the winner of a three-minute sex spree, frantically trying to cram every possible erotic experience into her sex shopping cart before time ran out.

She slid her fingers over his tight sacs, cradled them in her palms, touched them with her lips. One of her paintings had shown other things a woman could do with them. She didn't have time. Tracing their fullness with her tongue would have to be enough.

Justin's body was coiled tension as she touched his cock. Clasping it, she tried to hold the impression of heat and power for a future that seemed bleaker by the minute.

Her body clenched, an impatient warning that time and explosive orgasms waited for no man. With a sigh of coming home, she slid her lips over the head of his erection and absorbed his deep moan of pleasure. Closing her eyes, she took as much of him as she could, exploring the shape and essence of him with her tongue. She was lost in her own sexual nirvana when Justin's immense restraint snapped.

"One slave revolt coming up." His muttered warning came too late.

Serenity heard the thunk of his mask hitting the ring's mat at the same time she felt his hands on her hips, lifting her. Her eyes popped open.

"Ride me." His command offered no options. "Ride me with your spurs on and put me up wet, wicked woman." His hair was a tangled glory framing a face that rivaled his beautiful demon masks.

He slowly lowered her onto his shaft, his muscular arms bulging with the effort needed for a controlled descent.

"The hell with this." She planted her knees on either side of him. "I'll decide when it's time, Night Creature."

She paused for a minisecond. The head of his shaft stretched her open as every internal muscle contracted around wet and eager expectation of *immediate* gratification. And if she had any thoughts about denying them, they squelched the thoughts with strident screams of, "Sex! Now."

"It's time." She sank onto him, holding her breath while she reveled in the growing sense of fullness, the building pressure, the feeling of losing control before an inevitable force.

His shout punctuated her cry as he rose beneath her and drove deep into her. Everything beyond that was a sexual blur, a mindless driving for more, always more. She lifted and lowered her body onto his cock with a rhythmic intensity— harder, faster—only partially aware that he rose to meet each of her attempts to take more and more of him into her.

The pressure built. It expanded and filled her. It pushed out everything that had come before or would come after this moment. She hung for a thousand years on *The Moment*. The first ripples touched her, played with her, then receded.

Her cries grew in volume. Out of control ravings. Filled with words she wouldn't remember, hoped *he* wouldn't remember. And suddenly it was there. *The Moment*. Everything stopped. The world, her breath, her life. Every muscle in her body contracted. Waited.

She came in an avalanche of roaring sensual completion that was punctuated by Justin's shouts and her own screams. The sounds were a mere background, filtered through her splintering emotions. She saw nothing, felt only the spasms that shook her, giving her unspeakable pleasure. When they faded, they left her with a sense of unspeakable loss.

Serenity had no idea why she was lying with her head on Justin's chest, crying. He stroked her hair in slow, rhythmic motions and said nothing.

Finally, when her breathing had returned to normal and she didn't think she could stand another moment of the silence that stretched between them, Serenity made a token swipe at her eyes, then addressed the situation. "That was . . ."

"Right. That was . . ." He exhaled sharply, and she felt the reaction as her own.

"That was . . . indescribable." Serenity shifted from his body and sat up. Of course, she was lying. She was perfectly able to describe it. It was all the joy she'd ever experienced to the power of ten. It dimmed all her yesterdays and cast her tomorrows into doubt.

And since she was into a moment of truth, she might as well admit the big one. She was in love with Justin Hill.

There was nothing logical about her love in terms of what her society found admirable. He was emotional, over-whelmingly physical, and stubborn. She knew her lips were curved into a cat-with-cream smile. He was also amusing, unpredictable, and beautiful. Oh, and don't forget the sex. Sex was important. She *didn't* love him just for his mind. Serenity loved him for the total package.

Justin sat up and raked his fingers through his hair. "I'd like nothing better than to drag you off to bed and experiment with all the ways a man can die happy, but I have to work tonight."

Serenity's heart, which had been busily swelling with love, shriveled into puckered prune mode. "I see."

Laughter gleamed in his eyes, but he remained unsmiling. "I have to begin work on *The Flame*."

"Oh." Hope flared. Her heart, which was now about the size and consistency of a raisin, paused to listen. "I want to watch." *I want to watch moonlight bathe your naked body in silver and shadows. I want to explore your shadowed places.*

"Not a good idea, lemon drop." His gaze was a heated promise, letting her know he'd enlarge on the good idea theme later. "I'll need complete concentration. Can't concentrate worth a damn with you around."

"Really?" Her dedicated curator self applauded his decision. The woman in her wanted to test the limits of his concentration.

He smiled, and his smile lit the uncertain path she intended to take tomorrow at midnight.

"Yeah." He reached out and cupped her chin in his large

hand, forcing her to meet his gaze. "I learned something important in the last two days."

He paused, and she wanted to drag the words from him.

"The trip from head to heart was only a short drive after all." He rose, pulled on his trunks, picked up his gauntlets and mask, then headed for the door. "Oh, and after I finish concentrating on *The Flame*, I'll come for you . . ." she caught the corner of his smile ". . . in every way."

Her heart hummed happily as it plumped itself up again.

He paused before leaving. "Tomorrow's your last day in this time. I'd like to spend it with you. How about coming to the match with me tomorrow night?" His gaze drifted to the mask he held in his hand. "I think I'll be Upir. Something tells me two hearts might come in handy."

She dropped her gaze to hide her expression.

"Violence? Rabid mobs? Hot sweaty bodies?" She looked up and grinned. "Wouldn't miss it for the world."

CHAPTER SIX

Justin listened to the roar of the crowd. Serenity was out there. Waiting. His future hinged on whether she could accept this part of his life. He didn't know what he'd do if she couldn't.

Return with her to 2700? Probably not. He wouldn't be an asset to her life there. Hell, he didn't even know if she'd want him to go with her. She hadn't said the words.

He grinned. He hadn't given her much time to say anything today. They'd explored fantasies that Grandpa could never stuff into one of his dusty rooms. Justin had memorized the smooth slide of her skin against his, her warm woman scent, the husky heat of her voice crying his name, and he'd stored the memories away in case . . .

His grin faded. He hadn't said the words either, but he would. As soon as he saw whether she ran screaming into the night when the match began. Even if these three days were all he'd ever have of Serenity So-Fine, she'd changed his life. She'd nagged him until he'd called Grandpa. Amazing. His grandfather was flying in tomorrow to have a look at Justin's sculptures. He'd insisted on Clara picking him up at the airport and driving him up the mountain. Justin paused for a moment of conjecture about that.

His lips tightened. If he had anything to do with it, Serenity would be by his side tomorrow to greet the old tyrant. Justin wasn't a halfway kind of person. Three days or three years, it didn't make a difference. He loved Serenity, and he'd fight for her.

The crowd roared. Show time. Slipping on his Upir mask, he became Night Creature, hated and reviled and universally feared by the masses. Tonight, he'd earn the crowd's anger by using every dirty trick he knew to beat the reigning good guy, Chosen One, to a bloody pulp. He'd eventually lose, but, in the process, Chosen One would need to be carried from the ring on a stretcher while the crowd shouted encouragement to their injured hero and heaped curses on the Night Creature.

Drawing in a deep breath, he slid into his persona and strode out to meet his fate.

And, as lights flashed, white smoke billowed, and demon music blasted, he tried to see it all from Serenity's perspective. The crowd screamed for his blood and waved their signs while the usual hype went on over the intercom. God, Serenity would be in culture shock.

Everything fast-forwarded at that point. As he leaped into the ring, he caught a glimpse of Serenity in the front row. Wide-eyed, she had her bottom lip clamped between her teeth.

Justin didn't have a chance to glance at her again. The match rolled along as scripted until Chosen One flung him down and leaped on top of him.

All hell broke loose. A shrieking she-devil in a flowing black dress scrambled into the ring, raced past the open-mouthed referee, and kicked Chosen One in the butt.

Chosen One registered the assault with a surprised grunt, then rolled off Justin.

Justin lay on his back, shock holding him in place, as Serenity dropped to her knees beside him. Her blond hair fell around her flushed face in wild abandon while her blue eyes flashed with righteous anger. Before he could stop her, she slipped off his mask to the collective gasps of the audience riveted on the unfolding drama.

He closed his eyes. She'd just blown to hell his carefully constructed faceless horror act.

She patted his face and body as though she expected chunks of him to be missing. "Did he hurt you? I'll kill him if he touches you again." Her eyes widened. "Did I say that? I can't believe I said that."

Justin started to smile. Things were looking up. He glanced over at Chosen One, who winked at him then continued to writhe in mock agony. The referee was doing his arm-flapping, ineffectual act. They both must think he'd stuck this into the match without telling them and were going along with it.

Without warning, he flipped Serenity onto her back, pinned her arms above her head, and glared down at her. She stared up at him with wide blue eyes.

"That's right, look at me, Serenity. This is who I am. I enjoy this. The crowd, the physical part of it. I run on emotion, and this is one huge fuel tank. Understand?"

She swallowed hard, then nodded.

As the haze of battle faded, he realized what she'd done. She'd abandoned her society's rejection of violence to come to his rescue.

His woman. His love. He knew the fierceness of his conviction must be making him look pretty scary. He couldn't help it.

"Do you know what I'd like to do right now?" He didn't wait for her response. "I'd like to rip that dress from your body and—"

"I'm not wearing panties." She sounded hopeful.

Lord, give him strength. "And expose that beautiful body. Then I'd slip off your bra." He leaned down and touched his lips to the side of her neck. "After I tasted your breasts, your stomach, the soft flesh of your inner thigh, I'd spread your legs wide and—"

"Fuck me?" She sounded like she was trying the word on for size. She'd probably use the same inflection when she ordered a double cheeseburger. "It's an ugly word, but it conveys the graphic nature of sex in an interesting—"

"Who taught you that word?" His tone would clear the ring of pretenders to his evil demon crown.

She smiled up at him. Who was the real woman behind the smile? Serenity So-Innocent or Serenity So-Knowing? He loved both of them.

"You cried out the word every time we made love." Her glance dropped to his chest. Softened. She slid the tip of her tongue across her lower lip, and he almost lost it in front of thousands of screaming fans.

Her gaze shifted past him. "And that man in the front row must have a fixation with the word, because before the match we were talking, and he kept saying—"

"What man?" The unexpected stab of jealousy brought Justin to his feet as he searched the front row for the man who'd dare talk like that to his . . .

His what? She wasn't his. Serenity intended to leave him forever tonight. Justin stood in the middle of the arena, amid the chaos Serenity had caused, and absorbed the awful truth he'd managed to shove from his mind until this moment. She would return to her own time tonight unless he stopped her. Short of ripping that damned medallion from her neck, he didn't have many options. He had to get her back home to give it his best shot.

"I think your bad guy days are over, Night Creature." Chosen One's whisper reached him just as he contemplated slinging Serenity over his shoulder and racing from the arena. "They're loving it."

Startled, Justin glanced up to realize the mob had quieted, and every gaze seemed fixed on his face. Crap. No one was ever supposed to see his face.

He needn't have worried, because the crowd's attention shifted elsewhere almost immediately.

Serenity stepped past him to grab the microphone from a ringside announcer who was waving it at her. She spread her legs and stared out at the crowd. They stilled in anticipation.

Justin sucked in his breath at the militant gleam in her eyes.

"Ladies, men are savage beasts."

The women in the audience screamed their agreement.

"But you know something? I've just realized that I'm a savage woman."

The men roared their appreciation.

"I'm usually not a violent person, but if anyone tries to hurt my man, I'll . . ." Inspiration failed her.

The audience shouted their suggestions.

"Yes! All of those things." She smiled her thanks. "And

since I'm on a roll, I'd like to give my opinion on—"

Justin ripped the mike from her fingers while the crowd watched raptly. "No more opinions, Serenity."

She stared at him. "But I'm not finished."

He grinned at her. "You are . . . So-Finished."

As he dragged her from the arena past thousands of fans, who shouted their approval and slapped him on the back, he mourned the loss of his bad guy status. The thought of being the defender of justice, the protector of goodness and light, curdled his blood. But he'd worry about that later. He had more important things on his mind.

Serenity stood at the window and stared into the darkness. She could only see the dark silhouettes of trees, but Justin's mountain was more real to her than all her yesterdays in 2700.

He'd left her after they returned, saying he had something important to do. That was okay, because she had some things to work out alone. Like her future.

Almost midnight. And like in the ancient tale of Cinderella, she was about to return to the pumpkin-mice-and-evil-stepsisters reality of her time. Only she wouldn't leave behind a glass slipper to help the prince find her.

When had she started thinking of her time as the bad old days? She couldn't pin it down to a specific moment, but as Justin had filled more and more of her present, he'd pushed her past out.

With a resigned sigh, she unlocked that small, secret door in her mind. Truth flung it wide, then stood tapping its foot impatiently. *Admit it, you're not going anywhere at midnight.*

There's no place in 2700 for you anymore. You don't belong. You're emotional and violent, and you lust after Justin Hill's naked body. Oh, and you're not above stealing his heart if you get the chance.

Sitting down at the small desk, she took off her medallion, clicked open the back and entered a message. Then she put it back on.

As she started to rise, she noticed a sheet of paper that Justin had shoved under her door. Strange. She picked it up. He'd scrawled two words in a bold script. *I'm waiting.*

As arrogant as the man was his assumption that she'd know where he waited. But of course she did. He'd be in his other "heart" place.

All the way to the metal building beside the house, she wondered. *Hoped.* She didn't hesitate when she reached the door. Now that she'd made up her mind, she'd face her decision with no regrets.

She pushed open the door.

Darkness. Except for the large ring of fire, the already recognizable beginning of what would become *The Flame* . . . and Justin. He stood in the center of the ring. Naked. The fire's glow turned his skin molten gold, and his eyes gleamed silver as he watched her. A god of sin and temptation. One she'd never resist.

"I deal in things I can see and touch, Serenity So-Fine. I don't do abstracts. To make *The Flame live*, I have to experience it." His intensity, and his need, reached across the flickering tongues of fire and drew her toward him. "Come to me and help me touch the flame."

Even as he spoke, he switched off several of the gas jets

controlling the ring of fire. A path opened for her.

Serenity glanced down. Her medallion had begun to glow, a warning that her time in 2003 grew short.

With calm deliberation, she met his gaze. "Three days isn't long enough to learn about someone. I don't know if your parents are alive, or if you have brothers and sisters. I don't know what your favorite food is, or if you snore."

His smile gleamed white within the fire-lit circle. "Yes, yes, pizza, and no. Is that enough information?"

She returned his smile. "Sounds good to me."

Slipping her dress over her head, she kicked off her shoes and unsnapped her bra. She paused to consider her pantyless state, then met his disappointed gaze. "I know. You wanted to take them off with your teeth."

"Some things are worth waiting for."

He proved his point by waiting patiently as she slid the medallion off her neck, then held it in her hand while she stepped across the gas jets. The ring of fire closed behind her, a symbolic ending to her old life. She'd made her choice.

She went into his arms without hesitation, then gasped at the instant flare of heat and desire. He wrapped her in his embrace, branding her forever with all that made Justin Hill an irresistible temptation. A stomach-clenching mixture of clean male scent and sensual attraction that defied any kind of rational analysis. He just . . . *was*, for her.

He buried his face in the tangle of her hair, slid his fingers through the strands, and touched the hollow of her neck with his mouth. "I love you. In this time or any time you choose. I won't fit in your time, but I'm willing to give it a shot if it means I'll be with you."

She closed her eyes on the sacrifice he was willing to make. *For her.* Opening her eyes, she blinked hard to hold back tears. Why would she cry at this moment of supreme happiness? The logic eluded her.

He closed his fingers around the medallion, which was now flashing its imminent departure warning. A silent promise that he didn't intend to be left behind.

"Give me the medallion, Justin."

Reluctantly, he released it, then watched her with hooded eyes.

Turning, she flung it over the flames. As it hit the floor beyond the fire, it flashed brilliantly and was gone. And with it went all her life that had led to this moment and this man.

She turned back to him and met his stunned gaze. "I love you, Justin Hill. I love your heart, your body, and I definitely love going to your wrestling matches so I can kick some booty."

With an inarticulate roar, he lifted her off her feet, then held her tightly as he plundered her lips, his tongue touching and laying claim to every heated inch of her mouth.

Then he slowly let her slide down the length of his aroused body. She came to rest with her toes resting on his bare feet and her thighs spread to accept the hard, thick proof that he was definitely her man.

Wet and open to him, she settled onto his erection, glorying in the moment the head of his cock pushed into her, opening her wide, then sliding deep into all her tomorrows.

Even as her body clenched around the knowledge that he was hers, that the building explosion of pleasure would go on and on, he pulled her arms above her head and clasped her wrists in his strong hands.

Tears slid down her face as he drove into her with enough force to lift her off her toes. She met his savage need with her own, wrapping her legs around him and pounding onto his cock, writhing in a frantic attempt to take more of him.

And when she came, it was with a primal scream that echoed the cries of all women who loved and were loved.

No one in her time had ever seen the face of *The Flame*. She now knew that it was the face of love.

In the aftermath, he wrapped her in a protective embrace and murmured in her ear. "Did you send any explanation back with the medallion."

She nodded as she gazed into the flames.

"I said goodbye to my friends." She smiled up at him. "And I informed the Galactic Museum of Erotic Art that I was officially resigning my position as curator. I explained that I'd found my very own sex object and I wasn't giving him up."

His muffled laughter warmed her neck.

"You are *so* fine, lemon drop."

THE WEDDING NIGHT

by

CHERYL HOLT

CHAPTER ONE

London, 1815

"*Well, good night* then, Lord Banbury."

"Good night."

Stephen St. John, Viscount Banbury, eventually to be Earl of Stafford if his recalcitrant, impossible father ever dropped dead, glared at the interloper who'd now been his wife for all of ten hours. The silence extended; the farewell grew awkward.

What repartee, precisely, was a man supposed to express at a time such as this? *Sleep well? Pleasant dreams? See you in the morning?* Or how about more aptly, *What was I thinking, marrying a woman I don't know? Have I gone mad?*

Nothing seemed appropriate. Astoundingly, he blushed, his cheeks heating with an embarrassing dose of discomfort.

The wedding guests were gone, the house had been tidied by what was left of his domestic staff, and he'd been about to leave, too, when he'd stumbled upon her floating down the stairs. She was scarcely dressed, clad in a diaphanous green negligee and robe that hardly covered anything that ought to be covered. Apparently, as she'd concluded that he was already off to his merrymaking, she'd believed herself to be alone in the massive, drafty domicile. Unable to sleep, she'd descended to fetch a relaxing refreshment.

Her hair was blond, the shade of ripened wheat. It was unbound and hanging down her back to brush her bottom, and he was gravely troubled by the display. She was much too forward and assured, prancing about in her nightwear before an unfamiliar man, yet she didn't appear perturbed.

Yes, he was her husband, but nevertheless, they were strangers.

Even though he hadn't meant to, he evaluated her graceful figure. He was only human! He couldn't be expected to avoid looking at what was flaunted in plain sight.

She was much too shapely, and he squirmed uneasily and inspected the floor, only to be confronted by her feet.

Her toenails were painted red! The splash of bright crimson in the dull salon seemed immoderately sexy, out of place, incongruous and irreconcilable with the individual he pictured her to be.

Ordinarily, he was an urbane, sophisticated fellow, renowned and lauded for his aplomb, his polish and poise, and, most particularly, for his way with the ladies. Yet, with his new bride, he'd been transformed into a bungling, gauche oaf.

From the moment earlier in the day, when she'd waltzed into the parlor, promptly at eleven, he'd behaved like an ass. Throughout the abbreviated ceremony, then the afternoon of toasting and celebration, and the interminable meal that had wrapped up the festivities, he'd constantly tripped over himself, saying the wrong thing, doing the wrong thing, and generally making a fool of himself.

She likely presumed that she'd wed a moronic buffoon.

He was dawdling in the doorway, acting like a simpleton, powerless to depart, but incapable of maintaining any sort of intelligent conversation.

"Don't let me keep you," she obligingly said. Showing him her back, she strolled to the other side of the room, where surprisingly, she helped herself to a stout glass of brandy.

During the excessive, protracted gala, he'd covertly watched her. When his rowdy, wild friends had still been in attendance, she'd had naught to drink. While she'd ceaselessly had a beverage in her hand, he'd never seen her take so much as a sip. So why now?

He was used to consorting with a rather decadent type of lady, so he normally wouldn't have heeded whether she'd imbibed or not. Usually, he paid no heed to what a female did or didn't do. But it bothered him to discover that she was so nonplussed by events that she could blithely delight in a nightcap.

"Enjoy your . . . revelry," she added. "I'm sure it will be *most* entertaining."

From the beginning, he'd recognized that she had a husky, come-hither voice. When she talked, she always sounded as though she were on the verge of mentioning an indecent proposition. Thus, it was difficult to focus on the content of her speech, because the words kept getting lost in the sensual timbre of any utterance.

Narrowing his gaze, he studied her rounded behind, trying to deduce if she was mocking him with her flip *adieu*. Was she jesting? Was she serious?

She had to be joking. She had to be!

Though she'd readily and freely yielded to his ultimatum that theirs would be a marriage of convenience, how could she blandly acquiesce to his rushing out to cavort with others on their wedding night? Had she no feelings in the matter? Was she genuinely unconcerned about where he went or what he did? What woman—what wife!—could be so tolerant, so unmoved? What kind of person was she?

There was the crux of his problem. He had no idea.

She was an American, and he'd been acquainted with very few in his twenty-nine years, so the explanation for her peculiar apathy might be buried in the fact that she was a foreigner. Perhaps American women held their men to a lower standard. Though he doubted it. A contrary culture and upbringing couldn't alter basic feminine instincts that much!

By nature, females were possessive, jealous, and suspicious. Every one with whom he'd ever dallied had exhibited the invidious tendencies, and his wife—deep down—couldn't be any different. Reluctantly, he was forced to concede that she wasn't upset about his rudely trotting off because she didn't care about their marriage anymore than he did.

The realization vexed him enormously.

On his end, he'd perceived their speedy, abrupt courtship and union as a simple business transaction. She—Ellen Foster, twenty-five-year-old daughter of a wealthy Massachusetts cotton mill magnate—had wanted the English title that her daddy's money could buy. He—disowned, disinherited, impoverished scoundrel and libertine—had needed a quick infusion of cash so that he could thumb his nose at his stubborn father, and so that he could afford his pursuit of the depraved, wicked lifestyle on which he thrived.

The pragmatic solution conferred infinite benefits to both parties, but evidently, she'd embraced all the terms—those in writing, as well as those upon which they'd privately agreed.

How the notion galled!

She spun toward him, startling him with her stunning emerald eyes. Those eyes invariably took him unawares, amazing him with their intensity, their keen estimation and reflection. Whenever she peered at him straight on, he suffered the uncanny sensation that she discerned much more about him than she should, that she understood much more than was fitting or warranted.

She tipped her glass. "Would you like a whiskey before you go?"

"Why not?" he replied, pondering what would possess him to linger. She returned to the sideboard to fill a second tumbler, and he meticulously assessed her.

For many months, she'd been dawdling in London, flaunting her assets and sending out tentative inquiries to numerous potential suitors, but he hadn't crossed paths with her in the social whirl. His initial contact had come through a solicitor who'd approached him confidentially, and he'd been supplied with a financial contract and an astonishing, unforeseen overture of marriage.

No sane gentleman—especially one in his dire fiscal condition—would have balked at her offer.

Originally, he'd assumed her decision had been precipitate and inadvertently made. Upon further deliberation, he'd been left with the eerie conviction that her choice hadn't been random in the slightest, that she was a shrewd negotiator and schemer who'd been surveying the viable candidates, and who had settled on him for reasons that remained a complete mystery.

The dastardly wench had unquestionably known how to go about getting what she wanted, and she'd obviously wanted *him* and no other.

Prior to the wedding, he'd met with her only once, at the lawyer's office, but she'd been surrounded by her imposing father, a cadre of male relatives, and several bodyguards. Conservatively attired, she'd had her hair pulled up in a severe style, and, after he'd proposed, they'd been permitted to chat for a few fleeting minutes before he'd been brusquely hustled out. His memories of her, and the fateful appointment, were so disorganized, brief, and scattered that he'd recalled her as being a brunette!

She'd seemed conventional, suitable, polite, and average, and any hint that she might be pretty or appealing had been prudently disguised. As he gawked at her now, dissecting the silhouette and contours that were flawlessly outlined by her flowing robe, he was shocked to feel a stir of desire. The temperature in the stuffy chamber suddenly became warmer, his pulse beat a tad faster, and his pants grew unaccountably tight.

In all actuality, she was striking but, mystifyingly, upon their inaugural introduction, she'd scrupulously hidden her favorable characteristics behind a dour coif and an unflattering gown. She was an excellent height, neither short nor tall, and she was slim, yet curved where a female should be, and he couldn't keep from noticing how her unconfined breasts played against the fabric of her nightgown as she shifted and moved.

She was winsome. Not a grand beauty as were some of the women with whom he regularly fraternized, but she had pleasing features, winged brows, high cheekbones, a pert nose, a tempting mouth. And those magnificent eyes . . .

Previously, her distinctiveness hadn't registered, and, at

this late juncture, he didn't care to note it. Not when he had every intention of sticking to their platonic accord. When the bargain had been struck, he'd inferred that he was getting a plain, modest spouse, and he was unnerved to ascertain that he'd been mistaken.

If he'd misjudged her countenance so terribly—when he was repeatedly hailed for his abilities with the fairer sex—what else might he have overlooked in his haste to wed?

Twirling about, she walked toward him, holding out his libation, and, as she slipped the glass into his hand, her fingers trailed across his. He frowned. The gesture had been almost calculated, like a contrived caress.

"Would you like to sit with me for a bit?" she asked. "With everyone gone, the house is so quiet. I could use the company."

Without tarrying to learn his answer, she sauntered to the couch, her swift rotation making the hem of her robe flare out and graze across his knee and thigh. Furtively, he sniffed at her perfume, a clean, charming aroma that reminded him of summer afternoons and fresh cut flowers.

She drifted down onto the sofa, while he sat directly across, and, as she didn't tend to propriety in any fashion, he was furnished with a superb view as she nestled against the arm. Lounging, she curled her legs on the cushion, and her nightclothes rose up, revealing a slender foot, a smooth calf.

He couldn't quit staring.

Languidly, she sampled her brandy as she scrutinized him with a sly smile, and he couldn't stop speculating as to what was going on inside her head. Her dainty pink tongue flicked out and nipped at a droplet of liquor clinging to the edge of her glass. Just as with her scarlet-tinted toes, he was mesmerized by that tongue, held spellbound by its color and form, enchanted by the possibilities it represented.

He gave himself a good shake. Both mentally and physically. It had been a tedious day, with an arduous night still to come. He was merely weary from the rollicking, and fatigue was making him see things that weren't there, inducing him to surmise and hypothesize over details that were of no significance whatsoever.

"What a day!" she exclaimed, ostensibly reading his thoughts.

"Yes."

"I'm exhausted." She arched her back and stretched. "How about you?"

The motion thrust her bosom up and out and caused her robe to glide down, exposing a shoulder. Her silky hair ripped past in a glossy wave. She appeared wanton, inviting, as though she were awaiting a swain or had just wallowed in a clandestine romp.

He could make out every aspect of her breasts, the mass, the shape, the amplitude. Neither too large nor too small, they were just the right size for a man to appreciate. Her nipples were erect from the cool air in the room and from rubbing against the soft fabric of her robe. He could imagine what it would feel like to clasp the tiny nubs between his finger and thumb, how stimulating it would be to lave at them with his tongue.

She'd writhe and moan beneath him, and he'd pin her down while he . . .

Gad, but he really, really needed to go!

"I'm not tired in the least," he lied.

"Anxious to do up the Town?"

"Yes," he fibbed again.

In reality, he had no appetite for traipsing about London on his wedding night. What would he tell people? How would he explain?

Those who knew him—as well as those who didn't!—would anticipate that he, Stephen St. John, the notorious rake and user of women, would be snuggled between the sheets with his new bride. Not just for the night, but perhaps for days to come. What rational chap would pass up the chance to slowly and delectably initiate his virginal, rich spouse into her marital role?

He'd confided in no one the pact he'd made with her during their sole conversation before their nuptials. Bluntly, he'd informed her that he didn't want a wife, that he'd never fancied marrying at all, which meant that he'd require very little from her in the way of matrimonial obligation.

She'd been so eager for the match that she'd rashly acceded to his dictate, had latched on to his stipulations for solitude and independence with nary a complaint or objection, asserting that she had no problem with his demand that he be allowed to keep on with his bachelor habits.

At the time, her concurrence had seemed a godsend, and he'd insolently accepted her compliance with his mandate, but it wasn't the type of thing one could discuss with one's companions. Nor was it news he would relish having bandied about Town.

So once they finished their drinks, what the bloody hell was he to do with himself till dawn?

"Your friends are an *interesting* lot," she announced.

"You're remarkably generous in your description of them."

"I was wondering if you'll be entertaining them here at the house, or if you'll meet with them elsewhere? I was curious if—on occasion—I'll be compelled to serve as your hostess."

Inwardly, he groaned. Here was another facet of matrimony that he'd discounted in his impetuous alacrity to snag his heiress. Over the years, his domicile had been acclaimed as the scene for various and diverse lewd amusements. His covey of uncivilized, barbarous associates would overrun the residence, and he'd been more than happy to accommodate their vices, but he couldn't persist with his schedule of ribald parties now that his wife was on the premises and determined to make it into a home.

"No, I'll save you the aggravation."

"I don't mind if you have them over."

"Thank you, but we'll socialize at my club." The last thing he needed was Ellen getting to know any of his dissolute cohorts. The stories they might impart to her made him shudder.

"Should I ever plan on your being here for supper? Or will I be free to adjust my calendar with no regard to yours?"

She posed the query with a great deal of apathy, as though it was of no import if she ever saw him. Her audacity chafed. At his arrogance. At his pride. Didn't the blasted woman want him about? Wouldn't she fret over where he was or what he might be doing?

Pique and irritation had him retorting, "I'll join you for supper each and every night."

"You're certain?"

"Yes."

"Pity," she murmured.

He couldn't have heard her correctly! "I beg your pardon?"

"Well, I'd intended to—" She cut the sentence off, befuddling him with that cunning smile again, and she sighed, then leaned nearer. "We're both adults, so I guess I can be frank."

After her lengthy hesitation, he barked, "About what?"

"I have a few gentleman *friends* of my own whom I'd like to visit. Very discreetly, of course. And I'm sure you and your mistress—what's her name? Miss Poundstone?—would like to continue on with your customary routine."

He'd just taken a swallow of his whiskey, and he choked on it, coughing and gasping as he struggled to absorb all she'd just said. She was contemplating cuckolding him? She'd been apprised of his protracted affair with Portia Poundstone?

There were so many scathing responses he could make that he was dizzy from sorting them all out.

"You would take a . . . a . . . lover?" It had never occurred to him that she might, and he was infuriated at the prospect, so he strove to imbue casualness in his tone, refusing to let her detect how disturbed he was by her disclosure.

"I've encountered so many fascinating men while I've been in London, and I am married now. Where would be the harm?"

"Yes, but what will people say if you're perpetually gadding about with every available roué?" He shook his head, dumbfounded, unable to believe that the comment had spewed forth from his own mouth. "I don't have the most pristine reputation, but I'm afraid—in this instance—I must put my foot down. You absolutely can't."

"That sounds like a husbandly edict, Lord Banbury."

"Call me Stephen," he griped. She'd been *Banbury*-ing him all day, and it was beginning to grate. Throughout the reception, whenever she'd referred to him by his title, people's brows had raised.

"I thought we were to have a nontraditional marriage. That we would be at liberty to carry on as we pleased."

"Yes . . . well . . ."

He cleared his throat, his collar tight. He'd insisted on the autonomy for himself! Not for her! How could she have deemed otherwise? As she'd misconstrued on such a vital eventuality, there were—no doubt—all manner of situations over which they'd need to haggle. What else would he be constrained to clarify? "Some conduct is beyond the pale, Ellen. Surely, you grasp that fact."

"As you wish," she conceded graciously as she whirled a distracting finger round and round the rim of her glass. "If you would restrict my behavior, must I still suffer Miss Poundstone's presence? That hardly seems fair."

Bristling, he blushed anew, sustaining an absurd pang of embarrassment to be reviewing the topic of his paramour with her. Was she entirely devoid of decorum? Had she no concept of propriety and decency?

"Ellen," he gently chided, "it's not proper for you to mention the subject of Miss Poundstone to me."

"Why? We don't have an ordinary marriage. What's inappropriate about conferring over the conditions by which we'll progress?"

She looked so damned innocent. He scowled, feeling off-base and in the dark. Every statement she uttered seemed to be charged with enigmatic meaning and purpose.

"Be that as it may—" Lord, but he hadn't known that he had such a knack for being pompous and pretentious! "—my personal activities are just that: personal. You shan't question my comings and goings. It's not done."

"I will try my best not to, Lord Banbury."

"We'll get on much better that way," he contended.

"I'm positive we will."

Her submissive capitulation made him nervous. There wasn't a woman alive who was so subservient, so yielding. What was she up to?

As they chatted, she was toying with the strap of her negligee, sliding it up and down her nude shoulder. Her hand would descend, and the bodice dip slightly, baring the creamy swell of her breast. When she deliberately tugged it up, the cloth would constrict. The movement was overtly beguiling, and he locked his gaze on hers, declining to loiter on the enticing, hypnotic tempo of her hand.

She set her feet on the floor and deposited her empty glass on the table between them. As she yawned and stretched again, her breasts lifted, and her nipples were peaked and blatantly visible. Her neck, long and delicate as a swan's, was tipped back, and he could see her pulse thumping in an elevated rhythm at her nape.

"Well, I'm off to a nice hot bath, then my bed."

"How lovely," he said, for want of anything more profound, but a vision of her—wet and slippery all over—filled his mind, and he couldn't dislodge it. It was so vivid that his fingers tingled as he conjectured what it would be like to skim them over her slick, damp skin.

"Would you like me to replenish your whiskey before I retire?"

"Yes, thank you."

Why not have a tad more? He'd valiantly endeavored to keep up with his rambunctious guests, but, obviously, he hadn't had nearly enough alcohol. Total paralysis had been his goal, but he wasn't anywhere close to being numb.

As she reached for his glass, she bent across the table, and the alteration of her position loosened the front of her night-gown. Her breasts were swinging down, the bodice flopping. With a start, he realized that he could see her cleavage, the pink of her areola, her contracted nipples, her flat stomach.

Sweet Jesu, but if she advanced another inch, he'd be gawk-ing at the womanly hair shielding her mound!

He bit down a moan. Of delight. Of dismay.

In a flash, he was cocked as a pole. His undisciplined, im-polite phallus strutted to attention, rudely instructing him to alleviate the discomfort. He crossed one leg over the other and draped a hand across his lap. She was a virgin, so she wasn't likely to notice his inflamed predicament, or to un-derstand it if she did, but still, he was desperate to conceal his reaction.

Needing to calm himself, to gain control of his licentious impulses, he yanked himself away from the dangerous terri-tory she'd unwittingly revealed, focusing instead on her face. Which was a mistake.

Her skin was so smooth, her eyes so dazzling, her hair so alluring. And that mouth! Her lips were pouting, ruby red, moist, captivating. She made a man think about more than kissing, made him want to have her kneeling down before him and . . .

Frantic, he lurched backward.

He was sexually attracted to his wife! How could this be?

Not cognizant of the carnal effect she had on him, she strolled to the sideboard without so much as a glance in his direction. As she relocated, he breathed a sigh of relief. Surreptitiously, he observed her, and his trepidation escalated at an alarming rate.

There was something categorically erotic in how she walked. Her hips swayed adorably, and the material of her robe molded to her legs, bewitchingly outlining her petite waist, her curvaceous thighs, her gorgeous bottom.

She had a fantastic ass, the sort a man could really get a grip on when he was . . .

Yikes! He was a mess! Aroused. Titillated. Intrigued. And, under the circumstances, much too sober.

She offered him his drink, which he accepted, but he had to clutch the glass with both hands so that he could keep it steady. Quickly, he swigged the amber liquid, and tears welled into his eyes, but he managed to refrain from humiliating himself by hacking or sputtering.

"Good night again, Lord Banbury."

Did she address him as Banbury just to annoy him?

She ambled away, and, as she passed where he was sitting, the billowy sleeve of her robe grazed his cheek. Had she been more skilled at the art of coquetry, he might have assumed that the motion was practiced.

"Good night," he echoed to her well-proportioned, retreating derriere.

Long after she'd withdrawn, he stared at the spot where she'd been. He could smell her perfume, could feel the caress of her robe, and his manly instincts were stimulated by her lingering essence. His cock throbbed, his balls ached, and, suddenly, he was burning up with unassuaged passion. He wanted nothing more than to march up the stairs, boldly intrude into her room, and have a genuine wedding night.

Bloody hell! What was he considering? What was he hoping to achieve?

Reclining in his chair, he shut his eyes, quelling his careening emotions and his scattered musings, while trying to analyze the forces that were raging through him.

Rapidly, it was becoming apparent that she wasn't the type of woman a fellow could neglect. Nor was she the kind he could have a time or two and be shed of—as was his wont. There was a chemistry or magnetism about her that drew a man in, that lured him to his doom, that made him want to chase foolishly after her just to discover if she could be caught, which was exactly what he was eager to attempt.

Was he insane?

It was those vows, he decided. Speaking those wedding vows before the minister and his assembled colleagues had left him unsettled. His financial quandary had driven him to take a rich bride, and he'd entered into the union without much thought, deeming it to be a lark, an easy solution, an excellent jab at his overbearing tyrant of a father. Clearly, however, the improvident whim was a blunder of monumental proportions.

Since the day he'd turned eighteen and had moved out on

his own, his father had been subordinating him through adept manipulation of the purse strings.

Recently, the earl had been obnoxious, ordering Stephen to wed by his thirtieth birthday. Without garnering Stephen's permission, he'd gone so far as to select a potential fiancée and had commenced negotiations with the girl's father, even though she was a whiny, homely nag whom Stephen couldn't abide.

When Stephen had rebuffed the earl's scheme, the earl had halted Stephen's allowance.

Marriage to Ellen Foster had been a windfall, a stroke of luck that had plucked him out of the doldrums of economic despair and had immediately rectified all that was wrong with his life, but the event had transpired so swiftly that he hadn't had sufficient opportunity to acclimate to the ramifications of what he'd wrought.

Those vows weighed heavily, having sunk in and wedged themselves into his consciousness, and he couldn't discard their magnitude. He now had a wife. A comely, engaging, smart individual who would need and expect his courtesy, deference, and respect, yet he didn't want a wife! He'd liked his bachelor's existence just how it was!

A wife connoted stability and obligation, responsibility and monogamy, and he'd never been one who could commit to a single woman. Fidelity was a preposterous theory that was beyond his capabilities.

He was nettled, by his folly, by the impetuousness that had brought him a lifetime of tribulation and strife. At all costs, he *had* to have his own way, so he'd spent almost thirty years clashing with his father, but to no avail. Look where he'd landed himself! He was wed to a foreigner with whom he'd been acquainted for only a few hours, and he'd been accompanied at the ceremony by his crew of immature, boisterous friends, with nary a family member in attendance.

Standing, he adjusted his trousers, prodding at his cockstand, which wouldn't abate.

He needed a woman. Not his wife, of course, but a female nonetheless. Weeks earlier, he'd split with Portia. The grasping, avaricious vixen had had the gall to break it off merely because he'd been destitute.

What loyalty! What devotion!

The shrew!

Since their quarrel and his auspicious acquisition of Ellen's fortune, Portia had been trying to atone, to cozy up, claiming she hadn't meant the horrid insults she'd hurled, but he'd taken them to heart and had sworn off romantic entanglement altogether. Evidently, his body was strongly feeling the lack.

The deficiency had to be why he was experiencing such a dreadful corporeal gravitation toward Ellen, so some extensive, raucous fornication would suit him just fine. With an amenable partner, he could exhaustively slake his lust so that this asinine craving for Ellen would wane.

Absently, he cogitated on the changes a female would bring to the house, how different it would be to have her constantly about and underfoot. Although there would be advantages, too, he supposed. She didn't seem the type who would brook much nonsense from the retainers, so he could anticipate better meals, a cleaner residence, and more vigilant servants with her to superintend them.

And, naturally, there would be the chance to see her first

thing every morning, to come down to breakfast and find her sitting in the family dining parlor, with the sun shining like a halo around her flaxen hair, and her gown molded to her bosom, and he'd . . .

"Get a grip on yourself!" he petulantly grumbled.

He went to the foyer, ready to fetch his outergarments and depart for destinations unknown. After all, where could a married man receive succor and solace on his wedding night without the gossip—that he wasn't in bed with his wife—spreading like wildfire?

The anteroom was deserted, as were the hallways. The servants were absent. Ellen had given them the night off. He needed a hat and coat, though they all seemed to be conspicuously missing. Up in his bedchamber, he had many, and, vastly irked, he trudged up the stairs to retrieve them, wanting to be off, but having no enthusiasm for the journey.

CHAPTER TWO

"He's coming!" Ellen's younger sister, Alice, whispered the warning as she swiftly but quietly shut the bedroom door. "It looks as though our ploy was successful."

Ellen jumped to her feet. "You should have seen him when I leaned over that table in the parlor. Most of my breasts were visible. He almost fell over!"

"What if you'd given him an apoplexy?"

"I was afraid he might expire before having a chance to do the deed!"

They giggled like schoolgirls, then Alice sobered.

"Are you sure you're ready for this?"

"More ready than I've ever been for anything."

"At least I knew my husband on the big night. *And* I was madly in love with him. That definitely helped."

"I could picture myself falling in love with Stephen." Considering how her heart fluttered whenever he was near, the notion wasn't so far-fetched.

Six feet tall, with dark hair and eyes, he was dashing, handsome. His physique was broad at the shoulders, thin at the waist, with long legs and a lithe, muscled torso, but it wasn't his appearance that had captivated her. It was how he carried himself, the manner in which others deferred to him, how heads turned when he walked by.

Women coveted him for his swagger and sexy disposition. Men envied him for his status and confidence, his attitude and demeanor. Ellen wanted him—for all those reasons and more.

"I'm so worried about you," Alice said.

"Don't be. I'll be fine."

The two siblings clasped hands, linking their fingers and squeezing tight.

"I'll be in your *room*," Alice advised, which caused her to chortle with mirth. As if Ellen would have followed Stephen's silly order to use another suite! "If you need me . . . ?"

Alice's voice trailed off in a question, because they couldn't predict what was about to transpire. Ellen's new husband was a mystery over whom they'd tittered and fussed for weeks before Ellen had made up her mind to pursue him. Neither of them could say what he might or might not do.

"I won't," Ellen courageously maintained. However he might posture and preen, Stephen was a gentleman. A temperamental one, certainly, but a gentleman nonetheless. "Go now. Before he discovers that you're here."

Alice hugged her, and, surprisingly, tears flooded her eyes. "You're so pretty," she said. "He won't be able to resist."

"My fingers are crossed!"

"I hope it's as splendid for you as it was for me."

"It will be." Taking into account Stephen's scandalous reputation with the ladies, she reckoned that the event would be fantastic. By all accounts, she couldn't have chosen a more apt candidate to ease her through the loss of her virginity.

"Go!" she repeated, suddenly frantic to organize herself, to steady the tingle of excitement and calm her torrent of emotions before his arrival.

Grinning, Alice sneaked out, leaving Ellen to cope with the ordeal alone—as every bride had to do.

She went into the dressing room that divided the two principal bedchambers of the residence, even though it was an area she had no right to occupy. Stephen had tried his level best to keep her at a distance. Without asking her opinion, he'd relocated her accommodations to the other end of the hall, but it was a plan with which she had no intention of complying.

Her husband was about to learn a distressing fact about his wife: she was her father's daughter in all ways.

Because she was too intelligent, strong willed, and stubborn, she'd kept her tenacity prudently concealed from her spousal candidates. She'd wanted them to be complacent, to deem her tractable and meek, but she'd been raised to prevail and flourish as enthusiastically as her father had.

Years earlier, he'd been wrongfully convicted of theft. Then, in chains, he'd been transported from his beloved England. Disgraced, he'd journeyed to the New World. There, he'd toiled unbearably, never losing sight of his goals or objectives, and he'd ultimately thrived far beyond anyone's expectations.

Ellen had acquired perseverance from studying him, and, occasionally, she fancied herself to be more determined than he could ever be. She'd wanted Stephen and now she had him. Despite his blunt insistence that they would have a platonic marriage, her aim was deflowerment. Immediately!

After he'd proposed, she'd cordially listened to his drivel as to how he didn't want to wed, and she'd patiently suffered through his contention that he felt no compunction to execute his noble responsibility to his family and line by siring any children. Unfortunately for him, she wanted a houseful, as well as a loving husband to govern over the large flock she anticipated having.

Stephen was going to be that man. He just didn't realize it yet.

Anxious, but brimming with undaunted resolve, she stood next to the bathing tub that Alice had obligingly prepared. Insolently, she turned her back, pretending to tarry, waiting with bated breath, as he stomped into his bedchamber and cast about for the cloak and hat he'd had to retrieve—since she'd lugged them all upstairs in furtherance of her scheme.

She was so attuned to him she could feel his movements beyond the wall, could discern the moment he saw her, and she stiffened, her pulse hammering in her chest, her senses festering and overloaded.

Lord, give me strength, she silently prayed.

Steeling herself, her hands shaky and her knees weak, she untied the bow that bound the front of her robe, and it slid to the floor.

Stephen frowned. Could it be?

A light emanated from his dressing room. The door was ajar, and he got a whiff of warm water scented with rose oil.

The smaller room adjoined the next bedchamber, the one that would have belonged to the viscountess had his and Ellen's been a true marriage, but she couldn't be in it. As he hadn't wanted her to misconstrue proximity, he'd specifically advised her to put her possessions in the suite at the other end of the hall.

She wouldn't have flagrantly ignored his wishes as to where her apartment was to be. Would she?

Like the worst voyeur, he tiptoed to the door and peeked inside.

It was she! Taking off her clothes and preparing for her bath! She'd had his tub filled with steamy water. Towels and soaps had been laid out on a stool next to it. Facing the dressing table, her back to him, she slowly stripped, though there weren't many pieces to shed.

She removed her robe, easing it off so that it slid down and pooled in a pile of green silk at her ankles. Then the negligee followed. Almost as if she knew he was watching, as if she'd planned to torment and tease his male sensibilities, she worked the narrow straps down, over her breasts, her hips, then she slithered this way and that. The garment undulated, then whooshed past her buttocks, her legs.

He blinked. Blinked again. He gulped! She was completely naked! His heart pounded in his chest, his cock vibrated against the placket of his pants.

Chivalry required that he look away, that he sneak out and pretend he'd never seen her, or that he make some noise to announce himself, yet he couldn't force himself to action. He was frozen, rooted to his spot, and indiscreetly spying like the lowest cad.

She grabbed her hair and wound it into a knot, balancing the exquisite mass on the top of her head while she secured it with combs. With her hair up, her backside was fully visible, and, in silence, he exulted in the spectacle, careful not to give himself away.

Rubbing his phallus, he sought to reduce some of the torture she was inflicting unaware. Every time she fussed with a comb, she twisted to the side, providing him with a profile of her body, and he could study her all the way down. Chest, ribs, hipbone, thigh. Her breasts were ample and inviting, the nipples taut and jutting out.

Seductively, she spun toward the tub, which gave him an entire frontal glimpse of her torso. She was flawless, perfectly created for a man such as himself to corrupt. He allowed his torrid scrutiny to travel downward, from her breasts to her belly to her mound. Her cushion of womanly hair was as golden as the hair on her head, and he could imagine bending before her, delving into her with his fingers, with his tongue.

If he but dared, he could be her first. He could invade her pilfered boudoir and demand his husbandly due. She wouldn't be able to refuse him, nor would she try. Despite their dubious agreement, she was well raised and recognized her duties as a wife.

How sweet it would be to tantalize and explore! To sample and relish! Her virginal sheath would be a tight, lush haven. He would coax and cajole, persuade and beguile, until he had her writhing and crying out his name.

She would submit, but her surrender would be languid and luxurious.

As he was an accomplished lover, he'd had a succession of refined, worldly paramours join him in his bed. He knew how to introduce her to pleasure, could tutor and inveigle her to heights of passion that she, in her chaste state, could never have envisioned. It would take weeks—nay, months—to thoroughly indoctrinate her into carnality and vice.

The notion was so tempting, so provoking. All he need

do was brave that initial step, and she would be his. Forever.

He'd always eschewed the idea of permanence with a woman, but, as he tarried, peering at his enchanting, desirable wife, nude and preparing to slip into her bath, the concept of perpetuity didn't seem so bad.

What would he be giving up? A cadre of friends who weren't close? A string of blue-blooded women who were little more than whores? So far, he'd only viewed the onus presented by her arrival. He'd failed to reflect upon the benefits, and there abruptly appeared to be many.

She lifted her foot to clamber into the tub, and he tensed, zealously observing, when she halted. He'd thought himself to be hidden in the shadows, but, apparently, he'd been detected.

Their gazes linked and held. For a split second, he considered running from the room, escaping to loll in his old life, but something had him locked in place. He couldn't have left if wild horses had been dragging him away.

With a drive that bordered on madness, he *had* to know what it would be like to take her in his arms.

He walked to the door, pushed it wide, and entered.

Brazen as an ancient, conquering Viking, Stephen marched over the threshold. He strutted to her, so that their bodies aligned, so close that she could smell the starch in his shirt and the soap with which he'd bathed. His shoe was wedged between her feet. The lapels of his coat brushed her stomach.

He was fully clothed, fitted out to the nines, while she was naked as the day she'd been born. It took every ounce of

CHERYL HOLT

fortitude she possessed to keep from crossing her hands over her breasts and her lower womanly regions.

She met his sweltering glare with one of her own, refusing to have him assume she was timid or disturbed, because, in reality, she wasn't alarmed in the slightest. Thrilled, yes. Discomfited by his height and audacity, yes. Uneasy at having him behold her nudity, yes.

But she wasn't scared.

He looked like a predator that had swooped upon its prey, and his gaze rudely meandered down her anatomy, lingering on her breasts and her mound. Then, he traveled up, languidly, indecently appraising every aspect of what she'd willingly displayed for his enjoyment and enticement.

"This is *my* dressing room," he caustically pointed out. "What are you doing in here?"

"I'm about to take a bath."

"Your bedchamber is down the hall."

"I know."

"Why aren't you in it?"

"I'm having the suite remodeled, so I had the housekeeper move my things. Just until the work is completed." Valiantly, she strove to seem free of devious intent, but she needed to regain her equilibrium, so she sauntered away—from his stern scowl, his domineering presence—and casually strolled to the dressing table.

"How long will that be?"

"A few months, I'd guess."

"A few months!"

"Yes."

She bent over, peering into the mirror and examining her

face, when it dawned on her that she was furnishing him with an exceptionally naughty sight. Her bare bottom was sticking out, her thighs spread, the muscles taut and tight down the backs of her legs. His reflection was visible in the glass, though she doubted he'd noted it, and she paused, scrutinizing him, curious as to what he would do next.

He was directly behind her, by the tub, but transfixed, his attention riveted on her. The wanton position had impelled him to a higher vigilance, and he missed no detail. Furtively, she clutched the dressing table, buttressing herself so that she wouldn't nervously jump up and end the prurient spectacle before he was finished.

Stalking toward her, he traversed the floor in three quick strides. He reached out to seize her hips, but she straightened before his hands descended. She was too modest to have him touch her there so soon. Acting as if being naked was an ordinary occurrence was arduous enough. She wasn't about to allow him to manhandle her before she'd been kissed!

She needed more time to adapt!

He had her jammed against the dressing table, so she couldn't ward him off or escape. Her thigh and hip were crammed between his legs, and she could feel the protrusion in his pants that attested to how much he lusted after her.

The discovery should have been a victory, but she couldn't celebrate. She was panicked, her virginal naiveté rearing up and causing her to tremble.

Oh, how she hoped he hadn't perceived her quavering! She couldn't let him detect how apprehensive she was! Lest she lose this first round in their battle of wills, she had to maintain her cool facade of sophistication and shamelessness.

"I don't want you sharing this room with me," he said.

"I promise I won't be a bother." Smiling, she endeavored to be flirtatious, even though she wasn't very adept at coquetry. "You'll scarcely notice I'm about."

"Not bloody likely," he muttered, and he flexed his hips, further trapping her against the furniture, his titillation increasingly manifest.

Astoundingly, he commenced fondling her breast, massaging the mound and the elongated tip so that it peaked into a painful bud. She inhaled sharply, and her stomach clenched, but other than those minor recoils, she stood tall, imperious, comporting herself as though strange men caressed her breasts as a matter of course.

"What game are you playing?" he barked.

"I play no *game* with you," she haughtily alleged. "I'm merely seeing to my nocturnal ablutions. You've interrupted me, sir."

"I'm not a buffoon, Ellen. Don't toy with me." His hand slithered to her other breast, and he gripped the nipple between finger and thumb, pressing it so that she could feel a jerking motion in her womb.

"I'm not trifling with you, and you need not tarry. You may be off to your evening of women and frolic."

His fingers weaved through her hair, yanking out the combs that had secured it to her head, and it swished down. He wrapped much of the lengthy mane around his fist and used it as leverage to tilt her back. Obviously, he was trying to intimidate her—with his size, with his proximity—and he was succeeding. He balanced over her, his mouth inches away, his angry brown eyes searching hers for secrets he couldn't decipher.

As he contemplated her, he kept on with the manipulation of her nipple, squeezing it severely, though never enough to hurt.

"Perhaps, I won't go out." He thrust his loins against her. "Perhaps, I'd rather stay here."

Her heart did a flip-flop, and she yearned to throw her arms around him, to close the space between them and impertinently put her lips on his, but she managed circumspection. She wouldn't relent until she was positive he was far past the juncture where he could stop himself.

"I'm perfectly capable of washing myself. I require no assistance."

"I believe you'll have to forego your bath."

He rotated her so that she was facing him, so that her rear was braced on the dressing table, the wood digging into her buttocks. Deftly, he'd pushed her legs apart and finagled himself between her thighs. The nap of his trousers scratched her tender skin, and the friction began to stimulate the feminine areas of her body. At her center, she was growing damp.

His grip on her hair hadn't slackened, and he leaned even nearer. "Do you have any idea what happens between a man and a woman when they're alone?"

"Yes," she cheekily declared.

He tensed, overtly stunned by her response. "Are you a virgin, madam?"

"What an uncouth boor you are to pose such an indelicate question."

"I would hear your answer." Incensed by the prospect that

she might not be, he clasped her shoulders and gave her a firm shake. "Tell me!"

"There's one way to find out."

"Really? Do you have a fervent wish to be ravished? Or have you already been?"

She was determined to remain aloof and detached, which, under the circumstances, was extremely difficult.

"I'm twenty-five years old," she stated with a shrug. She was treading on a perilous ledge, but despite what she might say or do, he'd never abuse her physically. "Are you vain enough to suppose that you're the only man who's ever captured my fancy?"

When his brows quirked up, she knew that was precisely what he'd surmised. Most likely, he inferred that he'd been doing her a colossal favor by lowering himself to wed her. Arrogant, presumptuous Englishman! They'd all postulated that she was some shrewish, homely harridan who'd only been able to snag a spouse because of her father's fortune.

Pride and ire renewed her resolve and restored her lagging courage.

"I had better be," he warned.

"Or what?"

He bristled but didn't reply, so she persisted. "How could my chastity—or *lack* of it—possibly signify? You're not interested in a sexual relationship with me anyway. You made your feelings explicitly clear from the outset."

"Maybe I've changed my mind, and I've decided to impose a few wifely obligations upon you."

They would be no great burden, she longed to shout, but she bit her tongue.

She wanted him to embrace her, to take them to the next level—their asinine agreement be damned. He was holding her in his arms, but it was with an odd, confused sort of exasperation, as though he wasn't sure whether to kiss her or spank her.

Tugging on her hair, he dragged her backward so that he could survey her bosom and privates. Then, he dipped down, and she was certain he was finally going to kiss her. Instead, he nuzzled under her chin and licked her neck, right where her pulse beat so furiously, and she couldn't stifle a yelp of astonishment.

His lips were soft and warm, and he used them to marvelous effect, nibbling and biting her skin.

As he dabbled at her nape, his fingers crept down her chest, her stomach, until they arrived at the curly hair shielding her core. With no finesse or preparation, he slipped them inside her, and a cry of amazement and shock whizzed out of her lungs.

On discerning it, the cad chuckled, and she felt her cheeks flush bright red. Her foremost, unavoidable reaction was to scoot away, to press her legs together, so that she might halt the exotic incursion, but he had her splayed wide and crowded between himself and the dressing table. She couldn't evade the onslaught.

He stroked back and forth, exploring, delving in, then sliding out. Quivering, she was awhirl with dozens of peculiar sensations she'd never formerly endured. She wanted him to desist; she wanted him to continue on forever.

"You're wet for me, my darling bride." Abandoning his perch at her neck, he nipped upward to her cheek, which sent shivers down her arms, but just when he would have reached her lips, he pulled away, resting his hands on her thighs, and his fingertips were moist from where he'd touched her.

"Should I take you here? Against the dressing table?" He steadied her hips and thrust against her in a slow, repetitive rhythm. "Is that how you like it? Is that what you're angling for? Something rough and wild? Or should I take you to my bed and fuck you there?"

Though she was a virgin, she was hardly an innocent. She'd heard the crude word before, and she was repulsed that he would utter it in her presence. His disrespect was an indicator of how she'd misread the situation. She'd thought to attract him—with her nudity, with her budding ardor that had been developing since she'd first seen him—but he'd regarded her overture as a sign of base character.

"I wouldn't lie down with you now. Not when you're being such a horse's ass."

"You will if I command it."

He sounded stern, and he looked like a vicious adversary, but she was derisive. "You don't scare me, so don't try."

"I don't scare you?" he needled. "I should."

He took her hand and brazenly deposited it on his distended phallus. It was prodding at his trousers as though it might burst the seams. The appendage was enormous, much larger than she'd imagined, and though Alice had insisted it would easily fit into her sheath, she couldn't comprehend how.

Alice had told her what to do with it, how to handle it, and what he would like, but this encounter was too unusual, and she was at a loss as to how to proceed. Her hand lay there, limp and unequipped for any endeavor, so he grabbed it, and applied pressure, rubbing himself with the heel and using it to assuage the aroused tip.

"I'm a lusty man. I'll ride you like a stallion." She cringed with trepidation, and he smirked. "Isn't that what you want? Isn't that why you're prancing around naked in my private quarters?"

"I was minding my own business till you barged in."

"Come now," he cajoled, "let's be honest with one another." He hovered over her, forcing her back until her head was flattened to the mirror. He evaluated her, his gaze deceptively beguiling, his smile oozing false charm. "You're eager for an indiscreet romp with the viscount you purchased with all your lovely money."

"You flatter yourself. I'd never submit to a libertine such as yourself. I'd rather have a nice, quiet bath."

"Liar."

Narrowing the distance between them, he took her mouth in a stormy kiss. She parted her lips to register a protest, and he invaded with his tongue, plunging in as though it was his due, his lordly privilege. He crushed her loins to his so that he could dazzle her with the tempo of his phallus.

Her primary response was of awe and surprise, and she stiffened, but only for a moment. Before their wedding, she'd incessantly pondered what it would be like to be kissed by him, and she was ecstatic to report that the reality was much more extraordinary than any fantasy she'd been able to concoct.

As she was twenty-five, she'd been kissed occasionally, but

the handful of tepid gropings, instigated by vapid, indecisive swains, were nothing compared to this. Now that she'd been kissed by Stephen St. John, she wouldn't describe what she'd previously done as *kissing*.

This was zeal and tumult, fire and fury. His heart and soul were laid bare. He was a tempest, a gale of agitation and frustration, and she folded her arms around him and hugged him, needing to fortify herself, to hold on to something solid as the turbulence raged.

His mouth molded to hers, and his hands were everywhere, seeking and investigating her shoulders, arms, back, and chest. He dallied with her breasts, adeptly massaging the tender nubs until they were raw and inflamed and her womanly core began to weep with building desire. His fingers glided down, stretching and entering her once again, and his thumb toyed with her, bringing her exultant pleasure.

Shamed as she was to admit it, she was no stranger to the pinnacle that was approaching. In the dark of night, when she was horridly lonely, she knew how to slake herself, but the exhilaration she inflicted was paltry when weighed against such rapture. He was magic, his divine fingers wielding a wicked spell.

Ablaze, she was about to be swept away, and she frantically tamped down on her burgeoning need for release. Fighting it, she struggled to hide her dynamic escalation. He was too experienced with women. He'd know instantly if she'd found gratification, and she wasn't about to give him the satisfaction. Not when his worst traits were being exhibited.

Just when she could tolerate no more, when she was sure she was about to embarrass herself, he jerked away and stepped back, disengaging from her, and she nearly cried out at the deprivation. She was at the brink, teeming with the need for satiation, and it was all she could do to keep from begging him to let her finish.

He was taut as a bow string, his muscles straining and about to snap. His phallus had swelled to a gigantic length so that his trousers were tented and full. He poked at the front, trying to allay the confinement.

With infinite, scorching animosity, he analyzed her, then he insulted her by swiping his hand across his lips, as if attempting to wipe away her taste.

"You kiss like a skilled whore, Lady Banbury."

She probably should have been hurt by the contemptuous comment, but all she could focus on was the fact that he'd referred to her as his wife.

"So do you, *Lord* Banbury," she tartly retorted. "Your vast array of prior paramours has trained you well."

The outrageous remark was a direct hit—at his manly pride, at his masculine sensibilities. His formidable temper flared. "Let's see what else you can do with that mouth." He seized her hand and placed it on the placket of his pants. "Get down on your knees and open my trousers. I would have a French kiss."

There was very little about sexual diversion that her sister had neglected to mention, so she understood what he was demanding. When Alice had initially explained the raucous, lewd maneuver, she'd been appalled, but the more they'd discussed it, the more intrigued she'd been, and they'd squandered incalculable hours, dissecting technique and method.

Could she do it?

She felt acutely conflicted. It was an exploit that he shouldn't have requested until much later in their association, not until she'd been thoroughly indoctrinated into libidinous behavior and felt at ease with him as her partner. Yet, nothing would please him more. Her own body was electrified with unsated passion, and her titillation was inciting her to folly, urging her toward conduct she normally would never have considered.

He was watching her every move, waiting to discover what she would do, and she couldn't help suspecting that his dictate had been a dare, that he wanted to ascertain how far he could push her, how far she would go. Well, he could challenge her all he liked; she wouldn't back down.

She clutched at the waistband of his trousers, wrapping her fingers over the edge and drawing him toward her. Her thumb flicked the top button through its hole, then the second. He stood before her, rigid, irate, immobile, but, when she progressed to the third button, he slapped at her hand and leaped away.

Troubled and flustered, he assessed her as though she were a dangerous enemy. "What do you want from me?"

"Nothing," she fibbed. "Nothing at all."

"I won't be a true husband to you!"

"Have I asked you to be?"

"I don't want children. Ever!"

"Neither do I," she prevaricated.

"Then what do you think will happen if we keep on? Are you idiotic enough to presume that we'll go at it like a pair of rabbits, but there will be no consequences? I refuse to be shackled to you by some squalling, sniveling brood. I won't care for them! Or for you!"

She blanched at his vehement anger, then wondered why he was being so adamant. It seemed as though he was striving to convince himself—rather than her.

"Bully for you, Lord Banbury," she murmured.

"I have your money, Ellen. You have my title. We reviewed the terms, and you agreed to them: we will lead separate lives, and you will have no say over what I do or where I go. I will drink and carouse and dally with one woman after the next. It's the sort of man I am."

"No, you're not."

"How the bloody hell would you know?" he shouted. "I can't fathom any other life! I don't have the faintest idea how to carry on any other way!"

"You could learn a new way."

"I don't want to! I'm absolutely happy with how things are now!"

"I see." She was mumbling, mortified that she'd assumed she could persuade him otherwise.

"No, you don't. What were you hoping to gain out of this morass you've created with me? Are you scheming for us to become involved? To grow attached? Well, let me tell you something about myself that you don't seem to grasp: I am not about to practice fidelity for you!" He bent down, so that they were eye-to-eye, and he sneered at her preposterousness, at her lack of sophistication. "You can bait me into being your lover, and I'll acquiesce, but I will rapidly weary of you. Then, I will cheat on you each and every day of our marriage."

He was denigrating himself hideously, and she declined to concur with this dim portrait of his character. Deep down, he was a fine man, one who could be counted on by his friends, who honored his word, who made a vow and stuck to it.

"You would never do that to me," she asserted.

Scoffing, he laughed meanly. "If that's what you believe, Ellen, then you're a fool."

He stormed out, slamming the door behind, and she remained rooted to her spot, listening to him go.

CHAPTER THREE

Tormented and humiliated, Ellen froze, as he flew down the stairs and out of the house. He banged the door hard enough to rattle the windows. It seemed as if all the air had suddenly left her body, and she slumped against the dressing table.

She was crushed, unable to understand how she'd misread him so terribly. As he'd peeked through the dressing room door that she'd deliberately left ajar, she'd been so sure she could coax him into a tryst. His assessment had been as hot and potent as she'd imagined he, himself, would be, should she be clever enough to goad him past his idiotic, self-imposed restraint. But he hadn't been enticed.

The beguiling nightrail and robe she'd worn for her grand adventure hadn't worked, either. The outfit had been Alice's idea. In matters of passion, Alice was an expert, so Ellen had concurred with her suggestion of attire.

Alice was a widow, her brief, blissful marriage having come to a sorrowful end after her seafaring husband's mortal accident. Before they'd been betrothed, her spouse had been a randy fellow, vastly experienced from amorous flings in ports around the world, so the newlyweds had reveled in a bawdy, torrid physical relationship.

Alice was extensively versed in intimacy, having vivaciously mastered the techniques of marital duty about which Ellen had been totally unenlightened. Ellen was the older, spinster sister who had remained unwed simply because she was a romantic, searching for the man of her dreams. With very little prodding on Ellen's part, Alice had graciously divulged the particulars.

Their devoted father was eminently conservative and had shielded them from life's harsh lessons, protecting them from all dangers. His worst fears had been over the caliber of men who would eventually call on his daughters due to his accumulated wealth.

Ellen had been kept ignorant about many facets of living, and she was grateful that Alice had been kind enough to teach her, for though she'd agreed to Stephen's absurd clamoring for a marriage of convenience, she wasn't about to honor their arrangement.

This was love. This was war. And she'd intended to utilize every feminine wile in her immense arsenal to win his affection. How depressing to have blundered so utterly in the first battle.

Alice had avidly explained how she was to incite him until he was overwhelmed by lust, until he was inclined to take her without regard to the consequences, but she hadn't truly grasped what her sister had meant.

His menace and calculation had thrown her off balance, and his intensity was frightening.

She'd thought she knew more about Stephen St. John than just about any person on earth. Her decision to approach him with an offer of marriage hadn't been hasty or imprudent. Her father had brought her to London for the sole purpose of finding an impoverished, desperate peer of the realm who was in need of an heiress.

The dream of being a titled lady hadn't been her own, but her dear da's, and it had been fueled during the forty years he'd resided in America. He'd come from a distinguished family, his father having been an estate agent for a viscount. When he'd been arrested for stealing, the accusation had been made to hide evidence that the actual culprit had been the viscount's son.

While no more than a boy, he'd landed on the foreign shore, a forsaken, penniless felon.

In the beginning, hatred over the injustice had ruled him, but he'd used his rage for maximum benefit, laboring harder and saving more than any other individual could have done. Every accomplishment had been a move toward the day he'd be able to thumb his nose at the very people who'd ruined him.

With only a few conditions, he'd let her have her pick of the spoiled, available aristocrats, and her choice had been Stephen St. John. She'd been introduced to, had spied upon, and chatted with dozens of admirers, but, from the evening she'd set eyes upon him, she hadn't wavered.

She'd initially seen him at the theater. He'd been keeping company with his paramour, the voluptuous beauty Portia Poundstone. They'd been sitting together, holding court, across from her box. Throughout the tedious operatic presentation, she'd observed him. As the last aria was being sung, she'd sent her father's men scouring through London's clubs, brothels, and gaming hells to unearth every piece of information to be gleaned.

A proud man, he'd been coddled and pampered, and he wouldn't bend or compromise. He had to be in charge. Others bowed to his wishes and obeyed his commands. His father, the Earl of Stafford, was the only person with enough power and authority to order him about, but Stephen wouldn't come to heel. Because he wouldn't settle down and wed, he was at constant loggerheads with his family.

He always got his way. He always triumphed. No one countermanded his dictates or instructions. Tonight he'd stared her down, exuding a mixed combination of wrath and exasperation, making her wonder why she'd thought her seduction stratagem was a good idea.

She was intrepid, and she knew what she wanted. Alice had coached her on how to go about getting it, but when confronted with his fierce virility, she was no longer convinced she could best him.

How could he hie off to his other women? On her wedding night!

Of all nights, she wanted him home and in his own bed. Preferably with herself intimately snuggled by his side.

She was confused, upset, afflicted, not knowing what to do or where to turn. Though her sister was down the hall, she couldn't confer with her, couldn't confess what a dismal failure their ruse had been.

He'd desired her; his elevated craving had been unmistakable. But he hadn't wanted her! His rejection was harsh, degrading to endure, and her woe was excruciating.

Endlessly, she replayed every horrid insult they'd bandied, and she prayed that he'd return, but he didn't. Finally, she crawled into the bath and loafed till the water grew cold. With every creak of the old house, she jumped, anxiously assuming that it was he, that he'd changed his mind about their relationship or, at the least, that he'd resolved to express his regret over their argument.

What sort of people fought so viciously on their wedding night?

In despair, she inevitably admitted that he wasn't coming back, that he'd gone to celebrate his new fortune with an evening on the Town. She pictured him in the arms of the ravishing Miss Poundstone or another of the gorgeous women who flitted through his social circle, and she thought her heart might break.

While she was no acclaimed beauty, she was deemed by many to be winsome as well as educated, witty, and charming. She'd been eager to demonstrate that she could be an ideal mate and viscountess, enthused to share the end of their glorious day by making love, and the knowledge that he would rather carouse with his male friends—or worse yet, with one of his disreputable doxies—was an embarrassment too great to be borne!

She was too agitated to stay in her own room. Not without talking to him. Not without ascertaining that he was home, safe and sound. Though it was inappropriate and imprudent, she went to his bedchamber, needing to surround herself with his possessions.

Distractedly, lovingly, she explored his shaving equipment. She snooped through his drawers, fingering his scarves and undergarments, and she peeked in the wardrobe, counting and petting his shirts and coats.

Brimming with longing and remorse, she crawled onto his bed, ruminating over what to do, how to carry on after such a terrible misstep, and gradually, she drifted into a fitful sleep.

"Bloody, insane woman!" Stephen growled as he tromped down the stairs and banged out of the house.

A rented hansom was parked by the curb, the driver waiting patiently for his illustrious passenger to show. Stephen's own carriage had been sold long ago, and, with Ellen's marriage settlement only recently coming into his control, he hadn't had the chance to buy a new one.

In the shadows, the conveyance appeared cheap and seedy, but the driver understood his trade. He leaped to attention and held the door, but Stephen waffled. He knew he should get in, but he couldn't decide what direction to give. Should it be to his club where his friends could heckle him over his failed wedding night? How about to a gambling hall, where he'd waste a bit of his wife's fortune? Or maybe to a brothel, where he could slake some of the lust pounding through his veins?

As opposed to preceding months, he was flush with cash. Bidding the surprised man his thanks, he slapped too many coins into the driver's palm and stalked off, needing to be by himself, to walk off his fury.

Although his residence was situated in one of the better sections of town, London was hardly the place to go trekking about in the dark. Even in an exemplary area, mischief could befall a chap, but Stephen was scarcely concerned. His upset was so fierce that he was almost eager to blunder upon a few ruffians. Nothing would garner him greater pleasure, or provide him with a more suitable mode of letting off steam, than to have a nasty brawl with a pack of criminals who deserved a proper thrashing.

Head down, hands jammed in his pockets, he stomped down the street. A carriage pulled out from a neighbor's stable yard and, lest he bump into any of his acquaintances, he ducked and turned the corner. He'd rushed out so quickly that he hadn't bothered with hat or cloak, and he regretted his haste.

There was no way to disguise himself! What if someone saw him? How would he explain his wandering about shortly after the last guest had departed his wedding reception? All of London would theorize as to why he hadn't been snuggled in his wife's bed. He'd never hear the end of it!

He'd be a laughingstock! He'd be badgered and taunted, his manhood questioned.

The men would chaw over why he couldn't seduce his wife. They'd debate over exactly what he'd purchased by accepting all that money.

The women would be more vicious. They'd titter behind their fans, would gossip over whether he'd lost his infamous stamina, if he'd been unable to *rise* to the occasion. Or if— God forbid!—he hadn't satisfied her! They'd spread stories that she hadn't enjoyed it, that she'd tossed him out!

He could precisely imagine the crude gibes and banter.

Rounding another corner, he found himself on a particularly deserted tract where he was concealed from passersby, and he pressed at the front of his trousers, desperate to alleviate his erect phallus. His cockstand was so painful that his teeth hurt. It hadn't waned in the least. Neither the brisk stroll, nor the chilly evening air, had had any effect on the rude member at all.

Loitering, he thought of his wife, of how she'd looked as

he'd dabbled with her on the dressing table. He'd never witnessed a more glorious, erotic sight. Her curvaceous, well-proportioned body was his concept of feminine perfection. Wide where it should be and slim where it should be, too. Her skin was smooth and creamy, her blond hair luxurious and tempting. She was desire incarnate, every man's wildest fantasy, and she could have been his if he'd had the courage to proceed.

In agony, his rubbed his hand over his face, stopping abruptly when he realized he could smell her sex on his fingers. He suffered another stab of tormented longing, pondering her and what they might have done together.

Her taut nipples! Her tight sheath! He'd wanted her as he'd never previously wanted a woman, and he wished he'd had the nerve to progress to the natural conclusion, that he'd taken them both to heaven and beyond. No doubt he'd have spiraled to ecstasy in her arms.

Why had he halted? What had been his rationale? The sassy strumpet had virtually thrown herself at him, had practically implored him to ravish her, but he'd declined to cooperate. Merely because she was his wife. When had he ever denied himself? What had compelled him to start now? What purpose was served by refusing to copulate with her?

He could have her every night, every day, too, if he was so disposed. Whenever and wherever the mood struck him. She was an unfettered, bawdy wench, ripe for the plucking, who'd submit with a reckless abandon he rarely encountered among the jaded Jezebels of the *ton* who regularly warmed his bed.

So what if he had her, then took another woman later on? If he had a mistress or two or ten, it was no one's business but his own. It was his right. His due. He could have her routinely, and, when the sizzle dwindled, when he'd had enough and his appetite for her dissipated, he could entertain himself on the side.

If she learned of his infidelities, if she was distressed or humiliated by them, what did it signify?

Every gentleman of means had other lovers. It was the norm. Expected and allowed.

His personal gratification was the sole factor that mattered. The doctrine of his unadulterated superiority had been drilled into him since birth. He believed in it, had reveled in the prerogatives afforded him by his exalted status, had thrived on the unwritten tenets that guaranteed he could do as he pleased and damn the consequences.

Why, then, had it been so difficult to take what he'd wanted from her? Why had he been so unnerved? Usually, he frolicked heedlessly, cavorting and gamboling through an interminable stream of licentious, profligate amusements. Undeterred by morals, social mores, or others' opinions of propriety, he simply barged through life, seizing the moment, and relishing whatever diversion tickled his fancy.

Why hadn't he reached for her and the rapture he knew he would have derived?

Jesus! He was so conflicted!

Plodding on, slowing, he let the peace and quiet soothe him. Rambling, he trudged down various dim, indistinct streets, unsure of his destination. He couldn't visit any of his customary haunts, and he couldn't go home. *She* was there, and, in his disordered state, he couldn't conceive of venturing inside.

What if she was awake? What if he came face-to-face with her?

He'd been an ass, had dealt with her as if she were a whore, and he was extremely embarrassed. Gad, but he'd essentially accused her of being a harlot! He'd demanded to know if she was a virgin! On her wedding night!

What sort of despicable cad was he?

In spite of his faults, he had impeccable manners, and he knew how to act the consummate gallant when the situation called for it, yet she'd thrown him totally off balance, swaying from one indiscriminate remark to another when he hadn't meant any of them.

He'd just been so . . . so . . . curious, and awestruck and angry and . . . and . . . and . . .

Perversely, he felt a drastic need to persuade himself that he'd behaved appropriately. He never apologized, never expressed remorse, or tried to make amends. As he was a viscount who would inherit an earldom, he was so far above others that, without reflection or recompense, he could harm anyone who got in his way; yet, in this instance, he was besieged with guilt.

Dammit! He'd never be able to look her in the eye again!

After careful contemplation, he could only infer that she'd been intent on beguiling him, then being deflowered. Her tarrying in his dressing room and her propitious disrobing had been a ploy to lure him into debauching her.

But why?

What could her objective have been? They'd discussed their arrangement, had agreed to coexist and go about their separate lives. What was she really after? He'd asked her, and she'd maintained she wanted nothing, which was obviously a lie.

Evidently, she'd concocted a scheme to snare him into a physical relationship, to make their marriage genuine in every sense of the word, and the prospect scared the hell out of him. What kind of a husband would he be to the poor girl? Why should she want him to put forth the effort?

He was a spoiled, pampered ne'er-do-well, who did naught but trifle and lollygag. He couldn't be counted upon, couldn't be trusted, would do whatever benefited him—and only him— with no regard to others' sensibilities.

It was his nature, at the root of his personality, and the reason he'd wed with none of his family in attendance. No one could tell him what to do, coerce his compliance, or quash his stubbornness. He made his own decisions, selected his own path, and if others didn't like it, they could go hang.

What woman would deliberately bind herself to such a fellow? If she assumed he could make her happy, she was destined for a lifetime of disappointment.

Perhaps he'd just never go home! He'd spend the rest of his days, roving blindly through London, too much of a coward to confront his wife, beg her pardon, commence anew, or carry on.

Pausing to get his bearings, he checked out the row of wrought-iron fences, the neatly trimmed hedges, the majestic dwellings, when it dawned on him that he was standing on his own street, his residence down the block. While he'd presumed he'd been drifting aimlessly, apparently he'd traveled in a big circle, and his feet had automatically delivered him back to where he'd begun.

Was this a portentous sign? Had he wanted to return all along?

At his gate, he climbed the steps and lingered on the stoop. No light emanated from any of the windows. He hoped that meant she'd given up on her carnal quest and retired, so that he could slither to his room and crawl into his bed undetected.

Fumbling with the latch, he slunk into the foyer. The moon was high and flooding the stairs, so he didn't need a lamp, and he ascended to his bedchamber and sneaked in without meeting another soul.

Heaving a sigh of relief, he shut the door, turned, and . . .

There she was, dozing in the middle of his bed. She was lying atop the covers, as if she hadn't been brave enough to crawl under, but she'd staked out her spot in the center, and she seemed to belong just where she was.

Frowning, he dawdled, hands fisted on his hips, not certain of what to do. His first inclination was to march over and shake her, to reignite their quarrel, which wasn't a good idea. It was blatantly clear that she had a keen wit and could best him in any argument. He didn't want her here, but chagrin and perplexity forestalled him from barking out her name and sending her scurrying to her room.

He'd married the vexatious lady, and she wouldn't fade into the woodwork as he'd ordered, so he had to alter his plan of action.

Tiptoeing to the bed, he studied her. She was wearing her scanty negligee, the robe absent, and it had crept up past her knees, revealing her long, slender legs. Her ribs rose and fell in a leisurely rhythm. Dead to the world, she hadn't roused the slightest upon his entry, and it occurred to him that she was exhausted. It had been her wedding day, after all. The stress on her had to have been tremendous.

The entire afternoon and evening, he'd rued and fussed over the fact that he'd married a stranger, but he hadn't taken a second to conjecture as to how *she* had weathered the ordeal. She'd married a stranger, too, then she'd been constrained to host his cadre of daunting, exuberant associates, and she'd done so without a whimper of complaint.

Gracious, charming, she'd mingled and chatted. As his guests had left, he'd been repeatedly patted on the back, while his friends informed him how fortunate he was, what a catch he'd made, how he had the devil's own luck with women.

She looked young and dear, and his heart seemed to tumble erratically. He massaged over it, trying to ease some of the sudden ache. As she was pretty, smart, sexy, she was everything a man could possibly want in a wife. Why had he viewed her arrival as a millstone, an impediment? Why not dwell on some of the advantages?

He evaluated her a few minutes more, disconcerted, confused about what he wanted, and a soft voice niggled at him.

What if...? it queried. What if he grabbed for what she was offering? What if he forged on and made her his own?

In his prior ribald forays, he'd habitually felt as if he was searching for something, but he'd never found it. He was lonely and had no true friends. The women with whom he consorted were superficial and wanton, benumbed by their wealth and privilege. They had no more emotional attachment to him than he did to them. He was so alone, wanting companionship, craving contentment, but he never attained even a modicum of comfort.

What if the prize he'd perpetually been hunting for was her?

The notion swept over him like a bright ray of sunshine.

Appealing and irresistible, she had faith in him, in the type of spouse he could grow to be. She seemed to be aware of the less savory aspects of his character, yet she liked him anyway. If he dared to risk all, he'd gain a confidante, a comrade he could depend on and esteem, cherish and protect, and the concept didn't sound so bad.

Why . . . if he treated her decently, if he let her discover the man he was deep down, she might become fond of him. Eventually, she might come to . . . to . . . love him.

He smiled. It would be grand to be loved by Ellen Foster St. John.

Quietly, he went to the dressing room and removed his clothes. The tub from her ill-fated bath was in place, the water cooled, and he wondered if she'd washed in it after he'd strode off in a temper.

Taking a cloth, he dipped it and ran it over his heated skin. He hoped she *had* lain in it, for he liked to suppose that the water coating him had enveloped her, too. Finished, he dried with a towel, slipped into his robe, loosely looping the belt around his waist, then he strolled to his room.

He glided to the bed, but she hadn't stirred. Eager to observe everything that transpired, he lit a candle, watched the flame as it flickered and extended, then he dropped himself down. His hip was nestled to hers, his upper torso braced on an arm. He scrutinized her, dissecting her features.

She was so damned enticing, and she was his.

A wave of possessiveness rippled over him, and he was anxious to make her truly his own, to claim her and keep her. Resting a hand on her stomach, he caressed her belly in a languid circle. She smiled in her slumber, some unconscious part of her perceiving that it was he.

Leaning over, he kissed her, a brush of his lips to her velvety cheek.

"Ellen," he whispered.

Scowling, she rolled onto her back, stretching, gradually awakening. Her eyes fluttered open, but she scarcely recognized that he was hovering over her.

"Oh . . . I was sleeping so hard." She blinked, then alertness was restored in a rush. Her smile faltered. Tentatively, she ventured, "Hello."

"Hello."

"You're here."

"Yes."

"I was so worried about you."

"I took a walk," he inanely mentioned. "I needed some time to think."

She nodded. Plainly, she'd been endlessly cogitating their impasse, as well. "While you were gone, I made myself at home."

"I see that." Glancing around, he chuckled. A half-empty glass of wine stood on his dresser; her robe was draped over a chair; her slippers were next to the wardrobe. "It's quite all right."

"I don't want to fight anymore."

"Neither do I. I hadn't intended to. I was . . . was . . ." Was what? Irate? Bewildered? Aroused? Unsettled? All conditions applied. "I'm not sure what to do with you."

"We'll figure it out."

"Aye, I expect we will." Abashed, he blushed. "I didn't mean what I said to you earlier. I'm sorry. It's been a long day, and I was distraught. I shouldn't have—"

She pressed a finger to his lips, quelling the remainder of his confession. "I said several things I didn't mean, either." A mischievous grin creased her cheeks. "I might have been goading you. Just a tad."

"Minx."

A companionable silence descended as they perused one another, and he was overcome by the most peculiar sensation, that he'd always known her, that he'd been waiting for her forever.

Reeling with amazement and excitement, he kissed her. It was a gentle embrace that went on and on, and he shifted fully onto the bed, so that his body was touching hers all the way down. As he broke the kiss, she was gazing up at him so tenderly that he could barely stand to witness her affection. It was perceptible, real, and it poured over him. Like a blind man who'd been wandering in the desert, seeking an oasis, and had finally stumbled upon one, he soaked it in, thirsty for what she could give him.

Feeling adored and revered, he luxuriated in the possibility that she might have married him for himself, that she'd wanted *him* and no other.

"Let's start this night over," he suggested.

"I'd like that."

"Could we commence with your calling me Stephen?"

She quivered with mirth, a delectable rumbling shaking her tummy and chest. "You don't care for *Lord* Banbury?"

"If you *milord* me one more time, I just might strangle you."

"I'll try to restrain myself."

She laughed again, then it tapered off, and there was only the two of them, in the hushed, shadowed room. The moment grew intimate, agonizingly so, and a thousand words were perched on the tip of his tongue.

He wanted to make love to this woman—his wife. The proof was explicit by the cockstand that was wedged to her thigh, but he also wanted merely to talk with her. Surprisingly, he was desperate to learn all about her. Every detail, tiny and large, was abruptly paramount.

What was her favorite food? Her favorite color? What were her hobbies? He was curious about her home and life in America, why she'd journeyed to England in pursuit of a husband, why she'd chosen him over the others. Did she like to ride? To read? Could she play the piano-forte?

As fervently as he craved knowing about her, he was dying to prattle on about himself, and he was frantically praying she would inquire, so that he could explain the forces that had molded him. He longed to unburden himself about his horrid childhood, his deceased mother whom he didn't recall, his undemonstrative, aloof father, who had chastised and berated him at every turn, the parade of apathetic governesses and tutors who'd flowed past in a steady stream.

He wanted to tell her about the sweet-tempered nanny he'd had when he was eight or nine, how the woman had been fired for holding him as he'd cried after his kitten had been trampled by a horse.

His father had insisted she was transforming him into a sissy, that he'd develop into a gay blade under her tutelage, and he'd sent her away, had thrown her into the streets without permitting her to pack her bags. Stephen had never seen or heard from her again, and to this day, over twenty years later, he still speculated as to what had become of her.

Numerous events had coalesced to shape him into a harsh, indifferent man, and he was convinced that—if he apprised Ellen of his background—she would grasp why he was so impossible, so detached and solitary in the midst of so many. With an abiding certitude, he knew that she would understand, and, absurdly, her knowing would correct many of his afflictions, would cure much of what ailed him.

Detestable, forlorn memories were crowding into his head, so many of them that he couldn't keep track, and he felt nine years old once more. He was positive that if he uttered a single comment, he'd blubber like a baby, so he kissed her instead, needing to be close, to surround himself with her essence and femininity.

Her proximity was a healing balm, and, instantly, he was pacified.

"I would be most honored," he cautiously posed, "if I could make you my wife in every way."

"You'd like us to be lovers?"

"Aye."

"What brought about your change of heart?"

He couldn't elucidate the arduous rumination in which he'd engaged during his walk, or the stunning conclusions he'd reached. Before their wedding, he'd thought he could frivolously take a bride, that he could pick someone to flaunt at his father, but now that he'd done it, his perspective had altered.

She was his, despite his idiotic state of mind when he entered into the union, and he was duty-bound to succor and preserve, to respect and treasure.

It was those accursed vows! he grumbled to himself.

He'd recited them before God and the assembled company, so he'd been obligated, and, for once, he didn't chafe at the responsibility. A small part of him, one that seemed to be expanding with alarming rapidity, was excessively delighted that she'd waltzed into his life, but he'd never acknowledge so much. Not yet, anyway. A man had to be allowed some secrets.

"Let's chalk it up to temporary insanity."

"Let's do." She chortled, then laid her palm on his cheek. "Are you absolutely certain?"

"Yes."

"Then so am I."

"Have you ever . . . ?" he indelicately probed. After their previous bickering, he didn't know what he would encounter. If she was a virgin, he didn't want to rush or overwhelm her. If she wasn't? He'd be disappointed, but they'd deal with it, and he had to admit that her missing maidenhood would definitely make things easier!

"No. I never have." Genuinely chaste, she blushed prettily.

He hadn't anticipated being so exhilarated by the news, but his relief was so enormous that he felt as if he'd been hit with a battering ram. The air hissed from his lungs, and his pulse raced. He wanted to whoop with joy, but he managed to hide his exuberant reaction.

"I'll be your first." He couldn't keep from preening.

"I'm glad it will be you."

"Oh, Ellen," he murmured happily.

He was promptly panicked. What had she envisioned gaining in a husband? Would he match up? Would he compare with her maidenly fantasies?

How he yearned to satisfy her! To enchant her beyond measure!

"Do you know what's about to happen?"

"My sister Alice told me."

Briefly, he'd met her sister, and she'd seemed like a no-nonsense sort of individual, like Ellen herself, but what would Alice have imparted as wedding night advice? Concerned that he might have to rout imprudent apprehension, he asked, "Are you worried about what will transpire?"

"A little. But mostly, I'm excited."

"We'll take our time. I'll—"

"Don't hold back on my account," she interrupted. "I want you to show me how it can truly be."

How had he gotten so lucky? A beautiful, captivating bride who was wanton as hell! What a wedding night this was going to be! He was elated that he'd tossed aside his asinine reservations! Only a fool would have passed up this chance!

He searched her eyes for vacillation, anxiety, or dread, but he saw only curiosity and an eagerness to please that stirred his manly appetites and made him wild to proceed, mad to ascertain how glorious it could be.

Slow down! The warning rang out.

He was so provoked that he felt as if he could spill himself against her leg like a callow boy of fourteen. His cock surged to attention, pushing at the front of his robe, intent on being immediately serviced, but he couldn't progress as swiftly as his anatomy was ordering him to go. He needed to familiarize her, to let her accustom to his masculine physique.

Sliding over her, he covered her with his body, so that his weight pressed her down, his thighs cradled hers. He was hard, his cockstand excruciating, and she splayed her legs, so that she was open, adjusted. At her core, the fabric of her nightrail and his robe provided a cushion, and he held his hips stationary and began kissing her in earnest.

It started tamely, mildly, but his passion for her escalated, and he tantalized her, his tongue mating with hers in a torrid dance. His hands went to her breasts, kneading the soft mounds through the sleek material. He teased and toyed with her nipples, impatient to suckle at one of them.

Nibbling a path down her neck, he rooted and nuzzled at her cleavage. She smelled good, like soap and sleep and the rose-scented oil that had been added to her bath. He inhaled sharply, wanting to implant the aromas into his memory so he'd never forget.

Her breasts were so fine, and he massaged them, playing and shaping. Then, he tugged at the straps of her nightgown, yanking them down so that her bosom was exposed, so that the creamy flesh was offered up for his enjoyment and de-lection.

For a long while, he stared, his gaze potent and intense, making her writhe uncomfortably, then he dipped down and kissed her nipple, laving it, then sucking it into his mouth.

Like a babe, he nursed, soothed by the precious motion, but his hunger for her was too fierce, and the subdued indulgence fleetly augmented so that he was using her roughly, pinching and biting with enough pressure to make her squirm.

Merciless, he kept on to where her pulse was hammering at the base of her throat, her respiration labored and difficult, then he moved to the other nipple, giving it the same turbulent manipulation.

"I want you naked," he said, as he abandoned her inflamed bust and kissed down her stomach.

"Yes. Oh, yes," she moaned as he nipped at her navel.

Pulling at her nightgown, he drew it down inch by inch, to her waist, her hips, her thighs, and over her toes, then he pitched it onto the floor. Poised over her abdomen, he positioned himself between her legs as he burrowed across her belly and the silky tuft of her womanly hair.

"I'm going to kiss you here."

"Whatever you wish." She gulped, reminding him that, though she was game to try what he initiated, she was still an innocent.

With two fingers, he touched her, finding her saturated and slippery, and he delved inside, caressing her, preparing her for what was to come. She was tight and wet, and his cock inflated to an embarrassing length, hurling him to a frightening level of desire. To maintain his languid pace, he had to muster all his fortitude, and he fought against a savage impulse to pin her to the mattress and take her, brutally and crudely, while totally ignoring her virginal condition.

"You're so ready for me."

Unable to delay, he tasted her, and her erotic tang was an

ambrosia that called to his wicked instincts. The aphrodisiacal fragrance was one he recognized; it tempted him in a primal fashion that went far beyond rhyme or reason.

Flinging her thighs over his shoulders, he settled in, savoring her, then he chased after her sexual nub. It was taut and enlarged, and he grazed over it, brushing it with fast strokes. She panted and fidgeted as he held her down and inflicted thrilling punishment.

At the edge, she battled the rising tide even as her body propelled her toward the climactic end. She grappled against the onslaught, but he wouldn't let her evade the torrent. Straining, her hips worked against his mouth. She was so close. So close.

"Let go, darling."

"I can't." Delicious noises of want and need were emanating from the back of her throat. "It's too much. Too soon."

"Do it for me, Ellen. Let go." He reached up and grabbed for her nipples, squeezing them as he wrapped his lips around the tender morsel that would bring her the ultimate rapture.

"Stephen . . . oh . . ."

His lusty wife trusted him enough to leap into a powerful orgasm. As she bucked and thrashed, he rode the wave with her, embracing her and cherishing her as she spiraled up, up, then fell to earth, and he was there to catch her.

Lingering over her stomach, her bosom, her ruby lips, he let her sample the sex on his tongue, but he couldn't wait one more second to have her, and he loosened the belt on his robe, wrenched the lapels aside. Stimulation rocked him as his naked torso connected with hers.

"Stephen . . . that was . . . was . . . spectacular."

"Yes." He kissed her forehead, her nose. Her cheeks were flushed from their exertions, and she was smiling at him with a profound affection.

Near to love, he thought.

Could she grow to love him? What a marvelous notion! How he hoped she would. He'd spent his entire life avoiding attachment to any woman, but now, with his wife peering up at him, glowing from her inaugural experience toward intercourse, he couldn't imagine why he'd eschewed the situation.

"It's time, Ellen." Kissing her again, he clasped his cock, establishing himself at her very center.

Her virginal trepidation apparent, she beseeched, "Take me gently."

"Always," he vowed.

He eased himself in, the blunt crown stretching her, then he pushed in a tad more. Her eyes widened at his invasion, and he stopped, letting her acclimate, then he advanced until he was wedged inside, pressing against the maidenly barrier that blocked her passage.

"You're so big." A frown wrinkled her brow, and she twisted her hips from side to side, her innate response to flee from the incursion. "It hurts."

"The pain is normal." He was barely able to hold himself in check. "Lie still. Try to relax."

"Please . . . I . . ."

With a typical fear of the unknown, she was panicking, and he understood he should pause, perhaps retreat to let her adapt more fully, but he was beyond the point of logic or restraint. He *had* to be inside her.

"Don't be afraid."

Clutching her hips, he steadied himself, but she was wrestling with him, frantic to escape the inevitable. He knew it was wrong to be titillated by her struggles, but her alarm ratcheted his ardor a notch higher, and he braced her and plunged inside in a single, smooth thrust.

He was her first! Her very first! His pride and arrogance soared.

No matter what happened between them in the future, this one extraordinary fact could never be changed. A dangerous vigilance flooded through him, and he swore to himself, then and there, that she'd never intimately know another man. That he would care for her, would make her happy, so that she would remain his and his alone.

She arched up off the bed, crying with dismay, and he captured her wail with an ardent kiss.

"Ssh," he calmed, "that's the worst of it."

"I didn't believe you'd fit."

He quashed an insolent smirk. He was a strapping man, and hers was a narrow, slick haven that would cradle him through years of divine excess.

Her inner muscles contracted around his staff, her virgin's blood and sexual juice a steamy cauldron, urging him to the culmination, but he gritted his teeth, tamping down on his vehement need for satiation.

Eventually, she mellowed, the tension reducing, and he reposed with her, dropping down to rest on top of her, to feel her everywhere. Tentatively, her arms went around him, and tremulously, she smiled and hugged him. He placed a kiss of reassurance against her nape.

"Better?" he inquired.

"Much."

He raised up, balancing himself on his palms, and studied the carnal scene displayed below.

She was a prurient fantasy come true. Her blond hair was spread across his pillows, her body sundered and welcoming him. He glanced down to her breasts, to the peach-colored nipples that were erect and aroused. The golden hairs of her mound tickled and massaged his turgid cock. He was buried to the hilt, her anatomy having accepted every inch he had to bestow.

His gaze traveled up to meet her own, and she was looking at him with such fondness that his heart lurched in his chest.

I could love this woman, he realized, and the splendid prospect made him smile, too.

Overflowing with unbridled joy and devotion, he began to move.

"Let me show you how it ends."

CHAPTER FOUR

Ellen was jubilant.

She was a woman now. Stephen had made her so, and she was ecstatic. Both from the loss of her much-lamented virginity, and because he had been the one to relieve her of it.

To her enormous delight, he'd awakened her—with kisses and apologies and more—and she couldn't stop conjecturing as to whether she was in the middle of a blissful, erotic dream. She arched her pelvis, just so she could detect the pain between her legs.

His phallus was fully implanted. He'd taken her! He really had!

He lingered above her, his palms flattened on either side of her head. With each insertion, he probed exhaustively, her untried body shifting and adjusting to the novel sensations created by his entry.

The anticipation was over, her maidenhead obliterated, and she'd succeeded in bumbling through it without making a fool of herself. She was starting to adapt to his presence. Actually, his flexing was beginning to feel rather pleasant. A tingle ignited low in her belly and radiated from her womanly core to her nipples. She was becoming aroused, and considering how fervently she'd found release the first time, the second occasion—with him inside her—would be even more dynamic.

He was still clad in his robe, though it was open at the

front. His arms were covered, his thighs and legs, too, and she wanted him as naked as she, yearned to feast her eyes on his smooth flesh, to observe the mysteries of his delicious male torso.

"I want this thing off of you."

"Never let it be said"—he ceased his calculated penetrations—"that Lord Banbury denied a lady's request."

Urgent, she yanked at the garment, and he moved about, assisting her in undressing him. Shortly, the robe was dislodged, and he hovered over her, delaying, letting her look her fill.

He was magnificent. His shoulders were broad, his arms toned, his waist thin. His chest was coated with a thick matting of dark hair that dusted his nipples, then descended to his navel and downward to nest around his male parts.

Tentatively, she reached out and rested her hands on him, running across ridge and valley, sinew and muscle. The cushion of hair tickled, and she sifted through the intriguing pile, rubbed her nose in it. He laughed, a rumbling baritone that reverberated to her very pores.

He liked her handling—she could tell by his reactions—so she grew more bold, dipping down to fondle the spot where they were united, roving behind to cup his rounded, taut bottom.

Perched above her, tense and agile, he managed to suffer through her virginal journey of discovery until she decided to explore his nipples. When she took the tiny nubs between finger and thumb, she sent him over the edge upon which he'd been precariously poised.

Impatiently, he slapped her hands away. "Jesus, I've got to come," he said. "Now! I can't wait!"

"What should I do?"

"Hold me tight. Don't let go."

"I won't."

She snuggled him to her bosom as he settled himself down, kissing her and trifling with her breasts. Meticulously, rhythmically, he bore into her, each encroachment spurring him nearer and nearer to the precipice.

His rise of lust fueled her own, and, without warning, another stupendous orgasm swept her away.

As she'd suspected, with him inside her it was incredibly potent, and she grasped at him, needing him as her stable point as she flew across the universe. Even in his overly incited condition, he was cognizant of her drastic plight. He enfolded her in his arms, cradling her through the tumult.

"Stephen . . ." she wailed, the only word that appeared to matter in the torrid location to which she'd traveled.

"You're mine, Ellen," he intently maintained, bewitching her with his possessiveness. "All mine."

She discerned a voice crying out his name once more, and she vaguely recognized it as her own. Never seeming to attain the peak, she glided higher and higher, and he continued to plunge into her throughout the spiral.

He, too, approached the pinnacle, working himself into a frenetic dither. With no regard to her inexperienced circumstance, he'd taken her raucously. He couldn't get enough of her, couldn't propel forcefully enough or delve deeply enough. Sweat pooled on his brow and chest; his anatomy was rigid with strain.

Pushing into her, once, twice, thrice, he froze, his body stiff and unyielding. He tarried just there, his rod lusciously embedded. His climax commenced, and he twined an arm around her and clutched her to him, clenching her so fiercely that she was worried he might crack one of her slender bones.

A haunting moan echoed out, and he shuddered. Far inside, his phallus was throbbing as his hot seed surged from the tip and spewed across her womb. The fiery emission gushed out, again and again, his pleasure interminable, as though he couldn't find his way to the end.

Instinctively, she wrapped her legs around him, her fingers clasping his buttocks, and she pulled him in, hugging him to her as he emptied himself.

At last, with a jolting, violent quiver raking him, he was replete. He went slack and fell onto her, crushing her into the mattress, but he didn't feel heavy. He felt welcome, and she relished their connection and the opportunity to share such an intimate, private moment with him.

He'd held nothing back, had bared his soul, had shown her the most secret territory in his heart. The encounter had been stunning, remarkable, beyond her wildest dreams—and they had been quite tempestuous. He'd given her all that she'd pined for and more, and she was thrilled by how the assignation had progressed.

Alice had insisted that the marital act improved with repetition, that their sexual engagements would increase in satisfaction and enjoyment. If it could be this exciting, this unrestrained and exhilarating after their initial attempt, what lay in their future?

She saw years—nay, decades!—of stormy, impetuous love play as their destiny.

He'd been brutally distressed by his carnal spree. His forehead was buried in the pillow beside her; his lungs grappled for air. His heart hammered, bashing behind his ribs.

She massaged his shoulders and back and arms, easing him, helping him to regain his equilibrium. Ultimately, he heaved out a labored sigh, and his physical perturbation waned. He remained where he was, sprawled on top of her, his cherished masculine form pinning her down. The size of the unduly-large member had dwindled a bit, but, as though he was already contemplating another go-round, the stiffness hadn't totally abated.

Shutting her eyes, she let her senses soak it in, wanting to remember every detail, so that she'd always vividly recall every aspect of the fabulous event.

But as she dawdled, a disturbing notion occurred to her: What if he hadn't perceived their copulation to be extraordinary? What if it had been typical of his dalliances with his numerous other paramours?

How could she learn his answer? It wasn't as if she could simply blurt out her query!

If he characterized it as exceedingly normal, she would expire from humiliation!

He stirred and kissed her cheek. She could feel him smiling, and the insight brought a smile to her own lips. He rolled onto his side, turning her with him, so that they were facing one another. His cock was still firmly entrenched, scarcely softened, and his hand lay on her hip, making lazy circles up and down her flank.

For a long while, they stared, and Ellen was too flustered to speak. What was a woman to say after such a miraculous meeting of body and spirit? She studied him, trying to glean a clue to his mental state, but though she'd been thoroughly apprised about him on paper from the research her father's men had done before the wedding, she didn't know much about him personally, and she couldn't decipher his thoughts.

He seemed happy. Content. And intensely appeased. Yet, how could she be sure?

"When you're overwhelmed by passion, you call me Stephen." He traced a finger across her lips. "I like that."

She chuckled. As she'd been absurdly yearning for declarations of fondness and affection, his comment was notably diverse from what she'd been hoping to hear, but she shouldn't have been surprised. He was conceited, pompous, haughty, impossible. And he was hers.

She was so glad!

"You're proud that you can so easily goad me beyond my limits?"

"Absolutely."

"Vain beast."

He laughed again, and it was a joyous sound that made her stomach ripple with butterflies.

"You're going to be very good for my ego, *Lady* Banbury."

During the arduous day, she hadn't spent much time considering her title, and he was inordinately insolent as he tossed it at her.

"Bounder," she scolded. "I'm aware of your imperious tendencies, milord husband, and I don't think it will hurt for you to be put in your place every so often."

"No, I don't think it will."

The banter trailed off, and he persisted with assessing her, which had her acutely unnerved. She couldn't fathom why he would. Did he wish to confide in her? To unburden himself? On what topic?

Instead, he closed the distance between them, and kissed her, a sweet, chaste brush of his lips to hers. The precious gesture was so dear that tears welled to her eyes, and she hated that she would be inundated by emotion. Alice had counseled that she would be affected in ways she'd never imagined, but just as he was a proud man, so was she a proud woman. She didn't want him to see how moved she'd been by what they'd accomplished.

As he drew away, he gently probed, "Are you all right?"

"Definitely," she contended, but more tears threatened. She valiantly fought to keep them from toppling over, but one or two slipped onto her cheeks.

He rubbed them away with his thumb and kissed where they'd been. "Was I too rough?"

"No."

He blushed, appearing as ingenuous and unsophisticated as a young lad. "Are you positive? I am so enamored of you that I was carried away. I should have been more disciplined . . . I should have reined myself in . . . I should have . . ."

She cut off his litany of remonstrance. "It was marvelous, but a trifle disconcerting."

"It can be. Especially in the beginning."

She mustered her courage, then ventured, "Is it always like this?"

"No, my darling, Ellen. It never is."

"Then why . . . ?"

She couldn't verbalize what had transpired between them. She had no terms in her vocabulary that fit, and he came to her rescue, finishing the interrogatory for her.

"Then why was it so powerful?"

"Yes."

"We have an unusual affinity, you and I."

"Why?" she repeated.

"I don't know. It just happens. It's one of life's great mysteries."

Alice had asserted that people could fall in love in an instant, but Ellen hadn't believed her. Now, it seemed as if he was claiming the same, that they were made for each other, that they belonged together.

He was amazed and bewildered and was inspecting her strangely, as if he hadn't come to grips with their dramatic attraction himself.

Dare she assume that their assignation had been as profound for him as it had been for her?

Suddenly shy, which was silly in view of their nakedness and what they'd just done, she inquired, "Do you suppose we could do it again?"

"As soon as I catch my breath, you bawdy wench." Playfully, he swatted her on the rear. "We'll do it all night, if I can keep up with you."

"We've only been acquainted for a few hours, and you've transformed me into a wanton."

"Lucky me." He delivered another swat. Then, their mirth died down, and he sobered. "May I ask you a question?"

"Certainly."

"Well, you've been in London for months, searching for a husband, and you've been introduced to so many people. I wasn't even in the market for a wife, yet you set your sights on me, and now, here we are." He scowled, his vexation evident. "I was just wondering: When you could have had anyone, why did you pick me?"

"I had many reasons."

"What was the deciding factor?"

"You truly want to know?"

"Aye."

There'd been nothing random about her choice. She was tempted to acknowledge how frequently he'd been followed, how extensively they'd examined his background and finances, how deliberately she and her father had debated the pros and cons, how long and often she and Alice had dissected his likely sexual and other manly habits, but she'd save the entire story for another day.

He was abundantly narcissistic. No sense in letting him deduce how enchanted she'd been, or how desperately she'd wanted him, or how the others had paled in comparison.

She gave him a piece of the truth. "Because you have such a cute behind."

Incredulous, he glared at her, then he roared with laughter, shaking with merriment. He spun away from her, their bodies detaching as he flung himself onto his back to chortle uncontrollably.

When he could complete a sentence, he whirled toward her, once again. "And a . . . a . . . shapely derriere was important to you?"

"Extremely."

"And what other lofty attributes swayed you in my favor?"

"Well, you're a randy fellow. Very lusty, too."

"Randy *and* lusty?"

She wiggled her brows in naughty invitation. "My sister persuaded me that your licentious constitution pushed you to the top of the list."

Flabbergasted, he gulped in dismay. "You discussed my . . . my . . . lascivious propensities with your sister?"

"Incessantly."

Groaning, he flushed to the roots of his hair and flopped onto his back once more, slinging his arm over his eyes. "I'll never be able to face anyone in your family again." After a brief reflection, he peeked out at her. "Wait a minute. How do you know so much about my behavior?"

"You don't think I went into this blindly, do you?"

He rose up on his elbow. "Whatever do you mean?"

She winked at him, trying to look enigmatic, and he fastidiously perused her, his mind whipping through the possibilities.

"You saucebox! You had me investigated!"

"Maybe a little," she allowed. Hilariously, he was panicked and horrified, and she leaned forward and snuggled herself to him. "I wanted some excitement in my marriage. You wouldn't have had me wed some old goat, would you?"

"You devious scamp!"

Seductively, she rubbed herself against him, much like a contented cat, reveling in how they melded, how his bodily hair tickled and stroked her. He liked it, too. Down below, his cock began to harden.

"If you're really, really nice to me, I'll show you the files."

"The files!"

"Pages and pages. All about you and your antics."

"Oh, my Lord." Astonished and appalled, he twirled away again.

He had good reason to be aghast. The accumulated information painted a picture that was either grim or enticing— depending on one's point of view.

Fortunately for her, she'd wanted a spouse who was untamed, unencumbered by convention, and just a tad indecent. He'd fit the bill perfectly.

"I selected you because of the reports," she said, and she brazenly climbed onto his lap, his erect phallus a wedge between her legs. "From the details I'd gleaned, I knew you were the ideal man for me."

"You're joking."

She smiled down at him. How handsome he was. How appealing. How irresistible. "You'll make me a fine husband, Stephen St. John."

After a significant hesitation, he smiled in return. "I just might at that."

He tipped her so that she fell onto his chest, and he kissed her soundly, making her rejoice with happiness. Their embrace went on forever, and, when their lips parted, she was aroused anew, her heart pounding, her skin tingling, her nipples contracted and aching.

Though she was sore, she pulsated with need. She couldn't bear their separation, and she longed to have him join with her a second time.

"I do have one teeny confession to make."

"What's that?"

"When I told you I didn't want any children, I was lying." She sat on her haunches, lowering her privates, so that she could flex across his enlarged phallus. "I actually hope we have a dozen."

Intrigued, he perked up. "A dozen?"

"Yes."

"Well then, milady, we'd better get started."

He flipped her onto her back and applied himself to the task.

BURN, INC.

by

KIMBERLY RAYE

For Curt,
For helping me experience the magic of love at first sight,
And showing me firsthand that it really does happen.
I love you!

CHAPTER ONE

"*Should I* kiss him before or after he takes off his pants?"

"Before," a voice called out from the left side of the studio set, its source a petite brunette who carried a cardboard tray and dispensed Starbucks cappuccinos to the other women on the crew.

"After." The suggestion came from the opposite side of the set and a forty-something redhead who held several makeup brushes and a spritzer bottle, aka the instant sweat kit.

"Both," Geraldine Baxter announced, after giving each answer brief consideration.

"During." The comment came from Marty, Gerry's production assistant. The woman clutched a clipboard with her right hand and fingered the small ivory figurine that hung from a chain around her neck. A figurine worn by nearly every woman on the set.

The small statue, known among the crew as Trigger, looked like a miniature of Michelangelo's David—smooth and naked and perfect—and was held as the icon of all Women On Top—an organization promoting the erotic freedom of women everywhere.

"Roxeanne always has them kiss during the entire scenario," Marty went on. "With clothes. Without clothes. Peeling off clothes."

Gerry nodded, frantically crossing out her earlier suggestion and jotting down the new scene direction. She half-wished she had her own Trigger. But, despite her profession, she wasn't the type to caress a naked man in front of an entire set of people. Even if he wasn't the real thing.

She motioned for the lead actress to step toward the handsome man—the only man allowed on the set—who stood wearing nothing but a pair of raggedy jeans and dusty cowboy boots.

The Outlaw and the School Teacher would be the final production in Burn, Inc.'s ten-video fantasy series. The project consisted of breathing life into ten of the most popular female fantasies.

Over the past seventeen and a half months, Gerry had produced modern day versions of everything from the classic voyeur fantasy to a very tasteful bondage story to the ever-popular sex with a stranger, aka *The Outlaw and the School Teacher*, which they were currently filming.

Sort of.

They'd been on the set for four days, and so far they'd obtained only ten minutes of decent footage. The rest of the time had been spent debating the nuts and bolts of the actual scene. Who touches who first. Who kisses who when. Who says what and why.

"During's a very good idea." Not Gerry's idea, but then, the actual story never was. She handled the production side, while her business partner and best friend, Roxeanne Sinclair, took care of the creative aspect.

They were the dynamic duo. The driving force behind Burn, Inc., once a low-budget film company but now the leading producer of women's erotic videos. Together, they created tantalizing fiction made by women for women. With the exception of the actors, every person on the set was always female, from the key grip to the production assistants to the camera people. After all, who better to judge the success of a video aimed at women but women themselves?

Burn, Inc. had been a brilliant concept, one cooked up during late night pizza sessions back in college at UCLA-Berkley, where Gerry and Roxeanne had been roommates. Unfortunately, success had been slow in coming. With the majority of the industry aimed at men, Burn had had its work cut out for it convincing distributors that women had every right to be as erotically stimulated as men.

Despite the industry's resistance, however, Gerry and Roxeanne had pushed Burn into the market and created their own niche by providing tasteful erotica. They'd made a permanent place for themselves in both video stores and private catalogs, but it was time for something bigger.

After five years of struggling for every penny of profit, Gerry wanted to make some real money, to prove to her father that she was every bit as skilled in business as her two older brothers and every bit as worthy of his respect.

The owner of a very profitable investment firm, Morgan Baxter measured everyone's true worth, including that of his three children, according to dollars and cents.

After losing his wife to diabetes only months after Gerry's birth, he'd become a workaholic who'd pushed his children the way he did his employees. Grant, the oldest, was the owner of a nationwide computer manufacturing company. Gordon, the middle child, had made his money with his Fortune 500 financial consulting group.

And Gerry? She was the youngest and the only one who had a mortgage and a pile of debts and, therefore, zip in the respect department.

The fantasy series promised to change all of that. The series had been purchased by a major cable network who planned to debut the first video next month as part of their late-night programming, provided Burn could deliver the entire series by the scheduled deadline next week.

All or nothing.

Roxeanne had come up with the series idea and had written each of the scripts. Except for one.

This last one.

Gerry fought back a wave of anxiety and cued the music. "Ready and . . . action!"

Mimi Donovan, one of their best actresses, who was using her money from Burn to pay her way through law school, stepped forward and pressed her lips to those of the man in cowboy boots, an actor called Jeff. At the same time, she reached for the button on his pants.

The button slid free and the kiss deepened. The music played and Gerry yawned. She had spent another sleepless night tossing and turning and worrying over her present predicament. Roxeanne had left her hanging with her savings account depleted and her house mortgaged to the hilt in her efforts to help Burn, Inc., really take off.

They were in launch mode right now, on the verge of international cable success. *This* close to seeing a real profit, thanks to HBO, who'd purchased the series.

The entire series.

Ten videos and not one less.

Countdown . . . 5 . . . 4 . . . 3 . . .

"I'm just not feeling it," Mimi announced after a full five seconds into the kiss, her hand poised at Cowboy's zipper.

Houston, we have a problem.

"No offense to Jeff," Mimi went on as she let her hand fall away, "but this just isn't getting my juices flowing."

"Mine, either," the cappuccino girl announced. She twirled the Trigger hanging around her own neck. "Usually I'm craving a double-glazed donut with fudge filling from the pastry cart right about now, but truthfully, I would be happy with a plain glazed. No filling."

"Ditto, here," the makeup lady announced. Her own Trigger nestled comfortably in her deep cleavage and bobbed with every breath. "I always keep an extra bottle of water around during the love scene, for drinking rather than spritzing purposes, and, I have to admit, I'm not even thirsty."

"It just doesn't feel right," Mimi said as, she shoved her arms into her robe. "Something's missing."

Roxeanne.

She'd been missing in action for the past week, since attending a conference in Las Vegas, where she'd been scheduled to give a lecture about the erotic benefits of being a single woman to the West Coast chapter of Women On Top.

Yeah, right.

Miss I-Would-Never-Dream-of-Settling-for-Orgasms-with-One-Man had marched down the aisle at the Heartbreak Hotel Wedding Chapel with—surprise, surprise—*one* man. A man she'd just met in the hotel casino the night before.

Gerry still couldn't believe it.

Roxeanne. Married.

It didn't make any more sense now than it had when she'd gotten the phone call Monday morning.

She'd been pacing the set, wondering which Victoria's Secret catalog had snatched Roxeanne's attention that morning when her cell phone had rung.

"I did it!" Roxeanne's excited voice floated over the line. "Can you believe it?"

"What—"

"I met Stan," Roxeanne rushed on, "and it was love at first sight. I looked across the blackjack table and there he was. He laid down a straight flush, our eyes met, and bam!"

"Slow down." Questions whirled through Gerry's head as she sank into a nearby director's chair and tried to process the information. "You did what?"

"Stan won this gigantic hand, and we took the money and bought a monster of a ring, and then we just did it."

"Stan who?"

"Even my Trigger didn't ward him off. I took one look and it was like Trigger didn't even exist. I fell for Stan anyway!"

"Stan who?" Gerry asked again. "Who is he, and where does he come from, and what does he do, and what exactly did you do—"

"We're about to leave on our honeymoon. I know it's spur of the moment," Roxeanne hurried on, "but sometimes you just have to go with the flow."

"You're supposed to flow back here, remember? We're right in the middle of production."

"I can't spend my honeymoon working. What . . ." Her

voice faded, and Gerry heard a deep voice in the background. "Oh, don't worry. I wouldn't spend our special time fiddling around on an old video set."

"Hello? Video number ten? The last one in our contract? Our six-figure contract? The one that's going to let me get my house out of hock? The one my mother decorated herself before she passed on ?"

"Oh, no. I didn't get a chance to call my mother. Could you do it for me? She's lecturing at Oxford, but her secretary will be taking calls. Just leave a message and tell her—"

"I can't tell her anything," Gerry cut in, "because I don't even have this whole thing straight."

"It's great, isn't it? It's a wild and crazy ride and I've been missing out for so long, I just didn't realize it, but now—"

"Slow down," Gerry begged. "Please."

"Sorry. It's just that I've never felt this way before. My heart is pounding, and my nerves are jumping, and I can hardly stand up."

"It's called anxiety," Gerry told her. "I know because I'm having an attack of it right now. We're this close to the end of the series."

"Just film something, anything, and I'll see you soon."

"Soon? As in one day or one week or—" A loud click punctuated the sentence, and Roxeanne was gone for who knew how long.

The truth echoed through Gerry's head as the dial tone blared in her ear. She did the only thing a woman with her business and her home mortgaged to the hilt could do; she headed straight for her bottom desk drawer and her box of chocolate cupcakes.

Gerry drew in a deep breath and slid her hand into her pocket. The sound of plastic crinkling and crunching echoed around her as she pulled two empty wrappers free.

Two, when she'd vowed to limit herself to one a day, and only during extremely stressful situations. The chocolate was like the stress ball that sat on the corner of her father's desk. With every squeeze, the lines around his mouth would ease. Likewise, with every bite, Gerry felt her body relax.

Usually.

White cream smeared the clear plastic. She lifted it to her nose and took a long whiff. A sugary sweetness filled her nostrils and eased the throbbing in her temples for a full moment.

Until she opened her eyes to see Mimi preparing to walk off the set.

"Wait. Let's try something else." Gerry's mind rifled back through the past nine videos and all of the stimulating techniques she'd seen Roxeanne use. "Grab some of those tiny yellow flowers," she told Jeff, pointing to an old milk jug holding an array of wildflowers. "And trail them over her skin. We'll zoom in on that and maybe it will get everybody going."

Mimi looked skeptical, but she finally nodded. She slid off her robe, revealing an old-fashioned looking corset and bloomers. Gerry called for action, and the scene started. The camera panned in as Jeff caressed Mimi's cheek with a handfull of tiny flowers.

This is going to work.

She'd seen Roxeanne do the same thing with a red rose in

video number two, and, while she wasn't much for repetition, beggars couldn't be choosers.

"There, that's good. Mimi, are you feeling it?"

"I," the woman started. "I think I—achewwww!" The comment ended in a loud sneeze, followed by another and another. "Ohmigod," she blurted in between two more sneezes. "That's . . . that's ragweed." She sneezed again. "What is ragweed doing here in LA?"

"I told the florist I needed Texas wildflowers because the story takes place in Texas."

"I—I've got to get out of here." Mimi sneezed again and grabbed her robe. "Ragweed," she said again, the word punctuated with another sneeze as she rushed off the set, followed by Jeff.

"I guess we're calling it a day," Marty said as she came up to Gerry and pulled off her headset. "No leading couple, no love scene. That says day to me."

"How many minutes of film did we get?"

"About five, if you want to include that mediocre kiss and the sneezing."

"Cut the sneezing but leave the kiss. We'll try it again tomorrow."

Tomorrow.

Another chance.

Yeah, right. Try another dollar.

"Quitting time," she blurted. "I'll see everyone back bright and early in the morning." She rubbed her hands together. "And we'll put this love scene to bed, so to speak."

"Witty." Marty flipped off her camera and hooked her headset over the arm piece.

"I'd rather be creative, then I might be able to figure out what's wrong with this scene. It's got all the basics. Great characters. A good setting. But zip emotion."

"Don't forget the ragweed."

"How was I to know those harmless flowers were ragweed? I'm not a florist." She shook her head. "And I'm no Roxeanne. Where's a sexpert when you need one?"

"Take it easy. You'll figure it out, although it might be easier if you had Trigger."

"That's Roxeanne's department."

Marty smiled. "Not this time."

"You're not making me feel any better."

"Sorry. Look, so what? How hard can it be to pinpoint what women like even if you're not a Trigger-carrying Woman On Top like the rest of us?" She smiled and patted Gerry's shoulder. "You're *still* a woman."

"I *am* a woman," Gerry told herself later that day as she sat in the film room and watched and rewatched the five minutes of tape, including the lukewarm kiss and the ragweed incident. "I can do this."

I'm just not feeling it, Mimi had said.

Neither did Gerry, but she never felt it.

When she watched a piece of film, her attention was fixed on the setting and the camera angle. She didn't really pay attention to the action.

Or, in this case, lack of.

Okay, so there was zip emotion. That meant putting emotion into the scene and making viewers feel it.

Viewers, as in women.

As in Gerry.

She was a woman, albeit a stressed-out workaholic version of the female sex whose social life consisted of late nights spent unwinding with a pint of Ben & Jerry's and her favorite video, *Pretty Woman*. Heavens, she hadn't had a date in the five years since she'd invested every available penny into Burn, Inc.

Except for the Erotic Video Awards ceremony last year— her first and last social event since college. She'd gone with Marty, but that didn't qualify as a date since they were the same sex and both card-carrying heterosexuals.

She hadn't been turned on in who knew how long. It was no wonder she couldn't manage to light anyone else's fire. She had no matches. Heck, she couldn't even find her own pilot light.

But she could learn. She could get in touch with her inner vixen. Or so sayeth Dr. Love.

Dr. Love. LA's most renowned relationship therapist, author of the critically acclaimed *Seducing Your Senses*, and a running buddy of Roxeanne's. Gary had nerver actually met Dr. Love—they'd been earning different types of degrees— but he and Roxeanne had shared a lot of the same classes. They had graduated together from UCLA-Berkeley with so- ciology degrees and had both been made honorary lifetime members of Women On Top, complete with their very own Trigger figurines.

Gerry stared at the picture on Roxeanne's desk and the small, white, nude figurine hanging from a thin chain around her friend's neck. Trigger was the poster boy for Women On Top and Roxeanne never took him off.

While Dr. Love wasn't a woman, he'd made such a contribution to the movement that the Women On Top embraced him as one of their own. He had his very own Trigger, as well. Not to mention an arsenal of knowledge.

The moment the thought crossed her mind, an idea struck. If she needed her taxes done, she would call in an accountant. If she needed her brakes fixed, she would find herself a mechanic. Why not?

Gerry riffled through Roxeanne's Rolodex for several minutes before she finally found his number.

She dialed, but only managed to get his answering machine.

"This is Marc Love," said a deep, husky voice. "You know what to do at the beep."

"This is Geraldine Baxter. I'm Roxeanne's business partner. She's . . . ill right now and unable to be on the set. Since she's our relationship expert, we're sort of having a little trouble with one of our productions. I would love for you to come down and serve as a consultant until Roxeanne comes to her senses—that is, until she gets back on her feet. Please call me as soon as you get this message. Better yet, just come on down. I need all the help I can get."

She gave the phone number and address, sent up a silent prayer, and slid the receiver back into place.

She'd called in the cavalry and there wasn't much else to do but wait.

In the meantime . . .

She walked around Roxeanne's office, hoping to stimulate her own inner vixen.

The office was an extension of the diva of vixens—Roxeanne. The walls were painted a bright red. Everything from *Tantric Sex* to the *Kama Sutra* sat on the large ornate bookshelf against the far wall. A sofa, the fabric a rich red velvet, was placed in the middle of the room. The desk was a mammoth creation that took up half the room. The legs were carved versions of Eros.

The entire room oozed sensuality. It was no wonder Roxeanne could come up with such tantalizing ideas.

Gerry sank down onto the sofa and tried to absorb her surroundings. She rubbed her hand across the velvet settee, but nothing happened. No miraculous ideas. No bursts of creativity. No pangs of intense desire.

She paced around the room and touched the satin robe hanging from a hook in the far corner. Roxeanne was notorious for lounging around in nothing but the satin wrap and a smile. She said the feeling of near nakedness kept her in touch with her senses.

Gerry eyed the robe. Nah. She wasn't the lounging type, except when she pulled on her sweats, stuck Julia and Richard into the VCR, and opened some Ben & Jerry's.

Then again, that was the problem.

Five minutes later, she pulled on the robe. Satin slid against her bare flesh, but the sensation did little but make her feel uncomfortable and *naked*.

Almost.

She'd tried to morph into Roxeanne, but she hadn't been able to slide off her undies. Even with her panties in place, she still couldn't relax. There was too much of a breeze blowing on her bare thighs, reminding her that she was way out of her element.

She paced the room several more times, waiting for a spurt of creative thought, but nothing came.

Think outlaw, she told herself, but it was hard with so much red blinding her. While the room was intriguing, after a little while, it started to make her feel dizzy. As if she were stuck in a Valentine's Day nightmare and couldn't quite wake up.

It wasn't working.

Finally, she pulled Dr. Love's latest book from the bookshelf, grabbed her stash of cupcakes, and left the office behind in favor of the set.

She sank down onto the edge of the wrought-iron bed. Springs creaked, and the sound grated across her nerves. Flipping a button, she turned on the background, music, dimmed the lights, and propped herself up against the headboard. Maybe if she sat here and absorbed the feel of things, she might get a burst of ingenuity.

Five minutes and not a single burst.

Instead, she felt herself getting nervous, anxious, worried. Time was running out, and she did the only thing she could. She reached for the half-full box of cupcakes she'd set on the nightstand.

Desperate times called for desperate measures.

Logan Mackenzie expected almost anything as he walked onto the set of Burn, Inc. After discovering that his younger brother and lover of all things male, particularly his bachelorhood, had tied the knot with a woman he'd barely met, not much could surprise him.

Except a half-naked woman eating cupcakes.

Half-naked—he could understand. He was smack dab in the middle of the production set of a company that made erotic videos. That's what the security guard outside had told him when he'd asked about Roxeanne Sinclair.

Actually, the security guard had told him about the rules and regulations of a closed set, until he'd seen the naked man statue Logan had fished from his pocket while hunting for his driver's license. The man had smiled then, apologized for bothering Logan about ID, and told him to wear the idol like the rest of the crew in order to avoid any further hassles.

Logan had slipped it over his head and proceeded inside. Sure enough, the other guards had simply waved him along, and one had even engaged him in a friendly chat. That's when he'd gleaned that Roxeanne was one half of Burn, Inc., and this was, indeed, the place he was looking for, albeit mostly deserted.

Not that it mattered. Curiosity had driven him from a late night spent hunched over his desk, going over architectural plans, clear across town to a movie set. He hadn't been able to concentrate on work when all he could do was ask himself, *Why?*

No answer would be forthcoming until Stan came back. Until then, Logan could only wonder. Or he could come here and do a little investigative work that might help him understand why his brother had done such a ridiculous thing. What sort of a woman turned a man's head that fast?

A woman who made skin flicks for a living.

His attention shifted back to the brunette lounging on the bed. One of the actresses, he thought, judging by her lack of clothing.

She had shoulder-length brown hair that framed a heart-shaped face. She was pretty, but nothing spectacular.

No, the spectacular part was the rest of her.

She wore a short red satin robe and nothing else. His gaze

traveled from her toes, up over shapely calves and knees, to where the robe fell just past her rounded hips and brushed the tops of her thighs. The satin crisscrossed at the waist and tied.

She moved her arm to reach for the box on the table beside her, and the material shifted. The deep vee at her neckline parted, giving him a tantalizing view of the inside of one luscious breast tipped with a rose-colored nipple.

The air lodged in his chest for a long moment as he watched her breast tremble, the nipple quivering as she leaned and grasped . . .

The air eased from his lungs as she settled back down on the bed, the goodies on her lap and the robe back in place.

Half-naked made sense considering the nature of the business. But cupcakes?

As part owner and head crew boss for Mackenzie & Mackenzie Construction, he'd watched his guys scarf up every type of snack cake in existence, from Ding Dongs to Twinkies, HoHo's to Zingers, and not once had he considered the sight even remotely sexy.

In fact, with Bruce—his assistant crew chief and the best damned concrete layer ever to pour a slab—lunch itself could be downright scary.

She was far from the two hundred and fifty plus roughneck who toted two lunch kits to work everyday and belched *The Yellow Rose of Texas* after a foot-long chili dog.

Long, willowy fingers reached down and unwrapped a cake. She licked her lips and closed her eyes as she lifted the sweet. Straight white teeth sank into the chocolate. Her mouth closed around the bite and she chewed for several long moments that made his own mouth water for a taste.

Of her.

A soft sigh slid past her lips after she swallowed. She raised her hand and licked a spot of cream from one fingertip. Her moist pink tongue lapped at the filling, and his groin tightened.

Okay, he was beginning to see the erotic value of a cupcake.

His gaze stayed rooted on a small spot of cream at the corner of her mouth, and he had the insane urge to step forward and take a nice, slow lick—

"Thank God you're here." Her soft voice scattered his thoughts and jerked him back to the present.

To the fact that he'd driven through LA traffic to try to make some sense out of the terrible mistake his younger brother had just made.

Logan knew firsthand just how terrible a mistake it was. He'd made the same mistake himself, albeit he'd known the woman he'd taken the plunge with for several months before they'd walked down the aisle.

Time mattered little, he'd come to realize. A man could know a woman for years, and it wouldn't make any difference when it came to a wealthy neighbor who wore Speedos and drank margaritas at noon while everybody else was busting their ass for a living.

A working man just couldn't compete. Particularly this working man, who'd seen his bank account chopped in half when his significant other had hauled him through a brutal divorce.

That had been five years ago. The five longest, hardest

years of his life. He'd spent the time rebuilding his construction business with his little brother as his partner. Brothers didn't file for divorce. They were family. Reliable.

Unless they did something as stupid as waltzing down the aisle in Vegas without so much as a serious thought to the morning after.

Sex.

That's all Stan could have been thinking about. He'd been suckered in by some really hot mattress dancing and had traded his future for more. In the process, he'd compromised the both of them.

Logan wasn't about to see his hard work slaughtered by a bunch of divorce lawyers.

No way.

As soon as Stan got back, Logan was bringing his little bro to his senses before things got even more involved.

"I was trying to get into the mood," she said, motioning to her outfit. "I thought if I walked the walk and talked the talk, that maybe I could think of something on my own." She licked her bottom lip and he found himself mesmerized.

She had really great lips. Slightly puffy and pouty. The kind that begged for a nice, slow, deep kiss.

He shook the thought away. He wasn't here for kissing. He was here to look around.

"I don't mean to impose. I'm here for—"

"Gerry." She stood up, her hands clutching the edge of the robe together. "That's me, and I have to tell you, you've got your work cut out for you. Two hours of trying to get in touch with my inner sensuality, and the only thing I've realized is that I can eat a hell of a lot of cupcakes."

"I, um, saw that."

"Then you know how hopeless I am. I really need you."

"Need me?"

"For sex," she blurted. "Hot, stimulating, *moving* sex."

He tried to form a reply, but the line of communication from his brain to his mouth had suddenly shifted into shutdown. He was too busy listening and thinking and wondering if he'd actually heard her right.

But then she opened her mouth and left no mistake as to his hearing ability.

"Go ahead," she told him, folding her arms and eyeing him. "Turn me on."

And Logan Mackenzie knew beyond a doubt that he'd just been propositioned.

CHAPTER TWO

Relax.

The word whispered through Gerry's head as she stood face-to-face with Dr. Love, but she couldn't quite keep her knees from trembling.

You're in good hands. His reputation precedes him. The Eros hanging around his neck is proof of that. Not to mention he looks like a man who knows every nuance of a woman, with his deep, penetrating eyes and his rumbling voice and his hands, so strong and sure and stimulating.

She'd heard many things about him from Roxeanne, but she'd never actually seen him before.

He looked every bit the way she would have pictured a man with the name *Love*.

As if he'd been made for just that . . . making love.

He looked more physical than she would have imagined most men in his profession looked. He was tall and tanned, his arms muscular, stretching the sleeves of his white cotton T-shirt. Faded denim cupped his crotch and molded to strong, sinewy thighs. He had sun-kissed blond hair that barely brushed his collar and the bluest eyes she'd ever had the pleasure of gazing into.

He appeared more like a man who spent his days outdoors than one who was cooped up in a radio station or out in a three-piece suit, keeping the lecture circuits hot.

She tried to picture him in a tie, but the image wouldn't

quite come. Instead, she saw a vision of him bare chested and sweaty, the sun blazing down as he guzzled something ice cold to drink.

The picture stuck in her head, and the adrenalin pumped through her body at an alarming rate. Contrary to what a lot of men thought, women *were* visual. Burn's success proved as much. But while they liked visuals, they had to have emotional stimulation, as well.

That's where Roxeanne had come into the equation. She'd been keyed into the emotional sensuality of women everywhere because she'd been completely in touch with her own. Her entire life had centered around her own five senses, and so it had been easy for her to unlock the wants and desires of other women. She'd known just when to have the lead couple kiss, just how they should touch. She'd been a genius at making something as simple as a rose petal stroking bare flesh seem breathtaking and erotic.

Unlike Gerry's suggestion today with the ragweed.

Who knew something that pretty could be so devastating? She wasn't a florist, after all. Nor was she a card-carrying eroticist like her business partner.

Yet.

The urge to reach for another cupcake hit her, but she fought it back down and concentrated on the edges of the robe, which had become extremely hard to grasp when her palms were so sweaty.

Sweaty palms?

Why, she hadn't had sweaty palms since . . . She'd *never* had sweaty palms, not even with Roger.

Roger had been her first serious boyfriend, and her last.

The relationship had started on Halloween night at a fraternity party. She'd gotten a little tipsy, he'd gotten extremely drunk, and they'd ended up in bed together.

In hindsight, she could see that the sex hadn't been that great. But at the time, she'd imagined Roger to have hung the moon. She'd experienced her first orgasm, and, to a girl with a limited amount of experience, thanks to an overprotective father and two brothers, that Big O had made her fall head over heels for Roger. That and the fact that he'd paid so much attention to her and made her feel sexy and beautiful and all the other things every woman yearned for.

They'd dated for the entire four years of college and during that time he'd shown her firsthand that true love, the I'll-love-you-through-sickness-and-health kind, simply did not exist.

She'd felt the emotion for Roger. She'd nursed him through three cases of the flu, numerous colds, and even a very nasty episode of strep throat during finals. She'd made chicken soup and read lecture notes to him and simply been there, but he'd never once cared for her in return.

Luckily, she'd been fairly healthy and had only taken ill once with a terrible stomach virus. Had she seen even one spoonful of chicken noodle soup? A measly bowl of Jell-O?

Nada.

Zip.

Instead, he'd been out with another woman while she'd been home with dry heaves and sore ribs.

So much for the sickness part.

Lust was much better.

When one had time for lust, that is. Gun-shy and determined to live up to her father's expectations that his three children be successful in the business world, she'd invested all of her time and energy in Burn.

Now it had to pay off.

She wiped her palms on her robe and sent up a silent thank-you for bringing Dr. Love to her on such short notice. He'd done little more than look at her, and already he had her nerves jumping and her body reacting like a hormone-driven teenager.

"This is really good. You're going to have to break all of this down for me and get very specific on exactly what is causing the reaction. I mean, is it the hands, because you have really great hands. Or maybe your eyes. I've never had any-one look at me with such intensity. Or maybe it's your tone of voice. It's so deep and resonating. I can feel it all the way to my toes. Or maybe it's a combination of all three. Yes, it's probably all three doing it to me."

"I beg your pardon?"

"Making my heart pound."

"Your heart is pounding?"

"Of course." She came up to him and reached for his hand. She placed his palm against the furious flutter in her chest.

The robe separated skin from skin, but it didn't serve as a barrier against the heat of his touch. Warmth seeped into her, and the air actually lodged in her chest.

He looked surprised, his gaze drilling into her, as if he couldn't quite believe what he was feeling.

She felt a moment's hesitation. Something wasn't right.

But then the pad of his thumb found its way past the edge of her robe and stroked her bare skin, and every thought flew south for the winter. Electricity zipped through her and traveled to all her major erogenous zones. Her nipples pebbled, and moisture flooded between her legs.

As if he read the reaction, his gaze darkened. Forget darkened. They smoldered.

She laughed. "This is so incredible. Can you believe I'm actually nervous with anticipation?"

"Anticipation?"

"Sexual anticipation. You're really turning me on."

He shook his head as if, once again, he couldn't quite believe his ears. "I'm turning you on?"

"In a major way." Excitement rushed through her. He was so close and she was so aware and life was finally smiling down at her. "This is going to be so good for me. You're definitely the answer to every prayer."

"Maybe I'm a little slow, but I've been working all day, and I'm a little tired. So let's back up a second. I'm turning you on? That's what you're saying. That you're turned on, and I'm the one doing it?"

"Of course. You're turning me on in a major way, and I'm sure this isn't even your serious ammunition. You've probably got moves I could only dream of."

He regarded her with wary eyes. "You don't get out much, do you?"

"Is it that obvious?" She shook her head. "How can I when I work nearly twenty-four/seven? I do find some down time once in a while. I mean, I eat ice cream and watch *Pretty Woman*—my favorite video—but that's not the same thing as actually getting out. So, yes, I'm definitely starved for some sensual contact." She smiled. "But you're going to fix all of that."

"I am?"

"You're going to fill my empty well so that I ooze sensuality."

"Fill your empty well?"

He looked so surprised and skeptical that she had the fleeting thought that maybe he didn't intend to help her. Anxiety rushed through her. "You have to," she blurted. "I need you. By the time tonight's over, it's imperative that I be completely in touch with my sensuality. My time is running out. I've got a video to make. I have to turn women on everywhere in a major way. How am I supposed to do that if I don't even know what turns me on? But you do." She smiled. "You just looked at me, and bam, you turned me on."

"So you do make videos?"

Okay, so he knew his stuff when it came to sensuality but he seemed a little off at keeping all the facts straight.

"That's why I want you to help me," she said as patiently as she could manage, considering her pounding heart. "You're a sexpert." At his questioning gaze, she added, "You know everything about sex."

"I wouldn't say that."

"I would. You've been here all of five minutes and I'm practically buzzing."

He let his touch fall away and passed a hand over his face. "This is unbelievable."

"My thoughts exactly. I'm buzzing right now, and I can't quite believe it. I mean, no one's done this to me before. You're a genius. That's why I know tonight is going to help me so much. You'll be able to unlock a side of me I've never known. You can release my inner sensuality."

"You want me to give you *sex*?"

"Hot, *moving* sex. Not the boring kind. And you're just the man to do it to me. You're so stimulating."

Since that first hot night with Mary Ann Reynolds in the backseat of her daddy's Lincoln when Logan had been fifteen, he'd been called many things by many women. All of them flattering.

He'd had Mary Ann screaming out his name up at Blue Moon Creek, and the entire episode had set the stage for the next twenty-something years of his sex life. He'd developed a reputation for being good in bed. One he lived up to every time he bedded a woman.

But this woman wasn't anywhere near Blue Moon, Texas. She didn't know him or his reputation, yet she was still calling him a sexpert.

He made her heart pound, she'd said.

Okay, so maybe she didn't need rumor. He did have an effect on women. He shouldn't be surprised that she was instantly attracted to him. He'd been instantly attracted to her. They had chemistry. He'd felt it the moment he'd set eyes on her and watched her with the cupcakes. She'd made him hungry, and for a hell of a lot more than just a bite of her dessert.

He'd wanted a bite of her.

He still wanted one.

He wanted to taste her. To savor her. To see if she tasted as sweet as she smelled and felt as soft as she looked.

Hello? You're here to get a feel for the place, not feel up one of the actresses. You're a man on a mission. You've got priorities, and they don't include the eight-plus inches pulsing in your pants.

"I would really like to help you out, lady, but—"

"Gerry," she cut in. "My name is Gerry."

"I'd really like to help you out, Gerry, but I really don't have time for this." *Right. Time is all you have, buddy. Stan is nowhere to be found and you can't sleep for the questions driving you nuts.*

"It won't take much time. Just tonight. You show me as much as you can and that's it. Tomorrow, you go back to your life and I'll go back to mine."

She was determined. He had to give her that. And damned if he didn't want to give her exactly what she wanted. "One night? That's what you're suggesting?"

"I know it seems like a huge time commitment, but it would mean so much to me."

He'd had women flirt with him before. He'd seen everything from the seductive hair flip to the eyelash batting to the hotel key slipped into his pocket. He'd never, however, had any woman be quite so direct.

So open and honest. So eager.

He could see the desperation in her eyes, and he had the sudden need to give her any and everything she wanted.

Not to ease his own body, but to wipe the worry from her gaze.

Crazy. He hardly knew her. He shouldn't give a rat's ass if she needed help. He had his own agenda. He wanted information about Roxeanne.

But damned if all the questions seemed as important as they had the moment he'd walked onto the set. Not with the lights so dim and the soft music blaring through the speakers and the ripe woman standing so close to him.

Too close.

"I hate to be in such a hurry," she went on, "but we're really wasting time. Can we go ahead and get started?"

"Consider us officially started," he said as he stepped toward her and did the one thing he'd been wanting to do since he'd watched her eat the first cupcake.

He kissed her.

He was kissing her.

Shock rushed through Gerry at the first moment of contact. This wasn't supposed to be happening. She had an entire notebook ready for everything Dr. Love had to give her. She'd intended to take detailed notes.

To absorb as much of his expertise as possible.

But he seemed to have something a little more interactive in mind.

She started to pull away. This wasn't what she'd envisioned. Sure, it felt good, but they were too close. Too . . . *together*.

Then again, it *felt* good and that's what the entire point of tonight was about. For her to *feel*.

She was feeling, all right. In spades. He slid his hand down her back and his thumb rubbed the base of her spine and she all but melted into his embrace.

Interactive could be good. Besides, this was in the name of business and Gerry was always ready to give her all when it came to Burn, Inc.

For the next few moments, she drank in the taste and feel

of him, ran her hands up and down his solid arms, relished the ripple of muscle as he cupped her buttocks and pulled her closer.

He rocked her, his hardness pressing into her, and heat flowered low in her belly, spreading from one nerve ending to the next until every inch of her body burned like a wildfire in the dry California heat.

She moaned into his mouth, and, without breaking the kiss, he swung her into his arms and covered the distance to the bed.

A few seconds later, her feet touched down on the hard wood floor.

Through the thin fabric of her robe, he traced the slope of her breasts, changing course just shy of actually touching her nipples—throbbing, aching nipples that whimpered when his fingers caressed her sensitive breasts and cupped their fullness.

He was good, all right.

"Shouldn't we undress?"

"We will." But he didn't go for her robe or his own clothing. Instead, his dark, heated gaze slid from hers to roam down her body, pausing at key spots in between—her parted lips and heaving chest and quivering thighs barely concealed by the short covering—and back up again. And then, before she could take her next breath, he reached out, pulled the ties of her robe, and the edges parted.

She all but screamed at the first stroke of his callused thumb over her bare breast. He traced the slope, circled her areola without touching its center, cupped the fullness.

"They look as sweet as that cupcake," he said, his attention fixed on her nipples.

She waited breathlessly for his mouth, but he didn't seem of a mind to oblige her. Yet. Instead, the next several moments passed in a dizzying blur as he plucked and rolled the turgid tips until they were red and ripe and aching for more.

"Please."

"Close your eyes and just feel this, darlin'."

She obeyed, her eyelids fluttering closed as his hot fingertips traced the erect points. She forgot everything except the sensation assaulting her senses.

She relished the feeling, letting it flow over her, pick her up, and float her along for the next several frantic heartbeats.

"That's it." His deep voice filled her ears. "Go with it. Let it take you away." His hot mouth touched her neck, licking and nibbling as his fingers worked their magic.

Soon his hands slid down, skimming her rib cage and warming her stomach. He stopped just shy of her panties, a hot pink thong that Roxeanne had given her for Christmas last year. It was made of sheer, delicate lace and cut high on the thighs. It wasn't in keeping with the drawer full of conservative white undies she had at home, but then that's why she'd worn it today. For inspiration.

She sent up a silent thank you that she'd had such forethought. Otherwise, Dr. Love would know firsthand what a truly difficult case he'd taken on.

Then again, the magic his fingers were working, tracing slow, lazy, stimulating circles on her warm skin, showed that he was definitely up to the challenge.

A deep male growl vibrated from his throat when his hands

slid into her panties and found her wet and swollen and so ready for him. One fingertip parted her slick flesh and dipped inside.

Her eyes flew open, and she grabbed at his shoulders, clutching fabric as she fought to feel his bare skin against her own.

"Easy, honey. Calm down."

"Are you kidding? I can hardly breathe, much less be calm." She turned a pleading gaze on him. "I need to feel you."

He seemed surprised at the open request, as if he couldn't believe she would voice her feelings. But then he leaned back far enough and let her peel the material up and over his head. She tossed the T-shirt and went for his jeans, but he beat her to the punch. His tanned fingers worked at the zipper.

Metal grated, and the jeans sagged onto his hips. He stepped back far enough to push them down and kick them free until he stood before her wearing only a pair of briefs. He was rock hard beneath the soft white cotton. A heartbeat later, the full length of him sprang forward, huge and greedy, as he pushed his underwear down and kicked it to the side.

But it wasn't the sight of him naked and tanned and fully aroused that took her breath away; it was the heat burning in his gaze, making his eyes a bright, piercing blue.

Her hands went to her open robe, but he pushed her fingers aside to peel the fabric from her flushed skin and slide it down her shoulders.

His hand went to her panties, and he cupped her, his palm warm through the thin covering. He dipped one finger past the elastic, into the steamy heat between her thighs. He stroked and rubbed, and a sweet pressure tightened low in her belly.

Her teeth sank into her bottom lip as she struggled to keep her legs from melting. The effort was useless. She trembled and nearly went down. But he was there, surrounding her, holding her up and anchoring her when she would have dissolved at his feet.

He slid his finger into her slowly, tantalizingly, stirring every nerve to full, titillating awareness until he was as deep as he could go. He withdrew only to deliver the same delicious torture all over again. Advance, retreat. Back and forth. In and out. Until her heart pounded so hard and her breath came so fast, she thought she would hyperventilate. She could feel it coming. She was close. So very close . . .

"Not yet," he murmured, withdrawing his hand. In one motion, he swept her up into his arms.

She sank into the soft mattress as he let her down. He didn't join her on the bed. Instead, he stood over her and simply stared for a long moment, drinking in the sight of her and making her heart pound even faster.

No man had ever looked at her this way. As if he not only wanted her, but needed her.

Yeah, right. He's good at what he does and he undoubtedly gets a lot of practice, and this is just business.

She knew that. Yet, as she stared up at him, into him, it was easy to forget.

"The way you look at me," he murmured. "I can see you really want me."

"I do," she breathed. "More than anything."

He gave her another surprised look. Then, he leaned over

and touched his mouth to her navel, dipped his tongue inside. The small point of contact sent her skyrocketing, and she became centered on the soft, moist lips nibbling at her flesh, tasting. Savoring.

He moved his mouth lower. His tongue hooked under the waistband of her panties. He licked her bare flesh before drawing back to drag his mouth over her lace-covered mound. His lips feathered a kiss over her throbbing clitoris, and her legs jerked.

A warm laugh sent shivers down the insides of her thighs before he lifted his head and caught the waistband of her underwear with his teeth. He drew the material down, lips and teeth skimming her bare flesh in a delicious friction that made her burn all the hotter.

"Please," she gasped, needing him inside her more than she needed her next breath, but he wasn't ready to comply.

He shook his head. "Not yet, not until I do what I've been wanting to do since I first set eyes on you."

He reached onto the nightstand for a cupcake and bit into the treat. Morsels of cake drip-dropped onto her bare flesh. Leaning down, he lapped up crumbs, his tongue brushing the side of her rib cage, the underside of her breast, the tip of one throbbing nipple . . .

"You taste good so far, but let's see about the rest."

He slid down her body and parted her legs. Scooping a fingerful of cream from the inside of the cake, he rubbed it over the sensitive folds between her legs. Then he dipped his head.

His tongue flicked out and savored the treat. Gerry arched off the bed. Sensation rolled over her like a tidal wave, sucking the air from her lungs and stalling her heartbeat before she managed to come up for a breath.

He tasted and savored, licking her clean and pushing her so close to the edge that her entire body quivered.

"Not yet," he murmured when he finally finished.

He slid up her body and kissed her deeply. She tasted her own essence mingled with the cupcake, like ripe fruit dipped in sweet cream, and a spurt of hunger went through her.

"I want to take this a little slower," he said, his voice raw and husky and pained, when he finally dragged his mouth from hers, "but it's been a long time for me, as well. I'm afraid I don't have the patience to hold off any longer."

"That's okay. Patience is overrated anyway."

He grinned against her lips, and she returned his smile.

He wanted her. *Now.* The knowledge was more powerful than any touch and filled her with a wanton longing so fierce and potent that she wanted to weep. Instead, she drew in a deep, steadying breath as he leaned away from her.

He left the bed to retrieve his pants, and she took the opportunity to enjoy the view. With her eyes, she devoured every inch of him, from his well-developed biceps and six-pack abs to his narrow hips.

He was thick and long and pulsing, the bright purple head of his penis wet with a pearly drop of his essence. He stroked himself, once, twice, spreading the moisture before he rolled a condom over the turgid flesh. Then he stepped toward her. Her breath caught in her throat, and she restlessly licked her lips as she reached for him.

"Christ, you're wet," he said between clenched teeth as he sank, inch by throbbing inch, into her aching passage.

Her back arched off the bed and her hands grasped his hips and she held on as he started to move.

She marveled at the contrasting sensations of being completely filled by him yet eager for more. Voracious. She wanted him deeper and faster and harder with every thrust, and she lifted her body accordingly, eager to take everything he could give. And to give back, as well.

He complied, withdrawing only to plunge back into her. She dug her fingers into his firm buttocks and arched against him, drawing him more fully inside, clenching and unclenching around his glorious erection.

He let loose a colorful four-letter word that stirred her as much as the man himself, and she closed her eyes, concentrating on the sound of his labored breathing and the raw, guttural sounds vibrating from his lips.

Her nerves buzzed and her ears tingled and the hunger deep inside her grew. She'd never been so consumed, so desperate, so needy.

Business, a voice whispered, but she was beyond listening. She was relishing every sensation, conscious only of the man above her and the hot, thick erection filling her.

Sweat trickled from his brow, and his straight white teeth were clamped tight as he lifted himself and rocked into her over and over. His arms strained, every sculpted muscle standing out from the tension holding his body tight.

She struggled for air and touched his arms, fascinated by every bulge and ripple. He was so strong, so big and powerful, as he held himself above her and buried himself deep, deep inside.

She threw her head back and moaned, relishing the sound as it pulsed from her mouth.

She was extremely conscious of every feeling, her fingertips aware of his flesh, her eyes riveted on the sight of him, her ears tuned to the sounds of his lovemaking, her lips still ripe with the taste of him, her nostrils filled with the scent of raw male and hot, *moving* sex.

"Thank you, Dr. Love," she gasped as her body crested. "Thank you so much."

Her climax hit her hard and fast, crashing over her and turning her inside out and upside down. She shook violently, her internal muscles milking him.

He threw his head back and drove deep, riding his own release with a raw groan before collapsing against her. He buried his head in the curve of her neck, his heart pounding violently against hers.

"Now *that* was sex," she murmured after several long moments, when she could finally speak. She was still on fire, her body pulsing around his, and she relished the sensations.

"Hot, moving sex," he reminded her.

"Just as good as your book."

"My book?" He lifted his head and stared down at her.

"I was in tune with every sense. I could feel you, hear you, see you, taste you, smell you. It was incredible."

"My book?" he asked again.

"I didn't read the entire thing, but I started it and I've heard Roxeanne go on and on about how enlightening it was."

"My *book?*"

She pointed to the nightstand and the leatherbound volume sitting on top. "Yes, your book. You're Dr. Love and that's your book. *In Touch with Your Inner Sensuality*."

He shook his head. "I'm not Dr. Love."

"Yes, you are." Again, she had the unnerving sensation that something wasn't right. That the situation wasn't what she'd thought and she'd made a major mistake. "My senses are still buzzing," she said, as if that fact alone were enough to prove that he was the doctor himself.

"Thanks to me, not Dr. Love."

"You're Dr. Love. You have to be. You just walked in here, and bam, I was turned on."

"You're really good."

"What are you talking about?"

"You're a really good actress."

"I'm not an actress. I'm Gerry Baxter. I'm the producer for Burn, Inc."

"The producer?" He stared at her with disbelief.

"And you're Dr. Love."

"No, I'm not," he said again.

She scrambled from underneath him. "You *are* Dr. Love. I invited you here tonight. I begged you for help. That's why you came."

"You begged, but you weren't begging Dr. Love. You were begging me," he said again as he threw his legs over the side of the bed. He peeled off the condom and tossed it into a nearby wastebasket. "The producer?" He shook his head. "Un-friggin'-believable."

She tried to ignore the sight of him, so big and naked, his erection still thick and wet with cum. Instead, she concentrated on retrieving her robe and shoving her arms inside. "So what is it you're trying to say?"

"That I'm not Dr. Love." He stood and stepped toward her, backing her up against the nightstand as his gaze drilled into her. "You, Miss Producer, just had sex with Logan Mackenzie."

CHAPTER THREE

From the shocked look on her face, Logan might well have admitted to being from another planet.

"You *have* to be Dr. Love."

"Look, lady, I'm not, not anymore than you're an actress." The producer. He'd slept with the friggin' producer. Roxeanne's partner, no less.

"But you've got a Trigger." She pointed to the small idol hanging around his neck.

"Trigger?"

"The Eros statue. You're an honorary member of Women On Top. Because of all your hard work in promoting the erotic freedom of women."

"The only thing I promote is Mackenzie & Mackenzie Construction." He fingered the statue. "One minute, I'm going over architectural plans for a new shopping mall, and the next, I'm staring at this and reading a FedExed letter from my brother saying that he's tied the knot and his new wife won't be needing this. Then I get to this place and pull this thing out of my pocket and suddenly I'm in. That's the only reason I'm wearing this."

"All our employees have them. The guards probably thought you belonged here." She shook her head. "This is unreal. Your brother is Stan. Roxeanne's Stan." She closed her eyes. "I don't believe this."

"You and me both. He actually got married."

"I don't mean that. I mean, I do. I mean everything. Them. Us."

"You believed the *us* a few minutes ago."

She frowned. "You're Stan's brother, not Dr. Love." She shook her head. "But you had a Trigger."

"I told you. My brother sent it to me."

"Why didn't he just call you?"

"And risk me reaming him out over the phone?" He shook his head. "Stan isn't ready to face me with this one yet, but he still had to let me know. Otherwise, I would have expected him back for the Saunders project." At her questioning gaze, he added, "It's an office building we're starting. Stan put the deal together, and he's supposed to lead the crew first thing Monday morning."

"Next Monday?"

"Yesterday's Monday." He shook his head. "Married, of all the crazy things."

"You're telling me." She sat on the edge of the bed, the robe clutched tight around her. "I still can't believe she did it. She vowed never to get married. She's a Woman On Top and it goes against Number Five of the Erotic Eight."

"The Erotic Eight?"

"The proverbial Ten Commandments to all Women On Top. It's their creed. Their religion. They follow the teachings of Eros."

He fingered the statue. "You called him Trigger."

"It's his nickname. Because he's hung like a horse." At his raised eyebrow, she added, "They practice the Erotic Eight as if it were a religion, but Eros isn't their God. He's just a reminder of all the men out there and their attributes."

"Why do you think she did it?"

"Temporary insanity," she murmured as she searched through a pile of blankets for her undies. "I know the feeling."

"Here." He retrieved her panties and tossed them to her.

She took them and started to open her robe before she seemed to think better of it. She turned around. "I still can't believe this. I thought . . . I mean, you were supposed to be him and give me some pointers, and then, when you kissed me, I thought it was a little strange, but you tasted so good, and it's been so long, and I thought maybe this was just a hands-on demonstration for education's sake."

"I'm afraid I'm not following you."

"Dr. Love was supposed to come here tonight to give me some help on this latest video I'm working on. I didn't know who else to call. This is the first time Roxeanne's done something like this. She's usually pretty reliable."

"I'll bet."

"She is. I mean, she's a little off in her way of thinking because she's so in tune with her senses, if you know what I mean, but she's at least *here*."

"Not anymore, obviously. So, she called you?"

She nodded. "She said they were going on a honeymoon and she would be back soon. *Soon*, of all things. She knows we're on a deadline. I swear, she's lost all common sense."

"Then she's with the right guy. My brother is an idiot. Can you imagine marrying someone you just met?"

"I can't imagine Roxeanne marrying anyone. She's not the marrying kind."

"Neither is Stan. Not if he knows what's good for him.

Which he obviously doesn't. He can't marry someone like her."

She came up short and eyed him. "Someone like her? What exactly is that supposed to mean?"

"She's not his type."

"Well, he isn't her type if he's anything like you."

He frowned. "What's that supposed to mean?"

"She goes for more professional types. You know, a three-piece suit. You're more the T-shirt and jeans kind of guy."

"All the more reason they shouldn't be married. Look, I'm not here to argue with you. I just wanted to look around and see what kind of woman this Roxeanne is."

"Well, I just want to finish this series. I've got three days. That's why you're here. I mean, that's why Dr. Love was supposed to be here. To help me get in touch with my inner sensuality."

He couldn't help the grin that tugged at his lips. "Mission accomplished."

"What we did was not educational. It was crazy. I was crazy. I can't believe I didn't even ask your name. I just thought . . ."

"You wanted hot, moving sex. We had hot, moving sex. No harm done as long as we both keep what happened in its proper perspective."

"Amen to that." She nodded vigorously.

"We're two adults," he told her. "We can do what we want as long as we don't hurt anyone or have unrealistic expectations."

"Like you might feel something for me, or I might feel something for you. We don't even know each other. I mean,

I know that you like to have your neck licked and you like it when I stroke the small of your back, but that's not a basis for a relationship.

"Even if we are sort of related," she went on. "I mean, Roxeanne is my partner and Stan is your brother. That sort of hints at a relationship. A social relationship. Not a romantic one."

He shook his head. "I'm not looking for a romantic relationship. No way. No how. Not me." Never again.

"Me, either." She shivered. "I get the creeps just thinking about it. I'm definitely a non-romantic-relationship person."

"Me, too."

"And what we had certainly doesn't qualify as anything romantic. It was just sex."

"Great sex."

"Exceptional sex. But that's it." She glanced at a nearby clock. "I really should change and get home."

"I could drive you."

"No thanks. My car's in the parking lot. If I don't see you again, it was . . . nice."

"Uh, yeah." He watched her walk toward a row of offices on the opposite side of the set, and the sudden urge to go after her, pull her into his arms, and kiss her one more time nearly overwhelmed him. "When are they coming back?"

"Who?" She turned to face him, and he had the sudden vision of her lying beneath him, her lips open on a moan, her body arched in the throes of her orgasm.

He swallowed. "My brother and Roxeanne. When do you expect them back?"

"I told you, she only said soon. Nothing specific. Judging

from that, it could be tomorrow or it could be next month."

"It won't be next month. Stan and I have an appointment at the bank next Friday to sign a loan for a major project. He'll be back by then."

"I wish I could be as sure as you, but I'm not counting on anything. Besides, next Friday is too late for me. If you want to leave your number, I'll call you if I hear from them."

"Just ask him to call me. I've got a few things to say to him."

Forget a few. He had a helluva lot to tell his baby brother. He owed Stan for all the trouble he was causing. And he owed him double for the woman standing in front of him. She was Trouble with a capital T, because, as much as Logan promised himself to forget what had just happened, he couldn't.

Worse, he didn't want to, because he hadn't been with a woman like Gerry Baxter in a very long time.

Christ, he hadn't *ever* been with a woman like Gerry. A woman so open and honest and responsive.

Yep, the past few hours had been a mistake, all right. Women—all women—had trouble separating the emotional from the physical, and, while Gerry seemed to be the one exception, he wasn't taking her at face value.

He'd done that once before. He'd bought every line his ex-wife had fed him, and he'd wound up losing his shirt because of it.

It was better to let her walk away now and forget all about how she'd tasted, because he wasn't tasting her again.

No matter how much he suddenly wanted to.

o

A few hours later, back in her own apartment, Gerry tried to come to grips with what had just happened to her. She felt like Sleeping Beauty, as if she'd just awakened after a very long nap. If she hadn't known better, she would have sworn she could count every drop of spray that slithered over her ultra-sensitive skin. She could smell the subtle scent of chlorine mingled with her favorite green apple soap. She could hear the beat of her own heart and every deep, raspy breath that sawed past her swollen lips.

Her body seemed to be in a constant state of arousal. Her nipples were hard and turgid, the slick flesh between her legs throbbed, and she felt hollow and empty and hungry for more.

For him.

Before she could stop herself, she touched the erect tip of one nipple and circled the sensitive bud with her fingertip. She closed her eyes and, in her mind, she felt him.

His fingertip touched her, plucked at her nipple, trailed down over her belly, and slid into the slick flesh between her legs. He pressed just right, and she caught her breath, the sensation paralyzing and exquisite.

Another stroke and the pressure inside her built. He felt so good and she wanted him so bad and—

The shrill ring of the phone cut into her thoughts and pulled her back to reality. Gerry forced her eyes open to the empty shower stall. She stopped touching herself, turned the spray as cold as it would go, and tried to calm her aching flesh. In the other room, the answering machine picked up, and her father's voice floated over the line.

"I was just checking to see if you were going to make this

month's dinner, dear. Your brothers and I are anxious to see you and hear all about what's happening with your company. Gordon made an extra hundred thousand with his Coldwell stock. Can you imagine that? In this economy? Why, the boy's a genius. Anyhow, we hope to see you Friday night." *Click*.

They hoped to see her every month, or so her father said every time he called. But Gerry had been putting them off for the past six, making excuses to avoid seeing the three of them and having to answer questions about Burn's financial status.

She'd promised them that she would come this Friday. The cable deal was supposed to be finished by then, and she'd been so looking forward to answering everything they thought to ask. It would have been her shining moment. Her father and brothers would see the HBO series as a major coup, considering the current economy and the youngest Baxter as a genius for putting together such a great deal.

Go anyway. Face 'em like a man.

But she couldn't, not with everything up in the air. She'd sat through too many dinners already where she hadn't felt good enough. She wanted just one where she actually fit in. She wanted to feel like an equal. To feel important to them. Just once.

She flipped off the cold water, climbed from the shower, and reached for a towel. The soft cotton made her skin ache all the more as she rubbed the moisture away and tried to forget how good Logan Mackenzie's hands had felt rubbing her body.

She would forget. Their encounter had been a mistake.

One she couldn't undo. She could only move on and that meant facing another day of filming without Roxeanne.

". . . No, no. I completely understand," Gerry said into her cell phone as she sat on the set and prepared for another day of filming. "A kidney stone is definitely a good reason for not showing up last night." She listened as Dr. Love explained about his trip to the emergency room, thanks to a massive stone. "Don't worry about me. You take your pain medication and rest. I'll be okay. I've got a few ideas."

She said goodbye and shifted her gaze to the notebook in front of her.

Not one stinkin' idea.

Gerry gave herself yet another mental slap upside the head. What had she been thinking?

She hadn't been thinking, at all. That had been the trouble. She'd simply felt, and everything had felt so good that she'd been unable to keep her wits about her.

Now she had to deal with the morning after.

"Do you want to try the kiss again?"

Boy, do I ever.

Her mind rushed back through last night, and the way Logan's lips had nibbled at hers. His tongue had plunged deeply, exploring and tasting until her heart had pounded so fiercely. All the while, his fingers had splayed in her hair, holding her head close, angling her just right for the most thorough contact. . . .

"—earth to Gerry? Hello?"

She shook the memory away and tried to concentrate on

the couple standing on the set in front of her, where she'd stood just last night.

"What?"

"Do you want to start with the kiss again?" Mimi asked.

She nodded, and Mimi slid her arms around Cowboy Jeff's neck. His arms came up, one sliding around her shoulders, the other cupping her face—

"Hold it right there." Gerry motioned to the camera woman. "Get a close up of his hand where he's touching her cheek." The camera zoomed in and Gerry stared through the lens.

The stark contrast of tanned skin against creamy white flesh struck a chord deep inside her. Cowboy's thumb played over Mimi's cheekbone in a soft caress that wouldn't have been noticeable, were it not for the camera's narrow field of view.

"This is good," Marty mumbled from behind the camera. "This is really good."

"It is, isn't it?" Gerry smiled. "Now come out of the close-up really slow." The picture panned out, slowly bringing to life the couple whose lips touched each other's in a slow, deep, tantalizing kiss.

"I felt that," Mimi announced when the kiss ended. "I really felt that."

"Me, too." The sentiment echoed around the set, and Gerry smiled because she'd felt it herself, and it felt right.

Just like last night.

Crazy. You were horny; he was horny. Of course it felt good.

True, but it hadn't just felt good. It had felt incredible.

Earth shattering. *Moving*. As if there had been more in play than just two lusty appetites.

"—try shifting into the love scene?" Marty's voice pushed into Gerry's thoughts.

"What?"

"Are you all right?" The camera woman frowned. "You look flushed. You're not coming down with something, are you?"

Just a bad case of stupid, because Gerry was starting to think that maybe what she'd been feeling last night had been more than mere lust.

That she'd actually felt *like* for Logan Mackenzie. That she'd connected with the fear and hesitation she'd glimpsed in his eyes, and that she'd felt a connection to him that went beyond the heat that had roared between them. She'd understood him and sympathized with him.

Stupid, indeed.

They'd had a one-night stand, and to even think that anything could come of it was even more than stupid. It was downright dangerous.

And it wasn't happening.

Not this time.

CHAPTER FOUR

He'd never been attracted to a woman wearing glasses, but damned if he didn't get a massive hard-on watching Gerry Baxter.

She sat in the director's chair, her glasses riding low on her nose as she studied the notes in front of her. She looked up, calling out several stage directions, and then fixed her attention on a nearby camera. The smile that lifted her full lips sent a burst of heat straight to his already massive erection.

All part of the plan.

She probably didn't even need glasses. She'd merely slipped them on and smiled and looked so damned inviting just to tempt him.

But it wasn't happening. He was here strictly in a professional capacity. He had no doubt that Stan would be back in time to sign papers for the McMillan deal. They'd worked too long and hard and had too much riding on it for him to bail.

Besides, they were brothers. Blood. Stan had always been there for Logan. When they'd been kids, Logan had nearly got himself expelled from school for fighting. His brother had come through five minutes to expulsion time and admitted the truth—that he'd been the one fighting and Logan had merely stepped in to stop it. Again, when they'd been teenagers and Logan had been blamed for toilet papering old Mr.

Wilbur's barn because his rusted-out Mustang had been seen speeding away, Stan had stepped up and taken the blame for what he and his friends had done after sneaking out in Logan's car to go joyriding. Then again, when Logan had been fighting for his business in divorce court, Stan had arrived two minutes before Logan's scheduled testimony to lend his support.

Stan wouldn't let him down.

Logan knew that, yet, at the same time, he couldn't help wondering what had possessed his baby brother to marry a woman he hardly knew.

The question had kept him up tossing and turning all night, had haunted him all morning as he'd dispensed work orders and checked on his various crews, and had brought him back here.

His presence certainly had nothing to do with the fact that he wanted to see Gerry again. He simply needed to see her because she was the only person who could answer his questions about Roxeanne. Maybe she could clue Logan in as to why Stan would take the plunge with this particular woman.

He had his own theory. Sex. But as persuasive as the argument was, it didn't gel. Not with Stan. His brother had had his share of beautiful, experienced women, and not one had ever trapped him into marriage.

Until this one.

Why? That's what had brought Logan here instead of back to the office to spend his usual lunchtime eating a sandwich and going over tomorrow's schedule.

His gaze shifted to the woman sitting several feet away.

A vision of last night, of a similar smile that had curved

her face after she'd had a very loud, very explosive orgasm, popped into his head and sent a wash of heat through his already warm body.

His surroundings. That was the explanation for his aroused state.

He certainly wasn't hot for Gerry Baxter. They'd had their fun and now it was over.

You're preaching to the choir, buddy.

He knew it wasn't happening again, but he didn't buy the fact that she knew. Sure, she'd said as much. But he'd heard the same line before. She had her own agenda, and, judging by the way she was prancing around on the set, tantalizing him at every turn, that plan included *more*.

Every eye was riveted to the scene unfolding on the set—except Logan's. He watched Gerry, and damned if that weren't more of a turn-on than the heated kisses the on-set couple shared.

She looked so stiff and conservative with her black business suit and pin-striped blouse and low, clunky black pumps. Not at all the vixen she'd been when he'd happened upon her last night.

It's all part of the plan, guy.

Of course, today's image was probably meant to throw him for a loop, to make him believe she was exactly what she'd said—a workaholic interested in only one night of pleasure. He wasn't buying it. No woman who'd responded the way she had last night could be this stiff. And no one who'd turned him on to the point where he'd forgotten everything, including Mackenzie & Mackenzie, could be that much of a novice.

She knew what she was doing. Like every other woman

he'd ever known, she wanted something from him. He just wasn't sure what it was.

Yet.

"You're not supposed to be here." The soft voice pushed past his thoughts and he turned to stare at a forty-something redhead wielding what looked like an artist's palette. She wore the now-familiar Trigger around her neck. He started to point out the figurine hanging around his own neck, but unlike the night security guards, this woman knew he wasn't a crew member. "No men allowed."

"I'm here to speak with Gerry Baxter."

"She's got an office. Make an appointment."

"Not an option. I need to talk to her ASAP. It's very important."

"So are our rules. No men allowed. Leave now, or I'll call security."

"That won't be necessary." Gerry's voice came from behind Logan, and he turned to find her deep brown eyes fixed on him.

Chocolate syrup. That's what her eyes reminded him of. Dark, rich chocolate syrup that warmed him the way it would as it slithered over a cold scoop of vanilla ice cream.

"He was just leaving."

"No, I wasn't."

"Take five, everybody," Gerry called out before turning back to him. "What are you doing here besides interrupting a very important shoot?"

"I was going to wait until you finished."

"How diplomatic, but that's not possible. We don't allow any men on the set."

"What about the John Wayne wannabe?"

"He's an actor. That's different."

"How so?"

"We need him. Look, what are you doing here?"

"You actually talked to Roxeanne. Maybe she clued you in on something and you just don't realize it."

"She said they'd be home soon. That's it."

"Did you hear any sounds in the background?"

"'La Bamba.'"

"Maybe they went to Mexico."

"I've heard 'La Bamba' on the Top Forty station here. It was a popular song. It means nothing. Look, they'll come back when they come back. You need to face the fact that Stan flew the coop. He's probably not going to be here for your bank meeting, anymore than Roxeanne will be here to help me out of this mess. We're on our own."

"He'll be here."

"If you think so, great. Then there's no reason to worry and hunt him down."

"I'm not hunting. I just want to understand this. It's not like my brother."

"Well, it's not like Roxeanne either, but they did it, and now we have to deal with the consequences."

"Aren't you the least bit curious why?"

"Not really. Focusing on why isn't going to get this video made and my house out of hock."

"You're right. Let's go to lunch. You can tell me about Roxeanne and I'll tell you about Stan and maybe we can figure this out."

"I can't go to lunch. I'm busy."

"Your crew has to eat, don't they?"

"Yes."

"And you can't run everything by yourself, can you?"

"No."

"Then let's go to lunch."

"I'll be reviewing today's footage with a BLT in my office."

"Sounds good to me."

"I didn't offer."

She was really good. If he didn't know better, he would have laid down money that she really didn't want to have anything more to do with him. But, with the way his body was responding to her nearness, she had to be doing something to get him going. Something so subtle he couldn't even put his finger on it. Otherwise, he would have been as immune to her as he was every other woman who crossed his path.

"Lunch, and then I'll leave."

"You'll leave anyway if I call security."

"Why make a fuss when I promise to leave peaceably *after* lunch?"

"Because I don't want to have lunch with you."

Liar. The word whispered through Gerry's head as she stood face-to-face with the man who'd made passionate love to her only a few short hours ago.

A man who looked as if he read every thought racing through her mind, namely the desperate urge to reach out and press her lips to his.

She forced the notion away and started toward a small alcove off to the side, eager to escape the curious eyes and ears of the people milling about the set. Footsteps sounded behind her and she knew he was following her.

Once she'd reached her destination, and they were out of earshot, she turned on him. "Look, I'm busy, and I'm sure you're busy, so let's get right to the point. What do you want? And I know it's not lunch."

"I told you, I want to understand why Stan did this. He hardly knows Roxeanne. What would make him up and do something so crazy? It's not like she had time to lay a trap for him."

"For your information, Roxeanne would never trap any man. If a trap occurred, it was your brother who set it. She's a great catch. She's smart. Sexy. Financially solvent—Hey, maybe that's it." She pinned him with an accusing stare. "You guys need money. Maybe he saw Roxeanne as a means to an end."

"First off, we do not *need* money. The bank loan is for a very large project. It's standard operating procedure for any business undertaking this type of job. We've got everything worked out on our own. We don't need an outside investor. Besides, my brother isn't that way. Not to mention, my brother was the one who struck it big in Vegas. At least that's what you said. That he made enough to buy her a wedding ring."

She nodded. "A monster of a wedding ring."

"Maybe she needed money, and his big winnings attracted her."

"Roxeanne isn't the least bit interested in money. Believe me, I know that firsthand. She leaves all the finances to me, and the worry. Speaking of which, this is all really pointless.

They did what they did for whatever reason and we obviously didn't know them as well as we thought. There's no use second-guessing them. Trust me, I learned that the hard way."

"Meaning?" he prodded, and, as much as she wanted to clamp her lips shut, she couldn't.

"That I've been surprised before by people I thought I knew. People that were close to me. Sometimes we think we know people, but we don't." She shook her head and fought back a particular memory from her childhood. "Look, you really should leave."

"Finish what you started to say."

She wanted to. There was just something compelling about his liquid blue eyes that made her want to tell him everything about her past, her present, her future.

Ridiculous. She hardly knew him, and she wasn't about to get to know him. They'd had one night and it was over.

Of course, it was that one night compelling her to talk. They'd been intimate, and so she felt a false sense of closeness with him, as if he cared about what she thought as much as he'd cared about pleasuring her the night before.

He didn't.

If only his gaze didn't whisper otherwise.

"Come on. What were you going to say?"

Nothing. Not one single thing. "My father," she blurted. "Piano recital. Fourth grade. He said he would come, and I believed him because he was my father. But he forgot, because it wasn't important to him like it was to me. That was my mistake. Thinking that he held the same things in the same regard that I did."

"One piano recital and you're scarred for life?"

"Eighteen recitals in four years, and not once did I have a family member present. Not my father or my two brothers." She shook her head. "But it wasn't just piano. It was everything. They were busy doing their own thing, things that were important to them, and I was forgotten. They were at my college graduation, but only because that was important to them. They're all self-made businessman, very successful, and they wanted to see me use my MBA to join one of their firms. It was almost like a recruiting call. But I thought the vision that Roxeanne and I had was more important. So here I am, much to their dismay."

"Picking up the pieces because Roxeanne left you high and dry like everybody else."

She shrugged. "That's the way it is, but it's okay because I never expected anything different."

"But you should."

The words hung between them for a long moment, and, if she hadn't known better—that he was no different from everybody else because he, too, put his own priorities above all others—she might have actually believed the passion with which he said the words.

She might have believed *him*.

But Gerry had stopped putting her faith in other people a long time ago. She looked to herself for answers.

"I should, huh? You should practice what you preach."

"What's that supposed to mean?"

"That you're ready to believe the worst of Roxeanne. You've already tried and convicted her of trapping your brother and you don't even know her."

"I've known women like her, with their hidden agendas. They say one thing, but they really want something else. My mother did that. She wanted my father and his name, not because she loved him, but because she'd gotten pregnant, and he was the only one dumb enough to offer to marry her when she was carrying someone else's child. She ended up losing the baby, but then she was stuck. Her parents wouldn't hear of a divorce, and so she stayed, even though she didn't love him. My brother and I paid the price, because she ended up resenting us, just as she resented my father because of her own unhappiness."

"Are they still together?"

"No. My dad passed away from a heart attack about ten years ago. My mom's been remarried for the past five years. She's finally happy."

"I'm sorry about your dad. It's tough losing a parent."

"How do you know?"

"My mom died when I was a few months old. She had diabetes, and my birth was too much for her. It was just me and my dad and my brothers from then on."

"Sorry," he said, and the one word filled her with a strange warmth.

Warmth?

"Look, you really have to leave. I'm sorry that you have such a negative view of women because of your mother, but—"

"—and my ex-wife. We dated in high school. I wasn't thinking about anything more than getting into her pants. I thought she wanted the same thing. A little fun. Hell, we were just kids. But that fun came at a price. She said she loved me and that she wanted to be with me forever. But she only said that because she saw me as her ticket out of a desperate situation. Her family was very poor, and I was a step up since I actually had a job. My father did subcontracting work, and I helped him."

He shook his head and went on. "I really thought she was crazy about me, and I loved her for it, so I married her. The biggest mistake of my life. The feeling didn't go both ways. I knew it as the marriage wore on, but I had made a commitment, so I stuck it out. We were together for six years, until she found someone better than me and took the next step up, along with half of my business."

"That's terrible, but it's no reason to distrust every other female in the world."

"Oh, I don't distrust every female. Just the ones who use sex as a tool to manipulate men to get what they want. So what is it you want?"

"What do you mean?"

"You've been prancing around here looking so good I can't help but want to kiss you again."

"Prancing? I'm working, and as far as you wanting to kiss me, I think that's your problem. Not mine." She licked her dry lips and prayed for her voice to hold up.

"Aha. See there. You did the lip licking thing. You *are* trying to entice me."

"My lips are dry. You're paranoid."

"I'm on to you. You're not serious about forgetting last night. You're not the one-night stand type."

"How do you know what type I am?"

"You like *Pretty Woman*. You said so yourself."

"I love *Pretty Woman*. It's my favorite movie. So what?"

"It's a romantic movie. As in happily-ever-after, the opposite of a one-night stand. Not to mention, you don't wear one of these things." He fingered the Trigger hanging around his neck. "Like everybody else."

"Just because I'm a romantic at heart doesn't mean I have designs on you. I *can* sleep with a man and want no further connection with him." She just wasn't sure Logan Mackenzie was that man.

Because as much as she tried to keep everything in perspective and deny any further attraction, damned if she didn't want to kiss him again, too.

Worse, she wanted to keep talking to him. To sit down over coffee and simply visit.

Sex.

"I haven't met a woman yet who didn't have an ulterior motive."

"Yes, you have." She blinked back a sudden swell of tears. "You met me."

Logan watched her walk back to the set and barely resisted the urge to go after her. *Why?*

Answers. That's what he told himself. Now if he only believed it.

But talking to her, looking into her eyes, he'd not only seen her sincerity, he'd felt it, and now he felt like an asshole for dumping his past on her and letting her see just how cynical he'd become.

Hell, he hadn't even realized how cynical he'd become until he'd heard himself. While he'd believed as much, there was just something about saying it out loud and seeing the disbelief on her face that made him think maybe . . . just maybe he *was* wrong.

He watched her dismiss the crew, who immediately flocked toward a nearby pastry cart and started scarfing up chocolate glazed donuts. Meanwhile, Gerry grabbed the film from the camera and headed for a small room off to the side labeled "Cutting Booth."

So what if he was wrong?

That meant that last night had been just a one-night stand, and it was over. He should leave. Go back to work and wait for Stan. He had no further connection to Gerry Baxter. No reason to head over to the cutting booth to see her again.

Except that he wanted to.

He wanted to see her and touch her. Even more than that, he wanted to apologize and wipe the disappointment off her face because he couldn't help but think that this time, with this woman, maybe he was wrong.

He started across the set.

CHAPTER FIVE

Just sex.

That's what Gerry told herself as she walked into the cutting room and shut the door behind her.

Her only connection with Logan Mackenzie was the one night of great sex they'd had, and now it was over. She shouldn't care what he thought about her.

She blinked and wiped at her watery eyes. Worse, she shouldn't care about him, period. So what if he'd been soured by his past? It wasn't her job to change his mind on behalf of all womankind. They hardly knew each other.

She loaded the day's filming and punched the rewind button. When the tape had backed up, she hit "play" and tried to concentrate on the couple on the TV screen in front of her. Music filled the dim room and the sound of soft panting echoed in her head.

The camera zoomed in on the hero's hand, and her mind rushed back to last night, to the strong, tanned hands that had reached for her, massaged her, spread cupcake cream all along her soft folds before licking her clean. She was so lost in her thoughts that she didn't hear the door open and close behind her.

She felt his presence behind her a split second before she heard his voice.

"I didn't mean to hurt you."

She stood up, ready to confront him, but he was too close, the room too small. She couldn't turn. Instead, his body crowded hers, his groin pressing into the soft curve of her buttocks as he loomed closer. She had the brief urge to lean back into him, to rock against him until he hardened.

One night and now it's over.

She held herself rigid, determined to resist her newly awakened sensuality and Logan Mackenzie.

"It doesn't matter," she told him, desperately trying to focus on the screen rather than the man behind her. The trouble was, as the couple touched and kissed, all she could think about was touching and kissing Logan Mackenzie.

"It does. Just because I'm a little skeptical, doesn't mean I should have taken it out on you. It's just that last night was—"

"—just sex," she cut in. "That's all it was, regardless of what you think. I had fun, you had fun, now it's over."

"That sounds good to me except for one thing."

"Which is?"

"I really want to touch you again." And he did.

It was just a fingertip near her ear, but it was enough to send electricity skimming over her nerve endings, pulsing to every erogenous zone. The rough pad of his finger traced a lazy circle before sweeping down the length of her neck to the point where it disappeared into her blouse. But he didn't stop there. His touch continued over the thin material of her blouse.

"I want to touch you like that," he murmured, and her gaze was riveted on the screen where the hero was massaging the heroine's breasts through her white cotton chemise.

She wanted to tell him to stop, but she couldn't seem to find her voice, especially when his arms came up underneath hers and his fingertips traced her nipples through her blouse.

She closed her eyes and let her head fall back for a delicious moment as her nipples crested, reaching out, begging for more.

"And I want to touch you like that." His deep, husky voice drew her eyes open in time to see the hero pull the heroine's chemise over her head. His large hands went to her small breasts and she moaned. The sound vibrated in the air around them as Logan worked at the buttons of Gerry's blouse.

Soon, he slid the material free from her arms and dropped it to the floor. He dipped his hands into the cups of her bra and lifted her breasts free, his touch burning into her skin. His fingertips went to her already swollen nipples, and he plucked and rolled until a moan worked its way up her own throat.

Her legs trembled, and it was all she could do to hold herself upright. Her hands went to the counter in front of her, and she braced herself, the motion bending her over just a fraction.

He inched closer, and the bulge in his jeans nestled between her buttocks. He rocked against her and drew another shameless moan from her lips.

"Do you like that?" he asked.

"Yes," she breathed, "but I don't want to."

"Why is that?" His fingertips swept lower, to the button on her slacks. He slid the opening free and eased her zipper down. The material collapsed around her hips.

His hands shoved the soft fabric further down until she stepped free. She stood before him wearing little but a pair of lace panties cut high on the thigh—red ones this time, a birthday present from Roxeanne. Her bra was still fastened around her ribcage, but the cups were pushed aside, and her breasts plumped and bobbed with every movement.

Her gaze shifted back to the video screen in time to see the hero finish undressing the heroine. He was still fully clothed, his body dwarfing hers as she stood before him, naked and ripe and his for the taking.

Desire knifed through Gerry, and she trembled. She could feel the rough denim of Logan's jeans against her buttocks and the backs of her thighs. The soft cotton of his T-shirt cushioned her back as his arms came around her.

Together, they watched as the hero lifted the heroine and pinned her to the bed. He kissed her then, his hot mouth devouring hers as she opened for him and he settled over her, ready to claim what she so freely offered.

Gerry had watched many erotic videos, but they'd never affected her like this one. Then again, she'd never watched one while standing nearly naked with a hot, sexy man who wanted her.

A man she desperately wanted.

Again.

One night. The warning niggled at her conscience, and she drew a deep steadying breath, for, as much as she wanted his touch, she didn't.

She needed to keep things in perspective. Already, she wanted him with a need that went beyond anything she'd ever felt before. Deep down, she knew that need wouldn't be satisfied with another encounter.

It would only grow, and she would want more. More of his kisses and his touches.

More of him.

And Logan Mackenzie wasn't a man the least bit interested in giving more. On top of everything, she wanted to prove to him that she wasn't like all the other women in his past. She didn't have any designs on him. She'd meant what she'd said about last night.

Just sex.

"No," she murmured when his fingertips slid down her abdomen and trailed over her lace-covered mound.

"I want to." One finger pushed aside the elastic edge and dipped into the steamy heat between her legs. He traced the slick folds, circling her clitoris with a mesmerizing rhythm that destroyed all thought for several fast, furious heartbeats.

"I don't," she finally managed, but she didn't move his hand. She couldn't. She knew it and he knew it. "We shouldn't do this."

"I want you, and you want me." She didn't deny it. She couldn't. She was too wet for him, her body sucking at his probing fingertip. "Christ, you're hot." He slid his finger inside her, and the air caught in her lungs. Then he added another finger, stretching her, creating a delicious friction as he moved in and out.

She could feel his denim-covered erection pressing into her, desperate to get loose from its confines. She had the insane urge to turn, drop to her knees, and free him. To take him into her mouth and lave the thick purple head with her tongue and taste his salty essence until he trembled the way she was trembling right now.

"You do want me, Gerry. Admit it."

"You were wrong about me. I meant what I said. One night." She wasn't sure how she managed to say the words, but she did. Not that they would make much difference. He was too hard, and she was too hot. One more touch, and her resistance would melt.

He knew it, too, because he whispered, "I could change your mind." He withdrew his fingers to trace her slick folds and circle her pulsing clitoris again. Back and forth. Round and round. Mmm . . .

"If that's what you want," she finally breathed, knowing what he intended and ready to deal with the consequences. She'd been doing as much her entire life. She was used to seeing her own wants and needs put second to everyone else's, and she would deal with it the way she always did.

She would expect nothing more and make the best of it.

"But it's not what you want," he breathed and pulled away. "At least not what you're ready to admit."

She nearly cried out when he stepped away from her, but it was all she could do to hold herself upright, her arms braced on the counter. A few frantic heartbeats later, she heard the door open and close.

Gerry forced her eyes open to find the booth empty and Logan Mackenzie gone.

He'd stopped his seduction. He hadn't wanted to, but he had anyway because she'd wanted him to.

Her eyes filled with tears, and she blinked furiously. For the first time in her life, someone had actually put her needs first.

Just sex, she told herself yet again.

But she knew it was more, because it wasn't just her body that ached for him now, it was her heart. The trouble was, there wasn't a thing she could do about it, because Logan

Mackenzie didn't want a relationship. He distrusted women, and to pursue more with him would only confirm his suspicions that he couldn't trust her.

But she'd meant what she'd said. She hadn't wanted more than a one night stand with him, and, while she did, he would never know that.

It was payback time.

Logan had renewed her faith in people, and she was going to do the same for him.

Even if it meant letting him walk out of her life forever.

"This is really excellent." Roxeanne stabbed the off button on the video monitor and turned to Gerry. "You did it."

"I had to do it, because someone else wasn't here to do it for me like she should have been."

Roxeanne fingered the three-carat marquise-cut diamond on her left hand and smiled. "I'm sorry, Gerry, but I just couldn't help myself." She stared across the set at Stan, who stood talking to one of the production assistants.

They'd arrived early Friday morning, just as Logan had predicted. While it had been in plenty of time for Stan to make it to the bank with his brother, it had been too late for Roxeanne to finish up video number ten.

But it was already done. Fully cut and edited and ready to go.

"I knew you had it in you," Roxeanne told her.

"No, you didn't. You didn't even wonder if I had it in me. You didn't even think about me or this company."

A sheepish grin crossed Roxeanne's face. "Actually, I didn't." She turned a knowing look on her friend. "You should try it some time. I know this company is important, but it doesn't make the world go around. There's more to life. What is the saying? Man cannot live by bread alone? Well, woman cannot live by work alone. You've got to let your hair down. Relax. Fall in love."

At Gerry's surprised look, Roxeanne went on, "I know that sounds strange coming from me. I never expected to feel this way myself. I never believed all that bunk about love. I liked lust. It was dependable. It made you a little crazy, but you could control it. But love . . ." She shook her head. "Stan looked at me, and, just like that, my heart stopped beating. It was almost like a near-death experience, where you see your life flash before your eyes, but it wasn't my life. It was my future."

"I think my life is flashing before my eyes. That or I've been beamed up by aliens." Gerry shook her head and peered closely at her friend. "Are you really Roxeanne, or are we being invaded by pod people?"

Roxeanne laughed. "I've been wondering that, too. Especially when I had this weird vision of myself barefoot and pregnant and in the kitchen, *and* the vision didn't even bother me. I *liked* it. That's when I knew he was the one."

"It was all a little sudden, don't you think?"

"It feels like I've known him forever. That we've been meant for each other our entire lives. You know, when I was a little girl, I used to dream that I was a princess and this cowboy would ride up—"

"Don't you mean a white knight?"

"When I was about five, I had a major thing for Little Joe on *Bonanza*, so it sort of skewed my princess/knight fantasy.

Anyhow, this cowboy would ride up and look at me while I stared down from the barn loft—"

"Those had ladders."

"Not mine. I was stranded in the barn loft by these wicked *banditos*. Anyhow, along comes this cowboy, and he looks up at me with the bluest eyes I've ever seen and says, 'Howdy, ma'am, is everything all right?' and we live happily ever after." She shook her head. "And what do you know—I was sitting at that gambling table where I'd just lost two hundred dollars, and Stan looks over at me and guess what he says?"

"Howdy, ma'am, is everything all right?"

"Bingo. It was like he'd looked right into my head and knew my fantasy. And guess what else?"

"He had the bluest eyes you'd ever seen."

"That's right. How did you know?"

Because she'd stared into her own pair of bluer-than-blue eyes and felt her own heart stop.

Roxeanne sighed. "Love is so wonderful."

Gerry reached out and touched a palm to her friend's forehead. "No fever."

"I'm not sick." She smiled and shrugged. "Well, lovesick, but I've never felt better." She eyed her friend. "Look, I know this is somewhat of a shock, especially with my reputation. But people change. I hope you'll try to understand."

"Actually, I already do." She'd realized that on Friday night, when she'd met her father and brothers for dinner. She'd finished the video and had been hyped up to tell them all about the cable deal. But as she'd sat there and listened to their latest business ventures, she hadn't felt the same eagerness to join in and wow them with her own endeavors. For the first time, she hadn't felt the need to gain their approval, because she'd already gained her own.

She'd finished the video all by herself, and on Monday the deal would be sealed, and the satisfaction from that had been enough. While she'd spent most of her life blaming her father and brothers for their unrealistic expectations of her, she'd known at that moment that it was her own insecurity that had plagued her. She'd never felt smart enough or pretty enough or sexy enough, and that hadn't been anyone's fault but her own.

Things had changed. Her view of herself had changed.

She knew now that she was smart enough to succeed in business. And, thanks to Logan, she felt pretty and sexy enough to succeed in her personal life.

A vision of him pushed into her mind, and she did her best to push it back out, the way she'd been doing for the past week since he'd walked out of the cutting booth and out of her life.

"Why don't you tell him?"

At Roxeanne's words, Gerry's head jerked around and her gaze locked with her friend's.

"Logan told Stan that he met you, and, since you've been acting completely preoccupied and forgetful since I've been back, I'm assuming that it went a little further than just a meeting." Her eyes twinkled. "Did you finally take my advice, forget this company for five minutes, and have a little fun?"

"I did not have a little fun." She'd had a lot of fun. "Can we talk about something else?" While she'd shed her inhibitions in bed with Logan, she'd yet to declare herself a Trigger-wearing Woman On Top.

Roxeanne eyed her. "You like him," she finally said.

"I do not like him." She loved him, but she wasn't about to admit it to Roxeanne. To anyone, for that matter. It was her problem and, obviously, hers alone, since Logan Mackenzie had made no move even to contact her, much less make any declarations of his feelings.

Not that he had any.

"He likes you."

"Says who?"

"Stan." She eyed her husband, who stood across the room. As if he sensed her attention, he turned and caught her gaze. The look that passed between them, a combination of lust, tenderness, and deep admiration, sent a burst of envy through Gerry. What she wouldn't give to have Logan Mackenzie look at her like that.

The minute the notion pushed into her head, she pushed it right back out. *Just sex.*

"He said that Logan had this look in his eyes when he mentioned you," Roxeanne went on. "When Stan asked questions about you and Logan, Logan told him to mind his own business. In guy language, that equals intense liking. Guys always talk about women. Unless—" she paused and wiggled her eyebrows "—they like them."

"If he likes me, then why hasn't he called me?"

"Why haven't you called him?"

Because she'd made a promise. She was going to prove to Logan that she'd meant what she'd said. Despite his past experience with women, he could take her at her word. "Call him," Roxeanne pressed.

"I am not calling him, and would you please leave the subject alone?"

"I just want you to be happy."

"Then be on time for the meeting with the HBO people on Monday. That will make me the happiest woman on the planet."

"You're avoiding your real feelings. That's not healthy."

"It's not healthy for me to worry about whether this deal will finally go through. We hand over the series on Monday, and we both have to be there to endorse the check they're going to give us. I need you there."

"No problem, as long as we're done by ten A.M. I've got a dress fitting."

"A what?"

"A fitting. For my wedding dress. Stan and I are going to get married next Saturday."

"I thought you were already married."

"We want to share our happiness with our friends, and so we're renewing our vows in front of everyone. It's at seven o'clock. You're the maid of honor. Speaking of which, you've got a dress fitting right after mine, so don't be late."

"Thanks for telling me."

She grinned and signaled Stan that she was ready to leave. "Just don't be late."

"I still don't like this," Logan told his brother as he stood at the rear of the hotel ballroom and tugged on his tie.

The scent of pink roses nearly suffocated him, for the room was overwhelmed with arrangements of all sizes and shapes. Round tables surrounded the dance floor, the edges of the room flanked by buffet tables covered with all types of food, from egg rolls to pigs in blankets to an ice sculpture of a cowboy on horseback carrying a princess in front of him.

People milled about in front of the buffet tables, and others circulated around the room. Logan spotted a short, balding, fiftyish man wearing one of the Trigger statues. He knew even before the man turned to reveal a KLOV radio logo pinned on his lapel that this was the real Dr. Marc Love. He made a mental note to thank the man later. Because Love had stood Gerry up, Logan had had the best night of his life.

One that continued to haunt him.

"Would you give it a rest about the prenuptual agreement?" Stan's voice sounded next to him. "We're already married so it's too late for one of those things. Not to mention, I wouldn't ask her to sign one anyway. You'll just have to trust me on this."

"I do trust you." Logan had come to that conclusion over the past week as he'd observed the change in his little brother. "I was talking about the tux."

Stan grinned. "It's a one-time thing. We're done with the ceremony and pictures. You just have to make it through the rest of the reception and you're home free." The band started to warm up, a wail of feedback nearly deafening everyone. "I think it's almost time for the first dance."

Logan watched as his brother glanced in a nearby mirror. He slicked a piece of wayward hair behind one ear and straightened his tie.

Logan couldn't help but smile. This was the Stan who, before Roxeanne, couldn't have cared less if he washed his hair, much less combed it. The Stan who would just as soon turn his socks inside out and wear them twice as go to the laundromat. The same Stan who'd faked a stomach virus to get out of wearing a monkey suit to their cousin's wedding last year.

Stan had behaved more like a grown-up in the past week since he'd arrived, on time, to sign the loan at the bank, than he had his entire life.

"You really love her, don't you?" he asked Stan.

"I know it's hard for people to believe, but I took one look at her and I just felt it. I don't expect you to understand this love at first sight thing, but there's really something to it."

But Logan already knew that firsthand.

His gaze shifted to the woman who sat all alone across the room at a large round table, nursing a plate of vegetables from a nearby buffet table. She wore a pink dress that matched the color of the roses in her bouquet. It was the typical bridesmaid's nightmare—tea length with lots of ruffles and tulle—and damned if she didn't look good enough to eat. Like pink cotton candy.

"Talk to her," Stan said. "What have you got to lose?"

Everything.

Just like his brother, though damned if the thought seemed to bother Stan. He stood there, grinning like a cat who'd just snagged himself his very own mouse. He wasn't the least bit worried about the future because he was too excited about the present. Too caught up in the moment.

Too much in love.

The truth crystallized as Logan stood there staring at his younger brother who looked so calm and relaxed and *in love*.

That was the key. The love part. Stan felt it. Roxeanne who beamed at him from across the room felt it.

Logan felt it.

For the first time in his life, he truly felt the emotion.

He'd married his first wife because he'd thought that she loved him, not because he'd felt the same for her. After yearning for his mother's love all of those years, he'd been hesitant to let go of a woman who'd lavished so much affection on him.

But it had all been an act.

Things were different now, because Gerry was different. She was a woman who didn't put on an act or pretend to be something she wasn't. She'd meant what she'd said about keeping their encounter in perspective, and he couldn't help but admire her for it. At the same time, he hoped like hell she was just being stubborn about not wanting more.

He loved her, but did she love him?

There was only one way to find out.

He grabbed a piece of chocolate groom's cake and started across the room.

Gerry's gaze locked with Logan's the moment he started toward her. Panic rushed through her, and she did the only thing a woman who'd vowed off cupcakes could do. She bolted to her feet and raced for the nearest ladies' room.

The door rocked shut behind her, and she leaned against the sink, trying to calm her pounding heart. A slim escape, but she'd made it—

"Cake?" The deep voice came from the doorway.

Her head jerked up in time to catch his reflection as he

stepped inside the room, a gold-edged plate in his hand. He ducked, glancing beneath the two stalls to the right before locking the main door behind him.

"What are you doing?"

"Following you." He came up behind her.

He stood so tall and handsome in his tuxedo, his bow tie hanging loose from all the tugging she'd seen him doing whenever she'd chanced a glance his way. His blond hair was tousled, his jaw freshly shaven. He smelled of musky cologne and warm male, and her nostrils flared traitorously.

"You shouldn't be in here."

He grinned and held up the plate before sliding it onto the counter in front of her. "I thought you might want some cake."

"I'm not hungry."

"And here I thought chocolate was your favorite." His gaze caught and held hers, his blue eyes so dark and mesmerizing that her stomach hollowed out. He was so close she could feel the heat from his body.

Her heart pounded double time. "It was," she managed, summoning every ounce of control.

"As in past tense?"

"I've gone cold turkey. It just doesn't kill my craving the way it once did." She motioned to the Trigger idol he still wore around his neck. "Nice touch with the tuxedo."

He fingered the figurine. "Actually, I wore it tonight because I thought it might bring me good luck."

She smiled. "It's not a rabbit's foot. It's a symbol of erotic freedom. It tells the world that you're free and easy and looking for a good time."

"Really?" In one smooth motion, he ripped the necklace from around his neck and tossed it into a nearby trash. "So what is it?" he asked as he turned his attention back to her, his gaze meeting hers in the mirror.

Her heart pounded at the knowledge of what he'd just done and what it meant.

"I beg your pardon?"

"What is it that you're craving now, because I know what I'm craving."

"What?"

"You."

She swallowed and fought down a wave of desire. "I don't think it's a good idea for us to sleep together again."

"I'm not talking about sleeping together. I'm talking about making love. That's generally what two people do when they're *in*—" A loud pounding on the door cut him off mid-sentence.

"Is there anyone in there?" came a muffled voice.

"We're out of order," he shouted over his shoulder before turning back to her.

"What are you trying to say?"

"I want you. All of you." He slid his arms around her waist and lifted his hands. He cupped her breasts through her dress before moving higher to slip his fingers inside.

"I want your body," he went on. Warm, callused thumbs grazed her nipples, and she barely caught the moan that worked its way up her throat. He rubbed her a few glorious moments, and then he stopped.

His hands fell away, and she almost cried at the sudden

lack of warmth. That's how she felt without him now. Cold. Lonely. Needy.

His gaze held hers strongly and steadily as he lifted one hand and traced the curve of her neck. His fingertips went lower, trailing over her collarbone, down the slope of one aching breast until he reached the frantic thump in her chest. "And I want your heart," he added.

A smile touched her lips as she eyed him in the mirror. "You know, this kind of brings back memories. You behind me in the cutting booth."

"Unfinished memories. I stopped."

"Because I wanted you to."

"And now?"

"That depends on what you say next."

"How about if I say that you're different from every other woman I've ever known."

"Go on."

"But what you don't know is I'm different from every other man you've ever known."

"How's that?"

"Because I love you, and I'm betting that you love me."

She arched an eyebrow at him and grinned. "Are you sure you want to make that bet? You might lose your shirt."

He smiled. "Oh, I'm counting on that. My shirt and my pants and anything else that gets in the way of you and me."

She turned and faced him. "Then give it up."

"Does this mean we get to finish?" He shrugged out of his jacket and then his shirt. He tossed them both aside.

"I'm betting on it."

He grinned, hoisted her onto the counter, shoved the dress

to her waist, and reached for her panties. In one smooth motion, he slid the lace thong down her legs. It landed on top of his shirt as he stepped between her legs.

"And now your pants," she told him. "They're in the way, too."

"Whatever the lady wants." Tanned fingers worked at the button and zipper on his pants. He sprang hot and throbbing into her hands. "And what else does the lady want?" he murmured as he leaned down to kiss her.

"You. Your heart." She trailed her hands over his hair-dusted chest. "And your body." She grabbed his buttocks and pulled him closer. The tip of his erection pushed into her wet heat, and her breath caught.

"And, by the way, I do love you," she breathed as she leaned back to stare into his eyes. "Very, *very* much."

"It's about damned time," he murmured, and then he thrust deep, his body filling hers in one smooth motion.

POSSESSING JULIA

by

PATRICIA RYAN

To Nick "The Devil" DiChario
and Tim "The Goof"* Wright,
for the engagingly prurient zeal with which you
badgered me into letting you read this manuscript.
Not to mention the long, silly lunches, the insightful
critiquing, and the steadfast friendship.
I love you guys.

*Take a drink!

CHAPTER ONE

New York City, July 1867

"Mr. Van Lew, I have something rather difficult to confess," Julia Hughes told her reflection in the cloudy little toilet glass above her bedroom washstand. "I haven't been entirely . . ."

Entirely what? Forthcoming? Honest?

Julia drew in as deep a breath as her stays would allow, and tested another approach. "Mr. Van Lew . . . Emmett." Surely, by the time they were wed and retiring to their marital bed, he would have invited her to call him by his Christian name. "There's something you should know before we . . ."

Her gaze shifted from her own mirrored image to that of the high, half-tester bed behind her. She eyed the rumpled sheets and counterpane uneasily, imagining her wedding night two weeks from today . . . and Emmett Van Lew's certain outrage when he bedded her and discovered the truth. He would cast her out; the scandal would be ruinous, and her little family of three would resume their downward spiral into abject destitution. New York City was a cruel place to be homeless, especially for the very young and the very old. Julia shuddered to think of little Tommy and Aunt Eunice in that squalid almshouse on Blackwell's Island. With a sense of mounting desperation, she turned back to the mirror.

"Mr. Van . . ." She swallowed, her hands fisted in the oftmended skirt of her blue poplin day dress. "Emmett. Before we . . . retire, there's something I really should tell you. I'm sure, once I've explained why I . . . how it happened . . . that you'll understand and . . . forgive me for having let you think I was—"

"Fat chance."

Julia wheeled around to find Aunt Eunice in the doorway, one gnarled old hand gripping her cane and the other cradling her constant companion, Birdie—a wizened little mixed-breed terrier who'd come to Eunice as a stray fourteen years ago and grown to bear an unnerving resemblance to her mistress.

"How long have you been standing there?" Julia asked.

"Long enough to learn that you're still planning to break the news to him *before* the marriage is consummated instead of after, when he'll be all sleepy and satisfied and a good deal less likely to get his nose out of joint." Eunice's voice, vaguely British-inflected, like the rest of New York's "Upper Ten Thousand," had become tremulous with age and markedly sibilant from ill-fitting false teeth. "If you tell him beforehand, when he's still got his wits about him, he'll send you packing right then and there."

"If I wait to tell him, he'll find out on his own, just as soon as he . . ." Heat crawled up Julia's throat. "While we're . . . you know. That's what you told me, isn't it? That he'd be able to tell? Hardly the best time to try to explain why a widow with a five-year-old son is still a virgin."

"Not necessarily," Eunice said as she hobbled over to the bed and lowered herself onto it. The chairs and fainting couch had been sold off long ago, along with the Axminster carpet, cheval mirror and clothespress. Nesting Birdie in her billowing black skirts, she said, "Men can be most agreeable when they're in the throes of passion, you know. All I ever had to do to get my way with your Uncle Chester was to put on just his riding breeches and boots and nothing else. He knew what was coming. He'd be like a puppy panting for a bone."

"Aunt Eunice!" Julia exclaimed through shocked laughter.

"What every man secretly wants is a wife who's a perfect lady by day and a harlot by night. Be eager, seductive—and by the time he encounters that pesky maidenhead of yours, he'll be so smitten with you that he'll forgive you everything."

Eager? Seductive? Julia groaned and lowered her head in her hands, further disheveling her hair, which had been escaping in inky curlicues from its chignon all morning.

It was madness to imagine that she could forestall her bridegroom's wrath—by any means. Her seductive skills were nonexistent, and, as for the pleas for sympathy and understanding she'd been rehearsing, well . . . it wasn't as if he'd negotiated this union out of affection. All Emmett Van Lew really knew about Julia was that she was young, widowed, wellborn—albeit in reduced circumstances—and presumably fertile; Tommy was taken as proof of that. And all Julia really knew about her fiancé was that he was a middle-aged railroad tycoon with a mansion on Fifth Avenue and a country estate where he bred racehorses. And, of course, that he was determined to finally sire an heir, as determined as she was to rescue her family from genteel but increasingly desperate poverty. It was a match that would serve them both—assuming he didn't commence divorce proceedings the day after the wedding.

"Find out what gets his heart racing," Eunice was saying,

"and then tease him, entice him. Get him good and hard and keep him there for as long as you—"

"Auntie, for pity's sake!"

Julia's outburst startled Birdie, who leaped down from Eunice's lap and skittered out of the room, claws rat-a-tat-tatting on the bare wooden floors.

"Just offering a bit of friendly advice," the old woman sniffed as she flicked open the ivory fan that hung by a chain around her neck, along with her keys and spectacles. "Beastly hot up here." The high-necked, multilayered black crepe Eunice had worn since her husband's death nine years ago kept her in a state of quivering heat prostration in the summer.

"I couldn't begin to imagine how to tease and entice," Julia said.

Eunice eyed her great-niece balefully over her fluttering fan. "You're twenty-three years old."

"And never so much as been kissed."

The fan stilled. "Martin never kissed you?"

"Once—when Reverend Draper pronounced us man and wife."

"But he'd been courting you since you were that high."

"He was a seminarian." A good, sweet, darkly handsome seminarian—but a little shy and much too wary of offending her maidenly sensibilities. And there'd been no one since Martin—no sweetheart, not even a casual flirtation. Julia's maternal obligations and financial straits had kept her out of society for years. Her betrothal to Mr. Van Lew would never have occurred but for the machinations of mutual friends.

"Do you even know what men and women do together in bed?" Eunice asked.

"Of course," Julia bluffed as she twisted her engagement ring round and round. "The husband plants a seed in the wife's womb, and, if conditions are right, it grows into a baby."

Eunice regarded Julia with arid bemusement. "A seed."

So Julia had surmised from the hints and whispers she'd managed to piece together over the years, marital relations being a taboo subject in polite circles and decent literature. Had Julia's mother lived to see her daughter wed, she might have offered some preparatory counsel, but she had perished, along with her husband, in the cholera outbreak of '49. An orphaned only child with a healthy trust fund, Julia had spent vacations here in her aunt and uncle's Gramercy Park townhouse, and the rest of her formative years at the exclusive Foxton Hall School for Girls up on the Hudson. There, she'd fallen in love with the headmistress's son, Martin Hughes. The morning after their June wedding in 1861, Martin joined the 48th Regiment New York State Volunteers as an assistant chaplain. Four months later, he succumbed to typhus at Hilton Head Island, leaving Julia widowed and devastated at seventeen.

"A seed," Eunice repeated, studying Julia as she fanned herself. "I don't suppose you happen to know how this . . . seed gets implanted in the woman's womb."

"Certainly," Julia said, striving for a matter-of-fact tone to match Eunice's. "The man expels it from his . . . you know."

"And how much time do you imagine this takes?"

Julia thought about it: insertion of the male member, expulsion of the seed, withdrawal. "A few seconds?"

"Oh, my Lord." Eunice snapped the fan closed.

"I do realize a certain amount of kissing is customary."

"Kissing. Oh, you silly little goose. I had no earthly idea. Twenty-three years old . . . What did you and your little school chums whisper about after lights-out?"

"They knew even less than I did." Except, of course, for Libby Collier, but she preferred doing it to talking about it.

Eunice lifted her scrawny shoulders. "That's it, then. You're far too innocent and ill informed to sway Van Lew with your body. Your only hope is to throw yourself on his mercy and hope he's not as cold and pitiless as everyone says he is."

"Yes, well, now that we've established the full magnitude of my ignorance *and* my dilemma, I believe I'll get back to those handkerchiefs." Eight cents apiece; time was money.

Reaching out to grasp Julia's hand as she started to turn away, Eunice said, "I hate this. I'd always hoped you'd find someone wonderful, like my Chester, and make a love match."

"I did," Julia said soberly. She was about to add, "He died," when she was interrupted by a sudden squall in the form of a tow-headed boy who darted in a blur across the room, scrambled belly down under her bed, and took squinty-eyed aim at them with his wooden toy rifle.

"Take this, you stinkin' Rebs!" There ensued a battery of concussive mouth sounds of the type every male child was born knowing how to make.

"Tommy, come on out of there," Julia said. "I haven't had time to clean under there lately—you'll end up filthy."

Tommy squirmed out from under the bed, and Julia knelt down to dust him off, taking the opportunity to gather him into a big hug, which he was still young enough to return enthusiastically. How she loved the feel of his solid little body, the pressure of his downy cheek against hers, his unique, little boy scent. He was wearing Martin's Union Army forage cap, which they'd sent her after he died. It should have been huge on him, but he was such a big, sturdy boy that it fit almost perfectly; he was rarely without it.

"Mama," he asked, straightening his cap as she released him and stood, "who's that man downstairs?"

"There's no man downstairs, sweetie."

"Is so. I was running after Birdie to put this on her—" he dug a yellow neckerchief out of his pocket "—so she could be Johnny Reb, but when I got halfway down the stairs, I saw some man snooping around down there, so I came back up."

"Oh, dear, he's right!" Eunice exclaimed. "I almost forgot why I came up here in the first place. You have a caller."

"What? Auntie, you know we can't entertain visitors." They'd no proper food to serve, no decent gowns to receive in, and a home that had been very nearly stripped of furniture. "Send him away."

"I'm not sure I should." Planting her cane on the floor, Eunice hauled herself shakily to her feet. "It's . . ." She glanced at Tommy, hesitated, sighed. "It's Clay Redmond, dear."

Julia gaped at her aunt. "*Clay?* Why . . . why would he . . . ?"

"Why would he be paying you a visit after all this time?"

Eunice cast her niece a look ripe with significance. "I think I might try to find that out if I were you."

It *was* Clay. Dear God.

Martin's cousin, whom Julia hadn't seen—or wanted to see—since her wedding six years ago, had wandered out of the nominally furnished parlor and now stood, with his back to her, at the far end of the huge dining room in the rear of the house. Or rather, former dining room, since it was now entirely bare except for the watered silk wall coverings— stained with a ghostly patchwork of dark rectangles—and the window drapes. They couldn't sell those lest the neighbors see inside and realize the shameful extent of their poverty.

Clay had pulled aside both the heavy damask overdraperies and the net curtains beneath to gaze out at the back garden, releasing a glittering maelstrom of dust motes that whirled and spun in the streaming sunshine. Even silhouetted as he was against this blinding haze, he was instantly recognizable: those squared-off shoulders and rangy limbs, that nonchalant, hipshot stance. He had something in one hand that he slapped softly against his leg; Julia couldn't make it out. Birdie sat on the floor next to him, mimicking his contemplative posture.

Clay must have sensed Julia's presence in the hallway, because he turned to look at her. He regarded her in silence for a long moment, during which she wished she could see his expression. Finally, he walked toward her, Birdie bringing up the rear, his footsteps and her claw-clicks echoing in the vacant room. Pausing in the doorway, he inclined his head. "Julia."

She acknowledged his bow with a little nod. As a matron,

she could have properly offered her hand; she didn't. "Mr. Redmond. How good to see you after all these years."

He stepped into the central hall, where she could finally view him clearly. It was something of a shock. The last time she'd seen him, he'd been in white tie and swallowtail, his brown hair well combed and oiled, a sprig of lily of the valley gracing his satin lapel. He'd been twenty then, like the cousin for whom he'd served as best man that day, and a beautiful creature, almost indecently so, with those penetrating blue eyes and too lush mouth. Now . . .

Life must have thrashed him rather mercilessly over the past six years to have weathered him so. The striking contours of his face—sharp-hewn cheekbones, beard-roughened jaw—had been honed to bone and muscle, as if scoured over time by the elements. Years of harsh sunlight had bronzed his skin and gilded that overgrown thatch of hair. And then, there was his attire: navy reefer, baggy hemp trousers, a worn leather cap in his hand. A workingman's costume.

Clay's mild smile was at odds with the intensity of his gaze. "So it's 'Mr. Redmond' now, is it? Why not call me Clay, as you used to? After all, we *are* cousins by marriage."

She had to look away, inexplicably discomfited, as always, by this man she'd known since she was a child, but further rattled by something in his demeanor, a disquieting undercurrent that she couldn't quite get a bead on.

"Here you are," said Aunt Eunice as she joined them, having, as always, refused Julia's offer to help her down the stairs. As for Tommy, Julia had ordered him to confine his field of battle to the nursery until she came to get him. Eunice made a kissing sound at Birdie, who leapt into her embrace. "Touring the damage, are you?" she asked Clay.

Glancing around, he said, "What happened?"

Irked by his nosiness, Julia was searching for an appropriate way to put him off when Eunice said, "It was the Panic of Sixty-one. Our funds were invested in goods being shipped to southern ports, so of course we lost it all when the war broke out. Julia does some tatting and embroidery for a firm that offers fancywork to ladies in predicaments like ours—on a strictly confidential basis, of course."

Clay was looking at Julia as she contemplated the veins in the marble floor.

"Would you like some coffee, Clay?" Eunice offered. "I was just about to put a pot on."

"I'd love some, but I'll make it. I know how."

"You will not! Dr. Phipps says I should keep myself active, and besides, what kind of a hostess lets a gentleman make his own coffee?" She turned and trudged down the hall toward the kitchen, cradling Birdie and muttering, "The very idea."

Ushering Clay into the front parlor, Julia gestured him toward the best of the remaining armchairs. "What brings you to our doorstep after all this time, Mr. Redmond?"

He settled back, legs crossed, his cap on his knee. "I just got into town from Boston and someone told me you were getting married again."

She seated herself across from him, swallowing to ease the tightness in her throat. "You live in Boston now? A beautiful city. I'm quite fond of it."

"As am I. I build ships there."

"Really? I know a little about shipping." It was how she'd

lost all her money. "They tell me Donald McKay builds the finest clipper ships in Boston. I don't suppose you work for him."

He hesitated. "No."

Julia waited for him to offer the name of his employer, but he didn't. She wondered if he was a day laborer, taking whatever odd jobs were available in the shipyards.

As he rasped a hand distractedly over his chin, a shaft of sunlight ignited his scalding blue eyes. Julia shivered when he turned those eyes on her. "I suppose I should congratulate you on making such a lucrative match."

Lucrative? She kept her expression carefully neutral.

"I understand you have a son," he said, a bit too casually.

Julia's fingers tightened on the arms of her chair.

"I heard about it a couple of years ago, when I got back from the war," he said. "You can imagine how surprised I was, given your, uh . . . well, having presumed your . . . maiden condition."

Her heart pounded in her chest; she didn't move.

"Martin and I were as close as brothers," he said softly. "Closer. He told me everything—everything of any importance. Such as the fact that he'd spent his wedding night passed out from drink and wasn't able to . . ." He paused meaningfully.

She looked away, thinking yes, of course. Of course. They'd confided in each other about everything.

Clay said, "He was mortified about that, you know. But mostly sad. Anguished, really. He didn't think he'd ever—" His voice caught in his throat. "It was as if he knew he wouldn't come back. I felt . . ." He shook his head, swearing softly.

Julia stared out the window, willing her eyes to stop stinging, her throat to unclog. How fervently had she anticipated her wedding night. At last, she and Martin would unite their bodies, as they had already united their souls. What on earth had possessed him to drink all that whiskey that night? He'd been a teetotaler, with no tolerance for strong spirits.

The bridal dinner had been served that mild June evening beneath a canopy on Foxton Hall's croquet lawn overlooking the Hudson. When the garland-festooned carriage arrived to transport Julia and her new husband to the inn where they were to spend their wedding night, Martin was nowhere to be found; neither he nor Clay had been seen since the cake was cut.

Martin's choice of his cousin as best man had raised not a few eyebrows among the bluestockings and staid businessmen who dominated his family. Clay's own father led the protest, having disinherited his son for preferring fast sailboats and faster women to the family's iron foundry and a suitable marriage. A firebrand his whole life, Clay had given up on schooling after being kicked out of Andover, Exeter, and Harvard for disciplinary infractions. He and his pious cousin couldn't have been more different, yet they'd been friends and confidants since boyhood.

Martin always insisted that Clay had hidden depths, but Julia suspected that was just wishful thinking. She had to admit, though, that despite his reputation as a charming lothario, Clay had never overstepped himself with her. Indeed, he could be strangely taciturn, but perhaps that was simply a reflection of her own vague uneasiness whenever she was around him. Clay had an aura of raw virility—predacious, carnal—that made the little hairs quiver on the back of her neck. He was the quintessential male animal, bewildering and even a little frightening to an unworldly girl like Julia. She understood nothing about him and everything about her beloved Martin.

Julia, still clad in her organdy wedding gown and orange blossom coronet, had taken it upon herself to find her missing bridegroom. While searching the main academic building, she heard a warble of girlish laughter and muffled male speech from within the library. She opened the heavy oak door, breathing in the comforting redolence of linseed oil and old books—and something else tonight, an unfamiliar muskiness that sent a little buzz of awareness up her spine.

Libby Collier, Julia's pretty blond maid of honor, was sitting on the edge of the mahogany table in the middle of the dimly lit, book-lined room. She had her cage crinoline rucked up amidst a froth of pink tulle, exposing pale thighs and stockinged calves as she leaned over to pull up her drawers. An empty champagne bottle lay on its side next to her.

Libby's squeal of alarm upon seeing Julia dissolved into a flurry of giggles. "It's only you—thank God! No lectures, Julie, please. I love you—I hate it when you're cross with me."

Peering through the gloom, Julia saw him—whoever he was this time—standing in a dusky corner with his back to her, buttoning his trousers. He was in his shirtsleeves, silk braces dangling; tailcoat, vest and top hat tossed on a nearby couch.

Oh, Libby. Rich, sweet-natured, wildly wanton Libby. The

other girls sometimes asked Julia how she could be friends with a person of such low character, Libby's weakness for men, having blinded them to her warmth, her wit, her compassion, insight, loyalty . . . Libby Collier had innumerable sterling qualities. Unfortunately, sexual continence was not among them.

"Have you seen Martin?" Julia asked. "We have to go."

"He's passed out drunk somewhere." Before Julia could voice her incredulity at that, Libby looked toward her companion in the corner, who was shrugging his vest back on, and said, "Clay, where did you say he was?"

Clay? Of course: that height, the striking contrast between those titanic shoulders and lean hips. Without turning around, he lifted his sleek black coat with its knifelike tails, shook it out, and slipped it on. He glanced behind him then, flushed and grim, his gaze seeking out Julia for one brief, taut moment before he quickly looked away. "Out by the tennis courts," he said, his voice strained and a little thick tongued from drink.

Julia stuttered her thanks and fled the room, awash in baffling despondency. Clay and Libby barely knew each other! From out in the hall, she heard Libby erupt into giggles again. "Clay, you darling thing! You're even redder than she is!"

The following December, Libby Collier's mother invited Julia—reeling with grief over Martin—to accompany her and her daughter on extended holiday at a friend's château in the south of France. As their Cunard liner was steaming away from the South Street dock, Libby stunned Julia by confiding the real reason for this trip: she was pregnant. She was sure the father was Clay Redmond, who'd dropped out of sight after the wedding, since he was the first man she'd been with in several months—a rare period of chastity inspired by Julia's advice and example. Even if Clay could be found and coerced into marriage, he was notoriously dissolute and, since his disinheritance, all but penniless—hardly the kind of husband a family like the Colliers considered worthy of their only child.

The plan was for Libby to spend the months preceding the birth far from the prying eyes of New York society, settle the child with some worthy family, and return to her former life with no one the wiser. It would probably have worked out that way had not a stonemason who'd made repairs at the chateau commented to a client in Avignon—and that client's guests, who ran in the Colliers' social circle back in New York—about the two pretty *femmes Américaines* at Château Bartelais outside Aix-en-Provence, one of whom was expecting a child. When asked if he knew the girl's name, he said he thought it might be Collier.

When Libby's father, back in New York, cabled to report on the gossip flying around about Libby, Mrs. Collier and Julia put their heads together and came up with an amendment of the original plan. Rather than let Libby be ruined, Julia would take the baby and raise it as her own, on the pretense that it was her child by Martin. She promised the tearfully grateful Libby that she would keep her secret always—except from Aunt Eunice, in whom Julia had confided about her unconsummated marriage.

Libby gave birth the following March. Even as an infant, the robust baby boy looked indisputably like Clay Redmond. That summer, Julia returned home with little Tommy, while Mrs. Collier escorted her daughter to London for the summer social season. There, Libby met and married—to her mother's breathless delight—the second son of an earl. Julia's first order of business, upon her arrival in New York, was to invite every nabob and knickerbocker of her acquaintance to Trinity Church for the christening of Martin Thomas Hughes. To anyone who would listen, she related how comforting it had been, during her bittersweet confinement, to have the support of her good friend Libby Collier. Thus were the rumors forever silenced.

Clay yanked Julia out of her retrospection by saying, in a chillingly quiet voice, "Martin obviously can't be your son's father. I don't suppose you know who is."

CHAPTER TWO

She stared at him, too outraged to speak.

"Was it someone you'd been seeing on the side all along?" Clay asked. "Or just some street sweeper or lamplighter you fucked once and—"

"*What?* How—My God, how *dare* you speak to me like that?" she demanded, heat searing her face. Despite Clay Redmond's many flaws, she'd never once heard him swear in front of a woman. And to accuse her of . . . of . . . "You are the crudest, most loathsome man I've ever known. How could you *think* to say such things to me?"

"You can still blush?" he asked with a humorless smile. "That must come in handy, but don't think it'll work on me."

"Go to hell, Clay," she said evenly, the first time a vulgar phrase had ever passed her lips.

"Who'd you spread your legs for while Martin was at war, grieving because he never got to make love to you? Did you have a good laugh over that, you and the street sweeper?"

"My *God* . . ."

"Whose little by-blow did you give his name to—*his name, Julia!*—while he was lying in a grave on Hilton Head—"

"Get out." She stood and pointed a trembling finger at the door. "You sicken me. Get out of my house right now."

Clay rose lazily from his chair, but instead of leaving, he stalked toward her; it took all her strength of will to hold her ground. He said, "You know, I can't help but wonder how

Emmett Van Lew would react if he knew you've been passing off some other man's bastard as Martin's son all these years. How well do you know your fiancé, Julia? That man is carved out of ice. I can't imagine he'd be very eager to speak those vows, knowing how little they mean to you."

Her jaw dropped as it dawned on her what Clay was getting at, and why he'd really come here. "My God, you're blackmailing me!" she said through a sputter of incredulous laughter. "Do you think you can get blood from a stone? We've no money, no possessions . . . The bank will have the house within weeks."

He looked bitterly amused for some reason. "You'd pay me off in a heartbeat if you could afford to, though, wouldn't you? Anything to become Mrs. Emmett Van Lew. He's not a young man. If you're lucky, maybe he'll go under, too, and you'll have all that money without having to play the devoted wife, which I frankly doubt you could pull off. One good thing about Martin dying when he did—he never had to face the truth about you. You were probably relieved as hell when they told you he was dead, considering you were about to whelp another man's—"

Julia cracked her palm across Clay's face before she even realized she was doing it. The slap rang through the empty house like a rifle shot; her hand stung. A moment passed where she wondered, with odd dispassion, if he would strike back at her.

Clay, curiously calm, massaged his reddened cheek as he shifted his jaw back and forth. "That was a good one," he said. "Most women don't put enough muscle behind it."

In a voice quaking with restrained emotion, Julia said, "Not that I owe you any explanations, but I don't fancy the idea of your spreading vicious rumors that could end up hurting Tommy. It's true he's not Martin's child, but neither is he mine—not the child of my body, that is. He's most certainly the child of my heart, and he means the world to me."

"Are you saying he's adopted?" Clay asked skeptically. "If so, why this fiction about him being yours and Martin's?"

"You know how the 'right sort' feel about adoption within their ranks. Tommy would never be accepted. As for my . . . maiden condition, it is unfortunately still quite intact, regardless of your disgusting speculation."

He cocked his head. "Unfortunately?"

"I think that's as much explanation as you're entitled to, Mr. Redmond, considering the things you've accused me of and the language with which you've—"

"Oh, for pity's sake," came Eunice's quivering rasp.

Julia turned to find her aunt lurking in the doorway. How the devil did she manage to creep up on people so well with that cane and all that noisy old horsehair crinoline? Birdie jumped down from her mistress's arms to gaze up worshipfully at Clay, tail thump-thump-thumping on the floor.

"Her 'maiden condition' happens to be unfortunate," Eunice told Clay, "because Emmett Van Lew will toss her aside like so much trash when he beds her and realizes she couldn't have possibly have given birth to Tommy. He's already divorced two wives for failing to give him an heir. The only reason he proposed to Julia was because Tommy supposedly proves she's fertile. She's no more to him than one of those precious Arabian brood mares of his."

Clay's mouth twitched. "That might not be so bad. From

what I understand, he has the deepest love and admiration for those mares." To Julia, he said, "Have you considered the possibility that it's Van Lew himself who's infertile?"

"Of course I have. I insisted on a prenuptial agreement that guarantees me a settlement for living expenses and Tommy's education should he divorce me for not producing a child—providing I make a sincere effort for five years."

Clay looked impressed; she wished she didn't find that gratifying.

"You can see why I didn't want to tell you any of this," she said. "I beg you not to let on about Tommy being adopted—for his sake. Not only would it ruin him socially, but we'll be utterly destitute if my marriage to Mr. Van Lew falls through."

"Julia." Eunice clutched her niece's arm with surprising, talonlike strength. "Would you come into the kitchen and help me get the coffee tray set up?"

"Don't trouble yourself," Clay said. "I should really be—"

"You will stay right where you are until I come back, young man!" Eunice commanded as she prodded Julia down the hall.

"Auntie," Julia said as Eunice closed the kitchen door behind them, "what is this—"

"*Tell him.*"

"You can't mean—"

"He's Tommy's father. He deserves to know."

"Oh, you are utterly in his thrall. Have you forgotten what an amoral hound he is?"

"Because he fathered a child out of wedlock? Then I suppose your friend Libby is amoral, as well."

"I can't risk losing guardianship of Tommy to that man—he's no more father material than he is husband material. And have you forgotten that I promised Libby I'd keep her secret forever? It's not only her social standing that's at risk if he starts telling people—there's her marriage as well."

"Will you just think about—?"

"No! There's far too much at stake." Sighing unsteadily, Julia said, "I'm sorry, Auntie, but it would be disastrous. Come—let's show him out and be done with it."

They returned to the entrance hall to find Clay standing at the door, tapping his cap against his leg, his expression sober. He said, "There's something I need you to know, Jul—" A muscle in his jaw flinched. "Mrs. Hughes. I didn't come here to blackmail you, and if I'd wanted to question Tommy's paternity publicly, I would have done so long before this. I only wanted to . . . make you squirm a little, I guess. To punish you for what I thought you'd done to Martin, and for not being what I . . ." He averted his pained gaze. "What I always thought you were. You can't get much more petty, and if it's any comfort to you, I'm ashamed of myself." He tugged his cap on and turned to leave.

Birdie and Eunice both pounced on him as he reached for the doorknob. "Wait!" Eunice said. "I . . ." She glanced nervously at Julia. "I have a rather unorthodox proposal, but one which I believe will be of the utmost . . . Oh, bother. This is a bit awkward. Well." She spread her hands. "I'll just out with it."

Clay picked Birdie up to quell her whining, tucked her into one long arm, and gently rubbed her belly.

"Julia's virginity has obviously become a problem," Eunice

said starchily, "but it's a problem that can easily be rectified. Every man comes equipped with the necessary tool. It's just a matter of finding one who will perform the task capably and discreetly." She fixed her gaze on Clay.

"Oh, no," Julia said in dull, paralytic shock. "No. No."

Clay had paused in his petting to stare at Eunice.

"Why not?" Eunice demanded of her niece.

"You have to *ask*?" Julia was quivering head to toe.

"Here." Eunice wrestled off her magnificent diamond and sapphire ring and offered it to a nonplused Clay. "It's the only thing of value I've got left, but I'm sure you can get a pretty penny for it—it's Cartier. It's yours if you agree to perform this service for us. You appear to be in need of funds. There are worse ways to make a few thousand dollars."

"I don't believe this," Julia murmured dazedly. "That's your *engagement ring*, Aunt Eunice!" It was her aunt's most cherished possession, a memento of a long and loving marriage."

Still cradling the little dog, Clay took the ring. His cap shadowed his eyes, so Julia couldn't be sure, but they seemed to be focused not so much on the glittering bauble as on his own thoughts. His gaze lit on Julia briefly before he returned the ring to Eunice. "Take this back, Mrs. Sumner."

Eunice's face crumpled. Julia closed her eyes, battling competing emotions that didn't bear examination.

Clay said, "You can give it to me . . . afterward."

Julia's eyes flew open.

Eunice clasped her hands together. "You mean you'll do it?"

He stroked Birdie under the chin with his long, oddly

graceful fingers; she went blissfully limp. Looking up, he met Julia's eyes with an expression she couldn't read. "If Mrs. Hughes is agreeable."

"Of course I'm not agreeable!"

"But why not, dear," Eunice asked, "seeing as—"

"Oh, do stop asking me why not! My God, Aunt Eunice, there are a hundred reasons, even if one discounts common decency. Someone might find out, and I'd be ruined. No, *we'd* be ruined. And I could end up like Lib—" Her gaze shot to Clay, watching her intently as he scratched Birdie behind her ears. "I could end up . . . in a family way, couldn't I?"

"There are . . ." Clay returned his gaze to the dog ". . . precautions I can take."

"There!" Eunice said brightly. "You see? It's the ideal solution to our problem."

Julia said, "I hardly consider it 'ideal' to . . . to do what you're suggesting with a man who . . . a man I . . ." *A man who terrifies and intrigues me, a man I shouldn't even think about, much less . . .*

"You don't have to like me," Clay said quietly, misconstruing her meaning. "It isn't required."

"I know how you feel, child," Eunice said, taking both of Julia's hands. "But what choice do you have? Plead with Van Lew for understanding and forgiveness? Sway him with your feminine wiles? Neither of those tactics will work, and you know it. He'll cast you out, everyone will find out why, and then we'll be not only homeless, but disgraced."

"Speaking of Emmett Van Lew," Julia said, "what will he think about me disappearing before the wedding?"

"On the off chance that he even notices—which I doubt,

given how rarely he calls on you—I'll simply tell him you're visiting friends upstate."

Clay was pretending to be absorbed in petting the dog, but he was gazing sightlessly at the floor as he ran his fingers slowly through her fur . . . stroking, scratching. . . . Julia wondered how would it feel to be caressed like that on her own soft, untouched flesh, in those secret places where she'd never even touched herself. Her corset seemed to tighten, squeezing the very breath from her lungs; she felt drunk, needful, reckless. . . .

"Oh, God." She turned and strode several paces away, arms wrapped tightly around her, shaking her head.

Eunice followed after her, cane rap-rap-rapping, skirts crackling. "Do you want to talk about decency, Julia? Is it decent to let Tommy suffer because you're too timid to do what needs to be done to ensure his future? If Van Lew rejects you, the whole world will find that you've been lying about Tommy. Whether he ends up in an almshouse or not, he'll never be accepted. You'll have ruined any chance he ever had for—"

"*All right!*" Julia clapped her hands over her ears, head down, shaking like a rabbit. "All right. No more. I'll do it."

"I knew you'd see reason," Eunice said with a sigh.

Julia turned to find Clay, still standing at the door with his cap on and Birdie in his arms, regarding her with something that might have been compassion—if he were that sort. There was something else in his eyes, too—a quicksilver glint that made her wonder if this would end up being the most excruciating experience of her life . . . or the most ecstatic.

"I'll do it," she told him, "providing, of course, that I can count on your complete discretion . . . afterward."

"Of course."

Setting Birdie down, Clay doffed his cap and held out his hand. She took it, finding it very strong and very warm, the flesh of his palms and fingers as rough as the bark of a tree.

He must have sensed her reaction, because he smiled and said, "Shipwright's hands." The smile faded as he studied her, still gripping her much smaller, too stiff hand. "Are you sure about this? You do understand . . . what's involved."

"She has no idea," Eunice said.

Julia yanked her hand out of his grip. "I have *some* idea."

Eunice snorted. "She thinks the man takes a few seconds out of his day to plant some sort of little seed in the woman's—"

"Aunt Eunice!"

"All I'm saying is, it's not like digging a hole and shoving a tulip bulb in. If it's done right, it's more like . . ." the old woman's tone grew wistful ". . . creating a magnificent, fragrant garden that delights the senses and thrills the soul." Spots of pink bloomed on her softly creased cheeks; she cleared her throat. "Which is to say it can be quite a complicated undertaking, but a most diverting one." She smiled impishly. "Assuming the fellow helping you is a good man with the hoe."

Clay grinned. "I'd forgotten how taken I was with you when I met you at your niece's wedding, Mrs. Sumner. I remember thinking, if only I were a few years older . . ."

"Oh, what a lying dog you are. A splendid trait in a handsome man. Here." Prying a key off the chain around her neck, Eunice handed it to Clay. "You two will need a place to spend some time alone. My friends the Ashfords have an colossal new house they've built out on the south shore of Long Island. They're lovely people, but, well . . ." She lowered her voice and said "nouveau riche" in the same condemnatory tone with which she might have said "Irish." "They're related somehow to the—" again the damning whisper, for it was a family regarded by the Upper Ten as the worst sort of social climbing parvenus "—Vanderbilts. The house is surprisingly tasteful nonetheless, yellow with white trim, on ninety very secluded acres with a private beach. They call it Valhalla."

"How do you happen to have the key?" Clay asked.

"George Ashford has to spend the next year in London on business, so he took the family and staff with him. They closed up the house two weeks ago and told me I could use it any time I like. There are boats at your disposal, and Bellport Village is within walking distance. A gardener is to come on the first and third Friday of the month, so he would have been there yesterday. You'll have the place to yourselves until the wedding."

"That's two weeks from today," Julia said. "Surely it won't take that long to . . ."

"If it's to be done right, it will." Turning to Clay, Eunice said gravely, "I expect more than just a tulip bulb, young man."

He gave her knowing little smile. "That's understood."

CHAPTER THREE

Clay braced his hands on the balustrade that enclosed Valhalla's big second-floor veranda, his pulse quickening as he watched the shabby black brougham circle around to the front of the house. It was the same hired hack that had brought him here from the Bellport railroad station this morning; now, ten hours later, with a sanguine dusk descending, it was bringing Julia.

They had agreed to arrive separately for the sake of appearances; for added discretion, she'd transferred her wedding ring from her right hand to her left and would introduce herself as Mrs. Redmond, should anyone ask.

The hack paused directly beneath him, under an extension of the wraparound porch that formed a porte-cochere over the front entrance. Clay heard the driver step down and open the door; voices; clinking coins; then the snap of reins and the clop of hooves on the flagstone court as the big coach rattled away.

Clay breathed in a lungful of balmy salt air, let it out slowly. "Up here!" he called.

Julia stepped out onto the gravel drive to look up at him, a frayed and bulging carpetbag in one hand, reticule in the other. She looked so compact and tiny, like a perfect little porcelain doll with bisque white skin, raven hair clubbed at the nape, and impossibly huge, syrupy brown eyes. Her bolero-jacketed gray taffeta suit, like the blue dress she'd worn yesterday, was several years out of date, with a bell-shaped skirt, rather than the current back-weighted funnel. An unadorned pillbox hat and black gloves completed her traveling costume. No jewelry, feathers, fans or ribbons; she looked like a woman who was trying to be invisible. She looked scared.

He smiled to set her at ease. "Beautiful, isn't it?" He gestured toward the neatly cropped, sporadically treed lawn that terminated in a white sand beachfront. From the deck around the boathouse, a private dock jutted into placid Bellport Bay. Just visible where the water met the blushing sky was the narrow spit known as Fire Island, and beyond that, the vast Atlantic. A network of creeks surrounded the rest of the property, along with dense woods that extended all the way down to the bay on either side. Julia and Clay were utterly isolated.

She turned and, at last, favored him with a smile—the first he'd seen from her in six years, and it hit him like a quart of whiskey dumped straight into his veins. "It's lovely."

"I'll come down and bring your things up," he offered.

"No, don't bother—it's just this. I'll bring it up."

"Go up the stairs and through the master bedroom at the end of the hall, and you'll wind up here."

Clay lit the candles he'd massed in the middle of a cast-iron table laid out with cheese, bread, summer fruits, and fine local oysters, kept chilled thanks to the Ashfords' well-stocked ice house. He uncorked the bottle of Chateau Petit-Village Pomerol he'd brought with him from the city, smoothed his damp hair, and straightened his leather braces, hoping she wouldn't expect him to don a coat for dinner. It had been a sweltering day, and the heat showed no sign of letting up.

Hearing soft footsteps, he turned and watched through the open French doors as Julia surveyed the master bedroom, an airy haven done up with French and Japanese furnishings in shades of ivory, jade, coral, gold . . . Her gaze lit on the enormous canopied bed, which he'd made up himself with silky-soft, white-embroidered linen sheets, and then on his leather satchel next to it, open and empty.

"I've got a cold supper ready," he called in to her as he poured the wine, "so just set your things down and come on out. You can unpack later. I left the best dresser drawers for you."

She hesitated for a long moment, no doubt digesting the fact that he expected them to sleep in the same room—the same bed—and wondering whether to object. Even married couples often kept separate bedrooms, if they could afford to. To his relief, Julia set down her things and came out onto the veranda. "Mr. Redmond," she greeted him with a little duck of her head.

Swallowing a pinch of disappointment—would she be calling him that when he was inside her?—he bowed. "Mrs. Hughes."

She looked away and then back, a timorous smile flirting with her lips, cheeks prettily flushed—perhaps not entirely from the heat. "You're right, it's silly for us to be so formal. I mean, after all, we're . . ." She averted her gaze again.

We're what? Cousins by marriage? Lovers . . . almost? There was no name for what they were now. No decent name.

He handed her a glass of wine and raised his. "To the fates that brought us together here."

She clicked his glass with hers and raised it to her mouth, stealing a glance at him as she took a sip. "Your hair is wet."

"I've had a bath. Would you care to freshen up before you eat?" he asked, noting the tiny stray ringlets that clung damply to her temples—curlicues sketched in India ink. "There's a little gas furnace in the bathroom for making warm water."

"I'm fine, thank you. Where did this food come from?"

"I took a walk into the village after I got settled here. There's a little market and a bakery and, of course, fishmongers galore." But unfortunately no druggist or any other merchant in the provincial hamlet of Bellport who could sell him a French letter. Clay had left his in Boston, having had so little need of it lately that it never occurred to him to pack it. They were ten cents apiece in every corner shop in Manhattan, but he'd been busy yesterday cabling Boston about his unanticipated two-week absence and had just assumed he'd be able to buy one here.

"This must have cost you quite a bit," she said, tugging her gloves off as he pulled out a chair for her.

He shrugged as he sat. "I'm feeling indulgent."

They ate in near silence, to the gentle slap of waves in the distance and the occasional shriek of a gull. As darkness fell, there arose a chorus of insect chirps and trills.

"I've been having second thoughts."

Clay lowered his wineglass. "I'd be surprised if you hadn't. This is strange for me, too. I mean, granted, I've had more experience with . . ." He glanced through the French doors at the big bed with its down-filled mattress, lotus-patterned throw, and heaps of silken pillows. "But this arrangement is rather singular, to say the least."

"Have you ever been with a . . . a woman who's never—"

"Yes. I've been with virgins. I'll try to make it as good for you as possible. I'll do everything I can not to hurt you."

She stared at him uncomprehendingly.

Shit. Carefully he said, "You do know there's usually some pain the first time, for the woman? When the, um . . . maidenhead is breached. I'll be careful, take it slowly—and the next time or two as well, until your body is used to the, uh . . . to . . . me."

"That must be why Aunt Eunice suggested two weeks."

"That, and there are the finer points of physical intimacy, things that are difficult to describe unless one has experienced them, but which . . . well . . ."

"Yes, of course. Obviously, I mean, the more experience I gain, the better it will serve when the time comes."

For an addle-headed moment, he wasn't sure what she meant.

"My, um, wedding night," she said.

Clay nodded stiffly, absurdly dismayed by this reminder of his purpose. He felt suddenly foolish for the candles and the wine, and the oysters she hadn't even touched because, as it turned out, she'd never been able to stand the sight of them.

"Why don't I clear the table while you unpack?" he suggested, rising. "Then perhaps you'd like a tour of the house."

"This one's obviously a chaise longue," Julia said, taking hold of the sheet in which it was draped.

"Yes, but what color?"

"Red, like the ottoman." She lifted the sheet up and smiled to find an elegant swan chaise upholstered in crimson damask. "Your turn," she said as she lowered the sheet back over the chaise.

They were at the front end of the cavernous triple parlor that took up a good half of Valhalla's ground floor. The three rooms, made one by wide-open pocket doors, had clearly been designed to serve double duty as a ballroom. Julia had a hard time imagining this vast space brightly lit and filled with music and laughter and waltzing couples. With the gas jets down low, the curtains drawn, and all the furniture shrouded in white linen, there was a spectral dreaminess about the place.

"An armchair to match the leather one," Clay guessed as he tugged at another sheet. He grunted in disgust as the chair revealed itself to be crimson, like the chaise and ottoman. Whipping the sheet up, he let it float back down over the chair.

Julia grinned. "That's nine right for me and still just five for you."

He looked different today for some reason, more like the Clay she used to know—younger, with that compelling radiance that had always made him so magnetic to women. Of course, his demeanor was much different than it had been yesterday—thoughtful, almost courtly. But there was something more. . . .

Coming up behind her, he lightly gripped her arms and bent his head to the crook of her neck, his breath sending a hot shiver skittering deep inside her. "You smell so good, but

I can't pin down the scent—warm, not floral but sweet, almost like . . . marzipan?"

"Um, that's almond oil. It's in the skin cream I use after I bathe." This was the first time Clay had touched her since their handshake yesterday—and that had been the first time ever. His hands, warm even through the starched sleeves of her white cotton shirtwaist—at his prompting, she'd left her jacket and hat upstairs—felt unnervingly strong. Clay Redmond was a powerful man, driven by hungers that were utterly foreign to her: the pursuer, the ravisher. What had she been thinking when she'd agreed to this obscene arrangement?

She must have stiffened, because he chafed her arms and said, "I hate it that you're afraid of me."

"I'm not afraid of you," she lied, "but every time I stop to think about what I'm doing here . . ."

"Then don't think about it. Just let it happen. Trust me. Will you trust me?"

She took a deep, unsteady breath and nodded.

"Your turn." He stepped back, releasing her.

"This must be more sculpture," she said, pulling the sheet away from an irregular shape, about eighteen inches high, on a little pedestal table. It was a marble statuette of an embracing couple, both nude except for the man's helmet and shield. "Oh, it's lovely," she said.

"Aphrodite and Ares—the goddess of erotic love and the god of war." He smiled. "She's as petite as you are."

"And he's standing the way you do, with his weight on one hip. And he's tall, like you."

"Yes, well, there's one attribute I'm glad we don't share."

Julia tracked his gaze to the thumblike little appendage between Ares's legs.

"What's wrong with it?" she asked.

"Oh, you *have* been sheltered," he chuckled. "It's minus-
cule. They often are on these classical statues."

"Really?" Such statues had long provided her primary
frame of reference on such matters. "How—how big is it supposed to be?" Too late, when Clay started unbuttoning his
trousers, did she realize her mistake. "Stop that!"

He stilled, the pants half-unbuttoned. "You've obviously
never seen a man unclothed. Don't you think it's about time?"

"No!"

He gave her a bemused little smile and tempered his voice.
"Then what are we doing here, Julia?"

"Yes, I know, I just . . ." She lowered her burning face into
her hands. "Oh, God."

"The human body is the most beautiful thing in the world,"
Clay said, "but we hide it under all this armor, as if it were
not only shameful but frightening. I think you're more ter-
rified of seeing me naked than of taking me inside you."

It was the first time either one of them had so frankly
voiced their purpose in being here, and it took Julia aback.

"Let's just do this," he said, pulling down his braces. "Let's
take off our clothes—both of us. You're so beautiful, Julia.
I'm dying to see you without all those layers."

"I'm just . . . I'm not sure I'm ready."

"I'm not planning to take things that far tonight. But I
would like to start . . . easing us into things. Come on, sweetheart," he inveigled. "You said you trusted me."

Sweetheart. Julia wished her chest didn't clench at that.

Aunt Eunice was right; she *was* a silly little goose.

"I've got an idea," Clay said. "We can keep playing our little guessing game, but just make it more interesting. For every wrong guess one of us makes, that person has to shed an item of clothing. We play until both of us are naked or all the furniture's been uncovered."

"All the furniture in all three parlors?" Julia asked.

"That's right, but it's really not as much as it looks like, and you're good at this—you've been winning."

"If we get through all of it, and I'm not naked yet . . ." she wheedled, thinking of her complex strata of underclothing.

"Then you don't have to *get* naked," he said. "But assuming you do, there won't be any headlong dash from the room. You've got to stay right here after the last item comes off."

"For how long?"

With a cocksure grin, he said, "Till I've looked my fill."

She buried her face in her hands again, groaning in defeat. "I loathe you."

"I know. All right, whose turn is it?"

"Yours."

Clay uncovered a Hepplewhite console table that wasn't marble topped, as he'd thought, and kicked off his shoes; "Pairs count as one," he decreed. Julia's own shoes came off next, when she wrongly guessed that a Turkish-tufted, gold velvet settee would match the crimson armchair. However, for her next seven turns, she correctly predicted that the furniture grouped near the settee would go with it. Clay, meanwhile, lost his socks, trousers, and shirt—to her surprise, he wore no undershirt—leaving him in nothing but his drawers.

She was *not* surprised to see that he had the well-honed,

hard-packed body of a man who labored for a living. His muscles looked as if they'd been chiseled out of stone by a sculptor who'd gotten carried away and carved them just a little too deeply, etched in a few too many veins and cords and striations. The pronounced inward scoop of his torso enhanced the impression, despite his leanness, of explosive strength waiting to uncoil.

Maddeningly relaxed, he propped his hands on his slim hips, clad only in thin muslin drawers that hung low enough to expose a pair of sinewy hipbones and a too-intriguing fringe of dark hair. Julia looked away from the shadowy bulge beneath the muslin as she endeavored to prepare herself mentally for his—and her—complete and mortifying nudity.

Clay won his next three turns, while Julia lost hers. Off came her stockings, skirt, and petticoat. She felt absurd wearing nothing on her bottom half but knee-length drawers and a spring steel crinoline, but at least she was still covered up.

Finally, the moment came that Julia had been dreading—or rather, the first of the two she had been dreading. Clay guessed wrong about an ivory brocade chaise longue and, with perfect nonchalance, unbuttoned and kicked away his drawers.

Julia, of course, compounded her embarrassment by wheeling around and hiding her face, but not before an image of his private parts—*much* larger than Ares's and protruding from a mat of thick black hair—was indelibly seared on her mind's eye. "You think I'm an absolute ninny," she moaned.

"Turn around, Julia," he said, with only a hint of amusement. "It's not going to leap out and attack you."

She forced herself to lower her hands and turn, staring

fixedly at his face. "I *have* told you I loathe you."

"It's understood." He smiled. "They're all your turns now."

It took two more guesses for the crinoline to come off, three for her to lose the shirtwaist, and another three to shed the short-sleeved, prettily tucked petticoat bodice that covered her corset. She unbuttoned it with clumsy fingers, abashed at the prospect of a man seeing her in her stays and shimmy.

Clay just folded his arms and smiled. "Go on." To her dismay, the organ between his legs looked even longer and thicker than before; must be her nerves playing tricks on her.

So far, she'd worked her way through the front and middle parlors and halfway through the last, leaving only a dozen or so items to be uncovered. She guessed six in a row correctly; Clay did not look happy. The seventh, however—a stuffed hawk in a glass dome, which she'd taken for a bird cage—put an anticipatory smile back on his face. He watched with undisguised interest as Julia fumbled with the hooks and loops of the steel busk that fastened her corset in front.

"Need any help with that?" he asked.

"You stay right where you are." The busk parted; she grudgingly peeled it away, leaving herself in her all-too-thin chemise and loose drawers. The blessed relief she usually felt upon freeing herself from the unforgiving corset was absent this evening. Thankfully, the shimmy, which she'd stuffed into the drawers today, fell to midcalf when untucked; it would give her a few minutes of modesty toward the end— which might not even come, if she could manage more right guesses than wrong.

Five items left. Julia picked a rounded lump on a sideboard

that had to be another ancient marble bust; it turned out to be a Chinese cloisonné jar filled with rose petals. She took a deep breath, reached behind her, and untied her drawers, taking care, as she lowered them, to tug down her shimmy as she went.

Clay's gaze seemed to penetrate right through the bleached linen, which, in certain lights, could be nearly transparent. It would be all the more so tonight, given that it was damp with perspiration, clinging indecently to her breasts and hips. What was he seeing that sparked that dark glitter in his eyes, that speeded the rise and fall of his chest, and—

Dear God, it *had* grown, his masculine organ, distending to such an extent as to propel it slightly outward—a phenomenon she noted with more than a little dread. What *had* she gotten herself into?

"Four more to go," Clay said, his voice curiously gruff.

Licking her dry lips, Julia surveyed the remaining items and chose the most obvious. "It's a grand piano." It was: a beautiful, glossily lacquered new Steinway.

"Three left."

She took her time, but finally chose. "A candelabra."

He frowned when she whipped the sheet aside and saw that she'd been right. Unless she was mistaken, his manly part had lost a certain measure of bluster as well. "Two more."

She said, "This has to a bookcase." It was a glass-shelved étagère filled with Oriental curios. *No!*

Clay grinned and gestured toward her, as if to say, *Any time you're ready.*

CHAPTER FOUR

Julia's hands quaked as she gathered up the rumpled linen, scouring her desperate mind for a way out of this. But the shimmy was all she had on, unless one counted . . .

Why not? she thought as she raised her hands to her hair and unpinned the chenille net snood in which it was clubbed. He would taunt her, accuse her—quite rightly—of clutching at straws, but the ensuing debate would delay her fate by a few minutes, at least, and, right now, she'd take it.

Julia whipped off the snood, shook out her hair, and gave Clay a big, self-satisfied smile. She'd expected him to smirk, accuse her of trying to dupe him, demand the immediate removal of the shimmy. Instead, he studied her for a long, rapt moment, hands on cocked hips, gaze lingering on the black serpentine tendrils that cloaked her to the waist.

"I've never seen your hair down before," he said quietly. "It's beautiful."

She just looked at him, her smile dissipating.

He rubbed his chin, looking thoughtful, perhaps faintly amused . . . and something else, harder to define. "All right. You've got one last turn."

He was letting her get away with it? Julia could hardly believe her good fortune. Biting her bottom lip, she spun to face the last sheet-draped item: a perplexingly shaped form about her height. If she guessed this one right, she would walk away from this little game without having to strip down completely—a prospect that grew ever more harrowing as it approached. Was it another statue? A floor lamp? She studied its contours, sorting through the possibilities. . . .

"Are you hoping if you take long enough, I'll call it quits?" Clay asked. "If so, you have seriously underestimated my desire to see you naked." He folded his arms. "You've got five seconds before I rip that chemise right off your—"

"It's an easel," she said. "With a picture on it." She tore away the sheet, yelping in unladylike delight to find a small seascape propped on an ornate brass easel.

Clay opened his mouth in surprise, then closed it, his jaw rigid, his eyes—those keenly expressive eyes—betraying for the most fleeting moment the depth of his disappointment. Squaring his shoulders, he gave her a smile that didn't look forced but probably was. "Well done, Julia." He bent to scoop his drawers off the floor. "I hope you're up to a rematch tomorrow."

She'd won—in a manner of speaking. If he hadn't let her use her next-to-last turn to take off that snood, he would be reveling in his victory right now. He wasn't even going to mention her cowardly little ruse, though, much less shame her with it. Like all men of his class—his former class—he had been reared to be gracious in defeat. Possibly, too, he was motivated as much by mercy as by good sportsmanship; he knew how she dreaded the idea of standing naked before him. For whatever reason, he was letting her wriggle ignominiously out of losing.

He pulled on his drawers. "I'll help collect your things."

"Turn around."

He looked up, stilling when he saw her raising her chemise.

She paused with it gathered up to mid-thigh. "It's silly, I know, but I just don't want you looking at me while I . . . If you could just turn around for a minute . . ."

He did. He had a beautiful back, elegantly shaped and layered with muscle. "You don't have to do this, Julia."

"Stop talking and let me concentrate." She squeezed her eyes closed, counted to three, and yanked the shimmy off over her head. "Oh, God," she breathed, clutching it in front of her with quaking hands. Chills coursed through her, despite the heat.

"Is it off?" he asked.

She balled up the scrap of linen and tossed it at his feet. Evidently viewing this as a tacit invitation, he started turning around before she'd worked up the nerve to tell him to.

"No!" Julia dove beneath the piano, concealing herself behind its protective sheet, which hung all the way around to the floor. She crouched in the low, penumbral nook, the Turkish-patterned Savonnerie rug softly scratchy beneath her. Her heart was pounding and her face steaming. *Idiot! Idiot!*

About half a minute passed, and then she heard his voice, low and concerned, right outside the sheet. "Julia?"

"This whole thing was a terrible, terrible idea," she said, quivering on the verge of tears. "If I can't bear to let you see me naked, how could I ever let you . . . let you . . ."

"I'm coming in." The sheet started to rise.

"No!" She turned to scramble out the other side, but he was on her in a heartbeat, hauling her back against him with one long, determined arm. He held her tight, her naked back against his barely clothed front—all hard, unyielding muscle—as she struggled and squirmed.

"Stop this," he said so softly, so tenderly, that she obeyed him with a plaintive little mew of surrender.

Levering himself over her, he smoothed the hair off her face, cupped her cheek with his work-roughened hand. Her most private areas shielded by her hair and hands, she gazed up at him. He was luminous in the darksome, little lair: the lustrous skin, the radiant eyes. Why did he look so different?

"You ridiculous little thing," he murmured. "Don't you know how beautiful you are?" He brushed his thumb over her lips and dipped his head, his gaze on her mouth.

Julia wrested her head to the side, aborting the kiss. "No, Clay. No pretending—please." For him to deflower her in exchange for payment was one thing. To feign an intimacy of the heart while doing so . . . that would be more than she could tolerate. Meeting his eyes, she said, "This will all be so much easier for me if we keep it. . . ."

Clay nodded, not looking at her, his jaw set. No kissing; he understood, but he didn't like it. Was it that he was used to taking the reins during lovemaking and doing as he pleased, or was there more to it? Letting her go, he spun away to lie on his back, clawing the sweat-dampened hair out of his eyes.

She turned away from him and curled up on her side, blanketed by her hair and the comforting semidarkness. The air was hot and still in this intimate little niche. Julia breathed in a potpourri of new wool, clean sweat, and the piano's distinctive, almost sugary, rock maple tang.

"I hate being so *ignorant*," she said, puncturing the cumbersome silence. "I know so little that I don't even know how little I know. What I mean is—"

"I know what you mean."

"Aunt Eunice thought it was funny, what I said about . . . planting the seed." She looked over her shoulder at Clay, seemingly absorbed in the underside of the piano. "Why?"

He glanced at her, looked away. "They call it a man's seed, but it's not like a seed you plant in the garden."

"What is it like?"

"It's a fluid," he said, "somewhat like cream. It gathers in the . . ." He hesitated. "Here, turn around and I'll show you." Lifting his hips, he slid off his drawers.

"No," she said resolutely, facing away from him.

"You're braver than this," he said quietly.

Oh, God. Oh, God. "Close your eyes and I'll turn around."

A pause. "All right." If he was amused, he was careful to allow no trace of it in his voice.

Julia turned. Thanks to her small stature, there was just enough room to sit upright, legs curled beneath her. Clay was naked again, but she was, by now, more or less accustomed to that. Astounding how quickly one can get used to the most outrageous situation if there's enough at stake. His eyes were closed, so he couldn't see *her*; that was the important thing.

"Give me your hand," he said, reaching out blindly.

She hesitated, surmising what he had in mind.

"Give me your hand, or I'm opening my eyes right now." She gave it to him.

"It gathers here—" Clay cupped her left hand around a weighty pouch at the base of his instrument "—and comes out through here." He pressed her right hand to the shaft lying against his thigh. Its florid tip, shielded by a hood of skin, had a tiny, slit-like hole in it.

Julia swallowed hard, scarcely believing that she was touching him this way, in these places. His parts felt hot and heavy and vital. She kept her hands still, fighting the urge to jerk them away. "This, um, creamy seed," she said, "it just . . . what? Sort of drips out, or . . . ?"

He fell silent for a moment; she heard him breathing. "I can show you."

She fell silent then. Her heart thundered in her ears. He drew her fingers up his shaft in a featherlight caress. "Your hand is so small and cool. It feels . . ." he smiled ". . . even better than I'd imagined."

"What's happening to it?" she asked as the object of her scrutiny twitched and began to expand.

"Stimulation makes a man erect. He can't enter a woman otherwise. Here." He fisted her hand around him and urged it up and down in a slow but firm milking motion. "You can apply more pressure as it increases in size."

The organ seemed to come to life, rising out of its nest of hair to jut sharply upward, startling Julia. She'd realized it must get hard to perform its generative function; she just hadn't realized that it got *large* and hard. At least . . . not *this* large.

He released her hand; she hesitated, then continued stroking him, driven not just by curiosity but by something else, something that caused her breath to quicken along with the pattering of her heart. Clay lay perfectly still, his eyes still closed, although his chest rose and fell like a bellows. One hand gripped his crumpled drawers, the other a fistful of Julia's hair, bands of muscle in sharp relief on his forearms. He looked oddly vulnerable, as if he were straining against certain defeat at some Herculean labor, his body gleaming with sweat, his breath coming faster, faster. . . .

I did this to him, she thought, with a measure of awe and feminine pride. It was virginal little Julia Hughes to whom this powerful, strapping man was yielding in helpless need. That knowledge made her body hum with a kind of quivering heat that pooled deep in her lower belly. Her skin felt tight, her breasts heavy; every silken brush of her hair across her nipples made them tingle.

His body, and what was happening to it, fascinated her. Veins snaked along the shaft as it swelled and stiffened, feeling very much like marble sheathed in satin—except that marble was cool, and the flesh in Julia's hand fairly pulsed with heat. The little hood at the tip had drawn back, revealing a crown like a plum bursting ripe and ready.

This thing is too big, she thought—far too big to fit in her smallish body. A little tremor of fear scuttled through her as she recalled what he'd said about hurting her.

From the little hole on the tip there leaked a kind of sap that dripped onto the taut ridges of his belly. "Is that the seed?" she asked.

"No," he said hoarsely and cleared his throat. "That's just something that makes it easier to push into a woman and deposit the seed. Here . . ." He slid her fingertips over the syrupy emission, then down along his straining flesh. "You can sort of oil me with it. Yes . . . like that," he sighed as her slickened hand squeezed and pulled. "Oh, God, Julia."

He thrust into her fist, his ropy flanks quivering, his head thrown back. Sweat sheened him from head to toe, highlighting his taut and bulging muscles. The sac in her left hand, having also swollen somewhat, now tightened and drew up.

He arched his back, panting. Even in this dim light, she could see dark color flood his face. "Oh, God . . ."

"Are you all right?" she asked, letting go of him. "Am I hurting—"

"God, don't!" he gasped, seizing her hand. "Don't stop." He crushed her fist around him, squeezing so hard it hurt, and punched into it. "Don't—"

He shuddered, a strangled groan grinding out of his throat. The shaft in her hand jerked like a live thing as milky fluid shot from it, spattering Julia's hand and his chest. She flinched but kept stroking through another violent discharge, and another, and yet another. . . . With every hot spurt, there came another low, feral growl from Clay.

The emissions lessened in intensity and finally ceased; his trembling eased. The air sighed from his lungs as his body settled, damp and spent, onto the rug. Sweat beaded his upper lip, trickled in rivulets down his face and chest.

Clay opened his eyes and raised his heavy-lidded gaze to Julia's face. His smile was so dreamy, so disarmingly sweet, that she didn't even much care anymore about being naked with him here in this too-intimate little space; didn't even care about having done . . . whatever it was she'd just done to him.

"Here." Using his wadded-up drawers, he cleaned the still-hot seed first off her hand and then off his chest and belly.

He stroked her arm softly. "Let me do that for you, Julia—what you did just now for me."

She blinked in confusion. "How can you? I don't have a . . ." Her gaze lit on his now-quiescent member.

"Have you never climaxed?"

Climaxed?

He said, "You can, you know. It's different for women—they don't emit semen—but your body is made to reach a sexual crisis, just like a man's."

The word "crisis" gave her pause. "What happens?" she asked warily. "What does it feel like?"

"There's a kind of . . . mounting pleasure that's incredibly intoxicating. You'll feel the urge to push, as if you were joined with someone, even if you aren't. Women grow wet as the pleasure rises, and when it crests, it sort of . . . rolls through you like thunder, exploding over and over from within you. That part is almost impossible to describe."

Julia remembered how Clay had looked in the moments before he climaxed—the way he'd panted and groaned and shuddered, almost as if he'd been convulsing in agony. Pleasure didn't look like that—no pleasure she'd ever experienced, anyway.

Exploding over and over from within you . . . She tried to imagine it, and couldn't.

He rose on an elbow, caressed her face. "Lie down, Julia. On your back."

She hesitated, tempted to bolt from beneath this piano, grab her clothes, find a room that locked, and be done with this madness.

"Be brave," he quietly urged.

She lay on her back, part of her cringing at her nakedness, another part—some wanton side of her she'd never explored until now—finding it strangely exciting. Her lungs seemed to be working overtime, yet still she felt light-headed.

"Close your eyes. Feel my hand and nothing else." He brushed the hair out of her eyes and off her body, his callused fingertips raising prickles of sensation everywhere they touched. Her heart skittered as he molded her small breasts with a curious but gingerly touch, as if he were afraid of alarming her. "You're so soft here," he whispered. "You're soft everywhere. I can't wait to be inside you."

His fingers brushed her nipples, igniting currents of pleasure that crackled through her belly to the aching emptiness inside her. He followed that path with his hand, smoothing it downward until it rested on the fleecy patch between her legs; she throbbed at his touch. Her hands curled into fists, nails incising her palms, as she willed herself to lie still. "You're doing very well," he praised. "Open your legs just a bit . . . a little more."

She felt him part the tangled hairs at the seam of her sex, slowly and deliberately—an exquisite tugging and tickling that made her feel starved for air. Then came the whispery brush of a fingertip along the cleft itself, and another, and another . . . again and again, her flesh swelling and yawning as all her senses rushed there, her breath coming faster, a strange restlessness invading her hips, urging them upward. . . .

She sucked in a breath at his first probing foray into the liquid-hot, shockingly tender flesh within the cleft. "Easy," he breathed as he stroked the damp petals and the valleys between, rubbing, teasing. . . . "Easy."

His searching fingers found a knot of sensation so acutely sensitive that she jumped when he touched it, crying out for him to stop. "It's all right," he soothed. "It's all right. I'll be careful."

Her breath came in shuddery rasps as he continued the intimate caress, his fingers deft and quick, then agonizingly slow, massaging, inflaming, circling the turgid little knot and backing off . . . pushing inside her in a careful exploration, but not too far.

"Something's happening," she gasped as a strange, quivery charge gathered up in her limbs. "It feels . . ." As if she were going to fly apart. "I don't think it's supposed to feel like this." She tried to wrench his arm away with both trembling hands, but he captured them and held them tight.

"Shh, it's all right," he murmured in her ear. "It's all right. You'll see. Let it come."

"Oh, God," she moaned as the charge sizzled up her legs to her hips, which arched as if pulled by a string. . . .

"That's right. . . ."

Don't move, she thought, legs rigid, heart ramming painfully. *Don't move and it can't happen.* . . .

But then he stroked that little knot and pressed two fingers into her, and—

A sob tore from her lungs at the first sharp spasm.

"Oh, sweetheart, yes," Clay said breathlessly as she convulsed with pleasure, her body contracting around his fingers as if trying to draw him in. He said more things as she bucked, but the roar of blood filled her ears, and she couldn't hear him.

He gathered her up as the last tremor coursed through her,

stroking her hair and her sweat-slicked back as he murmured a comforting litany of praise and endearments. She was shaking; so was he. And he was hard again; she felt it against her belly, a warm, smooth pressure that incited, astoundingly, another little clench of the damp flesh between her legs.

"Do you want me to . . . touch you again?" she asked shyly.

She felt him smile against her hair, then shake his head. "It's not so bad to be left wanting a bit more. That way, the next time will be all the better. But I'm very gratified that you asked."

He nuzzled her, his chin only vaguely coarse against the tender skin of her temple and forehead, not prickly with beard stubble, as it had been yesterday. Drawing back from him a bit to confirm it with her eyes, she said, "That's why you look different. You shaved."

He folded her back into his embrace, his big shoulders twitching in a shrug that didn't seem as nonchalant as he probably meant it to. "I thought I'd be kissing you."

CHAPTER FIVE

"*Your husband* won't be faithful to you," warned Clay as he stood in the sun-washed bathroom scraping a razor over the final remnants of his morning stubble. He probably shouldn't bother, given her disinclination to kiss him . . . but he could always hope, couldn't he?

Julia, reclining up to her neck in a fragrant bubble bath, frowned but didn't look at him, clearly discomfited—despite yesterday evening's interlude beneath the piano—by the fact that he was naked and standing right next to her. He hadn't objected when she chose to wear a nightgown to bed last night, accepting that she'd reached a threshold of physical intimacy—for now. The safer she felt with him, the more receptive and comfortable she would be when he took her maidenhead—hopefully tonight, in that big, cozy feather bed, with the darkness helping to ease her out of any lingering inhibitions. Still, he was loath to humor her too much, lest he lose valuable, hard-won ground; hence his decision to barge in on her naked during her morning bath, an invasion she'd accepted without too much fuss.

"Emmett Van Lew is known to have a taste for . . . certain kinds of women," Clay said as he inspected his reflection in the mirror over the sink, rubbing his shaven lower face critically. "He has a reputation for frequenting the most notorious brothels in the city, regardless of his marital state."

"I've never quite understood the appeal of brothels for

married men," Julia said as she adjusted one of the pins securing her hair in a beguilingly unkempt topknot, seeming strangely unperturbed by this revelation. "What do they seek at those places that they can't get at home?"

Clay carefully wiped his razor on a towel. "At establishments such as the ones your fiancé prefers, well, let's just say a man's greenbacks will buy him anything he can imagine, and a few things he probably couldn't. But even the more conventional brothels flourish partly on the patronage of married men. There are certain acts that men simply don't like to ask of their wives—although perhaps they should."

"What acts?" she asked, leaning forward to scrub a sea sponge over a delicate foot.

"Acts of pleasure other than traditional intercourse."

"Like what we did last night?"

"No. Well, yes," he amended as he covered his milk glass shaving mug and rinsed out his badger brush. "But there are many other more . . . unorthodox routes to sexual release."

"Such as . . . ?"

Clay grinned slowly as he splashed water on his face, charmed by her childlike curiosity, such a refreshing reversal of her former diffidence. "Shall I demonstrate?" Without warning, he stepped into the ornately tiled tub.

"Clay! Oh, my God!" she giggled as he lowered himself into the steaming water behind her. Tucking her between his updrawn legs, he pulled her against his chest and lay back, luxuriating in her wet, warm, impossibly soft little body.

"I'll just describe them to you if you prefer," he said, urging her head back onto his shoulder so he could rub his clean-shaven face against hers. "And you can tell me which ones incite more curiosity in you than disgust."

"Disgust?"

"You have no idea, the tastes some men develop. Then, too, there are practices that repulse the uninitiated, but which can actually be rather . . ."

She craned her neck to look at him.

"Yes. Well. Where shall I begin?"

"Perhaps with the least distasteful acts," she suggested, settling back against him.

He nodded, suddenly not so sure this was a good idea. She *was* a virgin, after all, and a remarkably naïve one, to boot. But she seemed eager for tutelage, and she felt so good pressed up against him—particularly against his cock, snugged half-erect between the two cheeks of her firm little derrière.

"Let's start with the mouth, then," he said, skimming his hands lightly up her soapy, wet body—taut thighs, flat belly, high, resilient little breasts. "Lips, tongues, even teeth, can be incredibly stimulating on . . . certain parts of the body."

"You can't mean . . . *ugh!* That's the *least* distasteful?"

"To some. It's safe to say there's no part of the human body that hasn't been pressed into service for sexual gratification, and every man has his preferences. Some, if their lover is generously endowed, like to take their pleasure between her breasts." He molded Julia's breasts and thumbed the erect, darkly flushed nipples, making her breath come a little faster.

"Really?" she said, sounding more intrigued than disgusted. "Where—where else might a man . . ."

"Any place on a woman's body that can be penetrated. Here, for instance." Reaching between them, he slid a finger between the cleft of her bottom and his rigid shaft, until it met the tiny portal there.

She flinched. "That . . . that's utterly unnatural!"

"What sickens one person intrigues the next." He glided one hand beneath the water to the juncture of Julia's thighs while lightly squeezing her breasts with the other. "There are those whose tastes run to orgies."

"I've heard that word, but I'm not sure what it means."

"Sexual relations among a group. Two men might make love, or two women."

She digested that for a moment. "How is that possible?"

He shrugged. "By being creative. I've seen a woman use a—" He bit off the rest of it. What was he thinking?

"You've seen a woman use what?"

He sighed. "A sort of . . . well, it was a two-pronged ivory phallus, and she, um . . . was thrusting it into another woman while pleasuring her with her mouth." The memory made his erection throb.

Julia turned to gape at him. "What . . . In what situation would you possibly have witnessed—"

"I've done things, Julia. Many things. Not everything I'm describing to you, certainly, but . . . I've been with two women."

"When?"

"Once or twice . . . A few times. Shall I go on, or—"

"By all means. I can scarcely believe my ignorance!"

"You probably don't want to know about the whipping and spanking," he said, gently fondling her between her legs.

"Oh, my God."

He was glad she couldn't see him smile. "Or the tying up and gagging." He tightened his hips, pressing into her cleft as he probed between her legs. She was wet from being underwater, but there was a different wetness in her feminine slit—the slippery evidence of her arousal. "Or the various instruments and devices," he continued devilishly. "The slave auctions. The men who wear women's corsets. The leather masks and collars . . ."

"I don't want to hear anymore," she said breathlessly.

"I don't want to talk anymore." He explored her slick recesses with one hand as he caressed her breasts with the other, all the while thrusting against her, his cock sliding between the warm, perfect little peach halves of her bottom. Soapy water spewed in waves over the side of the tub, and their breath came fast and harsh . . .

It didn't take long—not for him, at least. He came hard, crying out in full-throated relief as she writhed against him, caught up in her own sensual delirium.

Gripping her around the waist with still-shaky hands, he rasped, "Turn around. Here—like this." He positioned her swiftly, lifting and turning her so that she was kneeling astride him, her sweet little quim an inch from his face.

"What are you . . . Clay? I don't think . . . Oh!"

He kissed her as he would have kissed her mouth, had she granted him that privilege, with purposeful lips and a gently probing tongue. The first tentative flick galvanized her. She clutched his shoulders as he explored her ever more deeply, her fingers digging into the muscles there, her hips trembling.

"Clay . . . oh, God."

He suckled her clit hungrily, using his busy tongue to enhance the sensation as he savored the soapy sweet, musky hot taste of her. He'd always loved doing this, could never get enough of it. It was like making a rosebud bloom just by kissing it; the more finesse one employed, the more luxuriant the final flowering. To be doing this to Julia, to feel her come apart like this and know it was his doing . . . Nothing in his twenty-six years had ever given him such savage gratification.

Julia groaned helplessly, pressing herself against his mouth. He gripped her hips to hold her still as she shuddered.

Her cry of release undid him; desire ambushed him with stunning force, considering he'd just spent himself, and most thoroughly. Never before had arousal revisited him so swiftly.

He gentled the ministrations of his tongue as she shuddered down to earth, breathing in the heady perfume of her arousal, nature's most potent aphrodisiac.

"God, you are something," he whispered, rubbing his face against her belly, his heart hammering. "You're killing me."

She combed his hair out of his eyes with unsteady fingers. "That was . . ."

He looked up.

She looked away, flushing hotly. ". . . actually rather nice."

He couldn't help chuckling. "I'm glad. Here." He lifted her easily. "Stand up. I'll rinse you off."

His waning erection seemed to fascinate her, which only made it spring back to life again. "Does it hurt?" she asked. "It looks as if it would hurt."

"Not usually." He adjusted the temperature of the water streaming from the spigot. "Only when one is forced to go too long without release."

Little furrows formed between her ink-stroke eyebrows. "I suppose it's considered poor form not to . . . reciprocate when someone has . . . done what you just did to me."

Clay smiled while filling a little Japanese wooden hand basin with water, touched both by her good manners and her trepidation at the prospect of fellating him. "One of the many wonderful things about lovemaking," he assured her as he poured the steaming water over her, "is that there are almost no real rules—and the few that do exist are so much fun to break. Put one foot up here on the side of the tub—that's right."

Julia braced her hands on Clay's shoulders as he rinsed between her legs, pleased that she didn't balk at the intimacy of it. "Don't worry, Julia. This—" he nodded toward his vexingly indefatigable member "—will most likely go away on its own. I'd rather wait until tonight for anything more, than ask you to do something you aren't ready to do. I want to make you embrace lovemaking, not dread it."

"So far," she said with a winsome little smile as he helped her from the tub, "I'd say you're doing a workmanlike job."

Clay's heart heaved against his chest wall as if trying to get out. God, how he ached to kiss her.

Settling back down in the water, he filled the basin, poured it over his head and grabbed the Castille soap. He washed up while Julia—delightfully unselfconscious about her nudity, considering her shyness last night—smoothed cream from a little cobalt blue Caswell & Hazard jar onto her face, throat, and arms. They talked about their plans for the day and settled on sailing, then Julia retired to the bedroom to get dressed.

"None of that blasted crinoline!" he called to her through the bathroom door after she'd closed it behind her. "No room for it on the bloody boat," he muttered, reaching forward to yank out the tub stopper, which he set on the sink next to Julia's face cream. She'd left it open. Clay scooped up a buttery dollop and rubbed it between his fingers, testing its lubricity. He brought his hand to his nose and inhaled the distinctive, almond-infused, soul-stirring perfume of Julia's skin.

Arousal surged through his veins like lava—and just when he'd finally started going limp again.

Clay shook his head resignedly. It was one thing to be left wanting a little more. It was another to spend an entire day in an agony of tumescence.

The frothy water had lowered to expose his erection. He brushed a cream-slicked fingertip over it, sucking in his breath as it flinched. It felt like red-hot steel, the skin stretched thin over flesh engorged to the bursting point.

Closing his eyes, he rammed into his greased fist and thought of Julia as she'd been only moments before, her hips trembling in his hands as she moaned and bucked. . . .

He ejaculated in seconds, one hand clutching the rim of the tub, the other pumping faster, faster, breath held tight in his chest, teeth clenched to keep from groaning, oh God yes, yes—

He gasped when he came in fierce, spasmodic arcs the length of the bathtub. *Yes…yes…yes…!*

Clay sank back in the almost empty tub, trembling as he

wrung the last of it out of him. Closing his eyes, he strove to steady his breathing, slow his heart, clear his mind. A raspy, unamused chuckle rose from his chest.

Oh, he was in trouble. Terrible, terrible trouble.

CHAPTER SIX

"*There's something* I've always wondered about women," Clay said as he gazed into the sputtering fire he'd built on their secluded stretch of beach when it had started getting dark.

Julia nearly choked on her chocolate truffle. "You mean there's actually something Clay Redmond doesn't know about women?"

"Insolent wench." Clay butted her lightly with his shoulder, causing the blanket tucked around them to slip. He righted it, wrapping his arm around her as he did so. She went boneless in his embrace, imprinting in her memory—so that she could relive it when he was gone and she was Mrs. Emmett Van Lew—the feel of his long, hard-muscled arm around her; the way he smelled of laundry starch underscored by something else, something warm and male that made her senses swim; and the way he looked at her when he thought she didn't notice.

Emmett Van Lew would never look at her like that. He would never have Clay Redmond's youthful luster, his passion, his sweet, heartbreaking solicitude. He would never coax her slowly to paroxysms of bliss, or take her sailing, or spend an hour collecting driftwood for a fire on the beach so that they could sit together beneath the stars, sharing a box of chocolate truffles and listening to the *hush...hush...hush* of the waves. It was Clay's way, she knew, of putting her in a tranquil state of mind before the deflowering that would occur, by tacit agreement, when they retired to that big, silken bed tonight.

No, her future husband would never give her a fraction of what Clay had given her just in the past twenty-four hours. But by marrying Julia, Emmett Van Lew would protect Tommy—the child she would sacrifice anything for, die for—from the living hell of Blackwell's Island. Tommy would grow up in a mansion on Fifth Avenue, have the best of everything, a future filled with promise. Tommy, whom she considered as much her son as if she had birthed him herself . . .

But you didn't, came the unbidden voice that had kept her awake for hours last night with Clay lying next to her, looking so boyish as he slept, so golden and guileless. *Libby Collier birthed Tommy,* the voice said. *He isn't your son at all.*

He's Clay's.

"You're shivering," Clay said, drawing her closer. "Was this a bad idea?"

"No, I love it out here. I'm glad we did this." But it was a good thing they'd thought to bring the two blankets, one to sit on and the other for warmth. The temperature had dropped during the day, while they were out on the little dinghy he'd liberated from the boathouse. As a result, it was a good deal cooler tonight than last night, but that was all right with Julia. It had given Clay the excuse for the fire; there was something about the tang of wood smoke mingled with sea air that both stirred and soothed her.

"So, what is it you've always wondered?" she asked, passing him the almost empty satin box. "You can have the last one."

He did, then drew the blanket tighter around them. "I've wondered how women can tolerate spending every waking hour laced up into all that godawful whalebone." He gave her corset a playful rap of his knuckles through her shirtwaist; the yellow striped one today, which she'd paired with her gray taffeta skirt—*sans* crinoline. "I should think it would be a challenge just to take a full breath."

"It is if one laces too tightly, but I don't." She grinned. "Who knows when I might end up eating half a pound of chocolate at one sitting?"

"Still . . ." He shook his head. "Why do you put up with it?"

"You aren't suggesting I go without it! I shouldn't have the nerve to set foot outside my house."

"Perhaps just when we're here alone."

"Next you'll be asking me to forego my drawers and shimmy."

"Now, there's an idea!"

"I think you're mad."

"I think I'm in—" He broke off and looked away, lifted the empty truffle box, grimaced, stuck it back in the sand. "I think I need to make another trip to the chocolate shop tomorrow." He smiled at her, tucked her up close. "And I need to talk you out of that pointless corset."

"It really doesn't bother me."

"You only think that because you're so used to it." He started unbuttoning her shirtwaist.

"What are you doing?" She batted at his busy hands.

"Taking the blasted thing off."

"It's chilly out here." She tried to scramble away, but he

banded an arm around her waist and arms to still her.

"Just the corset," he said, briskly flicking buttons. "You can keep the rest."

Julia squirmed in vain to free her pinioned arms, roused on some dark, unexamined level by his effortless mastery of her. "How—how can you take off just my corset without—?"

"Let's just say I have talents that I probably shouldn't. Now, hush before I tie you up and gag you." Opening her shirtwaist, he made short work of the tiny shell buttons of her petticoat bodice, then reached around her to unbutton her skirt and petticoat, leaving her not so much unclothed as undone. With a dexterity born, she was sure, of long practice, Clay unhooked the steel busk, wrestled the corset from its layers of disheveled clothing, and flung it out into the dark.

"Doesn't that feel better?" he asked.

"Not so much," she lied, pushing her hair—which he'd talked her into wearing loose—out of her face.

"Liar." He threw her on her back onto the blanket, rearing over her to admire her dishabille: the gaping shirtwaist and bodice, the old, embarrassingly threadbare chemise. "You're not squeezed into all that stiff boning," he said, massaging his hands upward, over her stomach and ribs, to cup her breasts, his palms hot and rough-hewn through the tissue-thin linen. "Isn't it better to be able to breathe and move and feel? Women's bodies were never meant to be shielded from sensation—they're so amazingly receptive. For example . . . ." He squeezed her nipples between his thumbs and forefingers, giving them a slow, firm twist that drew a soft moan from her. "Tell me where you feel this—aside from where I'm touching you directly."

She shook her head, unwilling to admit the sudden, little clutches of arousal between her legs.

With a too-knowing smile, he lay on top of her, one hand cradling her right breast while he lowered his head to the left, sucking her nipple into his mouth right through the shimmy.

"Oh . . ." She buried her hands in his hair—spun gold in the firelight—as he pinched and suckled, his fingers nimble, his mouth shockingly hot and wet and ravenous. Damn him, no man should know this much about women's bodies. . . .

"There are women who can be brought to climax just from having their nipples stimulated," he murmured against the damp linen as he nuzzled her.

"Have you . . ." She swallowed. "Have you ever made a woman climax that way?"

"No." But not, she suspected, from lack of trying.

"It isn't possible," she said. Not if *he* hadn't managed it!

"Isn't it?" Throwing up her skirts, he snaked a hand along her inner thigh until it reached the gap in her drawers where the center seam had been left open for convenience. She hitched in her breath when his fingers slid between the lips of her dewy sex, parting, probing.

"You're halfway there already." Tugging the other nipple into his mouth, he tongued it with firm, rhythmic strokes. When he shifted, she felt, against her stockinged leg, a ridge like cast iron behind the buttons on his trousers. He rubbed himself against her, hard and slow, as he pleasured her with his hand and mouth.

She writhed in concert with him, clawing at his hair, her heart hammering. Clay released her breast to unbutton his trousers, moving higher in order to align their bodies; he was already dripping. Spreading open her legs—along with the slit in her drawers—he notched himself in the cradle of her thighs and rocked against her.

She wrapped her arms around his back, reveling in the muscles churning beneath his shirt, his hot breath ruffling her hair. He felt so huge and hard, slicking back and forth along her drenched furrow. They churned together as if gripped in a fever of delirium, Clay molding a breast with one hand while the other cupped her bottom, enhancing the pressure against her most sensitive flesh. They grew ever more frantic as the fever escalated, glazing them with perspiration despite the temperature.

A log settled in the fire, touching off a plume of sparks that sizzled into the night air.

They lay still, hearts pounding, breath coming harsh and fast, much faster than the waves, his hands fisted in her hair.

"We should go inside," Clay panted.

"Yes."

He pressed against her, a tight, restrained movement that made them both shudder.

He nuzzled her cheek. "We should do this in a bed."

"Yes."

"I'll just . . ." He drew back a bit, then forward, a lubricious glide of steely flesh that drew a gasp of pleasure from her. "We'll go inside, just . . ." Another, harder lunge.

"Yes . . ."

And another, a little shaky this time. "Soon, just . . ."

"Yes," she gasped, thrusting to meet him. "Yes . . ."

They thrashed together, bodies straining, the fever a ravening firestorm now, too far gone to stop. A now familiar tingle crept up Julia's legs, speeding her heart and making her feel as if she couldn't take a full breath. *Yes . . . Oh, yes . . .*

In his frenzy, Clay drew back too far and missed his mark, thrusting into her in a sudden, burning intrusion. She flinched, sucking in a breath, even though she could tell he hadn't penetrated her very far.

"God, I'm sorry." He braced himself to withdraw.

"Shh, it's all right." She soothed, patting his back. "Just lie still for a minute."

He settled his body carefully, his sex snugged within her just past the crown, his heart ramming; she could feel it. They lay still for a few breathless heartbeats while Julia's body stretched to accommodate him; he felt like a fist pushing her open. They moved at the same time, just slightly—enough to sheath perhaps another half inch of him, which was as far as he could go, having encountered her maidenhead.

Clay pulled almost completely out; she arched her hips to draw him back in. Once again, he met the obstruction of her virginity. Another partial withdrawal; another guarded thrust.

Clay stilled, quaking all over, his throat working. He dipped his head to look at her, gasping for air, eyes glazed with raw need, hips quivering with the unmistakable urge to push. Julia lifted her own hips in answer, taking him deep enough to hurt but not caring, just needing this so desperately, now, for both of them. She pressed her hands to the small of his back in wordless invitation. He buried his face in her hair, kissed it, murmured something thankful that she couldn't quite hear.

With one hand curled protectively around her head and the other tucked under her bottom, Clay flexed his hips slowly, stopping when his efforts made her whimper. "Did I hurt you?"

"It's all right."

"Maybe if we were in a bed—"

"It's all right. It's all right." She rubbed his back, whispering words of encouragement. How strangely sweet, she thought, that *he* should be the one needing reassurance.

He pushed again, and again, butting ineffectually against the stubborn membrane. She tried to assist his progress with a sharp upthrust, whimpering at the resulting pain.

"Oh, honey." He went still, compelling her with his gaze to look at him. "Relax completely, Julia—don't strain. Let me do it all. Good girl," he praised when she went limp. "That's right. The hard part will be over soon."

Clay gripped her bottom with both hands to lift her up and dug his feet into the sand through the blanket. Whispering something—an apology?—he drove into her, a lunging stab that rent her virginity and seated him to the hilt in her snug passage. They both groaned; Julia trembled.

"Julia?" Clay said. "Are you—"

"I'm fine." Astoundingly, she was, despite the force with which he'd breached her and the sense she had of being impaled by something that couldn't fit inside her—and yet did. Despite the soreness, it felt incredible to be joined with him in such a deep and intimate way.

His first thrusts were achingly slow and gentle; Julia met them as if they were longtime lovers. She'd always thought she might feel shame doing this, but far from it. It felt like the most good and natural thing in the world, a dance every human being was born knowing the steps to. Her face level with his shoulder, she breathed in the laundry starch that she suspected would always act as an aphrodisiac for her, rubbed her cheek against the straining shoulder muscles beneath the soft cotton.

"I'm too close," he gritted out as his thrusts quickened and grew erratic. "It's going to be over too soon."

Too soon? He was waiting for her to climax, she realized. "No rules, remember?" she said.

Two more deep, searing lunges, and then a kind of pained moan rose from him as he seized her hips to steady her. Clay drew himself out, clearly trying to be careful, but the movement scraped her raw just the same. He flexed against her once through the gap in her drawers, hard and slippery, and then again. With the third thrust, the air left his lungs in a rush. He quivered as his seed flooded across her belly in a series of hot pulses, then collapsed, shaking.

He'd said he would take precautions against pregnancy; that must be why he pulled out. She scratched his back softly through his shirt, imagining how it would be if she didn't have to bear Emmett Van Lew's children, but could bear Clay's instead. They would be, by blood, Tommy's half siblings, she realized.

"I wish you had come," he mumbled into her hair.

"Come where?"

"Climaxed." Bracing himself on his elbows, he said, "I know it was painful, Julia. I'm really sorry. I—"

She touched his lips. "I'm not."

Clay looked grateful for that modest admission, perhaps even moved. He ducked his head just slightly, his gaze on her mouth, then seemed to remember, and stopped himself.

Buttoning himself back into his trousers, he said, "Oh, honey. You're bleeding." He dabbed her gently with his handkerchief, then used it to wipe off her belly. "Does it still hurt?" Tempted to lie and say no, she hesitated too long. Shifting so that he lay between her legs, he frowned at the abraded flesh there. "It *must*."

In a gesture she found inexpressibly touching, he dipped his head and licked her, not in the way he'd licked her this morning, to arouse her, but in the way an animal licks another animal who's wounded—long, gentle laps meant to soothe, to heal. He draped one of her legs over his shoulder, settling them both comfortably, half on their sides. She lost herself in the diamond-strewn sky, listening to the slap and suck of the waves as she luxuriated in his ministrations. He was like a wolf, she thought—predatory at times, yes, but capable of surprising tenderness toward those he considered his own.

Clay licked her patiently, the strokes gradually becoming slower, lighter, almost airy, forcing her to lift her hips to feel them. Her arousal renewed itself in such dreamy increments that she found herself shuddering and pushing before she was even fully aware of the reason. She felt so needful, an empty, pulsing chasm. Without interrupting what he was doing, Clay pried her fist free of her bunched-up skirts and squeezed her hand, as if to say, *Yes...let it come.*

It reared up like a wave building momentum...a slow heave of seawater that rises and crests, rolling home in a cataclysm of froth that tumbles...and tumbles...and tumbles....

Only to whisper quietly back into the sea, leaving glittering serenity in its wake.

CHAPTER SEVEN

"*How did* you happen to adopt Tommy?" Clay asked as he leaned back against the veranda's balustrade to sip the frosty '57 Mumm's that Julia had scolded him for spending too much money on this afternoon.

Julia looked down at her nearly empty champagne glass, seeming oddly distracted all of a sudden. "Is there any more?" she asked.

"Absolutely." Pushing off the railing, he plucked her glass from her hand and brought it to the cast iron table, where the bucket of iced champagne sat amid the remnants of the sumptuous dinner he'd ordered from a local restaurant. It was the one-week anniversary of their arrival at Valhalla, and he'd wanted to mark the occasion with a special meal.

Julia turned as he refilled her glass to gaze out thoughtfully at the bay. She was an extraordinary sight this evening, her flower-sprigged satin dress—a replica of a pre-Revolution French court gown—being nearly the same burnished gold as the sky. Clay wore fancy dress, too—fawn knee breeches with stockings and buckled shoes, lacy jabot shirt and cravat—but he'd long since discarded the brown satin frock coat and waistcoat in deference to the heat. They'd stumbled upon the costumes while exploring the attic this afternoon, and decided on a whim to wear them to their al fresco dinner.

In her small-waisted, swag-skirted gown, with its daring décolletage and lace-frilled sleeves, Julia could have passed for the daintiest of Marie Antoinette's retinue. Clay had struggled, throughout their leisurely supper, to keep his gaze from homing in on her creamy bosom, mounded high and plump above the gown's low-cut, stiff little bodice. Worse yet was the maddening knowledge of what she had on—and didn't have on—underneath, in addition to the ruffled petticoats and side-hoop paniers: a satin corset, stockings and shoes . . . and nothing else. No chemise, no pantaloons; none had been provided with the costume, and Clay had argued, with shameful opportunism, that she should go without rather than wear modern underpinnings with an eighteenth century ensemble. To his surprise, she'd readily conceded, perhaps intrigued by the very impropriety of it.

Funny . . . Six days ago, she'd reacted with outrage to his teasing suggestion that she dispense with those very undergarments. Yet, half an hour ago, during supper, she'd confided that the coarse canvas and wicker paniers against her bare skin made her feel deliciously wanton. When she said that, the cockstand Clay had endured throughout the meal swelled to the bursting point; if he'd so much as touched it, he would have gone off like a howitzer.

"This is the last of it," he said as he handed her the flute. It was a good thing, too. They'd drunk just enough champagne to effervesce the senses; any more, and their passions would be dulled rather than heightened. "So, how *did* it come about, your adoption of Tommy? It happened in France, I know, but how? Was his mother unwed? Was he an orphan?"

She took a slow sip, still staring out at the water, which rippled toward them like molten gold. "I'm not really sure."

"Found on the doorstep, was he?"

"Something like that."

"Illegitimate, most likely." Clay shook his head. "There are far too many of them in the world—innocent, unwanted little babes. That's why I'm always careful when I . . . when I'm with a woman."

She glanced at him curiously then, those graceful black brows drawn together in that pensive way she had. "Are you?"

"Oh, yes. It's been especially easy the past couple of years, because French letters have been so widely available since the war. Soldiers who never knew they existed before created a demand . . ." He trailed off when he noticed her look of bafflement. "A French letter is a condom." No help there. "A rubber sheath that fits over the man's organ. It catches the seed so that the lady is protected. I left mine in Boston."

"That's too bad," she said. "They sound very clever."

"Too clever, according to the religious authorities. I can't say I'm too keen on them myself, but for a different reason. The rubber is so thick and heavy, you see, that one feels only a fraction of the sensation one should. There are devices that women sometimes use—a little cup called a pessary, or a sponge with a string on it—but a man's only options are condoms and *coitus interruptus*."

She paused for a moment, obviously translating the Latin. "What you've been doing."

He nodded. "The surgeons say it's bad for a man's health, but I say an unwanted pregnancy is much worse for the lady's, and I'll be damned if . . . I beg your pardon." Having been brought up never to swear in the presence of women, Clay still burned with mortification at the memory of his speculation to Julia that Tommy had been fathered by some street sweeper she'd "fucked." "What I mean to say is, only the worst sort of blackguard would let a lady pay such a price for having indulged him. Not that I don't want children. I do, more so with every passing year."

That seemed to take her by surprise. She stared at him for a long, pensive moment, "You do?"

"Of course. It's only human to want offspring to carry on one's blood. It's the only form of immortality we mere mortals can hope for. I never wanted it under those circumstances, though—out of wedlock. Still, I've often thought . . ." He shrugged, slightly embarrassed by this revelation. "Suppose I never marry. Perhaps if I were a little less careful, I'd have a chance at fatherhood after all."

She looked away from him, pale and obviously distressed.

"If you're thinking I'm tempted to get you with child, well . . ." Clay couldn't resist a teasing grin. "Don't think it hasn't crossed my mind. I think you'd be . . . I'm sure you *are* an extraordinary mother. I've sometimes wished . . ." He stopped himself before he said something foolish. But then he said it anyway. "You would be the one. You know that, don't you?"

She closed her eyes, swallowed.

"But as I said," he went on quickly, "the circumstances . . ." He shook his head; now, it was he who looked away.

From the edge of his vision, he saw her look toward him, gripping the railing. For a moment, it seemed she was about to say something, but then she looked away again, her eyes glimmering darkly in the setting sun. "So you're saying . . ."

She cleared her throat, still gazing out at the bay. "You're saying you *have* always been careful, then."

"Yes. Well. I may have slipped up once or twice when I was younger and in my cups—but I don't drink like that anymore."

She nodded slowly. "Of course. If a man is intoxicated, he might not have the presence of mind . . ."

"It's hard enough to pull out when one is sober."

"Is it?" she asked.

"My God, yes. It ruins . . . well, no. It doesn't *ruin* one's climax, certainly, but it does diminish it. One must maintain a certain mental rigor as the critical point approaches, when one ought to be simply . . ." he shrugged ". . . lost in the moment."

"That's awful," she declared, with such depth of feeling that he ached, for the hundredth time this week, to kiss her. "I didn't realize . . . I mean, I'd just been assuming it was . . ." She ducked her head, her cheeks pinkening like a young girl's. "I'd been assuming you were . . . enjoying it as much as I was."

"You absurd little thing." Drawing her close, he laughingly nuzzled her hair, arranged tonight in an upswept riot of curls, some springing artfully loose to tumble down her back. "Does it seem as if I haven't been enjoying it? My God, it's been wonderful, never more so."

"But it could be better for you—much better, yes? If you didn't have to withdraw?"

He sobered, caressing her face. "That's not a risk I'm willing to take—or rather, let you take."

"No, I mean . . . I didn't mean I would want that. But it

wouldn't be risky if . . ." Her flush deepened; she looked down. "There would be no risk of pregnancy if we . . . didn't do it in the ordinary way. Perhaps if we were to try . . . that other thing?"

"Other thing?" he asked, his loins already quickening with renewed arousal.

"The thing I said was, um . . . unnatural."

"Ah." *Ah!* He grew fully erect.

"That way," she shyly explained, "you could . . . finish inside me. You wouldn't have to be thinking about withdrawal."

God, yes, Clay thought, but he forced himself to say, "You don't have to do that, Julia. I know you find it distasteful."

"I found that other thing distasteful, too—that, that thing where you . . . use your mouth. But then you did it, and I changed my mind."

Over the past seven days, Clay and Julia had engaged in the most ravenous, heartfelt lovemaking he had ever experienced. They'd utilized almost every room in the house and various spots on the grounds, as well as the dinghy rocking on the waves, employing most every position in Clay's repertoire and a few he'd never tried before. He had always sensed a certain banked passion in Julia, smoldering quietly beneath that placid facade. To his immense gratification, her sensual nature ran even deeper and hotter than he'd ever suspected. Coupled with a certain receptiveness for sexual variety, it made her the most compatible lover he'd ever had. The only act she still balked at—although she'd promised, unbidden by him, to try it before their week ended—was fellatio. He'd assumed, until just now, that she felt the same about the Greek mode of lovemaking as the French.

Evidently, he'd assumed wrong.

"Does it hurt?" she asked, her curiosity tinged only slightly with trepidation, as far as he could tell.

"Not so much if the man is careful."

"You've done it before." It wasn't really a question.

"There's not a great deal I haven't done, Julia—but there are many things I still haven't done with you, and all I can think about is having all the time in the world with you to do everything together that a man and woman possibly can."

Julia held his gaze for a moment with those big, soulful brown eyes, before looking away. She didn't say it—wouldn't say it—but he suspected she felt much the same.

"Are you sure about this?" he asked, lightly stroking her arms through the heavy satin of her dress. "You really don't have to."

"Yes. I'm sure." She set her glass down, nodded toward the bedroom through the open French doors. "Should we, um . . . ?"

"I'd like to stay out here, if you don't mind. It's such a warm evening, and the sunset is so beautiful." Taking her in his arms, he whispered, "Thank you for this," as he reached behind her to tug at the ribbon that laced her dress up in back.

He helped her off with the lavish gown, petticoats and paniers, leaving her in nothing but lace-trimmed stockings, high-heeled brocade slippers and her corset: an old-fashioned contraption fashioned of claret-colored satin, heavily boned and quilted, with elaborate gold embroidery on the wood-reinforced stomach panel. It tied at the shoulders, as opposed to being strapless, like her modern corsets—all the better to lift and squeeze her pale, proud little breasts. Had she been wearing a chemise, a lacy inch or so would have peeked out to conceal the tantalizingly exposed upper edges of her aureoles. The corset cinched in to a breath-stealing wasp waist, flaring out with a scalloped peplum that came to points front and back. It closed in back via a gold cord that criss-crossed through thirty little eyelets; Clay knew because he'd counted them all while lacing her up, a necessity due to the lack of a front busk. He'd tugged as hard as she could take it, fascinated by what the tight lacing did to her—the contraction of her waist, the swell of her bottom and breasts—and wanting her to feel it gripping her like a satin fist all evening.

"I could come just looking at you," he'd murmured into her ear as he tied her off.

She'd chuckled like the most accomplished courtesan. "I thought you didn't like corsets."

"I've changed my mind." He'd turned her around and tried to lift her against the attic wall then, but she'd teasingly thrown his own words back at him: "It's not so bad to be left wanting a bit more. That way, the next time will be all the better."

"Have it your way," he'd said as he set her down, "but I'm warning you—when I finally take you, it won't be gentle." Let her ruminate on that with every shallow breath she drew, he thought. Let her sex weep with anticipation, as would his own.

Of course, now that he knew *how* he would be taking her, it would have to be gentle. But just looking at her so provocatively attired, those lofty heels enhancing not only the shapeliness of her legs but the curves of her back and buttocks, made him think he just might explode before he got his breeches unbuttoned. It remained to be seen whether he could manage the restraint needed to do this right.

"Will you unlace me?" Turning, she rested her hands on the wide top railing of the balustrade.

"I think not," he said in voice gruff enough to make her smile knowingly at him over her shoulder. Coming up behind her, he skimmed his hands up her bare hips, around her crimped little satin-snugged waist and up to her breasts, which he scooped out of their confinement to squeeze and caress. He pressed her against the balustrade from behind, his hands covering hers as he pinned her there, but after three hard thrusts he backed off; he was simply too close to climax.

"There's something we need," he said, trying to keep his voice steady as he planted a soft kiss in her hair. "I'll be right back."

A shiver of apprehension coursed through Julia when Clay reappeared on the verandah bearing her little blue jar of Caswell & Hazard face cream. He unscrewed it and set it on the railing, then whipped off his cravat and unbuttoned his shirt, which he folded neatly next to the jar.

She warmed again at the sight of his narrow-hipped, long-legged body encased in those snug fawn breeches, his erection straining hard against the front flap, a spot of dampness having seeped through at the tip. And then there was that chiseled torso, those shipwright's shoulders, that breeze-ruffled, sun-streaked hair, those fiery eyes and burnished skin. He was so beautiful it made her chest hurt just to look at him.

He turned her to face the balustrade. "Just bend from the waist and hold onto the railing, like this. Don't let go. You can turn your face and rest it on the shirt. How's that?"

She nodded, her heart pounding. Her apprehension, visceral though it was, seemed to actually enhance her sense of anticipation. Arousal surged through her, but it was a different, more darkly exciting arousal than she'd ever felt before.

"You're incredible," he said huskily as he brushed her hair off the back of her neck and bent to place a tender kiss there. "No woman has ever looked more enticing."

"I feel . . . so exposed," she said tremulously, thinking of her naked hindquarters and intimate parts on such blatant display. "Vulnerable."

"Does it feel bad?" he asked, gently massaging the small of her back through her corset.

"It should—but it doesn't." Whatever embarrassment she felt was overshadowed by desire. A week ago, she would never have dreamed of desiring such a thing. Clay Redmond had cast a spell on her—one from which she feared she would never recover.

His hands left her; she sensed movement behind her and lifted her head to look. He was unbuttoning his front flap, an inverted U unconnected to the waistband of his breeches so that they stayed put after the panel fell open. Reaching into the jar for a dollop of the thick balm, he coated his shaft with half a dozen long, firm strokes, leaving it glistening in the amber-hued twilight.

"I love your round little bottom," he said as he dipped up a bit more of the cream. "Spread your legs a little wider.

You'll feel this," he warned softly as he pressed a fingertip to the surprisingly sensitive little aperture.

She hitched in a breath, astounded at the little flutter of pleasure his touch produced, even as her body instinctively resisted him.

"It's all right," he murmured. "I won't hurt you." He pressed until her body deemed fit to admit him, his finger sinking thick, fast, and, despite its lubrication, sandpaper-rough into this untried passage.

She flinched, but settled back down to accept the assault as he rubbed the cream into her, first with one finger, then two, pushing rhythmically at her inner walls as if trying to prepare her for him. It felt strange to receive pleasure from such an intrusion, and yet she couldn't deny her body's re-action. Moisture seeped from between her legs; her hips trembled.

Scooping up more cream with his other hand, he reached around her to stroke it into her sex with a firm, circular mo-tion that coaxed shameless moans from her almost immedi-ately. He caressed her in both places until she was frantic with need, her hips rocking in an ever-quickening rhythm.

Just when she felt the whispery hint of a climax beginning to build, like thunder rumbling softly in the distance, he slowed his caresses, easing his fingers from the slick embrace of her body. "Don't tense up now."

Julia felt him part the cleft of her bottom with one hand, and then came a smooth, thick, insistent pressure where his fingers had been. She gripped the railing harder, her heart drumming in anticipation.

"Arch your back a little. Yes . . ." He closed his greased

hands around her hips, tightly so he had some purchase.

She tensed, grimacing, as he pushed himself past the stubborn little gateway and into the snug conduit itself, grunting with the effort it took. The shock of penetration, even the discomfort of it, made her hunger for more. She wanted him to take her, claim her, consume her.

"Open yourself," he murmured breathlessly. "Let me in, sweetheart. I'll take it slow." He was trembling, though, probably with the strain of holding back. She felt that strain in the bite of his fingers as they gripped her, heard it in his harsh breathing.

Clay shoved again, harder . . . and again, his rock-hard shaft slowly coaxing, stretching, filling. He was shaking; so was she.

"Does it hurt?" he gasped.

"No, not . . . not really." It did, in a way, but pain and pleasure had united into something altogether different. He felt impossibly huge, searingly hard . . . yet she wanted him there, as deep as he could get. Turning her face into his shirt, she took comfort in the faint scent of him mingled with the warm salt air. She breathed a sigh of relief when he finally stilled, sheathed within her to the root, that other, saclike part of him full and heavy against her, the wiry little hairs prickling her sensitive bottom.

"Are you all right?" he panted, stroking her cheek.

"Yes," she said in a quavering whisper.

Slowly, carefully, he drew himself out just a bit and then edged back in again, and again, and again—short, suppressed strokes clearly meant to keep this from hurting her. He growled in gratification when Julia impulsively canted up her bottom to deepen the penetration. His thrusts lengthened then, growing steadily more forceful and urgent.

He abruptly stilled, his breathing ragged, body shuddering. "I have to stop for a minute, or I'll . . ."

She nodded, loving the way he pulsed inside her.

"How does it feel?" he asked.

"Wrong, in a way. But so right, too."

He chuckled; she felt that inside her, too.

"How does it feel for you?" she asked.

"Hot. And tight. So tight it almost hurts." He pushed in just a little deeper, then stopped; she heard him swallow. Again, he reached around her to renew his caress at the juncture of her thighs. His voice shuddering, he said, "Try to stay as still as possible when you come. I want to feel it inside you."

Oh, the effort it took not to grind against his hand as his deft, slickened fingers rubbed and stroked and fluttered. Her heart seemed to stop as the pleasure danced closer . . . closer . . . like flames licking at a crate of gunpowder.

"Oh . . ." she groaned, thrusting reflexively against his hand.

"Don't move!" he rasped, his fingers digging painfully into one hip as he leaned over, shifting the pressure inside her. She felt his teeth sink into her shoulder as he strove to hold her still.

That bite was all it took. The gunpowder ignited, detonating with jolting spasms that wrenched a hoarse shout from her. He shouted, too, as her body squeezed him like a fist, one sharp contraction after another. . . .

He rammed hard and deep, a growl rumbling from his

chest as his pleasure pumped convulsively into her. With a final strangled groan, he collapsed on top of her, his chest damp against her back, heart thundering, lungs sucking great gasps of air. He banded his arms around her, holding her tight, as the last few tremors coursed through them.

"My God," he breathed into her ear. "My God. Oh, my God." He pressed his lips to her cheek, rubbed his face against hers. . . . "Thank you."

"For what?"

"For trusting me. For letting me inside."

She knew he didn't mean inside her body.

"For everything," he said.

CHAPTER EIGHT

"*We never* talk about Martin," Clay said softly as they lay curled in each other's arms in the big, downy bed.

Julia thought about that as she listened to the measured thump . . . thump . . . thump of his heart through the warm wall of muscle on which her head rested. Outside, the storm that had awakened her a couple of hours ago still raged like a beast in the night. Her childish fear of lightning shamed her, but Clay took it in stride, teasing her only a little when she put on a nightgown because it would make her feel less vulnerable. Realizing she couldn't sleep, he'd lit the candles in the two French gilt wall sconces that flanked the bed, fetched a bottle of cognac and a bowl of fruit, and resolved to sit out the storm with her.

"We both loved him," Clay said, his slightly slurred speech attesting to the quantity of cognac he'd consumed—the most she'd ever seen him drink. She knew it was because they had only one more day here. Tomorrow evening—actually, *this* evening, because it was already the wee hours of the morning—she would return to the city to prepare for her wedding just twenty-four hours later. "He loved us, too. He would understand this." His arms tightened around her. "Us."

Julia nodded. Of course he would. He was . . . Martin. Martin had understood everything.

She winced at a sudden thunderclap, squeezing her eyes shut at the flutter of white light that followed. Clay tucked her more firmly into his embrace, murmuring soft words of reassurance, his breath tickling her scalp.

He sighed. "I really am sorry for the things I said to you that day I came to your house, and for the way I said them. Martin would have been appalled. He adored you. All he ever wanted, *really* wanted, even more than serving God or defending the Union, was to be your husband."

She nodded. "In his last letter to me, he wrote about a young soldier in his regiment who'd been caught trying to sneak out of camp. His excuse was that he'd just wanted to sleep with his wife one more time before he died. Martin told me he'd been tempted to do the same thing for the same reason. I cried for two days after I read that letter."

Clay's heartbeat quickened against her ear; he reached for his snifter.

"Clay? Are you all—"

"It was my fault," he said shortly. "I got him drunk. I did it on purpose, so he couldn't . . ." Swearing under his breath, he tossed back the remainder of his cognac in one gulp.

She sat up, staring at him. "You didn't want him to . . . make love to me?"

He closed his eyes and fell back against the mountain of silk pillows. "I shouldn't be telling you this. It's 'cause I've been drinking."

A woozy surge of shock greeted this revelation. All those years of wishing she'd had that one night with him, that they'd been able to share themselves that way, perhaps even start a baby, before the war ripped him out of her life. . . .

Clay opened his eyes, grabbed the bottle, and half-filled a glass meant to hold a couple of ounces. "I suppose I . . . admired you a bit more than I ought to have." Avoiding her wide-eyed gaze, he took a stiff gulp. "Of course, Martin deserved you far more than I did. He was good, virtuous. . . . He was like you. But that was little consolation, especially when I had to stand up for him while he made you his wife. And then knowing . . . what would happen between you that night. . . ." He shook his head, swallowed some more cognac. "I thought I was pretty clever, getting Martin so sotted, till the next morning, when he told me how devastated he was. And then, after he died, and I knew it was my fault that he'd never get to . . . *Christ.*"

"Oh, my God," she whispered. "I had no idea."

"How could you?" he asked. "People who don't have that kind of selfishness in them never really see it in others."

"No," she said softly, imagining Martin's reaction if Clay were to confess this to him. "No. It wasn't as simple as selfishness, don't say that. It wasn't right. It was a mistake, but . . . I think I understand. You mustn't flog yourself over it."

"Someone should. My reputation is well deserved, Julia. I don't merit your understanding in this, and certainly not your forgiveness."

"Martin would have forgiven you."

"He was the forgiving type. That's why he was the only one who'd have anything to do with me."

"What about Libby?"

He finally looked at her. "Who?"

"Libby Collier! My maid of honor. The girl in the library. The one you . . ." Heat crept into her cheeks.

"Oh, her." Another shrug. "I barely knew her. She was willing and I was . . ." he shook his head bleakly ". . . miserable. I closed my eyes and pretended she was you."

"Oh. Clay." She squeezed his hand.

"The Navy Department recruited me right after that, because of my facility with sailing. I spent the next four years helping to blockade the Southern seaports."

"Oh, so *you're* the reason I lost all my money," she said with mock severity, trying to lighten the mood.

"I don't suppose I helped. Anyway, I was at sea much of the time and pretty much out of touch with everyone. It wasn't until the war ended that I found out about Tommy, and . . ." He sighed heavily. "I jumped to conclusions. I think the real reason I was so furious at you was because I felt like a fool, having held you in such high esteem. At least it was easier, after that, to put you out of my mind for a time. But now . . ."

Yes. But now . . .

Julia chose a peach from the bowl and took a bite out of it. The honey-sweet juice trickled down her chin, and Clay brushed it off with a fingertip, which he touched to his tongue. Smiling, he proceeded to unbutton the front of her nightgown, looking like a clever little boy with an idea. She loved the relish with which he feasted on her body; she loved everything about him. And therein lay the problem.

She must have suspected from the beginning, on some subliminal level, that if she came here with Clay and let him take her virginity, she would end up losing her heart to him—and so she had. A cruel turn of events, considering what she had to lose if her engagement to Mr. Van Lew fell through.

After all, what could Clay Redmond offer her, even if he were the marrying kind? He was, by his own admission, something of a bounder, and almost certainly of limited re-sources—especially as compared to Emmett Van Lew. What they'd done together these past ten days, he'd been hired to do. Not that she deluded herself into thinking the money was all he cared about; if only it had been, this might be easier.

Having opened her gown just enough to expose her breasts, Clay took her half-eaten peach and rubbed it over a nipple, squeezing the fruit just enough to drizzle its syrup over the fleshy globe. Reclining half on top of her, he licked her clean with long, hot swipes of his tongue, the little bud puckering under the voluptuous assault, arousal sparking between her legs.

"Oh, yes," he murmured when she arched beneath him, her fingers digging into his scalp through his sleep-mussed hair. "I can't get enough of you," he sighed, grinding against her. "I'll never have enough." He suckled her hard, as if to savor every last drop of juice, his teeth scraping her nipple in a way that shot crackling little tendrils of pleasure throughout her.

His desire, his affection, his need for her . . . it was echoed in her own heart, her own body. It was so all-consuming, so hard to deny . . . yet one of them must make the effort, hard as it might be. She'd best remember that her marriage to Emmett Van Lew was all that stood between Tommy and Blackwell's Island.

Settling between her legs, his rigid shaft nudging her damp, little notch through the nightgown, Clay said, "I've been do-ing a lot of thinking these past few days, about . . . the future. About what will become of us after . . . this."

She said, "So have I."

Raising himself on his elbows, he looked at her. She saw too much in his eyes—anticipation? hope?—and looked away.

"I, um . . . I've been thinking about my marriage," she said.

He went very still, his gaze intense, his chest rising and falling a little too quickly.

"It's going to be a big change," she said in a voice that didn't sound like hers. "I'll have to get used to having servants again, and . . . and living in that Fifth Avenue monstrosity, and . . ." She forced a chuckle so patently hollow that she cringed inside. "I suppose I shall have to develop a deep love and admiration for Arabian brood mares."

A awful silence ticked by, and then he lifted one hand to lightly stroke some stray hairs off her face. With heartbreaking tenderness he said, in a voice slightly thick with drink, "Are you afraid, Julia? Of what's been happening here, between us? Is that why you're—"

"I don't know what you mean," she lied, lacking the courage to look directly at him. "I'm not afraid, I'm just . . . Well, perhaps a few prenuptial jitters . . ." Oh, Christ, she thought as heat flooded her face. He'll loathe me. She loathed herself.

Clay studied her for a long and excruciating moment, his jaw clenched, eyes desolate, erection waning. Without shifting from his position on top of her, he lifted his snifter, drained it, and set it clumsily back on the nightstand, not reacting when it toppled to the carpeted floor.

She had to say something, something real, something sincere, something far better than the fatuous twaddle that had just come out of her mouth. "Clay . . ."

"So, are you ready for Saturday?" The sadness was gone

from his eyes; they shone hard and bright, like shards of blue glass in the sun.

"What? Oh, um . . . yes. Yes. It—it's to be a house wedding at his country home in northern Manhattan." She was babbling, thrown by the sudden shift in mood. "Um, an evening affair, very formal. M-mayor Hoffman will be there, and—"

"No, I mean the wedding night. Are you all set, or do you need a few more good, hard fucks to get you ready for Emmett?"

She stared at him in dismay. "Clay, please . . ." she began in what she hoped was a pacifying tone, but her voice quavered.

"Please what? Please fuck me again, 'cause I need a little more practice? Hey, a job's a job," he said, yanking her nightgown up to her waist. He wrapped a fist around his organ, stroking it swiftly as he positioned himself.

"Oh, Clay, not like this," she implored, pushing at him with one hand and clutching her nightgown closed with the other.

He pressed into her, just barely erect enough to manage it. "What difference does it make, as long as you're broken in for Emmett?" Prying her hands off the gown, he wrenched it open; a seam tore; buttons popped. He pulled the rent garment down over her shoulders, partially immobilizing her arms.

He fondled her the way she imagined a man would fondle a whore, roughly kneading her breast, as if it were a *thing* that did not sit directly over her heart. Crude stimulus, but his body responded, swelling to fill her. Lifting her legs, he rammed hard. She tried to heave him off her, shoved at his sinewy arms, but she may as well have been trying to budge a marble statue.

"Please, Clay," she begged. "I hate this."

"You hate that I'm making things complicated," he said as he drove into her, his hair falling across his eyes with every snap of his hips. "That's what you *really* hate, isn't it? All you wanted was a little impersonal stud service, and I've gone and made an ass out of myself by falling for you."

Gripping her shoulders for leverage, he hammered her mercilessly, each fierce lunge stabbing her from within. Her head fell back; tears pricked her eyes.

"Clay, oh, God, don't. It—"

Thunder crashed overhead, rattling the house; lightning flared.

She burst into ragged sobs, tears streaming hotly down her cheeks. "It hurts, Clay. You're hurting me. Oh, God, Clay, please stop. Stop. Just stop."

He went still, gulping hoarse lungfuls of air, as she covered her face and wept, her nightgown torn halfway off her.

"Oh, Christ." Clay pulled out so quickly that she whimpered from the abrasion. "Oh, shit." Touching her face, he said, "Julia, I—"

"Go away," she pleaded, frantically disengaging from him.

"Please . . ." he raised both hands, looking stricken ". . . let me—"

"Go away," she tearfully implored him, scrambling into a fetal position as she pulled her tattered nightgown around her. "Please just go away."

He stood at the side of the bed, his hair in his eyes, his chest working, regarding her with a kind of shocked anguish, as if he couldn't quite grasp what had happened, what he'd done.

"Go away . . ." she whimpered. "Go away . . . go away . . ."

He backed away dazedly, paused as if to say something, then turned and left.

Time moved slowly as she lay there in the flickering amber half-light, reliving the events that had just transpired: Clay's inebriated musings about the future . . . *what will become of us* . . . the hopefulness in his eyes . . . her idiotic efforts to dismiss him—his pain, his need, his desire—with glib chatter about her wedding . . . his despair and bitterness and confounded rage.

Dawn was breaking when Julia finally yanked off her ruined nightgown, buttoned on her white cotton pique dressing gown, and went to look for Clay. After searching nearly every room in the house, she eventually found him in the front parlor, hunched naked on the edge of the sheet-draped swan chaise, his head in his hands. He'd opened the floor-to-ceiling curtains, uncovering a window that took up almost the entire wall. Rain sluiced down the leaded glass in rumbling sheets, bathing him in a watery luminescence that made it look as if he'd been carved out of translucent white alabaster. Except that he was trembling.

He looked like Ares mourning the loss of his Aphrodite.

Clay didn't realize Julia was there until he felt the cool brush of linen on his back and shoulders. He looked up to find her standing over him with a sheet she'd stripped off some piece of furniture, wrapping it around his shivering body.

It was her eyes that undid them—so quiet and soft and

dark. There was wariness in their depths, but none of the revulsion or rage that should, by rights, have been there.

His heart shattered like glass. Banding his arms around her, he pressed his face hard to her belly as she stroked his hair and whispered things he couldn't hear. He held her tight, rubbing his face against her roughly textured dressing gown, wondering why she had come to him after what he'd done.

"Christ, Julia, I'm sorry," he choked out. "I'm sorry. I'm sorry. I'm so sorry. What are you doing here? How can you not hate me?"

"I hate what you did, but I don't hate you," she said quietly. "I wish I hadn't said those things about—"

"No, you were right to remind me. You were just trying to . . . bring me back to earth." He looked up at her, incandescent in the silvery, rain-dappled light, her hair a wildly beautiful, snarled black mane. "I thought I could do this and it wouldn't . . . get to me. That *you* wouldn't get to me. But I'm still a selfish bastard. I just want you so much, and I can't—" His voice broke; he looked down, his throat clutching, striving for some semblance of self-control. "I can't believe I'm going to lose you. God, I hate this."

"So do I." She sat next to him, took her in his arms, urged him to lie down with her. "But let's not ruin the time we have left. Let's just be here for each other for as long as we have."

They held each other, their bodies snugged together as they listened to the rain drumming against the window, all the while stroking each other lazily through his sheet and her robe. Her eyes this close up were amazing, shot through with flecks of gold and rust that he'd never noticed before. He explored the contours of her face with his fingertips, needing to commit her to memory with every sense at his disposal. The trail of a dried tear coursed down her cheek; he licked it from her jawline to the outer edge of her eye, tasting salt and marzipan.

His loins stirred, possibly from their closeness, or perhaps the taste of her, or the aching fullness of her in his heart. She felt it and moved against him, the friction of their wrappings coaxing him to full arousal in seconds. Remembering that hellish scene upstairs, he said, "We don't have to—"

"Shh." She touched a finger to his lips, gave him that quiet little smile that always undid him, and shifted downward on the chaise, unwinding the sheet from him as she went. The silken weight of her hair on his rampant shaft made him shudder.

"Julia," he gasped as she pressed her lips to him. He moaned as the damp tip of her tongue traced a tentative path up the underridge. "You don't have to do this. Not after—"

"I want to," she said, her breath a hot tickle on his sensitized flesh. She closed her mouth over the crown, laved it with her tongue. "Is this all right? I'm trying to do what I think I'd like if I had . . . one of these."

He responded with a cross between a chuckle and a moan. "I'd say that's a remarkably effective strategy." Julia's very uncertainty enhanced her efforts, her airy kisses and delicate licks exciting him to a fever pitch of arousal.

A crack of thunder, accompanied by rivulets of lightning all too visible through the window, made her flinch.

"Come here." Reaching for her, he resettled her next to him, then shook out the sheet in which he'd been wrapped and draped it over them, covering them entirely. With the back of the chaise supporting the expanse of bleached linen, it formed an intimate little tent for two, hazily lit by a thin wash of dawn light. "There—we're in our own world now," he told her, tucking her back into his embrace and nuzzling her hair. "Nothing out there matters—not the lightning, not Emmett Van Lew, nothing. All that matters right now is us . . . just us."

"Just us . . ." She sighed.

"I'm a flawed man," he said, rubbing his chin on her head. "I don't really deserve you . . . or this time we've had together. But I want you to know it's been the best time of my life. I can't begin to tell you what it's meant to me."

"It's not over yet," she said as she unbuttoned her robe.

They coupled without shifting from their side-by-side embrace, her legs wrapped around him, his arms enfolding her like a fragile thing of great value—as, indeed, she was. It was a bittersweet joining, and as their pleasure crested, she began to weep.

Rolling her onto her back, he took her face in his hands and said, still moving within her, "Look at me, Julia. It's just us, remember? Just you and me. And this is our moment. Whatever happens in the future, whatever life brings us, there will always be this moment, where there's just the two of us, together like this. Just us," he whispered as they rocked together slowly, in dreamy, blissful union. "We'll always have this moment. Always . . ."

Clay awoke blinking at a flood of sunshine as he lay tangled alone in white linen sheets on a chaise longue. *What . . . ?*

And then he remembered. "Julia?" he called.

Much had transpired last night, some of it awful, but it had ended well, with the kind of lovemaking one always secretly yearned for, the kind that thrilled the heart as well as the loins. *Come inside me,* she'd whispered as their pleasure mounted. They'd reached the pinnacle at the same time, and in the same deep, rapturous way, neither of them making a sound. When it was over, they'd rolled onto their sides again, without uncoupling, and fallen asleep like that, joined body and soul.

It was while he was drifting off, lulled by the weight of her limbs entwined with his and the rhythm of their hearts beating as one, that he realized the truth. A moment, however perfect, however memorable, was not enough. Two weeks were not enough. A lifetime wouldn't be enough—but it would have to do.

I'll tell her tomorrow, he'd decided as sleep had drifted over him like a balmy breeze. . . . *I'll tell her about me—everything, the whole truth.*

He wanted her too much now, needed her too much, not to use every means at his disposal to keep her—even if it meant she'd be staying with him for the wrong reasons. It would save her from Van Lew, and he would have her. She harbored the same fierce love in her heart that swelled in his own. Why should they deny it? *How* could they deny it?

"Julia?" He sat up, looking around. It had to be close to ten o'clock; perhaps she'd gotten up to make them some eggs.

He could take her out on the boat today. They could drop anchor and make love on the deck to the rhythm of the waves. . . .

He would tell her then, while he was inside her. He would ask her—beg her—to be his. . . .

Something crackled under his hand when he braced himself to rise: a folded sheet of paper. He flicked it open while rubbing the morning grit out of his eyes. Something fell out, skittering across the Oriental carpet, something small and shiny.

He leaned over and picked it up, held it in front of his eyes. It was a ring: diamonds flanking a majestic sapphire. Eunice Sumner's engagement ring.

Clay's stomach contracted into a hard little knot as he turned his attention to the note:

Dearest Clay,

I'll be on the morning train back to New York by the time you read this. I'm so sorry to leave this way, but last night was a good ending, and I think we need a good ending more than we need another day.

You can hate me for this, and I won't blame you, but know that if I didn't care, I wouldn't have done this. And remember, too, that no matter what happens, we'll always have our moment.

Your Julia

Clay reread the note, and then he sat and stared out the window until he realized how long he'd been sitting there, naked and foolish, with an old woman's engagement ring in one hand and a crushed letter of final farewell in the other. Rising, he set the ring down on the nearest surface: the little

pedestal table that supported the statuette of Ares and Aphrodite.

She's as petite as you are.

And he's standing the way you do, with his weight on one hip.
And he's tall, like you...

Clay ran his hand over the cool white marble, lost in
thought. He tossed the wadded-up note aside and hefted the
statue, weighing it in his hands.

And then he turned and hurled it through the window in
an explosion of glass.

CHAPTER NINE

"*Another wedding* gift, and it's a heavy one this time," announced Caroline Astor as she thunked it on the Aubusson-carpeted floor of the guest room set aside by Emmett Van Lew this evening for his bride's prenuptial preparations.

"Thank you, Caroline." Julia, studying herself in the huge, gilt-framed mirror that dominated one wall of the warmly lit rosewood-paneled room, barely glanced at the unwrapped wooden crate. "Would you put it in the next room, with the others?"

"The gentleman asked that you open it while he waits. He's out in the hall."

"Tell him I'm too busy," Julia said. It was a lie. She'd been dressed and ready for over an hour, having been fussed over all day by a bevy of women with names like Astor, Roosevelt, Morgan, Whitney, DuPont—former acquaintances who hadn't spoken to her in years but now vied to ingratiate themselves with the future Mrs. Emmett Van Lew. She had enough time before the ceremony to open that gift and more, but her heart wasn't in it. It was all she could do to go through the motions, knowing what awaited her tonight . . . and for God knew how many years to come.

Caroline returned to the room shaking her head. "I'm sorry, Julia. He says he won't leave until you open it."

Aunt Eunice, busily adjusting the angle of the diamond tiara securing her niece's trailing lace veil, spat her mouthful of hairpins into her hand and hobbled out the door, muttering, "I'll take care of this."

Julia returned her attention to the mirror and the woman reflected in it, a refined little creature in a crystal-encrusted, champagne-colored satin gown with the elegant new princess skirt and a full court train. The gown, commissioned from the House of Worth in Paris at a cost estimated by her attendants at four thousand dollars, was one of four wedding gifts from Mr. Van Lew, the others being her tiara, a diamond and pearl necklace, and—to her bemusement—a thoroughbred mare. Everything Julia wore had been provided by her fiancé in a prettily wrapped and beribboned box: white kid gloves, silk stockings embroidered up the front, beaded grosgrain slippers, the most exquisite underpinnings she'd ever seen. . . . And, as an unintended but manifest reminder of her former poverty, a lace-edged handkerchief like those she'd embroidered a thousand times at eight cents apiece, with her initials stitched in one corner.

"Sorry," said one of her attendants as the door opened. "No men allowed."

"He's an exception," Eunice snapped as she escorted the visitor into the room. Julia caught a glimpse of him in the mirror and stared, heart tripping. Clay met her reflected gaze and stared back, achingly handsome in a double-breasted frock coat, winged collar and black tie, his hair lightly oiled and neatly combed, one arm curled around a silk top hat.

Julia's attendants, having gone quiet, were starting to exchange glances. "Why don't you girls go downstairs and make sure everything's ready for the ceremony?" Eunice suggested, herding them out with the aid of her cane. "Go on!" she said, following them into the hall. "Shoo! Shoo!" She turned and winked at Clay as she shut the door behind her, leaving them alone in the room.

"Julia," he said softly, taking in her attire. "My word."

"Wh-what are you doing here?"

"Bringing you a gift. I would have come sooner, but I had a broken window to fix." He crouched next to the crate and withdrew something—a crowbar?—from inside his coat. "May I?"

Julia nodded dully. He pried the lid off, hauled out a wad of straw, then gestured for her to look inside.

She did, gaping at what she saw. "The statue! Ares and Aphrodite. But . . . My God, Clay, you didn't *steal* this, did you?"

He gave her a look. "I cabled the Ashcrofts in London and arranged to buy it."

"You shouldn't be giving me this."

"Then I probably shouldn't be giving you this, either." He pulled a handkerchief out of his trouser pocket and unfolded it, revealing Aunt Eunice's diamond and sapphire engagement ring.

"Clay, I don't want that. That's yours. You . . ."

"Earned it?" He smiled wryly. "What happened between us out in Bellport wasn't about money, Julia. I didn't do it for the ring. I did it . . ." He looked down, color streaking his cheekbones, as he turned the ring over in his hands. "I did it because it seemed like the only way I would ever be able to have you, if only for a little while. I lied when I said I'd admired you a little too much. The truth is, I've loved you to the point of madness for as long as I can remember."

The air left Julia's lungs. "If . . . if that's really true," she said when she found her voice again, "why didn't you give that ring back to Aunt Eunice?"

"I tried to, just now out in the hall. But when I told her I wanted to buy one just like it for you, she said I should give you this one, because it had brought her so much happiness."

"You want to . . . You can't mean . . ."

He dropped to one knee, took her left hand in his, and started tugging off her glove. "I know I'm not what you bargained for in a husband, but I'm not quite as poor as you think. I started designing and building ships after the war—special ones, utilizing a combination of steam and sail power. Most of my profit I reinvest in the business, but I did buy some property in the Back Bay—that's a landfill where they're building Parisian-style townhouses. It's just a tidal flat right now, but . . . I'm yammering," he said as he stripped her glove off. "It's because I'm nervous."

He was nervous? Julia was shaking like a bird.

Taking her hand in both of his, he said, "It's not a glamorous life I lead. I may own the business, but I've got investors to answer to, and when I'm needed, I work right alongside my men in the shipyard. I'm no Emmett Van Lew, nor will I ever be. But I can support you and your aunt and Tommy—and any other children we might have. I was going to tell you all this yesterday. I would have told you before that, but I didn't want you to want me for . . . well, for the same reasons you wanted Van Lew. None of that matters anymore, though. I'm too desperate. I'll take you on any terms I can get you."

"Oh, my God." She was due to speak vows with another man in twenty minutes, and Clay Redmond was proposing!

"I know you love Boston—you told me so. Come back there with me, Julia. You won't be sorry. But if you stay here and marry that man, I guarantee you'll regret it every day for the rest of your life. Here." He slid the ring onto her finger. "How does that fit?"

"P-perfectly."

"You see?" He rose to his feet, smiling. "It's a good sign." He cradled her face gently in his big, rough hands. "Marry me, Julia. What happened between us in Bellport, that doesn't happen every day. It's special—too special for me to just turn around and hand you over to some other guy without a fight. Come on." He brushed his thumb down her cheek, across her lower lip. "Say yes."

"This is madness," she exclaimed through a nonplused little gasp of laughter.

He dipped his head, his gaze on her mouth, still caressing her lips. "Say yes, Julia. Just say it—it's easy," he murmured, his breath warm on her lips, his voice seductively deep and soft. "Say, 'Yes, Clay, I'll marry you. I'll live with you in Boston and have your babies and grow old with you.'" His lips a hairsbreadth from hers, he whispered, "Say it, Julia."

She inhaled that heady mixture of laundry starch and warm male, making her feel drunk, reckless. . . . Her head tilted back, as if it were too heavy for her neck. She had never let him kiss her. That felt suddenly very cruel and pointless. "Oh, Clay . . ."

"Say it. Say—"

The door slammed open; they both jumped and drew apart.

"Did you see her, Mama?" It was Tommy, out of breath from running, his five-year-old version of formal evening wear—accessorized with Martin's ubiquitous forage cap— badly disheveled, a big white satin bow dangling from his hand.

"Did I see who, sweetie?" Julia asked as she squatted down, shifting instantly into maternal mode.

"Birdie! I'm supposed to make her pretty for the wedding, but she keeps running away."

"Oh, Tommy, when will you learn that Birdie doesn't like having things tied around her neck?" Julia asked.

"Then why did Aunt Eunice ask me to catch her and do it?"

To keep him occupied during the preparations, Julia assumed. She was working on changing the subject when Clay braced his hands on his knees, smiled his most engaging smile, and said, "You must be Tommy."

Julia rose slowly, reeling with a sudden sick sense of vertigo as she realized that Clay and his son—the son he didn't even realize was his—were standing face to face! This was never supposed to happen.

Squatting on his haunches, Clay offered his hand. "I'm Clay Redmond."

Tommy put his sturdy little hand in Clay's much larger one and manfully shook it. "Martin Thomas Hughes. It's a pleasure to meet you, sir." The resemblance between them was startling, the only difference being Tommy's cornsilk hair—and Clay's had probably been much the same color at that age.

Anxious to separate the two, Julia opened her mouth to send Tommy after Birdie again, but Clay spoke before she could. "What excellent manners you have for such a young person, Martin Thomas Hughes. Your mother is to be commended."

"I'm not so very young. I turned five in March."

"My, but you're a strapping fellow for five!"

"Mama thinks it's because my father was big and tall."

"She does?" Clay glanced at her curiously, as well he might, since she'd claimed to know nothing of Tommy's parentage. He might have assumed she'd been referring to Martin—after all, she *was* pretending that Tommy was his son—except that Martin had stood perhaps five-nine, five-ten at the most.

"When did you hear me say that, Tommy?" she asked. "I never told you your father was tall."

"I heard you say it to Aunt Eunice when I was hiding under the dining table getting ready to ambush some gray-coats. You said I was a spitting image, but I haven't spat since you stood me in the corner for it."

Clay chuckled and reached out to finger-comb Tommy's tousled hair off his forehead, then stilled, his smile fixed in place, as he studied Tommy's features: the keen blue eyes and full lips . . . the sharply angled cheekbones . . . the robust curve of the jaw. Clay's smile slowly dimmed; she could see his mind working as he analyzed the little face in front of him. "So your birthday's in March, eh?"

Oh, God, Julia thought, gripping the back of a chair for

support. This was never supposed to happen. Not this way!

"March seventeenth, eighteen sixty-two!" Tommy said proudly, having just recently committed it to memory.

Clay took a moment to subtract nine months in his head, and then he looked up at Julia with an expression of wretched incredulity that begged her, wordlessly, to explain this away, to reveal why this was not as it seemed—that she hadn't kept this from him all this time. When she responded instead with a look of anguished contrition, he returned his astounded gaze to Tommy.

"Tommy, go downstairs and find Birdie," she ordered in a brusque, jittery voice as she ushered him out of the room.

The child turned in the doorway. "Mr. Redmond, are you the man who's going to marry my mama?"

Clay rose slowly to his feet, as grim as she'd ever seen him. After a long, excruciating pause he said, very softly, "No."

Tommy looked crestfallen as he walked away.

They stood in terrible silence as the grandfather clock in the corner ticked away the seconds.

"Were you ever going to tell me?" Clay asked in a quiet, strained voice.

She implored him with her eyes to understand, to not despise her. "I didn't want to lose him," she said tremulously.

Clay looked appalled. "You thought I'd take him from the only mother he's ever known?" He spun around, rubbing the back of his neck, then turned back as a thought seemed to occur to him. "Or were you just worried about what Van Lew would think if your son suddenly disappeared?"

"No," she said, biting back the sting of impending tears. "No."

"It's been about money all along, hasn't it, Julia?" he asked, his voice still soft—horribly soft. "The money's more important than anything, more than the bonds of fatherhood—or love."

"It's been about Tommy. Please, Clay, try to understand."

He looked down, raking a hand through his hair. "Remember that evening on the verandah, when I told you how much I wanted a child, how I wished you could be his mother? I opened my soul to you." When he looked back up, his eyes were red rimmed, and a vein stood out on his forehead. "You could have opened yours to me, Julia. You could have told me about Tommy. But you didn't."

"I wanted to."

"But you didn't." There came a little huff of bitter laughter. "Looks as if I had it right to begin with. You really *weren't* quite what you seemed."

"Clay . . ."

"I would like to see my son now and again, when I come to New York. That's every couple of months or so. Van Lew doesn't have to know, and you don't even have to tell Tommy who I am, that I'm his. . . ." Clay's throat moved as he swallowed. "I can meet him somewhere, perhaps at your aunt's house. You don't have to be there. It would probably be best if you weren't."

Watching him through the tears pooling hotly in her eyes, her chin quivering, she nodded. "Of course."

"All right, then." He picked his hat up off the floor and crossed to the door.

"Clay."

He paused in the doorway, his bleak eyes shining damply.

"Take this with you," she said, gesturing to the crate housing the statue. "Please."

"Keep it," he said gruffly as he turned away. "I sure as hell don't want it."

CHAPTER TEN

"*Excuse me,* sir," Julia called out to the driver of a tipcart heaped with raw lumber as it rumbled through the sprawling mayhem of the East Boston shipyards. "Sir?" Lifting her gray taffeta skirt with one hand and holding her pillbox hat down with the other, she jogged after him as one of the workmen whistled and made a suggestive comment about her ankles. "Sir? Can you tell me where I might find Mr. Clay Redmond?"

The old man halted his team and squinted at her, shielding his eyes against the searing midday sun. "Nice young lady like you shouldn't be wanderin' about amongst all these jack-tars and rowdies," he scolded around a mouthful of tobacco. He nodded over his shoulder at the burly laborers swarming over the ships under construction, some of the men scantily clad and all sweating profusely in the brutal heat. "Them types don't always watch their language like they ought." He punctuated this observation by spitting a stream of tobacco juice onto the hard-packed dirt not a foot from where she stood.

"Yes. Well. Be that as it may, I very much need to find—"

"Hop aboard." He slapped the seat next to him. "Redmond Shipbuilding's way down at the end there. I'll give you a ride so's you don't have to run the gauntlet of all them jackanapes."

He let her off at the site of a half-built ship rising up like the remains of some colossal beast, with its belly intact and ribs exposed. Log scaffolding buttressed the carcass, to which the shipwrights gained access by means of a makeshift gangplank cobbled together from what looked to be waste lumber. Workers trudged up this ramp in two-man teams, shouldering lengths of curved strakes to be nailed to the hull; none of them was Clay. More men labored on the ground, putting the finishing touches on lengths of timber supported by sawhorses.

Julia went still when she saw him, shirtless and drenched with perspiration as he scraped a plane over a massive oak beam. He put his entire body into it, muscles flexing and bulging, curls of wood shearing off with every long stroke. He kept his head down, sweat flying from his hair and face, a relentless machine comprised of sinew and fury.

For a minute, she just stood and stared, amid the roiling cacophony of the shipyard, stirred by the savage virility that had once so unnerved her. And, too, she had yet to decide what she could possibly say to him that would undo the acrimony of their parting two days ago.

Presently, a bearish fellow with a broad Irish brogue called out, "That's a fine lookin' chippy givin' you the eye there, boss. Looks like your dry spell might be over."

"What?" Without pausing in his efforts, Clay glanced at the bear, who nodded toward Julia.

He froze, then straightened, the plane forgotten in his hand, staring at her as if she were some sort of apparition. His men nudged each other, hooting with glee. "Look who's finally gotten all stupid over a wench! Never thought I'd see the day!"

Julia nodded to him, peeling off her gloves with trembling fingers.

Clay took a step in her direction, noticed the plane in his hand, and set it down. As he strode toward her, she saw that he was unshaven. His gaze flicked momentarily to the ring on her left hand, flashing in the sun.

"Mrs. Van Lew," he said with an unsmiling little bow, his hands resting on his cocked hips in that so-familiar stance of his. "To what do I owe this . . ." He suddenly frowned. "This isn't about Tommy, is it? Did anything happen to—"

"No! No, he's fine. He's with Aunt Eunice at the Union Oyster House, glutting himself." She gave him another wobbly smile. "He's always loved oysters. I never quite understood it."

He didn't return her smile, merely ducked his face, wiping his arm across his dripping forehead. One by one, the workmen paused in their labors to turn toward their employer and his mysterious lady visitor, watching as openly as if the couple were actors in a stage play.

"And it's not Mrs. Van Lew," Julia corrected. "I'm still Mrs. Hughes."

Clay looked up sharply, rubbing the sweat from his eyes as he focused once more on her left hand and the ring glittering there—not a wedding band at all, but Aunt Eunice's engagement ring, the one he'd tried to give her in New York.

"I got halfway through the vows," she said, "but I couldn't. I thought—" Her voice snagged. "I thought I had a plan, but it was a bad plan. You knew it. I wish I'd listened to you earlier. And I wish to God I'd told you about Tommy earlier." She cleared her throat. "I blurted out some kind of apology to Mr. Van Lew—I have no idea what I said—and then I picked up my skirts and raced out of there as if the place were on fire. Aunt Eunice and Tommy applauded me, but something tells me Caroline Astor will cut me cold if she ever sees me again."

Clay stared at her. "You left Emmett Van Lew at the altar."

"I love you, Clay," she said earnestly. "So much that it made it hard for me to think straight. It still does, in a way. I don't necessarily expect to . . . win you back just by saying that. You once told me you didn't deserve my understanding, nor my forgiveness. That's exactly the way I feel now."

He nodded slowly. "Martin would have forgiven you."

"He was the forgiving type," she said, echoing words Clay had spoken only days ago.

"Yes, a veritable saint." Clay rubbed his prickly jaw. "I'm not quite sure I measure up. Tell you what," he said, his mouth quirking just slightly. "I'll forgive you on one condition."

That got her attention. "What?"

"Well, now, if you can't guess, I'm not sure we're meant to be together after all." He was definitely fighting a smile as his gaze lit on her mouth, confirming his "condition."

She bit her lip. "Right now? But . . ."

"Here." Pulling a handkerchief out of his pocket, he wiped his damp face. "Is that better?"

"It's not that." She lowered her voice, glancing around them as she stepped closer. "All these men are watching." To kiss a man in public was scandalous enough, but with an audience of gawking shipwrights . . .

"Come now, Julia," Clay murmured with a smile. "You're braver than that."

He was right. She didn't used to be, but that, and many other things, had changed for good over the past two weeks.

Julia rose up on tiptoe to wrap her arms around Clay and pull him close, caring not a whit that he was sodden from head to toe. Gripping the back of his head to lower it, she gave him a long, deep, scratchy, sweaty, utterly heart-stopping kiss, which he returned with a passion that more than equaled her own. It went on and on, while his men laughed and clapped and cheered.

"Hey, boss!" someone shouted. "How long are you plannin' to keep that up?"

"Forever," Clay whispered against her lips.

AUTHOR BIOS

Nina Bangs's book *Night Games* was a *USA Today* bestseller. She has won many awards in the romance community and was an Honorable Mention *Romantic Times* Reviewer's Choice Award nominee in 2002.

National award-winning author Cheryl Holt is a lawyer, novelist, and mom who lives on the Oregon coast. Her writing has been critically acclaimed by *Romantic Times* magazine and many other publications. Her sixth novel, *Love Lessons*, was nominated as the Best Erotic Romance of 2001 by the National Readers' Choice Awards.

She is the author of nine books.

Kimberly Raye has always been an incurable romantic. While she enjoys reading all types of fiction, her favorites, the books that touch her soul, are romance novels. From sexy to thrilling, sweet to humorous, she likes them all. But what she really loves is writing romance—the hotter the better. She started her first novel back in high school and has been writing ever since. To date, Ms. Raye has published over twenty-four novels, one of them a RITA Award nominee, Romance Writers of America's award of excellence. She has also been nominated by *Romantic Times* magazine for three Reviewer's Choice awards, as well as for a career achievement award.

Born and bred in the Lone Star State, Ms. Raye still lives

deep in the heart of Texas with her real-life hero, Curt, and their young children.

PATRICIA RYAN, who writes in both the romance and mystery genres, has authored sixteen contemporary and historical romances and novels of romantic suspense, which have been critically acclaimed and published in over twenty countries. Among the awards her books have garnered are the Golden Heart, the *Romantic Times* Reviewers' Choice Award, and Romance Writers of America's top award, the RITA, for Best Long Historical Romance of 2000. She has also recently launched, under the name P. B. Ryan, the new Gilded Age historical mystery series, set in nineteenth-century Boston.

Ms. Ryan formerly worked in the publishing industry in New York City and in Rochester, New York, as both a marketing manager and editor. She lives in Rochester with her husband and daughters in a house that has somehow, over the years, become seriously infested with cats.